'Holdstock has a beautifully subtle imagination that conjures up worlds and events with enviable ease . . . a writer of both heart and fire'   Peter F. Hamilton

'For me, this is the outstanding fantasy book of the 1980s, something to read several times and to rediscover the same delight with every new reading'   Michael Moorcock

'Britain's best fantasist'   *The Times*

'Indescribably enchanting . . . a celebration of fantasy'
                                                                                  The Spectator

Also by Robert Holdstock

MYTHAGO WOOD

ROBERT HOLDSTOCK

This edition first published in Great Britain in 2014 by
Gollancz
An imprint of the Orion Publishing Group
Orion House, 5 Upper St Martin's Lane, London WC2H 9EA
An Hachette UK Company

5 7 9 10 8 6

A CIP catalogue record for this book is available
from the British Library

ISBN 978 1 473 20545 1

Printed and bound in Great Britain by Clays Ltd, Elcograf S.p.A.
The Orion Publishing Group's policy is to use papers that
are natural, renewable and recyclable products and made from
wood grown in sustainable forests. The logging and manufacturing
processes are expected to conform to the environmental
regulations of the country of origin.

www.orionbooks.co.uk
www.gollancz.co.uk

for Sarah
cariath ganuch trymllyd bwystfil

Contents

Introduction

The Wood is Full of Shining Eyes

Rob Holdstock is one of those people – *was* one of those people – who were so alive that even now, over five years after his death, it's hard to think of him as being gone for good. On some deep level I am certain that Rob will be sitting near the bar the next time I'm in the kind of place that writers of the fantastic gather. Rob is tall, good-looking, and comfortable in his own skin, in an awkward, English, happy-to-be-uncomfortable sort of way. He might look slightly older than the last time I saw him – a few more lines in his face, a little more grey in his beard – but that happens to all of us, and he will still be the Rob Holdstock I have known for over thirty years: easy, talkative, affable. The sort of person who seems delighted by his friends' successes and both baffled and pleased by his own. Someone who likes to be liked, and enjoys liking other people. A good person.

When I first met Rob he was an established writer – he had been writing for fifteen years at that point, since he was twenty – who was earning some of his living writing work he was proud of under his own name, and work he was (sometimes) less proud of under a variety of pseudonyms. He was well-liked, maturing in craft and skill. He took what he did utterly seriously, while always finding humour in the action and craft of writing, and the trappings that went along with it. When Rob wrote *Mythago Wood*, he seemed to mature and to find his identity as a writer, just as he found the story waiting in the wood.

It seems to me that the marvel of *Mythago Wood*, and the stories that followed it in the Ryhope Wood sequence, is that Rob created something that seemed, in retrospect, to have been there the whole time. Like a sculptor who takes his tools to an oddly shaped log and seems to do almost nothing to it, but now we see the dragon that was waiting there to be revealed the whole time. It was obvious, but we could not see it. It took an artist to show us what we should have known and should have seen, and once we had seen it we could not unsee it.

English woods are strange things. They do odd things with space and with time. Even the smallest woods seem to remember when the whole of the island was one huge forest, and contain that forest within themselves, just as every fragment of a broken hologram contains the full image, but fuzzier and less detailed. Rob Holdstock posited (and once he had posited it, we all knew, as if we had always known) that some of the old woods, the ones that remembered, that went all the way back to the dawn times, contained *mythagos*, mythic *imagos*: people and things that existed because they had been needed in the popular imagination, because enough of us had believed, and that these mythagos could gain power and existence from the mind of a living human.

Mythago Wood is a fantasy novel written by a science fiction writer, and, perhaps more importantly, by a former scientist. The magic in this book is science, of a sort, capable of being understood and interpreted and, most importantly, *used*. It's magic, only because we do not know how it works, because it is imprecise, because it deals with belief and with minds and woods and the past and the future. But the author knows the rules and the world, and is building something that feels right – historically, mythically and emotionally.

Holdstock is the only author of the last fifty years who can stand with Alan Garner, another author who combines what we know about the past, and what we conjecture, with the myths and romances known as The Matter of Britain, to give us something powerful that tells us new-old things about our past and ourselves.

The language is powerful and honest. *Mythago Wood* is a first person narrative, told in the years following the Second World War. Our narrator, Stephen Huxley, has been hurt, more than he knows, by his childhood and by his father. Now he will need to understand his family, and to try to rescue what he can, of his family and his life, from the wood. Holdstock picks his words with care – repressed, accurate, observant, pained, and uses them to create a place and people we will never forget.

Mythago Wood brought Rob Holdstock the acclaim that he deserved. The initial novella, written in 1981, won the BSFA award and the World Fantasy Award for Best Novella in 1982, an achievement repeated in 1985 when he expanded the novella into the novel you are about to read.

Rob Holdstock was to return to Ryhope Wood, and to these characters and their families, several times in the years that followed the publication of this book, as he filled in a mythic patchwork of events and people, some before this book takes place, most after. But *Mythago Wood*, a classic of the literature of fantasy, is the cleanest and the first expression of Rob's genius, and the perfect way to discover Ryhope Wood, a place which is, like so many other people and things, bigger and stranger and much more alive and dangerous the further in you go.

Neil Gaiman
on the edge of the dark woods
2014

Prologue

Edward Wynne-Jones Esq.
15 College Road
Oxford

Edward—

You *must* come back to the Lodge. Please don't delay for even an hour! I have discovered a fourth pathway into the deeper zones of the wood. The brook itself. So obvious now, a water track! It leads directly through the outer ash vortex, beyond the spiral track and the Stone Falls. I believe it could be used to enter the heartwoods themselves. But time, always time!

I have found a people called the *shamiga*. They live beyond the Stone Falls. They guard the fords on the river, but to my great satisfaction they are willing story-tellers, which they call 'life-speaking'. The life-speaker herself is a young girl who paints her face quite green, and tells all stories with her eyes closed so that the smiles or frowns of those who listen cannot effect a 'shape-change' upon the characters within the story. I heard much from her, but most important of all was a fragment of what can only be Guiwenneth's tale. It is a pre-Celtic version of the myth, but I am convinced that it relates to the girl. What I managed to understand of it goes thus:

'One afternoon, having killed a stag with eight tines, a boar twice the height of a man, and cured four villages of bad manners, *Mogoch*, a chieftain, sat down by the shore to rest. He was so mighty in deed and build that his head was half-covered by clouds. He spread his feet out in the sea at the bottom of the cliffs to cool. Then he lay back and watched a meeting take place between two sisters upon his belly.

'The sisters were twins, equally beautiful, equally sweet of tongue, and skilled with the harp. One sister, however, had married the warlord of a great tribe, and had then found herself to be barren. Her complexion had become as sour as milk left too long in the sun. The other sister had married an exiled warrior, whose name was *Peregu*. Peregu held his camp in the deep gorges and deadwoods of the far forest, but came to his lover as a nightbird. Now she had produced his child, which was a girl, but because of the exile of Peregu, her sour-faced sister and an army had come to claim the infant.

'A great argument occurred, and there were several clashes of arms. The lover of Peregu had not even named the child when her sister snatched the tiny bundle in its heavy cloth wrappings and raised it above her head, intending to name it herself.

'But the sky darkened as ten magpies appeared. These were Peregu and his nine sword-kin, changed by forest magic. Peregu swooped and caught his child in his claws, and flew upwards, but a marksman used slingshot to bring him down. The child fell, but the other birds caught her and carried her away. Thus she was named *Hurfathna*, which means "the girl raised by magpies".

'Mogoch, the chieftain, watched all this with amusement, but had respect for the dead Peregu. He picked up the tiny bird and shook the human form back into it. But he was afraid that he would crush whole villages if he prodded out a grave in the country with his finger. So Mogoch popped the dead exile into his mouth and twisted out a tooth to stand as a monument. In this way Peregu was buried beneath a tall white stone, in a valley which breathes.'

There can be no doubt that this is an early form of Guiwenneth's tale, and I think you can see why I'm excited. The last time the girl was here I was able to question her about her sadness. She was lost, she told me. She could not find the valley which breathed and the bright stone of her dead father. It is the same. I know it, I *feel* it! We must summon her again. We must go beyond the Stone Falls again. I need your help.

Who knows where and when this war will end? My eldest son will be called up soon, and Steven soon after. I shall have more freedom to explore the wood, and deal with the girl.

Edward, you *must come*.

With kind regards,

George Huxley.
December '41.

PART ONE

Mythago Wood

One

In May 1944 I received my call-up papers and went reluctantly away to war, training at first in the Lake District, then shipping over to France with the 7th Infantry.

On the eve of my final departure I felt so resentful of my father's apparent lack of concern for my safety that, when he was asleep, I went quietly to his desk and tore a page out of his notebook, the diary in which his silent, obsessive work was recorded. The fragment was dated simply 'August 34', and I read it many times, dismayed by its incomprehensibility, but content that I had stolen at least a tiny part of his life with which to support myself through those painful, lonely times.

The entry began with a bitter comment on the distractions in his life – the running of Oak Lodge, our family home, the demands of his two sons, and the difficult relationship with his wife, Jennifer. (By then, I remember, my mother was desperately ill.) It closed with a passage quite memorable for its incoherence:

A letter from Watkins – agrees with me that at certain times of the year the aura around the woodland could reach as far as the house. Must think through the implications of this. He is keen to know the power of the oak vortex that I have measured. What to tell him? Certainly not of the first mythago. Have noticed too that the enrichment of the pre-mythago zone is more persistent, but concomitant with this, am distinctly losing my sense of time.

I treasured this piece of paper for many reasons, but particularly for the moment or two of my father's passionate interest that it represented – and yet, it locked me out of its understanding, as he had locked me out at home. Everything he loved, everything I hated.

I was wounded in early 1945 and when the war finished I managed to stay in France, travelling south to convalesce in a village in the hills behind Marseilles, where I lived with old friends of my father. It was a hot, dry place, very still, very slow; I spent my time sitting in the village square and quickly became a part of the tiny community.

Letters from my brother Christian, who had returned to Oak Lodge after the war, arrived every month throughout the long year of 1946. They were chatty, informative letters, but there was an increasing note of tension in them, and it was clear that Christian's relationship with our father was deteriorating rapidly. I never heard a word from the old man himself, but then I never expected to; I had long since resigned myself to the fact that, even at best, he regarded me with total indifference. All his family had been an intrusion in his work, and his guilt at neglecting us, and especially at driving our mother to taking her own life, had blossomed rapidly, during the early years of the war, into an hysterical madness that could be truly frightening. Which is not to say that he was perpetually shouting; on the contrary, most of his life was spent in silent, absorbed contemplation of the oak woodland that bordered our home. At first infuriating, because of the distance it put between him and his family, soon those long periods of quiet became blessed, earnestly welcomed.

He died in November 1946, of an illness that had afflicted him for years. When I heard the news I was torn between my unwillingness to return to Oak Lodge, at the edge of the Ryhope estate in Herefordshire, and my awareness of Christian's obvious distress. He was alone now, in the house where we had lived through our childhood together. I could imagine him prowling the empty rooms, perhaps sitting in father's dank and unwholesome study and remembering the hours of denial, the smell of wood and compost that the old man had trudged in through the glass-panelled doors after his week-long sorties into the deep woodlands. The forest had spread into that room as if my father could not bear to be away from the rank undergrowth and the cool, moist oak glades, even when making token acknowledgement of his family. He made that acknowledgement in the only way he knew: by telling us – and mainly telling my brother – stories of the ancient forestlands beyond the house, the primary woodland of oak, ash, beech and the like, in whose dark interior (he once said) wild boar could still be heard, and smelled, and tracked by their spoor.

I doubt if he had ever seen such a creature, but that evening, as I sat in my room overlooking the tiny village in the hills (Christian's letter a crushed ball still held in my hand) I vividly recalled how I had listened to the muffled grunting of some woodland animal, and heard the heavy, unhurried crashing of something bulky moving inwards, towards the winding pathway that we called deep track, a route that led spirally towards the very heartwoods of the forest.

I knew I would have to go home, and yet I delayed my departure for nearly another year. During that time Christian's letters ceased abruptly. In his last letter, dated April 10th, he wrote of Guiwenneth, of his unusual marriage, and hinted that I would be surprised by the lovely girl to whom he had lost his 'heart, mind, soul, reason, cooking ability and just about everything else, Steve'. I wrote to congratulate him, of course, but there was no further communication between us for months.

Eventually I wrote to say I was coming home, that I would stay at Oak Lodge for a few weeks, and then find accommodation in one of the nearby towns. I said goodbye to France, and to the community that had become so much a part of my life. I travelled to England by bus and train, by ferry, and then by train again. On August 20th I arrived by pony and trap at the disused railway line that skirted the edge of the extensive estate. Oak Lodge lay on the far side of the grounds, four miles further round the road, but accessible via the right of way through the estate's fields and wood-lands. I intended to take an intermediate route and so, lugging my single, crammed suitcase as best I could, I began to walk along the grass-covered railway track, peering on occasion over the high, red-brick wall that marked the limit of the estate, trying to see through the gloom of the pungent pinewoods.

Soon this woodland, and the wall, vanished, and the land opened into tight, tree-bordered fields, to which I gained access across a rickety wooden stile, almost lost beneath briar and full-fruited blackberry bushes. I had to trample my way out of the public domain and so on to the south trackway that wound, skirting patchy woodland and the stream called 'sticklebrook', up to the ivy-covered house that was my home.

It was late morning, and very hot, as I came in distant sight of Oak Lodge. Somewhere off to my left I could hear the drone of a tractor. I thought of old Alphonse Jeffries, the estate's farm supervisor, and with the memory of his weather-tanned, smiling face came images of the mill-pond, and fishing for pike from his tiny rowing boat.

Memory of the tranquil mill-pond haunted me, and I moved away from the south track, through waist-high nettles and a tangle of ash and hawthorn scrub. I came out close to the bank of the wide, shadowy pool, its full extent hidden by the gloom of the dense stand of oak woodland that began on its far side. Almost hidden among the rushes that crowded the nearer edge of the pond was the shallow boat from which Chris and I had fished, years before; its white paint had flaked away almost entirely now, and although the craft looked watertight, I doubted if it would take the weight of a full grown man. I didn't disturb it but walked around the bank and sat down on the rough concrete steps of the crumbling boathouse; from here I watched the surface of the pool rippling with the darting motions of insects, and the occasional passage of a fish, just below.

'A couple of sticks and a bit of string . . . that's all it takes.'

Christian's voice startled me. He must have walked along a beaten track from the Lodge, hidden from my view by the shed. Delighted, I jumped to my feet and turned to face him. The shock of his appearance was like a physical blow to me, and I think he noticed, even though I threw my arms about him and gave him a powerful brotherly bear-hug.

'I had to see this place again,' I said.

'I know what you mean,' he said, as we broke our embrace. 'I often walk here myself.' There was a moment's awkward silence as we stared at each other. I felt, distinctly, that he was not pleased to see me. 'You're looking brown,' he said. 'And very drawn. Healthy and ill together . . .'

'Mediterranean sun, grape-picking, and shrapnel. I'm still not one hundred percent fit.' I smiled. 'But it *is* good to be back, to see you again.'

'Yes,' he said dully. 'I'm glad you've come, Steve. Very glad. I'm afraid the place . . . well, a bit of a mess. I only got your letter yesterday and I haven't had a chance to do anything. Things have changed quite a bit, you'll find.'

And he more than anything. I could hardly believe that this was the chipper, perky young man who had left with his army unit in 1942. He had aged incredibly, his hair quite streaked with grey, more noticeable for his having allowed it to grow long and untidy at the back and sides. He reminded me very much of father: the same distant, distracted look, the same hollow cheeks and deeply wrinkled face. But it was his whole demeanour that had shocked me. He had always been a stocky muscular chap; now he was like the proverbial scarecrow, wiry, ungainly, on edge all the time. His gaze darted about, but never seemed to focus upon me. And he smelled. Of mothballs, as if the crisp white shirt and grey flannels that he wore had been dragged out of storage; and another smell beyond the naphtha . . . the hint of woodland and grass. There was dirt under his fingernails, and in his hair, and his teeth were yellowing.

He seemed to relax slightly as the minutes ticked by. We sparred a bit, laughed a bit, and walked around the pond, whacking at the rushes with sticks. I could not shake off the feeling that I had arrived home at a bad time.

'Was it difficult . . . with the old man, I mean? The last days.'

He shook his head. 'There was a nurse here for the final two weeks or so. I can't exactly say that he went peacefully, but she managed to stop him damaging himself . . . or me, for that matter.'

'I was going to ask you about that. Your letters suggested hostility between the two of you.'

Christian smiled quite grimly, and glanced at me with a curious expression, somewhere between agreement and suspicion. 'More like open warfare. Soon after I got back from France, he went quite mad. You should have seen the place, Steve. You should have seen him. I don't think he'd washed for months. I wondered what he'd been eating . . . certainly nothing as simple as eggs and meat. In all honesty, for a few months I think he'd been eating wood and leaves. He was in a wretched state. Although he let me help him with his work, he quickly began to resent me. He tried to kill me on several occasions, Steve. And I mean that, really desperate attempts on my life. There was a reason for it, I suppose . . .'

I was astonished by what Christian was telling me. The image of my father had changed from that of a cold, resentful man into a crazed figure, ranting at Christian and beating at him with his fists.

'I always thought he had a touch of affection for you; he always told *you* the stories of the wood; I listened, but it was you who sat on his knee. Why would he try to kill you?'

'I became too involved,' was all Christian said. He was keeping something back, something of critical importance. I could tell from his tone, from his sullen, almost resentful expression. Did I push the point or not? It was hard to make the decision. I had never before felt so distant from my own brother. I wondered if his behaviour was having an effect on Guiwenneth, the girl he had married. I wondered what sort of atmosphere she was living in up at Oak Lodge.

Tentatively, I broached the subject of the girl.

Christian struck angrily at the rushes by the pond. 'Guiwenneth's gone,' he said simply, and I stopped, startled.

'What does that mean, Chris? Gone where?'

'She's just gone, Steve,' he snapped, angry and cornered. 'She was father's girl, and she's gone, and that's all there is to it.'

'I don't understand what you mean. Where's she gone *to*? In your letter you sounded so happy . . .'

'I shouldn't have written about her. That was a mistake. Now let it drop, will you?'

After that outburst, my unease with Christian grew stronger by the minute. There was something very wrong with him indeed, and clearly Guiwenneth's leaving had contributed greatly to the terrible change I could see; but I sensed there was something more. Unless he spoke about it, however, there was no way through to him. I could find only the words, 'I'm sorry.'

'Don't be.'

We walked on, almost to the woods, where the ground became marshy and unsafe for a few yards before vanishing into a musty deepness of stone and root and rotting wood. It was cool here, the sun being beyond the thickly foliaged trees. The dense stands of rush moved in the breeze and I watched the rotting boat as it shifted slightly on its mooring.

Christian followed my gaze, but he was not looking at the boat or the pond; he was lost, somewhere in his own thoughts. For a brief moment I experienced a jarring sadness at the sight of my brother so ruined in appearance and attitude. I wanted desperately to touch his arm, to hug him, and I could hardly bear the knowledge that I was afraid to do so.

Quite quietly I asked him, 'What on earth has happened to you, Chris? Are you ill?'

He didn't answer for a moment, then said, 'I'm not ill,' and struck hard at a puffball, which shattered and spread on the breeze. He looked at me, something of resignation in his haunted face. 'I've been going through a few changes, that's all. I've been picking up on the old man's work. Perhaps a bit of his reclusiveness is rubbing off on me, a bit of his detachment.'

'If that's true, then perhaps you should give up for a while.'

'Why?'

'Because the old man's obsession with the oak forest eventually killed him. And from the look of you, you're going the same way.'

Christian smiled thinly and chucked his reedwhacker out into the pond, where it made a dull splash and floated in a patch of scummy green algae. 'It might even be worth dying to achieve what he tried to achieve . . . and failed.'

I didn't understand the dramatic overtone in Christian's statement. The work that had so obsessed our father had been concerned with mapping the woodland, and searching for evidence of old forest settlements. He had invented a whole new jargon for himself, and effectively isolated me from any deeper understanding of his work. I said this to Christian, and added, 'Which is all very interesting, but hardly *that* interesting.'

'He was doing much more than that, much more than just mapping. But do you remember those maps, Steve? Incredibly detailed . . .'

I could remember one quite clearly, the largest map, show- ing carefully marked track ways and easy routes through the tangle of trees and stony outcrops; it showed clearings drawn with almost obsessive precision, each glade numbered and identified, and the whole forest divided into zones, and given names. We had made a camp in one of the clearings close to the woodland edge. 'We often tried to get deeper into the heartwoods, remember those expeditions, Chris? But the deep track just ends, and we always managed to get lost; and very scared.'

'That's true,' Christian said quietly, looking at me quizzically; and added, 'What if I told you the forest had *stopped* us entering? Would you believe me?'

I peered into the tangle of brush, tree and gloom, to where a sunlit clearing was visible. 'In a way I suppose it did,' I said. 'It stopped us penetrating very deeply because it made us scared, because there are few trackways through, and the ground is choked with stone and briar . . . very difficult walking. Is that what you meant? Or did you mean something a little more sinister?'

'Sinister isn't the word I'd use,' said Christian, but added nothing more for a moment; he reached up to pluck a leaf from a small, immature oak, and rubbed it between thumb and forefinger before crushing it in his palm. All the time he stared into the deep woods. 'This is primary oak woodland, Steve, untouched forest from a time when all of the country was covered with deciduous forests of oak and ash and elder and rowan and hawthorn . . .'

'And all the rest,' I said with a smile. 'I remember the old man listing them for us.'

'That's right, he did. And there's more than three square miles of such forest stretching from here to well beyond Grimley. Three square miles of original, post-Ice Age forestland. Untouched, uninvaded for thousands of years.' He broke off and looked at me hard, before adding, 'Resistant to change.'

I said, 'He always thought there were boars alive in there. I remember hearing something one night, and he convinced me that it was a great big old bull boar, skirting the edge of the woods, looking for a mate.'

Christian led the way back towards the boathouse. 'He was probably right. If boars *had* survived from mediaeval times, this is just the sort of woodland they'd be found in.'

With my mind opened to those events of years ago, memory inched back, images of childhood – the burning touch of sun on bramble-grazed skin; fishing trips to the mill-pond; tree camps, games, explorations . . . and instantly I recalled the Twigling.

As we walked back to the beaten pathway that led up to the Lodge, we discussed the sighting. I had been about nine or ten years old. On our way to the sticklebrook to fish we had decided to test out our stick and string rods on the mill-pond, in the vain hope of snaring one of the predatory fish that lived there. As we crouched by the water (we only ever dared to go out in the boat with Alphonse) we saw movement in the trees, across on the other bank. It was a bewildering vision that held us enthralled for the next few moments, and not a little terrified: standing watching us was a man in brown, leathery clothes, with a wide, gleaming belt around his waist, and a spiky, orange beard that reached to his chest: on his head he wore twigs, held to his crown by a leather band. He watched us for a moment only, before slipping back into the darkness. We heard nothing in all this time, no sound of approach, no sound of departure.

Running back to the house we had soon calmed down. Christian decided, eventually, that it must have been old Alphonse, playing tricks on us. But when I mentioned what we'd seen to my father he reacted almost angrily (although Christian recalls him as having been excited, and bellowing for that reason, and not because he was angry with our having been near the forbidden pool). It was father who referred to the vision as 'the Twigling', and soon after we had spoken to him he vanished into the woodland for nearly two weeks.

'That was when he came back hurt, remember?' We had reached the grounds of Oak Lodge, and Christian held the gate open for me as he spoke.

'The arrow wound. The gypsy arrow. My God, that was a bad day.'

'The first of many.'

I noticed that most of the ivy had been cleared from the walls of the house; it was a grey place now, small, curtainless windows set in the dark brick. The slate roof, with its three tall chimney stacks, was partially hidden behind the branches of a big old beech tree. The yard and gardens were untidy and unkempt, the empty chicken coops and animal shelters ramshackle and decaying. Christian had really let the place slip. But when I stepped across the threshold, it was as if I had never been away. The house smelled of stale food and chlorine, and I could almost see the thin figure of my mother, working away at the immense pine wood table in the kitchen, cats stretched out around her on the red-tiled floor.

Christian had grown tense again, staring at me in that fidgety way that marked his unease. I imagined he was still unsure whether to be glad or angry that I had come home like this. For a moment I felt like an intruder. He said, 'Why don't you unpack and freshen up. You can use your old room. It's a bit stuffy, I expect, but it'll soon air. Then come down and we'll have some late lunch. We've got all the time in the world to chat, as long as we're finished by tea.' He smiled, and I thought this was some slight attempt at humour. But he went on quickly, staring at me in a cold, hard way, 'Because if you're going to stay at home for a while, then you'd better know what's going on here. I don't want you interfering with it, Steve, or with what I'm doing.'

'I wouldn't interfere with your life, Chris—'

'Wouldn't you? We'll see. I'm not going to deny that I'm nervous of you being here. But since you are . . .' He trailed off, and for a second looked almost embarrassed. 'Well, we'll have a chat later on.'

Two

Intrigued by what Christian had said, and worried by his apprehension of me, I nonetheless restrained my curiosity and spent an hour exploring the house again from top to bottom, inside and out, everywhere save father's study, the contemplation of which chilled me more than Christian's behaviour had done. Nothing had changed, except that it was untidy, and untenanted. Christian had employed a part-time cleaner and cook, a woman from a nearby village who cycled to the Lodge every week and prepared a pie or stew that would last him three days. Christian did not go short of farm produce, so much so that he rarely bothered to use his ration book. He seemed to get all he needed, including sugar and tea, from the Ryhope estate, which had always been good to my family.

My old room was almost exactly as I remembered it. I opened the window wide and lay down on the bed for a few minutes, staring out and up into the hazy, late summer sky, past the waving branches of the gigantic beech that grew so close to the Lodge. Several times, in the years before my teens, I had climbed from window to tree, and made a secret camp among the thick branches; I had shivered by moonlight in my underpants, crouched in that private place, imagining the dark activities of night creatures below.

Lunch, in mid-afternoon, was a substantial feast of cold pork, chicken and hard-boiled eggs, in quantities that, after two years in France on strict rations, I had never thought to see again. We were, of course, eating his food supply for several days, but the fact seemed irrelevant to Christian, who in any case only picked at his meal.

Afterwards we talked for a couple of hours, and Christian

relaxed quite noticeably, although he never referred to Guiwenneth, or to father's work, and I never broached either subject.

We sprawled in the uncomfortable armchairs that had belonged to my grandparents, surrounded by the time-faded mementoes of our family . . . photographs, a noisy rosewood clock, horrible pictures of exotic Spain, all framed in cracked mock-gilded wood, and all pressed hard against the same floral wallpaper that had hugged the walls of the sitting-room since a time before my birth. But it was home, and Christian was home, and the smell, and the faded surrounds, all were home to me. I knew, within two hours of arriving, that I would have to stay. It was not so much that I belonged here (although I certainly felt that) but simply that the place belonged to me – not in any mercenary sense of ownership, more in the way that the house and the land around the house shared a common life with me; we were part of the same evolution. Even in France, even in the village in the south, I had not been separated from that evolution, merely stretched to an extreme.

As the heavy old clock began to whirr and click, preceding its laboured chiming of the hour of five, Christian abruptly rose from his chair and tossed his half-smoked cigarette into the empty fire grate.

'Let's go to the study,' he said, and I rose without speaking and followed him through the house to the small room where our father had worked. 'You're scared of this room, aren't you?' He opened the door and walked inside, crossing to the heavy oak desk and pulling out a large leather-bound book from one of the drawers.

I hesitated outside the study, watching Christian, almost unable to move my legs to carry myself into the room. I recognized the book he held, my father's notebook. I touched my back pocket, the wallet I carried there, and thought of the fragment of that notebook which was hidden inside the thin leather. I wondered if anyone, my father or Christian, had ever noticed that a page was missing. Christian was watching me, his eyes bright with excitement now, his hands trembling as he placed the book on the desk top.

'He's dead, Steve. He's gone from this room, from the house. There's no need to be afraid any more.'

'Isn't there?'

But I found the sudden strength to move, and stepped across the threshold. The moment I entered the musty room I felt totally subdued, deeply affected by the coolness of the place, the stark, haunted atmosphere that hugged the walls and carpets and windows. It smelled slightly of leather, here, and dust too, with just a distant hint of polish, as if Christian made a token effort to keep this stifling room clean. It was not a crowded room, not a library as my father would perhaps have liked it to be. There were books on zoology and botany, on history and archaeology, but these were not rare editions, merely the cheapest copies he could find at the time. There were more paperbacks than hardcover books; the exquisite binding of his notes, and the deeply varnished desk, had an air of Victorian elegance about them that belied the otherwise shabby studio.

On the walls, between the cases of books, were his glass-framed specimens: pieces of wood, collections of leaves, crude sketches of animal and plant life made during the first years of his fascination with the forest. And almost hidden away among the cases and the shelves was the patterned shaft of the arrow that had struck him fifteen years before, its flights twisted and useless, the broken shaft glued together, the iron head dulled with corrosion, but a lethal-looking weapon nonetheless.

I stared at that arrow for several seconds, reliving the man's agony, and the tears that Christian and I had wept for him as we had helped him back from the woodlands, that cold autumn afternoon, convinced that he would die.

How quickly things had changed after that strange, and never fully explained incident. If the arrow linked me with an earlier day, when some semblance of concern and love had remained in my father's mind, the rest of the study radiated only coldness.

I could still see the greying figure, bent over his desk writing furiously. I could hear the troubled breathing, the lung disorder that finally killed him; I could hear his caught breath, the vocalized sound of irritation as he grew aware of my presence, and waved me away with a half-irritated gesture, as if he begrudged even that split second of acknowledgement.

How like him Christian looked now, standing there behind the desk dishevelled and sickly, his hands in the pockets of his flannels, shoulders drooped, his whole body visibly shaking, and yet with the mark of absolute confidence about him.

He had waited quietly as I adjusted to the room, and let the memories and atmosphere play through me. As I stepped up to the desk, my mind back on the moment at hand, he said, 'Steve, you should read the notes. They'll make a lot of things clear to you, and help you understand what it is I'm doing as well.'

I turned the notebook towards me, scanning the sprawling, untidy handwriting, picking out words and phrases, reading through the years of my father's life in a few scant seconds. The words were as meaningless, on the whole, as those on my purloined sheet. To read them brought back a memory of anger, of danger, and of fear. The life in the notes had sustained me through nearly a year of war and had come to mean something outside of their proper context. I felt reluctant to dispel that powerful association with the past.

'I intend to read them, Chris. From beginning to end, and that's a promise. But not for the moment.'

I closed the book, noticing as I did that my hands were clammy and trembling. I was not yet ready to be so close to my father again, and Christian saw this, and accepted it.

Conversation died quite early that night, as my energy expired, and the tensions of the long journey finally caught up with me. Christian came upstairs with me and stood in the doorway of my room, watching as I turned back the sheets and pottered about, picking up bits and pieces of my past life, laughing, shaking my head and trying to evoke a last moment's tired nostalgia. 'Remember making camp out in the beech?' I asked, watching the grey of branch and leaf against the fading evening sky. 'Yes,' said Christian with a smile. 'Yes, I remember very clearly.'

But the conversation was as tired as that, and Christian took the hint and said, 'Sleep well, old chap. I'll see you in the morning.'

If I slept at all, it was for the first four or five hours after putting head to pillow. I woke sharply, and brightly, in the dead of night, one or two o'clock perhaps; the sky was very dark now, and it was quite windy outside. I lay and stared at the window, wondering how my body could feel so fresh, so alert. There was movement downstairs, and I guessed that Christian was doing some tidying, restlessly walking through the house, trying to adjust to the idea of my moving in.

The sheets smelled of mothballs and old cotton; the bed creaked in a metallic way when I shifted on it, and when I lay still the whole room clicked and shuffled, as if adapting itself to its first company in so many years. I lay awake for ages, but must have drifted to sleep again before first light, because suddenly Christian was bending over me, shaking my shoulder gently.

I started with surprise, awake at once, and propped up on my elbows, looking around. It was dawn. 'What is it, Chris?'

'I've got to go. I'm sorry, but I have to.'

I realized he was wearing a heavy oilskin cape, and had thick-soled walking boots on his feet. 'Go? What d'you mean, go?'

'I'm sorry, Steve. There's nothing I can do about it.' He spoke softly, as if there were someone else in the house who might be woken by raised voices. He looked more drawn than ever in this pale light, and his eyes were narrowed – I thought with pain, or anxiety. 'I have to go away for a few days. You'll be all right. I've left a list of instructions down-stairs, where to get bread, eggs, all that sort of thing. I'm sure you'll be able to use my ration book until yours comes. I shan't be long, just a few days. That's a promise . . .'

He rose from his crouch and walked out of the door. 'For God's sake, Chris, where are you going?'

'Inwards,' was all he said, before I heard him clump heavily down the stairs. I remained motionless for a moment or two, trying to clear my thoughts, then rose, put on my dressing-gown and followed him down to the kitchen. He had already left the house. I went back up to the landing window and saw him skirting the edge of the yard and walk-ing swiftly down towards the south track. He was wearing a wide-brimmed hat, and carrying a long, black staff; on his back he had a small rucksack, slung uncomfortably over one shoulder.

'Where's inwards, Chris?' I said to his vanishing figure, and watched long after he had disappeared from view.

'What's going on, Chris?' I asked of his empty bedroom as I wandered restlessly through the house; Guiwenneth, I decided in my wisdom, her loss, her leaving . . . how little one could interpret from the words 'she's gone'. And in all our chat of the evening before he had never alluded to his wife again. I had come home to England expecting to find a cheerful young couple, and instead had found a haunted, wasting brother living in the derelict shadow of our family home.

By the afternoon I had resigned myself to a period of solitary living, for wherever Christian had gone (and I had a fairly good idea) he had said clearly that he would be gone for some time. There was a lot to do about the house and the yard, and there seemed no better way to spend my time than in beginning to rebuild the personality of Oak Lodge. I made a list of essential repairs, and the following day walked into the nearest town to order what materials I could, mostly wood and paint, which I found in reasonable supply.

I renewed my acquaintance with the Ryhope family, and with many of the local families with whom I had once been friendly. I terminated the services of the part-time cook; I could look after myself quite well enough.

And at last I visited the cemetery; a single, brief visit, coldly accomplished.

The month of August turned to September, and I noticed a definite crispness in the air by evening, and early in the morning. It was a season I loved, the turn from summer to autumn, although it bore with it associations of return to school after the long holiday, a memory I didn't cherish.

I soon grew used to being on my own in the house, and although I took long walks around the deep woodlands, watching the road and the railway track for Christian's return, I had ceased to feel anxious about him by the end of my first week home, and had settled comfortably into a daily routine of building in the yard, painting the exterior wood-work of the house ready for the onslaught of winter, and digging over the large, untended garden.

It was during the evening of my eleventh day at home that this domestic routine was disturbed by a circumstance of such peculiarity that afterwards I could not sleep for thinking about it.

I had been in the town of Hobbhurst for most of the afternoon, and after a light evening meal was sitting reading the newspaper; towards nine o'clock, as I began to feel ready for an evening stroll, I thought I heard a dog, not so much barking as howling. My first thought was that Christian was coming back, my second that there were no dogs in this immediate area at all.

I went out into the yard; it was after dusk, but still quite bright, although the oakwoods were melded together into a grey-green blur. I called for Christian, but there was no response. I was about to return to my paper when a man stepped out of the distant woodland, and began to trot towards me. He was holding on a short, leather leash the most enormous hound I have ever seen.

At the gate to our private grounds he stopped, and the dog began to growl; it placed its forepaws on the fence, and in so doing rose almost to the height of its master. I felt nervous at once, keeping my attention balanced between the gaping, panting mouth of that dark beast, and the strange man who held it in check.

It was difficult to make him out clearly, for his face was painted with dark patterns and his moustaches drooped to well below his chin; his hair was plastered thickly about his scalp; he wore a dark woollen shirt, with a leather jerkin over the top, and tight, check-patterned breeches that reached to just below his knees. When he stepped cautiously through the gate I could see his rough and ready sandals. Across his shoulder he carried a crude-looking bow, and a bundle of arrows, held together with a simple thong and tied to his belt. Like Christian, he bore a staff.

Inside the gate he hesitated, watching me. The hound was restless beside him, licking its mouth and growling softly. I had never seen a dog such as this, shaggy and dark-furred, with the narrow pointed face of an Alsatian, but the body, it seemed to me, of a bear – except that its legs were long and thin, an animal made for chasing, for hunting.

The man spoke to me, and although I felt familiar with the words, they meant nothing. I didn't know what to do, so I shook my head and said that I didn't understand. The man hesitated just a moment before repeating what he had said, this time with a distinct edge of anger in his voice. And he started to walk towards me, tugging at the hound to prevent it straining at the leash. The light was draining from the sky, and he seemed to grow in stature in the greyness as he approached. The beast watched me, hungrily.

'What do you want?' I called, and tried to sound firm when I would rather have run inside the house. The man was ten paces away from me. He stopped, spoke again, and this time made eating motions with the hand that held his staff. *Now* I understood.

I nodded vigorously. 'Wait here,' I said, and went back to

the house to fetch the cold joint of pork that was to last me four more days. It was not large, but it seemed an hospitable thing to do. I took the meat, half a granary loaf, and a jug of bottled beer out into the yard. The stranger was crouched now, the hound lying down beside him, rather reluctantly, it seemed to me. As I tried to approach them, the dog growled, then barked in a way that set my heart racing and nearly made me drop my gifts. The man shouted at the beast, and said something to me. I placed the food where I stood and backed away. The gruesome pair approached and again squatted down to eat.

As he picked up the joint I saw the scars on his arm, running down and across the bunched muscles. I also smelled him, a raw, rancid odour, sweat and urine mixed with the fetid aroma of rotting meat. I felt sick, but held my ground watching as the stranger tore at the pork with his teeth, swallowing hard and fast. The hound watched me.

After a few minutes the man stopped eating, looked at me, and with his gaze fixed on mine, almost challenging me to react, passed the rest of the meat to the dog, which growled loudly and snapped at the joint. The hound chewed, cracked and gulped the entire piece of pork in less than four minutes, while the stranger cautiously – and without much apparent pleasure – drank beer, and chewed on a large mouthful of bread.

Finally this bizarre feast was over. The man rose to his feet and jerked the hound away from where it was licking the ground noisily. He said a word I intuitively recognized as 'thank you'. He was about to turn when the hound scented something; it uttered first a high-pitched keen, and then a raucous bark, and snatched itself away from its master's restraining grip, racing across the yard to a spot between the ramshackle chicken houses. Here it sniffed and scratched until the man reached it, grabbed the leather leash, and shouted angrily and lengthily at his charge. The hound moved with him, padding silently and monstrously into the gloom beyond the yard. They ran at full speed around the edge of the woodland, towards the farmlands around the village of Grimley, and that was the last I saw of them.

In the morning the place where the man and beast had rested *still* smelled rank. I skirted the area quickly as I walked to the woods and found the place where my strange visitors had emerged from the trees; it was trampled and broken, and I followed the line of their passage for some yards into the shade before stopping and turning back.

Where on earth had they come from? Had the war had such an effect on men in England that some had returned to the wild, using bow and arrow and hunting dog for survival?

Not until midday did I think to look between the chicken huts, at the ground so deeply scored by that brief moment's digging. What had the beast scented, I wondered, and a sudden chill clawed at my heart. I left the place at a run, unwilling, for the moment, to confirm my worst fears.

How I knew I cannot say: intuition, or perhaps something that my subconscious had detected in Christian's words and mannerisms the week or so before, during our brief encounter. In any event, late in the afternoon that same day I took a spade to the chicken huts, and within a few minutes of digging had proved my instinct right.

It took me half an hour of sitting on the back doorstep of the house, staring across the yard at the grave, to find the courage to uncover the woman's body totally. I was dizzy, slightly sick, but most of all I was shaking; an uncontrollable, unwelcome shaking of arms and legs, so pronounced that I could hardly pull on a pair of gloves. But eventually I knelt by the hole and brushed the rest of the dirt from the corpse.

Christian had buried her three feet deep, face down; her hair was long and red; her body was still clad in a strange green garment, a patterned tunic that was laced at the sides and, though it was crushed up almost to her waist now, would have reached to her calves. A staff was buried with her. I turned the head, holding my breath against the almost intolerable smell of putrefaction, and with a little effort

27

could gaze upon the withering face. I saw then how she had died, for the head and stump of the arrow were still embedded in her eye. Had Christian tried to withdraw the weapon and succeeded only in breaking it? There was enough of the shaft left for me to notice that it had the same carved markings as the arrow in my father's study.

Poor Guiwenneth, I thought, and let the corpse drop back to its resting place. I filled in the dirt again. When I reached the house I was cold with sweat, and in no doubt that I was about to be violently sick.

Three

Two days later, when I came down in the morning, I found the kitchen littered with Christian's clothes and effects, the floor covered with mud and leaf litter. I crept upstairs to his room and stared at his semi-naked body: he was belly down on the bed, face turned towards me, sleeping soundly and noisily, and I imagined that he was sleeping enough for a week. The state of his body, though, gave me cause for concern. He was scratched and scarred from neck to ankle, filthy, and malodorous to an extreme. His hair was matted. And yet, about him there was something hardened and strong, a tangible physical change from the hollow-faced, rather skeletal young man who had greeted me nearly two weeks before.

He slept for most of the day, emerging at six in the evening wearing a loose-fitting grey shirt and flannels, torn off just above the knee. He had half-heartedly washed his face, but still reeked of sweat and vegetation, as if he had spent the days away buried in compost.

I fed him, and he drank the entire contents of a pot of tea as I sat watching him; he kept darting glances at me, suspicious little looks as if he were nervous of some sudden move or surprise attack upon him. The muscles of his arms and wrists were pronounced. This was almost a different man.

'Where have you been, Chris?' I asked after a while, and was not at all surprised when he answered, 'In the woods. Deep in the woods.' He stuffed more meat into his mouth and chewed noisily. As he swallowed he found a moment to say, 'I'm quite fit. Bruised and scratched by the damned brambles, but quite fit.'

In the woods. Deep in the woods. What in heaven's name

could he have been doing there? As I watched him wolf down his food I saw again the stranger, crouching like an animal in my yard, chewing on meat as if he were some wild beast. Christian reminded me of that man. There was the same air of the primitive about him.

'You need a bath rather badly,' I said, and he grinned and made a sound of affirmation. I went on, 'What have you been doing? In the woods. Have you been camping?'

He swallowed noisily, and drank half a cup of tea before shaking his head. 'I have a camp there, but I've been searching, walking as deep as I could get. But I still can't get beyond . . .' He broke off and glanced at me, a questioning look in his eyes. 'Did you read the old man's notebook?'

I said that I hadn't. In truth, I had been so surprised by his abrupt departure, and so committed to getting the house back into some sort of shape, that I had forgotten all about father's notes on his work. And even as I said this I wondered if the truth of the matter was that I had put father, his work and his notes, as far from my mind as possible, as if they were spectres whose haunting would reduce my resolve to go forward.

Christian wiped his hand across his mouth and stared at his empty plate. He suddenly sniffed at himself and laughed.

'By God, I do stink. You'd better boil me up some water, Steve. I'll wash right now.'

But I didn't move. Instead I stared across the wooden table at him; he caught my gaze and frowned. 'What is it? What's on your mind?'

'I found her, Chris. I found her body. Guiwenneth. I found where you buried her.'

I don't know what reaction I expected from Christian. Anger, perhaps, or panic, or a sudden babbling burst of explanation. I half hoped he would react with puzzlement, that the corpse in the yard would turn out not to be the remains of his wife, and that he had no involvement with its burial. But Christian knew about the body. He stared at me blankly, and a heavy, sweaty silence made me grow uncomfortable.

Suddenly I realized that Christian was crying, his gaze not wavering from my own, but moistened now by the tears that coursed through the remaining grime on his face. And yet he made no sound, and his face never changed its expression from that of bland, almost blind contemplation.

'Who shot her, Chris?' I asked quietly. 'Did you?'

'Not me,' he said, and with the words his tears stopped, and his gaze dropped to the table. 'She was shot by a mythago. There was nothing I could do about it.'

Mythago? The meaning was alien to me, although I recognized the word from the scrap of my father's notebook that I carried. I queried it and Chris rose from the table, but rested his hands upon it as he watched me. 'A mythago,' he repeated. 'It's still in the woods . . . they all are. That's where I've been, seeking among them. I tried to save her, Steve. She was alive when I found her, and she might have stayed alive, but I brought her out of the woods . . . in a way, I did kill her. I took her away from the vortex, and she died quite quickly. I panicked, then. I didn't know what to do. I buried her because it seemed the easiest way out . . .'

'Did you tell the police? Did you report her death?'

Christian smiled, but it was not with any morbid humour. It was a knowing smile, a response to some secret that he had not so far shared; and yet the gesture was merely a defence, for it faded rapidly. 'Not necessary, Steve . . . the police would not have been interested.'

I rose angrily from the table. It seemed to me that Christian was behaving, and had behaved, with appalling irresponsibility. 'Her family, Chris . . . her parents! They have a right to know.'

And Christian laughed.

I felt the blood rise in my face. 'I don't see anything to laugh at.'

He sobered instantly, looked at me almost abashed. 'You're right. I'm sorry. You don't understand, and it's time you did. Steve, she had no parents because she had no life, no real life. She's lived a thousand times, and she's never lived at all. But I still fell in love with her . . . and I shall find her again in the woods; she's in there somewhere . . .'

Had he gone mad? His words were the unreasoned babblings of one insane, and yet something about his eyes, something about his demeanour, told me that it was not so much insanity as obsession. But obsession with what?

'You *must* read the old man's notes, Steve. Don't put it off any longer. They will tell you about the wood, about what's going on in there. I mean it. I'm neither mad nor callous. I'm just trapped, and before I go away again, I'd like you to know why, and how, and where I'm going. Perhaps you'll be able to help me. Who knows? Read the book. And then we'll talk. And when you know what our dear departed father managed to do, then I'm afraid I shall have to take my leave of you again.'

Four

There is one entry in my father's notebook that seems to mark a turning point in his research, and his life. It is longer than the other notes of that particular time, and follows an absence of seven months from the pages. While his entries are often detailed, he could not be described as having been a dedicated diarist, and the style varies from clipped notes to fluent description. (I discovered, too, that he himself had torn many pages from the thick book, thus concealing my minor crime quite effectively. Christian had never noticed the missing page.) On the whole, he seems to have used the notebook, and the quiet hours of recording, as a way of conversing with himself – a means of clarification of his own thoughts.

The entry in question is dated September 1935, and was written shortly after our encounter with the Twigling. After reading the entry for the first time I thought back to that year and realized I had been just eight years old.

Wynne-Jones arrived after dawn. Walked together along the south track, checking the flux-drains for signs of mythago activity. Back to the house quite shortly after – no-one about, which suited my mood. A crisp, dry autumn day. Like last year, images of the Urscumug are strongest as the season changes. Perhaps he senses autumn, the dying of the green. He comes forward, and the oakwoods whisper to him. He must be close to genesis. Wynne-Jones thinks a further time of isolation needed, and it must be done. Jennifer already concerned and distraught by my absences. I feel helpless – can't speak to her. Must do what is needed.

Yesterday the boys glimpsed the Twigling. I had thought him resorbed – clearly the resonance is stronger than we had believed.

33

He seems to frequent the woodland edge, which is to be expected. I have seen him along the track several times, but not for a year or so. The persistence is worrying. Both boys clearly disturbed by the sighting; Christian less emotional. I suspect it meant little to him, a poacher perhaps, or local man taking short cut to Grimley. Wynne-Jones suggests we go back into woods and call the Twigling deep, perhaps to the hogback glade where he might remain in the strong oak vortex and eventually fade. But I know that penetrating into deep woodland will involve more than a week's absence, and poor Jennifer is already deeply depressed by my behaviour. Cannot explain it to her, though I dearly want to. Do not want the children involved in this, and it worries me that they have now twice seen a mythago. I have invented magic forest creatures – stories for them. Hope they will associate what they see with products of their own imaginations. But must be careful.

Until it is resolved, until the Urscumug mythago forms from the woodland, must not let any but Wynne-Jones know of what I have discovered. The completeness of the resurrection essential. The Urscumug is the most powerful because he is the primary. I know for certain that the oakwoods will contain him, but others might be frightened of the power they would certainly be able to feel, and end it for everyone. Dread to think what would happen if these forests were destroyed, and yet they cannot survive for ever.

Thursday: Today's training with Wynne-Jones: test pattern 26: iii, shallow hypnosis, green light environment. As the frontal bridge reached sixty volts, despite the pain, the flow across my skull was the most powerful I have ever known. Am now totally convinced that each half of the brain functions in a slightly different way, and that the hidden awareness is located on the right-hand side. It has been lost for so long! The Wynne-Jones bridge enables a superficial communion between the fields around each hemisphere, and the zone of the pre-mythago is excited accordingly. If only there were some way of exploring the living brain to find exactly where the site of this occult presence lies.

Monday: The forms of the mythagos cluster in my peripheral vision, still. Why never in fore-vision? These unreal images are mere reflections, after all. The form of Hood was subtly different – more brown than green, the face less friendly, more haunted, drawn. This is certainly because earlier images (even the Hood mythago that actually formed in the woodland, two years ago) were affected by my own confused childhood images of the green-wood, and the merry band. But now, evocation of the pre-mythago is more powerful, reaches to the basic form, without interference. The Arthur form was more real as well, and I glimpsed the various marshland forms from the latter part of the first millennium AD. Also, a hint of the haunting presence of what I believe is a Bronze Age necromantic figure. A terrifying moment. The guardian of the Horse Shrine has gone, the shrine destroyed. I wonder why? The huntsman has been back to the 'Wolf Glen'; his fire was quite fresh. I also found evidence of the neolithic shaman, the hunter-artist who leaves the strange red ochre patterns on tree and rock. Wynne-Jones would love me to explore these folk heroes, unrecorded and unknown, but I am anxious to find the primary image.

The Urscumug has formed in my mind in the clearest form I have ever seen him. Hints of the Twigling in shape, but he is much more ancient, far bigger. Decks himself with wood and leaves, on top of animal hides. Face seems smeared with white clay, forming a mask upon the exaggerated features below; but it is hard to see the face clearly. A mask upon a mask? The hair a mass of stiff and spiky points; gnarled hawthorn branches are driven up through the matted hair, giving a most bizarre appearance. I believe he carries a spear, with a wide, stone blade . . . an angry-looking weapon, but again, hard to see, always just out of focus. He is so old, this primary image, that he is fading from the human mind. He is also touched with confusion. The overlaying of later cultural interpretation of how his appearance would have been . . . a hint of bronze particularly, mostly about the arms (torques). I suspect that the legend of the Urscumug was powerful enough to carry through all the neolithic and on into the second millennium BC, perhaps even later. Wynne-Jones thinks the Urscumug may pre-date even the neolithic.

Essential, now, to spend time in the forest, to allow the vortex to interact with me and form the mythago. I intend to leave the house within the next week.

Without commenting on the strange, confusing passages I had read, I turned the pages of the diary and read entries here and there. I could clearly recall that autumn in 1933, the time when my father had packed a large rucksack and wandered into the woods, walking swiftly away from my mother's hysterical shouting, flanked by his diminutive scientist friend (a sour-faced man who never acknowledged any-one but my father, and who seemed embarrassed to be in the house when he came to visit). Mother had not spoken for the rest of the day, and she did nothing but sit in her bedroom and occasionally weep. Christian and I had become so distraught at her behaviour that in the later afternoon we had penetrated the oak-woods as deeply as we dared, calling for our father and finally panicking at the gloomy silence, and the loud, sudden sounds that disturbed it. He had returned weeks later, dishevelled and stinking like a tramp. The entry in his notebook, a few days subsequently, is a short and bitter account of failure. Nothing had hap-pened. A single, rather rambling paragraph caught my attention.

The mythogenetic process is not only complex, it is reluctant. I am too old! The equipment helps, but a younger mind could accom-plish the task unaided, I'm sure. I dread the thought! Also, my mind is not at rest and as Wynne-Jones has explained, it is likely that my human consideration, my worries, form an effective barrier between the two mythopoetic energy flows in my cortex – the *form* from the right brain, the *reality* from the left. The pre-mythago zone is not sufficiently enriched by my own life force for it to interact in the oak vortex.

I fear too that the natural disappearance of so much life from the forest is affecting the interface. The boars are there, I'm sure. But perhaps the life number is critical. I estimate no more than forty, moving within the spiral vortex bounded by the ashwood intrusions into the oak circle. There are few deer, few wolves, although the most important animal, the hare, frequents the woodland edge in profusion. But perhaps the absence of so much that once lived here has thrown the balance of the formula. And yet, throughout the primary existence of these woods, life was changing. By the thirteenth century there was *much* botanical life that was alien to the *ley matrix* in places where the mythagos still formed. The form of the myth men changes, adapts, and it is the later forms that generate most easily.

Hood is back – like all the Jack-in-the-Greens, is a nuisance, and several times moved into the ridge-zone around the hog-back glade. He shot at me, and this is becoming a cause of great concern! But I cannot enrich the oak vortex sufficiently with the pre-mythago of the Urscumug. What is the answer? To try to enter more deeply, to find the *wildwoods*? Perhaps the memory is too far gone, too deep in the silent zones of the brain, now, to touch the trees.

Christian saw me frown as I read through this tumble of words and images. Hood? Robin Hood? And someone – this Hood – shooting at my father in the woods? I glanced around the study and saw the iron-tipped arrow in its long, narrow glass case, mounted above the display of woodland butterflies. Christian was turning the pages of the notebook, having watched me read in silence for the better part of an hour. He was perched on the desk; I sat in father's chair.

'What's all this about, Chris? It reads as if he were actually trying to create copies of storybook heroes.'

'Not copies, Steve. The real thing. There. Last bit of reading for the moment, then I'll go through it with you in layman's terms.'

It was an earlier entry, not dated by year, only by day and month, although it was clearly from some years before the 1933 recording.

I call those particular times 'cultural interfaces'; they form zones, bounded in space, of course, by the limits of the country, but bounded also in time, a few years, a decade or so, when the two cultures – that of the invaded and the invader – are in a highly anguished state. The mythagos grow from the power of hate, and fear, and form in the natural woodlands from which they can either emerge – such as the Arthur, or Artorius form, the bear-like man with his charismatic leadership – or remain in the natural landscape, establishing a hidden focus of hope – the Robin Hood form, perhaps Hereward, and of course the hero-form I call the Twigling, harassing the Romans in so many parts of the country. I imagine that it is the combined emotion of the two races that draws out the mythago, but it clearly sides with that culture whose roots are longest established in what I agree could be a sort of *ley matrix*; thus, Arthur forms and helps the Britons against the Saxons, but later Hood is created to help the Saxons against the Norman invader.

I drew back from the book, shaking my head. The expressions were confusing, bemusing. Christian grinned as he took the notebook, and weighed it in his hands. 'Years of his life, Steve, but his concern with keeping detailed records was not everything it might have been. He records nothing for years, then writes every day for a month. *And* he has removed and hidden several pages.' He frowned slightly as he said this.

'I need a drink of something. And a few definitions.'

We walked from the study, Christian carrying the notebook. As we passed the framed arrow I peered closely at it. 'Is he saying that the real Robin Hood shot that into him? And killed Guiwenneth too?'

'It depends,' said Christian thoughtfully, 'on what you mean by real. Hood came to that oak forest, and may still be there. I think he is. As you have obviously noticed, he was there four months ago when he shot Guiwenneth. But there were many Robin Hoods, and all were as real or unreal as each other, created by the Saxon peasants during their time of repression by the Norman invader.'

'I don't comprehend this at all, Chris – but what's a "ley matrix"? What's an "oak vortex"? Does it mean anything?'

As we sipped scotch and water in the sitting-room, watching the dusk draw closer, the yard beyond the window greying into a place of featureless shapes, Christian explained how a man called Alfred Watkins had visited our father on several occasions and shown him on a map of the country how straight lines connected places of spiritual or ancient power – the barrows, stones and churches of three different cultures. These lines he called leys, and believed that they existed as a form of earth energy running below the ground, but influencing that which stood upon it.

My father had thought about leys, and apparently tried to measure the energy in the ground below the forest, but without success. And yet he had measured *something* in the oakwoods – an energy associated with all the life that grew there. He had found a spiral vortex around each tree, a sort of aura, and those spirals bounded not just trees, but whole stands of trees, and glades.

Over the years he had mapped the forest. Christian brought out that map of the woodland area, and I looked at it again, but from a different point of view, beginning to understand the marks made upon it by the man who had spent so much time within the territories it depicted. Circles within circles were marked, crossed and skirted by straight lines, some of which were associated with the two pathways we called south and deep track. The letters HB in the middle of the vast acreage of forest were clearly meant to refer to the 'hogback' glade that existed there, a clearing that neither Christian nor I had ever been able to find. There were zones marked out as 'spiral oak', 'dead ash zone' and 'oscillating traverse'.

'The old man believed that all life is surrounded by an energetic aura – you can see the human aura as a faint glow in certain light. In these ancient woodlands, *primary woodlands*, the combined aura forms something far more powerful, a sort of creative field that can interact with our unconscious. And it's in the unconscious that we carry what he calls the pre-mythago – that's unconscious that we carry what he calls the pre-mythago – that's *myth imago*, the image of the idealized form of a myth creature. The image takes on substance in a natural environment, solid flesh, blood, clothing, and – as you saw – weaponry. The form of the idealized myth, the hero figure, alters with cultural changes, assuming the identity and technology of the time. When one culture invades another – according to father's theory – the heroes are made manifest, and not just in one location! Historians and legend-seekers argue about where Arthur of the Britons, and Robin Hood *really* lived and fought, and don't realize that they lived in *many* sites. And another important fact to remember is that when the mind image of the mythago forms it forms in the *whole* population . . . and when it is no longer needed, it remains in our collective unconscious, and is transmitted through the generations.'

'And the changing form of the mythago,' I said, to see if I had understood my sketchy reading of father's notes, 'is based on an archetype, an archaic primary image which father called the Urscumug, and from which all later forms come. And he tried to raise the Urscumug from his own unconscious mind . . .'

'And failed to do so,' said Christian, 'although not for want of trying. The effort killed him. It weakened him so much that his body couldn't take the pace. But he certainly seems to have created several of the more recent adaptations of the Urscumug.'

There were so many questions, so many areas that begged for clarification. One above all: 'But a thousand years ago, if I understand the notes correctly, there was a country-wide *need* of the hero, the legendary figure, acting for the side of Right. How can one man capture such a passionate mood? How did he *power* the interaction? Surely not from the simple family anguish he caused among us, and in his own head. As he said, that created an unsettled mind and he couldn't function properly.'

'If there's an answer,' said Christian calmly, 'it's to be

found in the woodland area, perhaps in the hogback glade. The old man wrote in his notes of the need for a period of solitary existence, a period of meditation. For a year now I've been following his example directly. He invented a sort of electrical bridge which seems to *fuse* elements from each half of the brain. I've used his equipment a great deal, with and without him. But I already find images – the pre-mythagos – forming in my peripheral vision *without* the complicated programme that he used. He was the pioneer; his own inter-action with the wood has made it easier for those who come after. Also, I'm younger. He felt that would be important. He achieved a certain success; I intend to complete his work, eventually. I shall raise the Urscumug, this hero of the first men.'

'To what end, Chris?' I asked quietly, and in all truth could not see a reason for so tampering with the ancient forces that inhabited both woodland and human spirit. Christian was clearly obsessed with the idea of raising these dead forms, of finishing something the old man had begun. But in my reading of his notebook, and in my conversation with Christian, I had not heard a single word that explained *why* so bizarre a state of nature should be so important to the ones who studied it.

Christian had an answer. And as he spoke to me his voice was hollow, the mark of his uncertainty, the stigma of his lack of conviction in the truth of what he said. 'Why, to study the earliest times of man, Steve. From these mythagos we can learn so much of how it was, and how it was hoped to be. The aspirations, the visions, the cultural identity of a time so far gone that even its stone monuments are incom-prehensible to us. To learn. To communicate through those persistent images of our past that are locked in each and every one of us.'

He stopped speaking, and there was the briefest of silences, interrupted only by the heavy rhythmic sound of the clock. I said, 'I'm not convinced, Chris.' For a moment I thought he would shout his anger; his face flushed, his whole body tensed

41

up, furious with my calm dismissal of his script. But the fire softened, and he frowned, staring at me almost helplessly. 'What does that mean?'

'Nice-sounding words; no conviction.'

After a second he seemed to acknowledge some truth in what I said. 'Perhaps my conviction has gone, then, buried beneath . . . beneath the other thing. Guiwenneth. She's become my main reason for going back now.'

I remembered his callous words of a while ago, about how she had no life yet a thousand lives. I understood instantly, and wondered how so obvious a fact could have remained so doggedly elusive to me. 'She was a mythago herself,' I said. 'I understand now.'

'She was my father's mythago, a girl from Roman times, a manifestation of the Earth Goddess, the young warrior princess who, through her own suffering, can unite the tribes.'

'Like Queen Boadicea,' I said.

'Boudicca,' Christian corrected, then shook his head. 'Boudicca was historically real, although much of her legend was inspired by the myths and tales of the girl Guiwenneth. There are no recorded legends about Guiwenneth. In her own time, and her own culture, the oral tradition held sway. Nothing was written; but no Roman observer, or later Christian chronicler, refers to her either, although the old man thought that early tales of Queen Guenevere might have drawn partly from the forgotten legends. She's lost from popular memory—'

'But not from hidden memory!'

Christian nodded. 'That's exactly right. Her story is very old, very familiar. Legends of Guiwenneth rose out of stories from previous cultures, perhaps right back to the post-glacial period, or to the time of the Urscumug itself!'

'And each of those earlier forms of the girl will be in the wood too?'

Christian shrugged. 'The old man saw none, and nor have I. But they *must* be there.'

42

'And what *is* her story, Chris?'

He looked at me peculiarly. 'That's hard to say. Our dear father tore the pages about Guiwenneth from his diary. I have no idea why, or where he hid them. I only know what he told me. Oral tradition again.' He smiled. 'She was the child to the younger of two sisters, by a young warrior banished to a secret camp in the wildwoods. The elder sister was the wife of one of the invaders, and she was both barren and jealous, and stole the girl child. The child was rescued by nine hawks, or somesuch, sent by her father. She was brought up in the forest communities all around the country, under the guardianship of the Lord of Animals. When she was old enough, and strong enough, she returned, raised the ghost of her warlord father, and drove the invaders out.'

'Not much to go on,' I said.

'A fragment only,' Christian agreed. 'There is something about a bright stone, in a valley that breathes. Whatever else the old man learned about her, or from her, he has destroyed.'

'Why, I wonder?'

Christian said nothing for a moment, then added, 'Anyway, legends of Guiwenneth inspired many tribes to take offensive action against the invader, whether they were Wessex Chieftain, which is to say, Bronze Age, Stonehenge and all that; Belgic Celts, which is to say Iron Age; or Romans.' His gaze became distant for a moment. 'And then she was formed in this wood, and I found her and came to love her. She was not violent, perhaps because the old man himself could not think of a woman being violent. He imposed a structure on her, disarming her, leaving her quite helpless in the forest.'

'How long did you know her?' I asked, and he shrugged.

'I can't tell, Steve. How long have I been away?'

'Twelve days or so.'

'As short as that?' He seemed surprised. 'I thought more than three weeks. Perhaps I knew her for no time at all, then,

43

but it seems like months. I lived in the forest with her, trying to understand her language, trying to teach her mine, speaking with signs and yet always able to talk quite deeply. But the old man pursued us right to the heartwoods, right to the end. He wouldn't let up – she was *his* girl, and he had been as struck by her as had I. I found him, one day, exhausted and terrified, half buried by leaves at the forest edge. I took him home and he was dead within the month. That's what I meant by his having had a reason for attacking me. I took Guiwenneth from him.'

'And then she was taken from you. Shot dead.'

'A few months later, yes. I became a little too happy, a little too content. I wrote to you because I had to tell *someone* about her . . . clearly that was too much for fate. Two days later I found her in a glade, dying. She might have lived if I could have got help to her in the forest, and left her there. I carried her out of the wood, though, and she died.' He stared at me and the expression of sadness hardened to one of resolve. 'But when I'm back in the wood, her myth image from my own subconscious has a chance of being formed . . . she might be a little tougher than my father's version, but I can find her again, Steve, if I look hard, if I can find that energy you asked about, if I can get into the deepest part of the wood, to that central vortex . . .'

I looked at the map again, at the spiral field around the hogback glade. 'What's the problem? Can't you find it?'

'It's well defended. I get near it, but I can't ever get beyond the field that's about two hundred yards around it. I find myself walking in elaborate circles even though I'm convinced I've walked straight. I can't get in, and whatever's in there can't get out. All the mythagos are tied to their genesis zones, although the Twigling, and Guiwenneth too, could get to the very edge of the forest, down by the pool.'

But that wasn't true! And I'd spent a shaky night to prove it. I said, 'One of the mythagos has come out of the wood . . . a tall man with the most unbelievably terrifying hound. He came into the yard and ate a leg of pork.'

Christian looked stunned. 'A mythago? Are you sure?'

'Well, no. I had no idea at all what he was until now. But he stank, was filthy, had obviously lived in the woods for months, spoke a strange language, carried a bow and arrows . . .'

'And ran with a hunting dog. Yes, of course. It's a late Bronze Age, early Iron Age image, very widespread. The Irish have taken him to their own with Cuchulainn, made a big hero out of him, but he's one of the most powerful of the myth images, recognizable all across Europe.' Christian frowned, then. 'I don't understand . . . a year ago I saw him, and avoided him, but he was fading fast, decaying . . . it happens to them after a while. Something must have fed the mythago, strengthened it . . .'

'Some *one*, Chris.'

'But who?' It dawned on him, then, and his eyes widened slightly. 'My God. Me. From my own mind. It took the old man years, and I thought it would take me a lot longer, many more months in the woodlands, much more isolation. But it's started already, my own interaction with the vortex . . .'

He had gone quite pale, and he walked to where his staff was propped against the wall, picked it up and weighed it in his hands. He stared at it, touched the markings upon it.

'You know what this means,' he said quietly, and before I could answer went on, 'She'll form. She'll come back; my Guiwenneth. She may be back already.'

'Don't go rushing off again, Chris. Wait a while; rest.'

He placed his staff against the wall again. 'I don't dare. If she has formed by now, she's in danger. I have to go back.' He looked at me and smiled thinly, apologetically. 'Sorry, brother. Not much of a homecoming for you.'

Five

As quickly as this, after the briefest of reunions, I had lost Christian again. He was in no mood to talk, too distracted by the thought of Guiwenneth alone and trapped in the forest to allow me much of an insight into his plans, and into his hopes and fears for some resolution to their impossible love affair.

I wandered through the kitchen and the rest of the house as he gathered his provisions together. Again and again he assured me that he would be gone for no more than a week, perhaps two. If she was in the wood he would have found her by that time; if not, then he would return and wait a while before going back to the deep zones and trying to form her mythago. In a year, he said, many of the more hostile mythagos would have faded into non-existence, and she would be safer. His thoughts were confused, his plan that he would strengthen her to allow her the same freedom as the man and the hound did not seem supportable on the evidence from our father's notes; but Christian was a determined man.

If one mythago could escape, then so could the one he loved.

One idea that appealed to him was that I should come with him as far as the glade where we had made camp as children, and pitch a tent there. This could be a regular rendezvous for us, he said, and it would keep his time sense on the right track. And if I spent time in the forest I might encounter other mythagos, and could report on their state. The glade he had in mind was at the edge of the wood, and quite safe.

When I expressed concern that my own mind would begin to produce mythagos, he assured me that it would take months for the first pre-mythago activity to show up as a haunting presence at the edge of my vision. He was equally blunt in saying that, if I stayed in the area for too long, I would certainly start to relate to the woodland, whose aura – he thought – had spread more towards the house in the last few years.

Late the following morning we set off along the south track. A pale yellow sun hung high above the forest. It was a cool, bright day, the air full of the scent of smoke, drifting from the distant farm where the stubbly remains of the summer harvest were being burned. We walked in silence until we came to the mill-pond; I had assumed Christian would enter the oak woodland here, but wisely he decided against it, not so much because of the strange movements we had seen there as children, but because of the marshy conditions. Instead, we walked on until the woodland bordering the track thinned. Here Christian turned off the path.

I followed him inwards, seeking the easiest route between tangles of bracken and nettles, enjoying the heavy stillness. The trees were small, here at the edge, but within a hundred yards they began to show their real age, great gnarled oak trunks, hollow and half-dead, twisting up from the ground, almost groaning beneath the weight of their branches. The ground rose slightly, and the tangled undergrowth was broken by weathered, lichen-covered stubs of grey limestone. We passed over the crest and the earth dipped sharply down, and a subtle change came over the woodland. It seemed darker, somehow, more alive, and I noticed that the shrill September bird-sound of the forest edge was replaced, here, by a more sporadic, mournful song.

Christian beat his way through bramble thickets, and I trudged wearily after, and we soon came to the large glade where, years before, we had made our camp. One particularly large oak tree dominated the surrounds, and we laughed as we traced the faded initials we had once carved there. In its branches we had made our lookout tower, but we had seen very little from that leafy vantage point.

'Do I look the part?' asked Christian, holding his arms out, and I grinned as I surveyed his caped figure, the rune-inscribed staff looking less odd, now, more functional.

'You look like something. Quite what I don't know.'

He glanced around the clearing. 'I'll do my best to get back here as often as I can. If anything goes wrong, I'll try and leave a message if I can't find you, some mark to let you know . . .'

'Nothing's going to go wrong,' I said with a smile. It was clear that he didn't wish me to accompany him beyond this glade, and that suited me. I felt a chill, an odd tingle, a sense of being watched. Christian noticed my discomfort and admitted that he felt it too, the presence of the wood, the gentle breathing of the trees.

We shook hands, then embraced awkwardly, and he turned on his heels and paced off into the gloom. I watched him go, then listened, and only when all sound had gone did I set about pitching the small tent.

For most of September the weather remained cool and dry, a dull sort of month that enabled me to drift through the days in a very low-key state. I worked on the house, read some more of father's notebook (but quickly tired of the repetitive images and thoughts) and with decreasing frequency walked into the woodlands and sat near, or in the tent, listening for Christian, cursing the midges that haunted the place, and watching for any hint of movement.

With October came rain and the abrupt, almost startling realization that Christian had been gone for nearly a month. The time had slipped by, and instead of feeling concerned for him I had merely assumed that he knew what he was doing, and would return when he was quite ready. But he had been absent for weeks without even the slightest sign. He could surely have come back to the glade once, and left some mark of his passing.

Now I began to feel more concern for his safety than perhaps was warranted. As soon as the rain stopped I trudged back through the forest and waited out the rest of the day in the miserable, leaking canvas shelter. I saw hares, and a wood owl, and heard distant movements that did not respond to my cries of 'Christian? Is that you?'

It got colder. I spent more time in the tent, creating a sleeping-bag out of blankets and some tattered oilskins I found in the cellar of Oak Lodge. I repaired the splits in the tent, and stocked it with food and beer, and dry wood for fires. By the middle of October I noticed that I could not spend more than an hour at the house before becoming restless, an unease that could only be dispelled by returning to the glade and taking up my watching post, seated cross-legged just inside the tent, watching the gloom a few yards away. On several occasions I took long, rather nervous sorties further into the forest, but I disliked the sensation of stillness and the tingling of my skin which seemed to say repeatedly that I was being watched. All this was ima-gination, of course, or an extremely sensitive response to woodland animals, for on one occasion, when I ran scream-ing and yelling at the thicket wherein I imagined the voyeur was crouched, I saw nothing but a red squirrel go scampering in panic up into the crossed and confused branches of its home oak.

Where *was* Christian? I tacked paper messages as deep in the wood, and in as many locations, as I could. But I found that wherever I walked too far into the great dip that seemed to be swallowing the forest down, I would, at some point within the span of a few hours, find myself approaching the glade and the tent again. Uncanny, yes, and infuriating too; but I began to get an idea of Christian's own frustration at not being able to maintain a straight line in the dense oak-wood. Perhaps, after all, there *was* some sort of field of force complex and convoluted, that channelled intruders back on to an outward track.

And November came, and it was very cold indeed. The rain was sporadic and icy, but the wind reached down through the dense, browning foliage of the forest and seemed to find its way through clothes and oilskin and flesh to the cooling bones beneath. I was miserable, and my searches for Christian grew more angry, more frustrated. My voice was often hoarse with shouting, my skin blistered and scratched from climbing trees. I lost track of time, realizing on more than one occasion, and with some shock, that I had been two, or perhaps three days in the forest without returning to the house. Oak Lodge grew stale and deserted. I used it to wash, to feed, to rest, but as soon as the worst ravages of my body were corrected, thoughts of Christian, anxiety about him, grew in my mind and pulled me back to the glade, as surely as if I were a metal filing tugged to a magnet.

I began to suspect that something terrible had happened to him; or perhaps not terrible, just natural: if there really were boars in the wood, he might have been gored by one, and be either dead or dragging himself from the heart-woods to the edge, unable to cry for help. Or perhaps he had fallen from a tree, or quite simply gone to sleep in the cold and wet and failed to revive in the morning.

I searched for any sign of his body, or of his having passed by, and I found absolutely nothing, although I discovered the spoor of some large beast, and marks on the lower trunks of several oaks that looked like nothing other than the scratchings of a tusked animal.

But my mood of depression passed, and by mid-November I was quite confident again that Christian was alive. My feelings, now, were that he had somehow become trapped in this autumnal forest.

For the first time in two weeks I went into the village, and after obtaining food supplies, I picked up the papers that had been accumulating at the tiny newsagents. Skimming the front pages of the weekly local, I noticed an item concerning the decaying bodies of a man and an Irish wolfhound, discovered in a ditch on farmland near Grimley. Foul play was not suspected. I felt no emotion, apart from a curious coldness, a sense of sympathy for Christian, whose dream of freedom for Guiwenneth was surely no more than that: a fervent hope, a desire doomed to frustration.

As for mythagos, I had only two encounters, neither of them of much note. The first was with a shadowy man-form that skirted the clearing, watching me, and finally ran into the darkness, striking at the trunks of trees with a short, wooden stick. The second meeting was with the Twigling, whose shape I followed stealthily as he walked to the mill-pond and stood in the trees, staring across at the boathouse. I felt no real fear of these manifestations, merely a slight apprehension. But it was only after the second meeting that I began to realize how alien the wood was to the mythagos, and how alien the mythagos were to the wood. These creatures, created far away from their natural age, echoes of a past given substance, were equipped with a life, a language and a certain ferocity that was quite inappropriate to the war-scarred world of 1947. No wonder the aura of the woodland was so charged with a sense of solitude, an infectious loneliness that had come to inhabit the body of my father, and then Christian, and which was even now crawling through my own tissues, and would trap me if I allowed it.

It was at this time, too, that I began to hallucinate. Notably at dusk, as I stared into the woodlands, I saw movement at the edge of my vision. At first I put this down to tiredness, or imagination, but I remembered clearly the passage from my father's notebook in which he described how the pre-mythagos, the initial images, always appeared at his peripheral vision. I was frightened at first, unwilling to acknowledge that such creatures could be resident in my own mind, and that my own interaction with the woodland had begun far earlier than Christian had thought; but after a while I sat and tried to see details of them. I failed to do so. I could sense movement, and the occasional manlike shape, but whatever field was inducing their appearance was not yet strong enough to pull them into full view; either that, or my mind could not yet control their emergence.

On the 24th of November I went back to the house and spent a few hours resting and listening to the wireless. A thunderstorm passed overhead and I watched the rain and the darkness, feeling wretched and cold. But as soon as the air cleared, and the clouds brightened, I draped my oilskin about my shoulders and headed back to the glade. I had not expected to find anything different, and so what should have been a surprise was more of a shock.

The tent had been demolished, its contents strewn and trampled into the sodden turf of the clearing. Part of the guy rope dangled from the higher branches of the large oak, and the ground hereabouts was churned as if there had been a fight. As I walked into the space I noticed that the ground was pitted by strange footprints, round and cleft, like hooves, I thought. Whatever the beast had been it had quite effectively torn the canvas shelter to tatters.

I noticed then how silent the forest was, as if holding its breath and watching. Every hair on my body stood on end, and my heartbeat was so powerful that I thought my chest would burst. I stood by the ruined tent for just a second or two and the panic hit me, making my head spin and the forest seem to lean towards me. I fled from the glade, crashing into the sopping undergrowth between two thick oak trunks. I ran through the gloom for several yards before realizing I was running *away* from the woodland edge. I think I cried out, and turned and began to run back.

A spear thudded heavily into the tree beside me and I had run into the black wood shaft before I could stop; a hand gripped my shoulder and flung me against the tree. I shouted out in fear, staring into the mud-smeared, gnarled face of my attacker. He shouted back at me.

'Shut up, Steve! For God's sake, shut up!'

My panic quietened, my voice dropped to a whimper and I peered hard at the angry man who held me. I was Christian, I realized, and my relief was so intense that I laughed, and for long moments failed to notice what a total change had come about him.

He was looking back towards the glade. 'You've got to get out of here,' he said, and before I could respond he had wrenched me into a run, and was practically dragging me back to the tent.

In the clearing he hesitated and looked at me. There was no smile from behind the mask of mud and browning leaves. His eyes shone, but they were narrowed and lined. His hair was slick and spiky. He was naked but for a breechclout and a ragged skin jacket that could not have supplied much warmth. He carried three viciously pointed spears. Gone was the skeletal thinness of summer. He was muscular and hard, deep-chested and heavy-limbed. He was a man made for fighting.

'You've got to get out of the wood, Steve; and for God's sake don't come back.'

'What's happened to you, Chris . . . ?' I stuttered, but he shook his head and pulled me across the clearing and into the woods again, towards the south track.

Immediately he stopped, staring into gloom, holding me back. 'What is it, Chris?'

And then I heard it too, a heavy crashing sound, something picking its way through the bracken and the trees towards us. Following Christian's gaze I saw a monstrous shape, twice as high as a man, but man-shaped and stooped, black as night save for the great white splash of its face, still indistinct in the distance and greyness.

'God, it's broken out!' said Christian. 'It's got between us and the edge.'

'What is it? A mythago?'

'*The* mythago,' said Christian quickly, and turned and fled back across the clearing. I followed, all tiredness suddenly gone from my body.

'The Urscumug? That's *it*? But it's not human . . . it's animal. No human was ever that tall.'

Looking back as I ran, I saw it enter the glade and move across the open space so fast I thought I was watching a speeded-up film. It plunged into the wood behind us and was lost in darkness again, but it was running now, weaving between trees as it pursued us, closing the distance with incredible speed.

Quite suddenly the ground went out from under me. I fell heavily into a depression in the ground, to be steadied, as I tumbled, by Christian, who moved a bramble covering across us and put a finger to his lips. I could barely make him out in this dark hidey hole, but I heard the sound of the Urscumug die away, and queried what was happening.

'Has it moved off?'

'Almost certainly not,' said Christian. 'It's waiting, listening. It's been pursuing me for two days, out of the deep zones of the forest. It won't let up until I'm gone.'

'But why, Chris? Why is it trying to kill you?'

'It's the old man's mythago,' he said. 'He brought it into being in the heartwoods, but it was weak and trapped until I came along and gave it more power to draw on. But it was the old man's mythago, and he shaped it slightly from his own mind, his own ego. Oh God, Steve, how he must have hated, and hated *us*, to have imposed such terror on to the thing.'

'And Guiwenneth . . .' I said.

'Yes . . . Guiwenneth . . .' Christian echoed, speaking softly now. 'He'll revenge himself on me for that. If I give him half a chance.'

He stretched up to peer through the bramble covering. I could hear a distant, restless movement, and thought I caught the sound of some animal grumbling deep in its throat.

'I thought he'd failed to create the primary mythago.'

Christian said, 'He died believing that. What would he have done, I wonder, if he'd seen how successful he'd been.' He crouched back down in the ditch. 'It's like a boar. Part boar, part man, elements of other beasts from the wildwood. It walks upright, but can run like the wind. It paints its face white in the semblance of a human face. Whatever age it lived in, one thing's for sure, it lived a long time before man as *we* understand "man" existed; this thing comes from a time when man and nature were so close that they were indistinguishable.'

He touched me, then, on the arm; a hesitant touch, as if he were half afraid to make this contact with one from whom he had grown so distant.

'When you run,' he said, 'run for the edge. Don't stop. And when you get out of the wood, don't come back. There is no way out for me, now. I'm trapped in this wood by something in my own mind as surely as if I were a mythago myself. Don't come back here, Steve. Not for a long, long time.'

'Chris—' I began, but too late. He had thrown back the covering of the hole and was running from me. Moments later the most enormous shape passed overhead, one huge, black foot landing just inches from my frozen body. It passed by in a split second. But as I scrambled from the hole and began to run I glanced back and the creature, hearing me, glanced back too; and for that instant of mutual contemplation, as we both moved apart in the forest, I saw the face that had been painted across the blackened features of the boar.

The Urscumug opened its mouth to roar, and my father seemed to leer at me.

PART TWO

The Wild Hunters

One

One morning, in early spring, I found a brace of hare hanging from one of the pothooks in the kitchen; below them, scratched in the yellow paintwork on the wall, was the letter 'C'. The gift was repeated about two weeks later, but then nothing, and the months passed.

I had not been back to the wood.

Over the long winter I had read my father's diary ten times if I had read it once, steeping myself in the mystery of his life as much as he had steeped himself in the mystery of his own unconscious links with the primeval woodland. I found, in his erratic recordings, much that told of his sense of danger, of what – just once – he called 'ego's mythological ideal', the involvement of the creator's mind which he feared would influence the shape and behaviour of the mythago forms. He had known of the danger, then, but I wonder if Christian had fully comprehended this most subtle of the occult processes occurring in the forest. From the darkness and pain of my father's mind a single thread had emerged in the fashioning of a girl in a green tunic, dooming her to a helplessness in the forest that was contrary to her natural form. But if she were to emerge again, it would be with Christian's mind controlling her, and Christian had no such preconceived ideas about a woman's strength or weakness.

It would not be the same encounter.

The notebook itself both perplexed and saddened me. There were so many entries that referred to the years before the war, to our family, to Chris and myself particularly; it was as if my father had watched us all the time, and in that way *had* been relating to us, had been close to us. And yet all the time he watched, he was detached, cold. I had thought him unaware of me; I had imagined myself a mere irritation in his life, a nagging insect that he waved aside brusquely, hardly noticing. And yet he had been totally aware of me, recording each game I played, each walk to, and around, the woodland, recording the effects upon me.

One incident, written briefly and in great haste, brought back a memory of a long, summer's day when I had been nine or ten years old. It involved a wooden ship, which Chris had fashioned from a piece of fallen beech, and which I had painted. The ship, the stream we called the sticklebrook, and a raging passage through the woodland below the garden. Innocent, childish fun, and all the time my father had been a sombre, dark shape, observing us from the window of his study.

The day had begun well, a bright, fresh dawn, and I had awoken to the sight of Chris, crouched in the branches of the beech tree outside my room. I crawled through the window in my pyjamas, and we sat there, in our secret camp, and watched the distant activity of the farmer who managed the land hereabouts. Somewhere else in the house there was movement, and I imagined that the cleaning lady had arrived early, to benefit from this fine summer's day.

Chris had the piece of wood, already shaped into the hull of a small boat. We discussed our plans for the epic journey by river, then scampered back into the house, dressed, snatched breakfast from the hands of the sleepy figure of our mother, and went out into the workshed. A mast was soon shaped and drilled into the hull. I layered red paint on to the planking, and daubed our initials, one set on either side of the mast. A paper sail, some token rigging, and the great vessel was ready.

We ran from the yard, skirting the dense, silent woodland, until we found the stream where the launching of the vessel would take place.

It was late July, I remember, hot and still. The brook was low, the banks steep and dry, and littered with sheep droppings. The water was slightly green where algal life was growing from the stones and mud below. But the flow was strong, still, and the brook wound across the fields, between lightning-blasted trees, into denser undergrowth, and finally below a ruined gate. This gate was much overgrown with weed, bramble and shrubby tree life. It had been placed across the stream by the farmer Alphonse Jeffries to stop 'urchins' such as Chris and myself from floundering into the deeper waters of the pool beyond, where the brook widened and became more aggressive.

But the gate was rotten, and there was a clear gap below it, where the ship of our dreams would pass quite easily.

With great ceremony, Chris placed the model on the waters. 'God speed to all who sail in her!' he said solemnly, and I added, 'May you come through your great adventure safely. God speed the HMS *Voyager*!' (Our name, suitably dramatic, was pinched from our favourite boy's comic of the day.)

Chris let the vessel go. It bobbed, spun and whirled away from us, looking uncomfortable on the water. I felt disappointed that the boat didn't sail like the real thing, leaning slightly to the side, rising and falling on the swell. But it was exciting to watch the tiny ship go spinning towards the woodland. And at last, before vanishing beyond the gate, it *did* sit true upon the ocean, and the mast seemed to duck as it passed the barrier and was swept from our sight.

Now began the fun. We raced breathlessly round the edge of the wood. It was a long trek across a private field, high and ripe with corn, then along the disused railway track, across a cow field. (There was a bull, grazing the corner. He looked up at us, and snorted, but was well content.)

Beyond this farmland we came to the northern edge of the oakwood, and there the sticklebrook emerged, a wider shallower stream.

We sat down to await our ship, to welcome it home.

In my imagination, during that long afternoon as we played in the sun and earnestly scanned the darkness of the woods for some sign of our vessel, the tiny ship encountered all manner of strange beasts, rapids, and whirlpools. I could see it fighting valiantly against stormy seas, outrunning otters and water rats that loomed high above its gunwales. The mind's journey was what that voyage was all about, the images of drama that the simple boat-trip inspired.

How I would have loved to see it come bobbing out along the sticklebrook. What discussions we might have had about its course, its journey, its narrow escapes!

But the ship did not appear. We had to face the hard reality that somewhere in the dark, dense woodland, the model had snagged on a branch and become stuck, there to remain, rotting into the earth again.

Disappointed, we made our way home at dusk. The school holidays had begun with a disaster, but the ship was soon forgotten.

Then, six weeks later, shortly before the long car and train journey back to school, Christian and I returned to the northern spread of the woods, this time walking our Aunt's two Springer spaniels. Aunt Edie was such a trial that we would welcome any excuse to leave the house, even when the day was as overcast and damp as that Friday in September.

We passed the sticklebrook and there, to our amazed delight, was the HMS *Voyager*, spinning and racing along in the current; the brook was high after the rains of late August. The ship rode the swell nobly, continually straightening and forging rapidly into the distance.

We raced along the bank of the stream, the dogs yapping ferociously, delighted with this sudden sprint. At last Christian gained on the spinning vessel and reached out across the water, snaring our tiny model.

He shook off the water and held it high, his face bright with pleasure. Panting, I arrived beside him and took the model from him. The sail was intact, the initials still there. The little object of our dreams looked exactly as when we had launched it.

'Stuck, I guess, and released when the waters rose,' said Chris, and what other explanation could there have been?

And yet, that very night, my father had written this in his diary:

Even in the more peripheral zones of the forest, time is distorted to a degree. It is as I suspected. The aura produced by the primal woodland has a pronounced effect upon the nature of dimensions. In a way, the boys have conducted an experiment for me, by releasing their model ship on to the brook that flows – or so I believe – around the edge of the woodland. It has taken six weeks to traverse the outer zones, a distance, in real terms, of no more than a mile. Six weeks! Deeper in the wood, if the expansion of time and space increases – which Wynne-Jones suspects – who can tell what bizarre landscapes are to be found?

During the rest of the long wet winter, following Christian's disappearance, I increasingly frequented the dark, musty room at the back of the house: my father's study. I found a strange solace among the books and specimens. I would sit at his desk for hours, not reading, nor even thinking, merely staring into the near distance, as if waiting. I could visualize my peculiar behaviour quite clearly, snapping out of the mindless reverie almost irritably.

There were always letters to be done, mostly of a financial nature, since the money on which I was living was rapidly dwindling to a sum insufficient to guarantee more than a few months' idle seclusion. But it was hard to focus the mind upon such humdrum affairs when the weeks passed, and Christian remained vanished, and the wind and rain blew, like living creatures, against the smeared panes of the French windows, almost calling me to follow my brother.

I was too terrified. Though I knew that the beast – having rejected me yet again – would have followed Christian deeper into Ryhope Wood, I could not face the thought of a repeat of that encounter. I had staggered home once, distraught and anguished, and now all I could do was walk around the forest edge, calling for Christian, hoping, always hoping, that he would suddenly appear again.

How long did I spend just standing, watching that part of the woodland which could be seen from the French windows? Hours? Days? Perhaps it was weeks. Children, villagers, the farm lads, all were occasionally to be seen, figures scurrying across the fields, or skirting the trees, making for the right of way across the estate. On each occasion that I sighted a human form my spirits leapt, only to subside again in disappointment.

Oak Lodge was damp, and smelled so, but it was in no sorrier a state than its restless occupant.

I searched the study, every inch of it. Soon I had accumulated a bizarre collection of objects which – years before – had been of no interest to me. Arrow and spear heads, both of stone and bronze, I found literally *crammed* into a drawer, there were so many of them. Beads, shaped and polished stones, and necklaces too, some made from large teeth. Two bone objects – long thin shafts, much inscribed with patterning – I discovered to be spear throwers. The most beautiful object was a small ivory horse, much stylized, its body strangely fat, its legs thin but exquisitely carved. A hole through its neck showed that it was meant to be worn as a pendant. Scratched within the contours of the horse was the unmistakable representation of two humans *in copula*.

This object made me check again a short reference in the journal:

The Horse Shrine is still deserted, I think now for good. The shaman has returned to the heartlands, beyond the fire that he has talked about. Left me a gift. The fire puzzles me. Why was he so afraid of it? What lies beyond?

I finally discovered the 'frontal bridge' equipment that my father had used. Christian had destroyed it as much as he could, breaking the curious mask and bending the various electric gadgetry out of shape. It was a strangely malicious thing for my brother to have done, and yet I felt I understood why. Christian was jealous of entry into the realm in which he sought Guiwenneth, and wanted no further experimentation with mythago generation.

I closed the cupboard on the wreckage.

To cheer myself up, to break the self-obsession, I reestablished contact with the Ryhopes, up at the manor house. They were pleased enough with my company – all, that is, except the two teenage daughters, who were aloof and affected, and found me distinctly below their class. But Captain Ryhope – whose family had occupied this land for many generations – gave me chickens with which to repopulate my own coops, butter from his own farm supplies, and best of all, several bottles of wine.

I felt it was his way of expressing his sympathy for what must have seemed to him to be a most tragic few years of my life.

Concerning the woodland he knew nothing, not even that it was, for the most part, unmanaged. The southern extent was coppiced, to supply farm poles, and firewood. But the latest reference he could find in his family's accounts to any sort of woodland management was 1722. It was a brief allusion:

The wood is not safe. That part which lies between Lower Grubbings and the Pollards, as far as Dykely Field, is marsh-ridden and peopled by strange common-folk, who are wise to woodland ways. To remove them would be too costly, so I have issued orders to fence off this place and clear trees to the south and southwest, and to coppice those woods. Traps have been set.

For over two hundred years the family had continued to ignore that immense acreage of wild-grown wood. It was a fact I found hard to believe and to understand, but even today, Captain Ryhope had hardly given a second thought to the area between those strangely named fields.

It was just 'the wood', and people skirted it, or used the

tracks round the edge, but never thought about its interior. It was 'the wood'. It had always been there. It was a fact of life. Life went on around it.

He did show me a written entry in the manor's accounts for 1536, or 37, it was not clear which. This was before his family's time, and he showed me the entry more out of pride at its allusion to King Henry the Eighth than for the reference to Ryhope Wood's strange qualities:

The King was pleased to hunt the woodlands, with four of his entourage and two ladies. Four hawks were taken, and a canter across the wild fields. The King expressed admiration for the dangerous hunt, riding without due care through the underwood. Returned at dusk to the Manor. A stag had been killed by the King himself. The King talked of ghosts, and was entertaining on the manner of being haunted in the deeper glades by the figure of Robin Hood, which apparently loosed an arrow at him. He has promised to hunt upon the estates in another season.

Shortly after Christmas, whilst I cooked in the kitchen, I detected movement beside me. It was a shock to my system, a moment of fright that made me twist around, adrenalin making my heart race.

The kitchen was empty. The movement remained, a hesitant flickering at the edge of vision. I raced through the house to the study, and sat behind the desk, my hands on the polished wooden surface, my breathing laboured.

The movement disappeared.

But it was a growing presence that had to be faced. My own mind was now interacting with the aura of the woodland, and at the edge of vision the first pre-mythagos were forming, restless, ill-defined shapes that seemed to vie for my attention.

My father had needed the 'frontal bridge', the strange machine, paraphernalia out of Frankenstein, to enable his own ageing mind to generate these 'stored' mythic presences from his racial unconscious. His journal – the log of his experiments with Wynne-Jones – and Chris, too, had hinted that a younger mind might interact with the wildwoods more simply, and very much faster than my father had ever imagined possible.

In the study there was a brief escape from these clamouring, frightening forms. The woodland had reached its dark, psychic tendrils only to the nearer rooms of the house – the kitchen and dining-room – and to pass beyond that zone, through the stuffy lounge, along the passage to my father's studio, was somehow to shake off those insistent movements.

In time, in a matter of weeks, I became less afraid of the images from my unconscious that were slowly materializing. They became an intrusive, but rather un-threatening part of my life. I kept clear of the woods, imagining that by so doing I was not causing the generation of mythagos which might later emerge to haunt me. I spent a great deal of time in the local village, and journeyed to London, to friends, on as many occasions as I could manage. I avoided making contact with the family of my father's friend, Edward Wynne-Jones, despite my growing awareness of the necessity of finding the man and speaking to him about his research.

In all these ways I suppose I was cowardly; and yet, in retrospect, it was more a result of my unease, my distraction at the incomplete nature of events with Christian. He ought to come back at any time. Without knowing for sure whether he was dead, or just totally lost, there was a great tendency to move neither forward nor back.

Stasis, then: the flow of time through the house, the endless routine of feeding, washing, reading, but without direction, without goal.

The gifts from my brother – the hares, the initials – provoked something akin to a panic reaction in me. In early spring I ventured for the first time close to the encroaching woodlands, calling Christian's name.

And it was shortly after this break in routine, perhaps in the middle of March, that occurred the first of two visitations from the woodland which were to have a profound effect upon me in later months. Of the two emergences it is the second that was most immediately important; but the first would become of increasing significance to me later, even though, on that windy, cold dusk in March, it was an enigmatic haunting that passed through my life like a cold breath, a fleeting encounter.

I had been to Gloucester for the day, visiting the bank where my father's affairs were still managed. It had been a frustrating few hours; everything was in Christian's name, and there was no evidence that my brother had agreed to pass the handling of affairs across to me. My pleas that Christian was lost in distant woodlands were listened to with sympathy, but precious little understanding. Certain standing orders were being paid, certainly, but my financial predicament was growing acute, and without some access to my father's account I would be forced back upon my education. Honest employment was something I had once looked forward to. Now, distracted and obsessed with the past, I wanted nothing more than to be allowed to govern my own life.

The bus was late, and the journey home through the Herefordshire countryside was slow and continually held up by cattle being moved along the roadways. It was late afternoon before I cycled the final miles from the bus station to Oak Lodge.

The house was cold. I pulled on a thick, Shetland jumper and busied myself at the fire-grate, cleaning the ashes of the wood fire from the previous day. My breath frosted and I shivered violently, and at that moment I realized there was something unnatural in that intense chill. The room was deserted; through the lace-covered windows, the front gardens were a blur of brown and green, a fading vision in the gathering gloom of dusk. I put the light on, wrapped my arms around my shoulders and walked quickly through the house.

There could be no doubt. This cold was not right. Ice was

already forming on the insides of the windows, on both sides of the house. I scraped at it with a fingernail, peered through the lesions so made, out across the back yard.

Towards the woodland.

There was a movement there, a vague stirring, as tenuous, as intangible as the flickering motions of the pre-mythagos which, though they occupied my peripheral vision, had ceased to concern me. I watched that distant stir in the forest as it rippled through the trees and undergrowth, and seemed to cast a moving shadow across the thistle-covered field that separated treeline from the edge of the garden.

There was something there, something invisible. It was watching me, and slowly approaching the house.

Not knowing what else to do, terrified that perhaps the Urscumug had returned to the woodland edge in search of me, I picked up the heavy-hafted, flint-bladed spear that I had made during the December weeks. It was a coarse and primitive means of defence, but was satisfyingly secure in a way that no gun could have been. What else, it had occurred to me, should one use in offence against the primitive but a primitive tool?

Passing down the stairs, I felt a breath of warm air on my frozen cheeks, a touch like the quick exhalation of breath of someone close by. A shadow seemed to hover about me, but it disappeared quickly.

In my father's study the haunting aura vanished, perhaps unable to compete against the powerful residuum of intellect that was my father's own ghost. I peered through the French windows at that woodland which could be seen from here, rubbing at the frosted glass, watching as my father had once watched, frightened, curious, drawn to the enigmatic happenings beyond the human limit of the house and grounds.

Shapes darted about the fence. They seemed to pour from the woodland edge, spiralling and leaping, grey, shadowy forms that vanished as quickly as they came, like the tongues of grey smoke from a gorse fire. From the trees, and back to the trees, something reaching, feeling, prowling about the grounds.

One of the tendrils passed over the fence and extended to the French windows themselves, and I drew back, startled, as a face stared at me from the outside, then vanished. The shock had made my heart race and I dropped the spear. Reaching down for the heavy weapon, I listened as the French windows were rattled and banged. The woodshed door was struck a violent blow, and a sudden fury swept among the startled hens.

But all I could think of was that face. So strange: human, yet with qualities that I can only describe as elfin; the eyes had been slanted, the inside of the grinning mouth a glowing red; the face had possessed no nose, nor ears, but a wild, spiky growth of fur or hair had sprouted from cranium and cheeks.

At once mischievous, malevolent, funny, frightening.

Abruptly the light drained from the sky, and the land outside became grey and foggy; the trees had become shrouded in a preternatural mist, through which an eerie light shone from a direction towards the sticklebrook.

My curiosity at last outweighed my apprehension. I opened the windows and stepped into the garden, walking slowly through the darkness towards the gate. To the west, in the direction of Grimley the horizon was bright. I could clearly see the shapes of farmhouses, copses and the roll of hills. To the east, towards the manor house, the evening was similarly clear. It was only above the woods, and Oak Lodge itself, that this storm-dark pall of gloom hovered.

The elementals came in force, then, emerging from the very ground itself, rising about me, hovering, probing, and making strange sounds very like laughter. I twisted and twirled, trying to glimpse some rational form to the gusting creatures, occasionally glimpsing a face, a hand, a long, curved finger, the nail a polished claw that jabbed towards me, but curled away before contact could be made. I glimpsed female shapes, lithe and sensuous. But mostly I saw the grimacing faces of something more elfin than human; hair flowed, eyes sparkled, broad mouths parted in silent cries. Were they mythagos? I hardly had time to question it. My hair was touched, my skin stroked. Invisible fingers prodded my back, tickled me below the ears. The silence of the grey dusk was interrupted by abrupt and brief bursts of wind-shrouded laughter, or the eerie cries of night birds that hovered above me, broad-winged, human-faced.

The trees at the edge of the wood swayed rhythmically; in their branches, through the hanging mist, I saw further shapes, shadows chased each other across the sunless fields about. I was surrounded by poltergeist activity of uncanny and immense proportions.

Swiftly, then, the activity died away, and the light from the sticklebrook grew more intense. The stillness was frightening, chilling. The cold was numbing, and my body was racked with cramp. I watched the light as it emerged from mist and woodland both, and was astonished when I saw its source.

A boat came sailing from the trees, moving steadily along a stream far too small to contain its width. The boat was painted with bright colours, but the glowing light came from the figure which stood upon its prow, peering intently towards me. Boat and man, both were among the strangest things I have ever seen. The boat was high-prowed and high-sterned, with a single sail set at an angle; no wind took the grey canvas or the black rigging; symbols and shapes had been carved upon the wood of the hull; bizarre figurines surmounted both prow and stern, and each of those carved gargoyles seemed to twist to watch me.

The man glowed with a golden aura. He stared from beneath a bronze-bright helmet, its crown elaborately crested, half-hidden between the twisting cheek guards. A flowing beard, chalk-white with streaks of red, reached to his broad chest. He leaned upon the railings of the ship, his patterned cloak wrapped about his body, the light that surrounded him glinting on the metal of his armour.

About him played the ghouls and ghosts of the forest edge, and they seemed to be pushing and tugging at the ship, accounting for its movement forward on the shallow waters of the stream.

This mutual regard across a distance of no more than a hundred yards lasted for a full minute. Then a strange wind began to blow, filling out the broad sail of the eerie vessel; the black rigging tugged and twanged, the boat rocked and the glowing man glanced up to the sky. Around him, the dark forces of his night-time entourage gathered, clustering about the boat, whining and crying with the voices of nature.

The man tossed something towards me, then raised his right hand in that universal symbol of acknowledgement. I stepped towards him, but was blinded by a sudden dust-laden wind. Elementals swirled around me. I saw the golden glow disappear slowly back towards the wood, the stern now the prow, the sail filled with a healthy breeze. Try as I might I could not step forward through the barrier of protective forces that accompanied the mysterious stranger.

When at last I was free to move, the ship had gone, the dark pall of mist above the land was suddenly sucked away, like smoke swirling towards a fan. It was a bright evening; I felt warm. I walked to the object the man had thrown and picked it up.

It was an oak leaf the size of my palm, fashioned out of silver, a masterful piece of craftmanship. As I stared down at it, I saw the shallowly inscribed letter C within the outline of a boar's head. The leaf was pierced, a long thin tear, as if a knife had been thrust through the metal. I shivered, although why the sight of this talisman should fill me with such dread I was not, at that time, able to understand.

I went back to the house, to think about these most bizarre mythago forms yet to have emerged from the edgewoods.

Two

Rain swept across the land, a drenching shower that seemed to come from a sky too bright to have carried the downpour. The fields became slick and treacherous as I raced back towards Oak Lodge. The rain penetrated my thick pullover and flannels, and was cold and irritating on my skin. I had been caught unawares, strolling down from the manor house after a few hours gardening, undertaken in exchange for a cut of mutton from their supplies of salted meat.

I ran across the garden and flung the heavy piece of meat into the kitchen, then stripped off my saturated jumper, still standing in the rain. The air was heavy with the smell of earth and woodland, and as I stood there, shedding my wet clothes, so the storm passed, and the sky brightened slightly.

Sun broke through cloud, and for a few seconds a wave of warmth encouraged me in my thinking that as late April was about to give way to early May, the first signs of summer were at hand.

Then I saw the fragmentary carnage near to the chicken coop, and a chill of apprehension made me dart to the side of the kitchen door . . .

Before I left I had closed the door, I was certain of that. But it had been open as I had scampered out of the wet weather.

Wringing out my jumper I walked cautiously to the chicken coop. Two chicken heads lay there, their necks still bloody where they had been struck from the bodies with a knife. In the rain-softened soil round about were the marks of a small-footed human being.

Entering the house I could see at once that I had entertained a visitor in my absence. The drawers to the kitchen table were open, cupboards were open, and tins and jars of preserved foods had been scattered, some jars opened and sampled. I walked through the house and observed the muddy prints of feet as they toured through the sitting-room, into the study, up the stairs and through the various bedrooms.

In my own bedroom the prints, a vague outline of toes and heels, stopped by the window. The pictures of myself, Christian and my father, that were placed on my bureau, had been moved. By holding the framed photographs to the light I could see the smudges of fingerprints on the glass.

The prints of both fingers and feet were smallish, but not like a child's. I suppose, even at that moment, I knew who my mystery visitor had been, and felt not so much apprehensive as intensely curious.

She had been here within the last few minutes. There was no blood in the house, which I felt there should have been had she carried the spoils of her raid about with her, but I heard no disturbance as I had come across the fields. Five minutes before, then, no more, no less. She had come to the house under the cover of the rain, had toured the establishment, poking and prying with admirable thoroughness, and had then raced back to the woods, stopping in her passage to strike the heads swiftly from two of my precious hens. Even now, I thought, she was probably observing me from the woodland edge.

In a fresh shirt, my trousers changed, I walked out into the garden and waved, scanning the dense undergrowth, the shadowy recesses that were the several pathways into the forest. I could see nothing.

I resolved, then, that I would have to learn to go back into the woodland.

The next day was brighter, and considerably drier, and I equipped myself with spear, kitchen knife and oilskin wrap and walked cautiously into the woods, as far as the clearing where I had made my camp, some months before. To my surprise there was hardly a fragment of that camp site left.

All the tent canvas had gone, the tins and pots purloined. By carefully feeling the ground I discovered a single, bent tent peg. And the glade itself had changed in a remarkable way: it was covered with oak saplings. They were no more than two or three feet high, but they clustered in the space, too many to survive, but too high by far to have grown in that space of a few months . . .

And winter months too!

I tugged at one of the saplings and it was deeply rooted; I skinned my hand, and tore the tender bark, before the plant at last relinquished its fervent grip upon the earth.

She did not return that day, nor the next, but thereafter I became increasingly aware that I was entertaining a visitor during the dark hours of night. Food would vanish from the pantry; implements, ordinary items of kitchen-ware, would be misplaced, or replaced. Also on some mornings there was a strange smell in the house, neither earthy, nor female, but – if you can imagine this bizarre combination – something that was a little of both. I noticed it most powerfully in the hallway, and would stand for long minutes, just letting the peculiarly erotic aroma seep into my system. Dirt and leaf litter were always to be found on the ground floor and stairs of the house. My visitor was becoming bolder. I imagined that, whilst I slept, she stood in the doorway and watched me. Strangely, I felt no apprehension at the idea.

I tried setting my alarm clock to awaken me in the dead hours, but all this succeeded in doing was giving me a restless night and a bad temper. On the first occasion I used the alarm I discovered I had missed my visitor, but the pungent smell of woodland female filled the house, thrilling me in a way that I felt almost ashamed to acknowledge. On the second occasion, she had not visited. The house was silent. It was three in the morning, and the only smell was of rain; and onions, part of my supper.

And yet I was glad, on that occasion, to have set the alarm so early, for though my imagined woodland nymph was not in evidence, I *was* being visited. The sound of chickens being disturbed came to me as I climbed back into bed. Immediately I raced down the stairs to the back door, and held the oil lamp high. I had time to glimpse two tall, thickly built man-shapes before the glass of the lamp shattered and the flame was extinguished. Thinking back on that incident I can remember the *whoosh* of air as a stone was slung, a shot more accurate than is rationally believable.

In darkness I watched the two shambling figures. They stared back at me; one had its face daubed with white, and appeared to be naked. The other wore wide pantaloons and a short cloak; his hair was long and richly curled, but that detail may have been wrongly imagined. Each held a living chicken by the neck, stifling the animal's cries. As I watched, each wrenched the head from its animal, then turned and walked stiffly to the fence, lost in the gloom of night. The one in the baggy pantaloons turned, just as he entered obscurity, and bowed to me.

I remained awake until dawn, seated in the kitchen, picking idly at bread and making two pots of tea that I really didn't want. As soon as it was light I dressed fully and investigated the chicken coops. I was now down to two animals, and they walked irritably about the grain-scattered arena, almost resentfully clucking.

'I'll do my best,' I told them. 'But I have a feeling you're destined to go the same way.'

The hens walked stiffly from me, perhaps requiring to enjoy their last meal in peace.

An oak sapling, four inches tall, was growing in the middle of their ground, and – surprised and quite fascinated – I reached to it and plucked it from the earth. Intrigued by the way nature itself seemed to be infiltrating my own jealously guarded territory, I toured the grounds, more alert than previously, to what was emerging from the soil.

Saplings were springing up all over the part of the garden next to the study, and the thistle-field which connected that area with the woodland itself. There were more than a hundred saplings – each less than six inches tall – in a scattered band across the small lawn that led from the study's French windows to the gate. I went through the gate and noticed how the field, sparsely grazed for several years and quite wild, was now richly dotted with seedlings. Towards the woodland edge they were taller, some almost at my own height. I plotted the width and extent of that band of growth, and realized with a chill that it formed a sort of tendril of woodland, forty or fifty feet wide, reaching to the house by way of the musty library.

The vision, then, was of a pseudopod of woodland trying to drag the house itself into the aura of the main body. I didn't know whether to leave the saplings, or crush them. But as I reached to tug one of them from the ground, so the pre-mythago activity in my peripheral vision became agitated, almost angry. I decided to leave this bizarre growth. It reached to the very edge of the house itself, but when the saplings grew too large they could easily be destroyed, even if they grew at an abnormal pace.

The house was haunted. The thought of it fascinated me, even as it sent shivers of fear down my spine; but the feeling of terror was one step removed, as it were; it was the same haunting, terrifying feeling that one gets when seeing a Boris Karloff film, or listening to a ghost story on the Home Service. It occurred to me that I had become a *part* of the haunting process that was enveloping Oak Lodge, and that as such I could not respond normally to the overt signs and manifestations of the spectral presences.

Or perhaps it was simply this: I wanted her. *Her*. The girl from the wildwood who had obsessed my brother, and whom I knew to have visited Oak Lodge again, in her new life. Perhaps much of what would follow was caused by this desperate need in me for love, to find the same degree of commitment to the female creation of the woodland that Christian had found. I was in my early twenties, and save for a brief, physically exciting, but intellectually empty liaison with a girl from the village in France where I had been after the war, I was inexperienced in love, in the communion of mind and body that people *call* love. Christian had found it. Christian had lost it. Isolated at Oak Lodge, miles from anywhere, it is not surprising that the thought of the return of Guiwenneth began to obsess me.

And eventually she came back as more than a transient aroma, or watery footprint on the floor. She came back in full body, no longer afraid of me, as curious of me, I like to think, as I was of her.

She was crouched by the bed; sparse moonlight reflected from the sheen of her hair, and when she glanced away from me, nervously I thought, that same light glinted from her eyes. I could get no more than an impression of her, and as she rose to her full height I could discern only her slender shape, clad in a loose-fitting tunic. She held a spear, and the cold metal blade was against my throat. It was sharpened along the edges, and each time I moved her slightest prod caused the skin on my neck to part. It was a painful encounter and I was not prepared for it to be a fatal one.

So I lay there, in the hours after midnight, and listened to her breathing. She seemed slightly nervous. She was here because she was . . . what can I say? Seeking. That is the only word I know to explain it. She was seeking me, or something about me. And in the same way I was seeking her.

She smelled strong. It was the sort of smell I would come to associate with a life in the forests and remote places of a barren land, a life where regular washing was something of a luxury, and where one was marked by aroma as clearly as, in my own day, one was marked by the style of clothes.

So she smelled . . . earthy. Yes. And also of her own secretions, the sharp, not unpleasant smell of sex. And sweat too, salty, tangy. When she came close to me and peered down I got an idea that her hair was red, and that her eyes were fierce. She said something like, 'Ymma m'ch buth?' She repeated the words several times, and I said, 'I don't understand.'

'Cefrachas. Ichna which ch'athab. Mich ch'athaben!'

'I don't understand.'

'Mich ch'athaben! Cefrachas!'

'I wish I *did* understand, but I really don't.'

The blade dug deeper into my neck and I flinched, and raised a hand slowly to the cold metal. Gently I eased the weapon away, smiling, and hoping that in the darkness she could see my willing subservience.

She made a sound, like frustration, or despair, I'm not sure which. Her clothing was coarse. I took the brief opportunity to touch the tunic she wore and the fabric was rough, like sacking, and smelled of leather. Her presence was overwhelming and quite overpowering. Her breath on my face was sweet, though, and slightly . . . nutty.

'Mich ch'athaben!' she said, and this time it was almost with a tone of hopelessness.

'Mich Steven,' I said, wondering if I was on the right track, but she remained silent. 'Steven!' I repeated, and tapped my chest. 'Mich Steven.'

'Ch'athaben,' she insisted, and the blade nicked sharply into my flesh.

'There's food in the pantry,' I offered. 'Ch'athaben. Downen. Stairen.'

'Cumchirioch,' she retorted savagely, and I felt myself insulted.

'I'm doing my best. Do you have to keep prodding me with the spear?'

Abruptly and unexpectedly, she reached out and grabbed my hair, jerking my head back and peering at my face.

A moment later she was gone, running silently down the stairs. Although I followed her swiftly, she was fleet of foot, and became absorbed by night's shadows. I stood at the back door and searched for her, but there was no sign.

'Guiwenneth!' I shouted into the darkness. Was that the name by which she knew herself, I wondered? Or only Christian's name for her? I repeated the call, changing the emphasis in the name. 'Gwinn*eth*! G*win*eth! Come back, Guiwenneth. Come back!'

In the silence of those early morning hours my voice carried loudly, hollowly, reflected back at me from the sombre woodland. Movement among the blackthorn scrub cut off my cry in mid-name.

By the sparse moonlight it was hard to see properly who stood there, but it was Guiwenneth, of that I was sure. She stood quite motionless, watching me, and I imagine that she was intrigued at my use of her name.

'Guiwenneth,' she called softly, and it was a throaty, sibilant sound, a pronunciation more like *chwin aiv*.

I raised my right hand in a gesture of parting and called, 'Goodnight then, *Chwin aiv*.'

'Inos c'da . . . Stivven . . .'

And the enfolding shadows of the forest claimed her again, and this time she did not reappear.

Three

By day I explored the woodland periphery, trying to penetrate deeper but still unable to do so; whatever forces were at work defending the heartwoods, they regarded me with suspicion. I tripped and became tangled in the rank undergrowth, ending up time and time again against a mossy stump, bramble-covered and impassable, or finding myself facing a wall of water-slick rock, that rose, dark and daunting, from the ground below, itself eroded and covered by the twisting, moss-furred roots of the great sessile oaks that grew here.

By the mill-stream I glimpsed the Twigling. Near to the sticklebrook, where the water swirled more rapidly below the rotting gate, there I caught sight of other mythagos, moving cautiously through the undergrowth, their features barely discernible through the paint they had daubed on their skins.

Someone had cleared the saplings from the centre of the glade and the remains of a fire were pronounced; rabbit and chicken bones were scattered about, and on the thistle-covered grass were the signs of a weapons industry, flakes of stone, and the peelings of bark from young wood, where a shaft for a spear or arrow had been fashioned.

I was conscious of the activity around me, always out of sight, but never out of earshot; furtive movement, sudden rapid flight, and a strange, eerie calling – bird-like, yes, but clearly of human manufacture. The woods were alive with the creations of my own mind . . . or Christian's – and they seemed to be clustering around the glade, and the stream, moving from the woodland at night along the oak tendril that reached to the study.

I longed to be able to reach deeper into the forest, but it was a wish that was constantly denied me. My curiosity as to what lay beyond the two hundred or so yards of the periphery began to peak, and I created landscapes and creatures as wild, in my imagination, as had been the imaginary journey of the *Voyager*.

It was three days after Guiwenneth's first contact with me that an idea for seeing deeper into the woodland occurred at last; why I hadn't thought of it before I cannot say. Perhaps Oak Lodge was so remote from the normal stream of human existence, and the landscape around Ryhope so far from the technologically advanced civilization at whose heart it lay, that I had been thinking only in primitive terms: walking, running, exploring from the ground.

For several days I had been aware of the sound, and occasional sight, of a small monoplane as it circled above the land to the east of the wood. On two days the plane – a Percival Proctor, I think – had come quite close to Ryhope Wood, before turning and disappearing into the distance.

Then in Gloucester, on my way to the bank, I saw the plane again, or one very like it. It was photographing the city for a land survey, I discovered. Operating out of Mucklestone Air Field, an area of some forty square miles was being photographed aerially for the Ministry of Housing. If I could just convince the air crew to 'loan' me the passenger seat of one of their planes for an afternoon, I could fly above the oak woodland and see the heart-woods from a vantage point where surely the supernatural defences could not reach . . .

I was met at the perimeter gate of Mucklestone Field by an air-force sergeant who led me, silently, to the small cluster of white-washed Nissen huts that served as offices, control buildings and mess buildings. It was colder inside than out. The whole area was unpleasantly run-down and lifeless, although a typewriter clattered somewhere, and I could hear distant laughter. Two planes stood on the runway, one clearly being serviced. It was a brisk afternoon, the wind was blowing from the south-east, and most of it seemed to whistle through the corners of the cramped little room into which my guide conducted me.

The man who smiled uncertainly at me as I entered was in his early thirties, perhaps, fair-haired, bright-eyed and hideously burn-marked around his chin and left cheek. He wore the uniform and insignia of an RAF Captain, but had the collar of his shirt open, and wore plimsolls instead of boots. Everything about him was casual and confident. He frowned, though, as he shook my hand and said, 'Don't quite understand what exactly it is you want, Mister Huxley. Sit down, won't you?'

I did as he bade me and stared at the map of the surrounding landscape that he had spread out on the desk. His name was Harry Keeton, that much I knew, and he had clearly flown during the war. The burn scar was both fascinating and hideous to look at; but he wore it proudly, like a medal, apparently not in the least bothered by the grotesque marking.

If I regarded him curiously, he was equally puzzled by me, and after a moment or two's hesitant exchange of looks he laughed nervously. 'I don't get many requests to borrow a plane. Farmers, mostly, wanting their houses photographed. And archaeologists. They always want photographs at dusk or dawn. Sun shadows, you see? It shows up field markings, old foundations, things like that . . . but you want to fly over a wood . . . is that right?'

I nodded. I couldn't actually make out where, on the map, the Ryhope estate lay. 'It's a woodland by my house, quite extensive. I'd just like to fly across the middle of it, and take a few photographs.'

Keeton's face registered something like worry. He smiled, then, and touched his scarred jaw. 'Last time I flew over a wood a sniper made the best shot of his life and brought me down. That was in 43. I was in a Lysander. Lovely plane, lovely handling. But that shot . . . straight to the fuel tank, and wallop. Down into the trees. I was lucky to get out. I'm

83

nervous of woods, Mister Huxley. But I don't suppose there're any snipers in yours.' He smiled in a friendly way, and I smiled back, not liking to say that I couldn't guarantee such a thing. 'Where exactly is this wood?' he asked.

'It's on the Ryhope estate,' I said, and stood and bent over the map. After a second I saw the name. Strangely, there was no indication at all of the woodland, just a dotted line indicating the extent of the massive property.

Keeton was looking at me peculiarly when I straightened up. I said, 'It isn't marked. That's odd.'

'Very,' he said. His tone was matter of fact . . . or perhaps slightly knowing. 'How big is the place?' he asked then. 'How extensive?' Still he stared at me.

'Very extensive. A perimeter of more than six miles . . .'

'Six miles!' he exclaimed, then smiled thinly. 'That's not a wood, that's a forest!'

In the silence that followed I became certain that he knew at least *something* about Ryhope Wood. I said, 'You've been flying close to the place yourself. You or one of your pilots.'

He nodded quickly, glancing at the map. 'That was me. You saw me, did you?'

'It's what gave me the idea of coming to the air field.' When he added nothing, but just looked very slightly cagey, I went on, 'You must have noticed the anomaly, then. Nothing marked on the survey map . . .'

But instead of addressing himself to the statement, Harry Keeton just sat down and toyed with a pencil. He studied the map, then me, then the contours again. All he said was, 'I didn't know we had any mediaeval oak woodland of that extent left uncharted. Is it managed woodland?'

'Partly. Most of it is quite wild, though.'

He leaned back in his chair; the burn scar had darkened slightly and I thought he seemed to be restraining a growing excitement. 'That in itself is amazing,' he said. 'The Forest of Dean is immense, of course, but it's well managed. There's a wood in Norfolk that's wild. I've been there . . .' He hesitated, frowning slightly. 'There are others. All small, all

84

just woodland that has been allowed to *go* wild. Not real
wildwood at all.'

Keeton suddenly seemed quite on edge. He stared at the
map, at the area of the Ryhope estate, and I thought he
murmured something like, 'So I was right . . .'

'Can you help me with a flight over the wood, then?' I
asked and Keeton glanced at me suspiciously.

'Why do you want to over-fly it?'

I started to tell him, then broke off. 'I don't want this
talked about—'

'I understand.'

'My brother is wandering somewhere inside it. Months
ago he went exploring and hasn't come back. I don't know if
he's lost or dead, but I'd like to see what can be seen from the
air. I realize that it's irregular . . .'

Keeton was immersed in his own thoughts. He had gone
quite pale, now, all save the burn scars on his jaw. He
focused on me suddenly and shook his head. 'Irregular?
Well, yes. But I can manage it. It will be expensive. I'll have
to charge you for fuel . . .'

'How much?'

He quoted a likely figure for a sixty mile jaunt that made
the blood drain from my face. But I agreed, and was relieved
to discover that there would be no other costs. He would fly
me out himself. He would turn the cameras on Ryhope
Wood and add it to the landscape map that he was com-
piling. 'It would have to be done eventually, might as well do
it now. The earliest I could fly you out is tomorrow, after
two o'clock. Is that all right with you?'

'Fine,' I said. 'I'll be here.'

We shook hands. As I left the office I glanced back. Keeton
was standing quite motionless behind his desk, staring at the
survey map; I noticed that his hands were shaking slightly.

I had flown only once before. The journey had lasted four
hours and had been in a battered, bullet-ravaged Dakota,
which had taken off during a thunderstorm and landed on
deflated tyres on the runway at Marseilles. I had known little

of the drama, being drugged and semiconscious; it was an evacuation flight arranged with great difficulty, to the place of convalescence where I would recover from the shrapnel wound in my chest.

So the flight in the Percival Proctor was effectively my first trip skywards, and as the flimsy plane lurched and seemed almost to leap into the skies, I clutched hard to the handholds beside me, closed my eyes, and concentrated on fighting down the sudden package of innards that seemed about to burst from my throat. I don't think I have ever felt so potentially sick in my life, and how I remained in equilibrium is beyond me. Every few seconds my body parted company with my stomach as a gust of wind – a thermal, Keeton called them – seemed to grasp the plane with invisible fingers and shift it upwards or downwards at alarming speeds. The wings buckled and flexed. Even through the helmet and headphones that I wore I could hear the creaking complaint of the aluminium fuselage as this tiny model structure fought the mindless elements.

We circled the airfield twice, and at last I risked opening my eyes. It was an initially disorientating feeling, as I suddenly became aware that the view from the side window was not a distant horizon, but farmland. My mind caught up with my inner ear, and I adjusted to the idea of being several hundred feet above the ground, hardly conscious of the confusion of my body in relationship to gravity. Then Keeton banked sharply to the right – and there was no disorientation then, merely panic! – and the plane slipped quickly away to the north; bright sun obscured all vision to the west, but by peering hard through the cold, rather misty side window, I could see the shadowy field structure below, with the bright scattered clusters of white buildings that were hamlets and towns.

'If you feel sick,' Keeton called back, his voice a grating rasp in my ears, 'use the leather bag beside you, would you mind?'

'I feel fine,' I said back, and felt for the reassuring

container. The plane was buffeted by a cross wind and part of me seemed to rise within my chest cavity before catching up with its companion organs. I clutched the bag more tightly, felt the sting of sharp saliva in my mouth, that awful cold feeling that precedes nausea. And as quietly, and as quickly, as possible – and humiliated totally – I gave in to the violent need to empty my stomach.

Keeton laughed loudly. 'Waste of rations,' he said.

'I feel better for being rid of them.'

At once I *did* feel better. Perhaps anger at my weakness, perhaps the simple fact of being empty, allowed me a more cheerful approach to the terrifying act of flying hundreds of feet above the ground. Keeton was checking the cameras, his mind on them, not on our passage through the sky. The semi-circular steering wheel moved of its own volition, and though the plane seemed struck by giant fingers, flipping it to right and left, then pushing it down with alarming speed, we seemed to maintain a straight course. Below us, farmland blended with dense green woodland; a tributary of the Avon was a muddy band winding aimlessly into the distance. Cloud shadow chased like smoke across the patchwork pattern of the fields, and all in all everything below seemed lazy, placid, peaceful.

And then Keeton said, 'Good God, what's that?'

I looked forward, over his shoulder, and saw the dark beginnings of Ryhope Wood on the horizon. A great cloud seemed to hang above that part of the land, an eerie darkness as if a storm were raging above the forest. And yet the skies were quite clear, cloud *could* be seen, as sparse and summery as that above the whole of the west of England. The sombre pall seemed to ebb upwards from the wildwoods themselves, and as we approached the vast expanse of the forest, that darkness nagged at our own moods, darkening us, filling us with something approaching dread. Keeton voiced it, banking the tiny plane to the right, to skirt the edge of the wood. I looked down and saw Oak Lodge, a grey-roofed, miserable huddle of a building, its entire grounds looking black, morose, the sapling growth spread thickly towards the house's extension where the study was located.

The forest itself looked tangled, dense and hostile; I could see away across the foliage tops, and they were unbroken, a sea of grey green, rippling in the wind, looking almost organic, a single entity, breathing and shifting restlessly beneath the unwelcome aerial gaze.

Keeton flew at a distance from Ryhope Wood, around the perimeter and it seemed to me that the expanse of primal woodland was not as vast as it had first appeared. I observed the trickle of the sticklebrook, a winding, quite erratic flow of grey-brown water, occasionally sparkling in the sun. It was possible to see the stream's journey into the wood for some way, before the tree tops closed over it.

'I'm going to make an overpass from east to west,' Keeton announced suddenly, and the aircraft banked, the forest tilted before my fascinated eyes, and suddenly seemed to lurch drunkenly towards me, flowing below me, and spreading out widely, silently before me.

At once the plane was taken by a storm-wind of appalling strength. It was flung upwards, almost tilting nose over tail as Keeton struggled at the controls trying to right the vehicle. Strange golden light streamed from wingtip and propellor blur, as if we flew through a rainbow. The plane was struck from the right, and pushed hard towards the edge of the forest, back towards open land. Around the cabin a ghostly, banshee-like wailing began. It was so deafeningly loud that Keeton's cries of rage and fear, coming to me through the radio headphones, were almost inaudible.

As we left the confines of the woodland, so a relative calm reappeared, the plane straightened, dropped slightly, then banked as Harry Keeton turned back for a second attempt to fly over the forest.

He was quite silent. I wanted to speak, but found my tongue tied as I fixed my gaze on the wall of gloom ahead of us.

Again, that wind!

The plane lurched and looped over the first few hundred yards of woodland, and the light that began to enshroud us grew more intense, crawling along the wings and playing, like tiny shreds of lightning, over the cabin itself. The screaming reached an intensity that made me cry out, and the plane was buffeted so hard that I felt sure it would be broken, shredded like a child's model.

Looking down through the eerie light, I saw clearings, glades, a river flowing . . . it was the briefest of visions of a woodland almost totally obscured by the supernatural forces that guarded it.

Suddenly the plane was turned over. I'm sure I screamed as I slipped heavily in my seat, only the heavy leather belt stopping me from being crushed against the ceiling. Over and over the plane rolled, while Keeton struggled to right it, his voice a desperate rasping sound of anger and confusion. The howling from outside became a sort of mocking laughter, and abruptly the tiny aerial vessel was *flung* back across the open land, righting itself, looping twice, and coming perilously close to impacting with the ground below.

It zipped up, bouncing across copses, farmhouses; running scared almost, away from Ryhope Wood.

When at last Keeton was calm, he took the plane up to a thousand feet and stared thoughtfully into the far distance, where the woodland was on the horizon, a gloom-covered place which had defeated his best efforts to explore it.

'I don't know what the devil caused that,' he said to me, his voice a whisper. 'But right now I'd prefer not to think about it. We're losing fuel. There must be a tank rupture. Hang on to your seat . . .'

And the plane skipped and darted southwards, to the landing field, where Keeton unloaded the cameras and left me to my own devices; he was badly shaken and seemed quite keen to be away from me.

Four

My love affair with Guiwenneth of the Greenwood began the following day, unexpectedly, dramatically . . .

I had not returned home from the airfield at Mucklestone until mid-evening, and I was tired, shaken, and very ready for bed. I slept through the alarm, waking abruptly at eleven-thirty in the morning. It was a bright, if overcast day, and after a snatched breakfast I walked out across the fields, and turned to regard the woodland from a vantage point some half mile distant.

It was the first time I had seen, from the ground, the mysterious darkness associated with Ryhope Wood. I wondered whether or not that appearance had developed recently, or if I had been so embroiled, so enveloped by the aura of the woodland that I had merely failed to notice its enigmatic state. I walked back towards the house, slightly cold in just my sweater and slacks, but not uncomfortable in these late spring, early summer days. On impulse I took a stroll to the mill-pond, the site at which I had met Christian for the first time in years, those scant months before.

The place had an attraction for me, even in winter, when the surface of the pool froze around the reeds and rushes of its muddy extremities. It was scummy now, but still quite clear in the middle. The algal growth that would soon transform the pond into a cesspool had not yet shaken off its winter hibernation. I noticed, though, that the rotten-hulled rowing boat which had been tethered close to the decaying boathouse for as long as I could remember, was no longer in evidence. The frayed rope that had held it moored – against what fierce tides, I wondered? – reached below the water's level and I imagined that at some time during the rainy winter the corrupted vessel had simply sunk to the muddy bottom.

On the far side of the pool, the dense woodland began: a wall of bracken, rush and bramble, strung between thin, gnarled oak-trunks like a fence. There was no way through, for the oaks themselves had grown from ground too marshy for human transit.

I walked to the beginning of the marsh, leaning against a sloping trunk, staring into the musty gloom of the edgewood.

And a man stepped out towards me!

He was one of the two raiders from a few nights before, the long haired man wearing wide pantaloons. I saw now that his appearance was that of a Royalist from the time of Cromwell, the mid-seventeenth century; he was naked to the waist, save for two leather harnesses crossed on his chest, attached to which were a powder horn, a leather pouch of lead balls, and a dagger. His hair was richly curled, the curls extending even to his beard and moustaches.

The words he spoke to me sounded curt, almost angry, and yet he smiled as he spoke them. They seemed foreign to me, and yet afterwards I was able to realize that they were English, spoken with an accent akin to broad country. He had said, 'You're the outsider's kin, that's all that matters . . .' but at the time his words had been alien sounds.

Sound, accent, words . . . what mattered more at the time was that he raised a bright-barrelled flintlock, wrenching back the lock itself with considerable effort, and discharged the piece towards me from a position halfway between his waist and his shoulder. If it had been a warning shot, he was a marksman whose skill would earn the greatest admiration. If he had intended to kill me, then I count myself truly lucky. The ball struck the side of my head. I was moving backwards, raising my hands in a defensive gesture, crying out, '*No!* For God's sake—!'

The noise of the discharge was deafening, but all was swiftly lost in the pain and confusion of the ball striking my head. I remember being thrust backwards as if thrown, and the ice-cold waters of the pond gripping me and sucking me down. For a moment, then, there was blackness, and when I came to my senses again I was swallowing the foul mill-pond waters. I splashed and struggled against the clinging mud, and the weeds and rushes which seemed to wind about me. Somehow I surfaced and gulped air and water, choking violently.

Then I saw the gleaming haft of a decorated stick, and realized that I was being offered a spear to grasp. A girl's voice called something incomprehensible in all but senti-ment, and I clung on to the cold wood gratefully, still more drowned than alive.

I felt my body dragged from the clutches of the weeds. Strong hands gripped my shoulders and hauled me all the way out, and as I blinked water and mud from my eyes I focused upon two bare knees, and the slim shape of my rescuer, leaning towards me and forcing me down on to my stomach.

'I'm all right!' I spluttered.

'B'th towethoch!' she insisted, and the hands strongly massaged my back. I felt water surfacing from my guts. I choked and vomited the mixture of chyme and pond water, but at last felt able to sit upright, and I pushed her hands aside.

She backed off, still crouching, and as I rubbed the muck from my eyes I saw her clearly for the first time. She was staring at me and grinning, almost chuckling at my filth-ridden state.

'It's not funny,' I said, glancing anxiously beyond her at the forest, but my assailant had gone. Thoughts of him faded quickly as I stared at Guiwenneth.

Her face was quite startling, pale-skinned, slightly freckled. Her hair was brilliant auburn, and tumbled in unkempt, wind-swept masses about her shoulders. I would have expected her eyes to be bright green, but they were a depth-less brown, and as she regarded me with amusement, I felt drawn to that gaze, fascinated by every tiny line on her face, the perfect shape of her mouth, the strands of wild red hair that lay across her forehead. Her tunic was short and of cotton, dyed brown. Her arms and legs were thin, but the muscles were wiry; a fine blonde down covered her calves and I noticed that her knees were badly scarred. She wore open sandals of crude design.

The hands that had forced me down, and pumped water from my lungs so powerfully, were small and delicate, the nails broken short. She wore black leather wrist bands, and on the narrow, iron-studded belt around her waist she carried a short sword in a dull grey sheath.

So this was the girl with whom Christian had become so helplessly, hopelessly enamoured. Looking at her, experiencing a rapport with her that I had never before encountered, the sense of her sexuality, of her humour, of her power, I could well understand why.

She helped me to my feet. She was tall, almost as tall as me. She glanced round, then patted me on the arm and led the way into the undergrowth, heading in the direction of Oak Lodge. I pulled back, shaking my head, and she turned and said something angrily.

I said, 'I'm sopping wet, and very uncomfortable . . .' I brushed hands against my mud and weed-saturated clothes, and smiled. 'There's not a chance that I'm going home through the woodland. I'll go the easy way . . .' And I started to trot back round the path. Guiwenneth shouted at me, then slapped her thigh in exasperation. She followed me closely, keeping within the tree line. She was certainly expert, since she made practically no sound, and only when I stopped and peered hard through the scrub could I occasionally glimpse her. When I stopped, so she stopped, and her hair caught the daylight in a way that must surely have betrayed her presence endlessly. She seemed to be swathed in fire. She was a beacon in the dark woods, and must have found survival hard.

When I reached the garden gate I turned to look for her. She came scampering out of the forest, head low, spear held firmly in her right hand while her left clutched the scabbard of her sword, stopping it from bouncing about on her belt. She raced past me, ran across the garden and into the lee of the house, turning against the wall, looking anxiously back towards the trees.

I sauntered after her and opened the back door. With a wild look, she slipped inside.

I closed the door behind me and followed Guiwenneth as she strolled through the house, curious and commanding. She tossed her spear on to the kitchen table and unbuckled her sword belt, scratching through her tunic at her taut flesh below. 'Ysuth'k,' she said with a chuckle.

'Itchy too, no doubt,' I agreed, watching as she picked up my carving knife, snickered, shook her head and dropped the implement back on the table. I was beginning to shiver, thinking of a nice hot bath; but there would only be a lukewarm one, the water heating in Oak Lodge being primitive in the extreme. I filled three pans with water and put them on to the stove. Guiwenneth watched, fascinated, as the blue flame sprang to life. 'R'vannith,' she said with a tone of weary cynicism.

As the water began to heat I followed her through the sitting-room, where she looked at pictures, rubbed the fabric covers of the chairs, smelled the wax fruit and made an astonished, slightly admiring sound, then giggled and tossed the artificial apple to me. I caught it and she made a gesture as in eating, questioning, 'Cliosga muga?', and laughed.

'Not usually,' I said. Her eyes were so bright, her smile so youthful, so mischievous . . . so beautiful.

She kept scratching the belt sores around her waist as she explored further, entering the bathroom and shivering slightly. I wasn't surprised. The bathroom was a slightly modified section of the original outhouse, grimly painted in now fading yellow; cobwebs festooned every corner; old tins of Vim scouring powder, and filth-laden rags, were clustered below the cracked porcelain basin. It amazed me, as I looked at the cold, unwelcoming place, that all through childhood I

94

had washed here quite contentedly – well, contented, that is, with everything except the gigantic spiders that scuttled across the floor, or emerged from the plug-hole of the bath with alarming frequency. The bath was deep, of white enamel, with tall stainless steel taps that attracted Guiwenneth's attention more than anything. She ran her fingers across the cold enamel and said that word again: 'R'vannith.' And laughed. And I suddenly realized that she was saying *Roman*. She was associating the cold, marble-like surfaces, and the special heating techniques, with the most advanced technology of society as she – in her time – had known it. If it was cold, hard, ease-making, decadent, then of course it was Roman, and she, a Celt, despised it.

Mind you, she could have done with a bath herself. Her odour was quite overwhelming and I was not yet used to experiencing so powerfully that particular animal part of a human. In France, in the last days of the occupation, the smell had been of fear, of garlic, of stale wine, too often of stale blood, and of damp, fungus-infested uniforms. All of those smells had somehow been a natural part of the war, part of technology. Guiwenneth had a woodland, animal aroma that was startlingly unpleasant, yet strangely erotic.

I ran the tepid water into the bathtub and followed her on her perambulations towards the study. Here again she shivered, walking around the edge of the room, looking almost anguished. She kept glancing at the ceiling. She walked to the French windows and stared out, then stomped around on the floor in her open sandals before touching the desk, the books, and some of my father's woodland artefacts. Books did not interest her in the least, although she peered at the page structure of one volume for several seconds, perhaps trying to puzzle out exactly what it was. She was certainly pleased to see pictures of men – in uniform, it happened, in a book on nineteenth-century army uniforms – and showed me the plates as if I had never seen them before. Her smile proclaimed the innocent pleasure of a child, but I was not distracted by anything other than the adult power of her body. She was no naïve youth, this.

I left her browsing in the gloomy study and topped up the bath from the freshly boiled pans. Even so, the water was only just lukewarm. No matter. Anything to scrub away the revolting residue of algal growth and slime. I stripped off my clothes and stepped into the tub, and became aware that Guiwenneth was standing in the doorway, smirking as she stared at my grimy, but essentially pallid and weedy torso.

'This is 1948,' I said to her, with as much dignity as possible, 'not the barbarian centuries just after Christ.'

Surely, I said to myself, she couldn't expect me to bristle with muscle, not a civilized man like me.

I washed quickly and Guiwenneth dropped to a crouch, thoughtfully silent. Then she said, 'Ibri c'thaan k'thirig?'

'I think you're beautiful too.'

'K'thirig?'

'Only on weekends. It's the English way.'

'C'thaan perin avon? Avon!'

Avon! Stratford-upon-Avon? Shakespeare? 'My favourite is *Romeo and Juliet*. I'm glad you have *some* culture at least.'

She shook her head, that beautiful hair drifting about her features like silk. Dirty though it was, lank – I could see – and greasy, it still shone and moved with a rich life of its own. Her hair fascinated me. I realized that I was staring at it, the long-handled scrubbing brush poised halfway to a position where I could get to my back. She said something that sounded like an instruction to stop staring, then she rose from her haunches, tugging down her brown tunic – still scratching! – and folded her arms as she leaned against the tiled wall, staring out through the small bathroom window.

Clean again, and revolted by the appearance of the bathwater, I took my courage into my hands and stood in the bath, reaching for my towel, but not before she had glanced at me . . . and sniggered again! She stopped herself laughing, the twinkle in her eye quite infuriatingly attractive, and regarded me, staring up and down at the white flesh she could see. 'There's nothing wrong with *me*,' I said, towelling myself vigorously, slightly self-conscious but determined not to be transparently coy. 'I'm a perfect specimen of English manhood.'

'Chuin atenor!' she said, contradicting me totally.

I wrapped the towel around my waist, and prodded a finger towards her, then at the bath. She got the message, and answered me with one of her own, her right fist irritably struck twice towards, but not against, her own right shoulder.

She went back into the study and I watched her for a moment as she flipped through the pages of several books, looking at the colour plates. I dressed then, and went to the kitchen to prepare a pot of soup.

After a while I heard water being run into the bath. There was the briefest period of splashing, coupled with sounds of confusion and amusement as an unfamiliarly slippery bar of soap proved more elusive than functional. Overwhelmed by curiosity – and perhaps sexual interest – I walked quietly to the cold room and peered round the door at her. She was already out of the tub, tugging her tunic into place. She smiled thinly at me, shaking back her hair. Water dripped from her legs and arms, and she gave herself an elaborate sniff, then shrugged as if to say, 'So what's the difference?'

When I offered her a bowl of the thin vegetable soup, half an hour later, she refused, seeming almost suspicious. She sniffed the pot, and dipped a finger into the broth, tasting it without much appreciation as she watched me eat. Try as I might, I could not get her to share this modest fare. But she was hungry, that much was clear, and she did eventually tear off a piece of bread and swirl it in the soup pot. She watched me all the time, examining me, examining my eyes in particular, I thought.

At length she said quietly, 'C'cayal cualada . . . Christian?'

'Christian?' I repeated, saying the name as it should be pronounced. She had made it sound like *Kreesatan*, but

I had recognized the name with something of a thrill of shock.

'Christian!' she said, and spat on the floor angrily. Her eyes took on a wild expression and she reached for her spear but used the haft to prod me on the chest. 'Steven.' A thoughtful pause. 'Christian.' She shook her head as she came to some conclusion. 'C'cayal cualada? Im clathyr!'

Was she asking if we were brothers? I nodded. 'I've lost him. He went wild. He went to the woods. Inwards. Do you know him?' I pointed at her, at her eyes, and said, 'Christian?'

Pale though she was, she went a touch paler. She was frightened, that much was clear. 'Christian!' she snapped, and flung the spear expertly and effortlessly across the kitchen. It thudded into the back door and hung there, quivering.

I got up and wrenched the weapon from the wood, somewhat annoyed that she had effectively split through the grain, leaving a fair-sized hole to the outside world. She tensed slightly as I pulled the spear out and examined the dull, but razor-edged blade. It was crenulated, but not like a leaf; the teeth were recurved hooks, running right around each edge. The Irish Celts had used a fearsome weapon called the *gae bolga*, a spear that was supposed never to be used in honour, for its recurved teeth would wrench the innards out of a man it struck. Perhaps in England, or whatever part of the Celtic world that had birthed Guiwenneth, no such considerations of honour were important in the use of weapons.

The haft was inscribed with little lines at different angles; Ogham, of course. I had heard of it, but had no idea how it worked. I ran my fingers along the incisions, and queried: 'Guiwenneth?'

She said, 'Guiwenneth mech Penn Ev.' She said it with pride. Penn Ev would have been her father's name, I supposed. Guiwenneth, daughter of Penn Ev?

I passed her the spear, and reached cautiously for the blade in its scabbard. She moved away from the table, watching me carefully. The sheath was hard leather with strips of very thin metal almost stitched into the fabric. Bronze studs decorated it, but a heavy leather thread had been used to bind the two sides together. The sword itself was totally functional: a handle of bone, wrapped round with well-chewed animal skin. More bronze studs gave an effective finger grip. The pommel was almost non-existent. The blade was of bright iron, perhaps eighteen inches long. It was narrow at the pommel, but flared out to a width of four or five inches, before tapering to a precise point. It was a beautiful, curvaceous weapon. And there were traces of dried blood upon it that testified to its frequent use.

I sheathed the sword again, then reached into the broom cupboard for my own weapon, the spear I had made from a stripped and crudely shaped branch, with a large, sharp chipping of flint for the point. She took one look at it and burst out laughing, shaking her head, apparently in disbelief.

'I'm very proud of this, I'll have you know,' I said, with mock indignation. I fingered the sharp stone point. Her laughter was bright and easy, a genuine amusement at my paltry efforts. She seemed slightly humbled, then, covering her mouth with her hand, even though she still shivered with amusement. 'It took me a long time to make. I was quite impressed with myself.'

'Peth'n plantyn!' she said, and giggled.

'How dare you,' I retorted, and then did something very foolish.

I should have known better, but the mood of humour, of peace, was too conducive to complacency. I made a pretend attack upon the girl, lowering the spear, jabbing it easily towards her as if to say, 'I'll show you . . .'

She reacted in a split second. The mirth vanished from her eyes and mouth and an expression of feline fury appeared there. She made a throaty sound, an attack sound, and in the brief time it had taken me to thrust my pathetic child's toy in her general direction she had swept her own spear down twice, savagely, and with astonishing strength.

The first blow fetched off the spear head, and nearly knocked the haft from my hand; the second strike snagged the wood, and the whole decapitated weapon was wrenched from my grip and flung across the kitchen. It knocked pots from the wall, and clattered down among the china storage vessels.

It had all happened so fast that I could hardly react. She seemed as shocked as me, and we stood there, staring at each other, our faces flushed, our mouths open.

'I'm sorry,' I said softly, and tried to lighten the mood. Guiwenneth smiled uncertainly. 'Guirinyn,' she murmured by way of her own apology, and picked up the severed spear head and handed it to me. I took the stone, which was still attached to a fragment of wood, peered at it, made a sad face, and we both burst into spontaneous, light laughter.

Abruptly she gathered together her belongings, buckled on her belt and walked to the back door.

'Don't go,' I said, and she seemed to intuit the meaning of my words, hesitating and saying, 'Michag ovnarrana!' (I have to go?) Then, head low, body tensed for rapid flight, she trotted back towards the woodland. As she vanished into the gloom she waved once and emitted a cry like a dove.

Five

That evening I went to the study and drew out the torn and tattered journal that my father had kept. I opened it at random, but the words defied my efforts to read them, partly, I think, because of a sudden mood of melancholy that had surfaced at around the dusk hour. The house was oppressively quiet, yet echoed with Guiwenneth's laughter. She seemed to be everywhere, yet nowhere. And she stepped out of time, out of the years gone by, out of the previous life that had occupied this silent room.

For a while I stood and stared out into the night, more conscious of my own reflection in the dirty glass of the French windows, illuminated by the desk lamp. I half expected that Guiwenneth would appear before me, emerging through the shape of the lean, tousle-haired man who gazed back at me so forlornly.

But perhaps she had sensed the need – the need in *me*, that is – to establish something I had come to know as a fact . . . in all but the reading.

It was something I had known, I suppose, since I had first skimmed the journal. The pages in which the bitter details had once been recorded had long since been torn from the diary, destroyed no doubt, or hidden too cleverly for me to discover. But there were hints, insinuations, enough for the sadness to have suddenly registered upon me.

At last I went back to the desk and sat down, slowly leafing through the leather bound book, checking dates, edging closer to that first encounter between my father and Guiwenneth, and the second, the third . . .

The girl again. From the woodland, close to the brook, she ran the short distance to the coops, and crouched there for a full ten minutes. I watched from the kitchen, then moved through to the study as she prowled the grounds. J aware of her, following me silently, watching. She does not understand, and I cannot explain. I am desperate. The girl affects me totally. J has seen this, but what can I do? It is the nature of the mythago itself. I am not immune, any more than were the cultured men of the Roman settlements against whom she acted. She is truly the idealized vision of the Celtic Princess, lustrous red hair, pale skin, a body at once childlike yet strong. She is a warrior. But carries her weapons with awkwardness, as if unfamiliar.

J is unaware of these things, only the girl, and my attraction. The boys have not seen her, though Steven has talked twice, now, of visions of the antlered 'shaman' form that is also active at this time. The girl is more vital than the earlier mythago forms, which seem mechanical, quite lost. She is hardly recent, but behaves with an awareness that is uncanny. She watches me. I watch her. There is more than a season between each visitation, but her confidence appears to be growing, I wish I knew her story. My surmise must be close, but the details remain elusive since we cannot communicate.

And a few pages later, written some two weeks after the previous event, but not dated:

Returned in less than a month. Indeed, she must be powerfully generated. I have decided to tell Wynne-Jones about her. She came at dusk, and entered the study. I remained motionless, watching her. The weapons she carries are violent looking. She was curious. She spoke words, but my mind is no longer fast enough to remember the alien sounds of lost cultures. Curiosity! She explored books, objects, cupboards. Her eyes are unbelievable. I am fixed to my chair whenever she looks at me. I tried to establish contact with her, speaking simple words, but the mythago is generated with all its embedded language, and perception. Nevertheless, WJ believes that the mythago mind will be receptive to education, language also, because of its link with the mind that created it. I am confused. This record is confused. J arrived in the study and was distraught. The boys have begun to be upset by J's decline. She is very ill. When the girl laughed at her, J almost hysterical, but left the study rather than confront the woman she thinks I am betraying her for. I must not lose the interest of the girl. The only mythago to emerge from the woodland. This is an opportunity to be grasped.

Pages are missing thereafter, pages of immense relevance since they certainly deal with my father's efforts to follow the girl back into the woodland, documenting the passages and pathways that he used. (There is, for example, a cryptic line in an otherwise routine account of the use of the equipment that he and Wynne-Jones had devised: 'Entered through hog path, segment seven, and moved more than four hundred paces. There is a possibility here, but the real way in, if not the obvious way, remains elusive. Defences too powerful, and I am too old. A younger man? There are other pathways to try.' And there it breaks.)

The final reference to Guiwenneth of the Green is brief and confused, yet contains the clue to the tragedy that I had only just come to recognize.

September 15th, 42. Where is the girl? Years! Two years! Where? Is it possible for one mythago to have decayed, another to have replaced it? J sees her. J! She has declined, she is close to death, I know she is close. What can I do? She is haunted. The girl haunts her. Images? Imagination? J more often hysterical than not, and when S and C around, she remains coldly silent, functioning as a mother but no longer as a wife. We have not exchanged . . . (this latter is crossed out, though not illegibly). J fading. Nothing in me hurts at the thought of this.

Whatever illness had afflicted my mother, the condition had been exacerbated by anger, jealousy, and ultimately, perhaps, by grief at the way a younger and astonishingly beautiful woman had stolen my father's heart. 'It is the nature of the mythago itself . . .'

The words were like siren calls, warning me, frightening me, and yet I was helpless to heed them. First my father had been consumed, and after, what tragedy had ensued when Christian had come home from the war, and the girl (by then, perhaps, well established in the house) had changed her affections to the man who was closer to her own age? No wonder the Urscumug was so violent! What fights, I wondered, what pursuits, what anger had been expressed in the months before my father's death in the woodland? The journal contained no reference to this period in time, no reference to Guiwenneth at all after those cold, almost desperate words: *J fading. Nothing in me hurts at the thought of this.*

Whose mythago was she?

Something like panic had affected me, and early the next morning I ran around the woodland, until I was breathless and saturated with sweat. The day was bright, not too cold. I had found a pair of heavy walking boots, and carrying my 'sawn off' spear, I had patrolled the oakwoods at the double. I called for Guiwenneth repeatedly.

Whose mythago was she?

The question haunted me as I ran, a dark bird darting about my head. Was she mine? Or was she Christian's? Christian had gone into the woods to find her again, to find the Guiwenneth of the Green that his *own* mind had generated as it interacted with oak and ash, hawthorn and scrub, the whole complex life form that was ancient Ryhope. But whose mythago was *my* Guiwenneth? Was she Christian's? Had he found her, pursued her, and forced her to the woodland edge, a girl who was afraid of him, contemptuous of him? Was it from Christian that she hid?

Or was she *mine*? Perhaps my own mind had birthed her, and she had come to her creator as once before she had gone to my father, child drawn to adult, like to like. Christian, perhaps, *had* found the girl of his dreams, and even now was ensconced in the heartwoods, living a life as bizarre as it was fulfilling.

But the doubt nagged at me, and the question of Guiwenneth's 'identity' began to become an obsession.

I rested by the sticklebrook, a long way from the house, at the place where Chris and I had waited for the tiny ship to emerge from its forest journey, all those years before. The field was treacherous with cow-pats, although it was only sheep who grazed here now, clustered along the overgrown stream bank, watching me sideways, and with suspicion. The wood was a dark wall stretching away towards Oak Lodge. On impulse I began to follow the sticklebrook back along its course, clambering over the fallen trunk of a lightning-struck tree, forcing my way through the tangle of rose briar, bramble and knee-high nettles. Early summer growth was well advanced, even though the sheep penetrated as deep as this to graze the clearings.

I walked for some minutes, against the flow of the water, the light dimming as the canopy grew denser. The stream widened, the banks became more severe. Abruptly it turned in its course, flowing from the deeper wood, and as I began to follow it so I became disorientated; a vast oak barred my way, and the ground dropped away in a steep, dangerous decline, which I circuited as best I could. Moss-slick grey rock thrust stubby fingers from the ground; gnarled young oak-trunks grew through and around those stony barriers. By the time I had found my way through, I had lost the stream, although its distant sound was haunting.

Within minutes I realized I was seeing through the thinner wood at the edge to open land beyond. I had come in a circle. Again.

I heard, then, the call of a dove, and turned back into the silent gloom. I called for Guiwenneth, but was answered only by the sound of a bird, high above, flapping its wings as if to make mockery of me.

How had my father entered the woodland? How had he managed to penetrate so deeply? From his journals, from the detail on the map that now hung upon the study wall, he had managed to walk some considerable distance into Ryhope Wood before the defences had turned him around. He had known the way, I was sure of that, but his journal had been so pillaged by the man in his last days – hiding evidence, hiding guilt, perhaps – that the information was gone.

I knew my father quite well. Oak Lodge was a testament to many things, and to one thing in particular: his obsessive nature, his need to preserve, to hoard, to shelve. It was unthinkable, to me, that my father would have destroyed anything. Hidden, yes, but never obliterated.

I had searched the house, I had been to the manor, and asked there, and unless my father had broken in one evening to use the vast rooms and silent corridors to his own ends, then he had hidden no papers at the manor house either.

One possibility remained, and I sent a letter of warning to Oxford, hoping that it would arrive before I did, something that could not be guaranteed. The following day I packed a small bag, dressed smartly, and made the laborious journey by bus and train to Oxford.

To the house where my father's colleague and confidant, Edward Wynne-Jones, had lived.

I had not expected to find Wynne-Jones himself. I could not remember how, but at some time during the previous year – or perhaps before I went to France – I had heard of his disappearance, or death, and that his daughter was now living in the house. I didn't know her name, nor whether she would be receptive to my visit. It was a chance I would have to take.

In the event, she was most courteous. The house was a semi-detached on the edge of Oxford, three storeys high, and in a bad state of repair. It was raining as I arrived, and the tall, severe looking woman who answered the door ushered me quickly inside, but fussily made me stand at the end of the hall while I shrugged off my soaking coat and shoes. Only then did she exercise the usual courtesies.

'I'm Anne Hayden.'

'Steven Huxley. I'm sorry about the short notice . . . I hope it's convenient.'

'Perfectly convenient.'

She was in her mid-thirties, soberly dressed in grey skirt and a grey cardigan over a high-necked white blouse. The house smelled of polish and damp. All the rooms were bolted on the corridor side: a defence, I imagined, against intruders coming in through the windows. She was the sort of woman who summons, unbidden, the epithet 'spinster' in untrained, inexperienced minds, and perhaps there should have been cats clustered about her feet.

In fact, Anne Hayden was far from living in a style that appearance would have suggested. She had been married, and her husband had left her during the war. As she led me into the dark, leathery sitting-room, I saw a man of about my own age reading a paper. He rose to his feet, shook hands and was introduced as Jonathan Garland.

'If you want to talk quietly, I'll leave you for a while,' he said, and without waiting for an answer went away, deeper into the house. Anne made no more explanation of him than that. He lived there, of course. The bathroom, I noticed later, had shaving things lining the lower shelf.

All of these details may perhaps seem irrelevant, but I was observing the woman and her situation closely. She was uncomfortable and solemn, allowing no friendly contact, no touch of rapport that would have allowed me to begin my questioning with ease. She made tea, offered me biscuits, and sat totally silently, for a while, until I explained the reason for my visit.

'I never met your father,' she said quietly, 'although I knew of him. He visited Oxford several times, but never when I was at home. My father was a naturalist and spent many weeks away from Oxford. I was very close to him. When he walked out on us I was very distressed.'

'When *was* that, can you remember?'

She gave me a look part-way between anger and pity. 'I can remember it to the day. Saturday, April the 13th, 1942. I was living on the top floor. My husband had already left me. Father had a furious argument with John . . . my brother . . . and then abruptly left. It was the last I saw of him. John went abroad with the forces and was killed. I remained in the house . . .'

By dint of careful questioning, gentle prompting, I pieced together a story of double tragedy. When Wynne-Jones, for whatever reason, had walked out on his family, Anne Hayden's heart had broken for the second time. Distressed, she had lived as a recluse for the years following, although when the war ended she began to move in social circles once more.

When the young man who lived with her brought a fresh pot of tea, the contact between them was warm, briefly expressed and genuine. She had not ceased feeling, even though the scar of her double tragedy was blatant.

I explained in as much detail as I felt necessary that the two men – our two fathers – had worked together, and that my father's records were incomplete. Had she noticed, or discovered, journal extracts, sheets, letters that were not Wynne-Jones's?

'I have hardly looked at anything, Mr Huxley,' she said quietly. 'My father's study is precisely as he left it. If you find that a touch Dickensian, you are welcome to think so. This is a large house, and the room is not needed. To clean it, and maintain it, would be unnecessary effort, so it is locked and remains so until he returns and tidies it up himself.'

'May I see the room?'

'If you wish. It's of no interest to me. And, provided you show me the items, you may borrow anything you like.'

She led the way up to the first floor, and along a dark corridor whose flower-patterned wallpaper was peeling badly. Dusty pictures lined the walls, dim prints by Matisse and Picasso. The carpet was threadbare.

Her father's study was on the end; the room overlooked the city of Oxford. Through its filthy net curtains I could just make out the spire of St Mary's. Books lined the walls so heavily that cracks had appeared in the plaster above the sagging shelves. The desk was covered by a white sheet, as was the rest of the furniture in the room, but the books themselves laboured below a depth of dust as thick as a fingernail. Maps, charts and botanical prints were stacked against one wall. Stacks of journals and bound volumes of letters were thrust to choking point into a cupboard. Here was the antithesis of my father's meticulously laid out studio, a cluttered, confused den of labour and intellect, which confounded me as I stared at it, wondering where to begin my search.

Anne Hayden watched me for a few minutes, her eyes narrow and tired behind the horn-rimmed spectacles she wore. 'I'll leave you for a while,' she said then, and I heard her make her way downstairs.

I opened drawers, leafed through books, even pulled the carpets back to check for loose floorboards. The task would have been gigantic, examining every inch of the room, and at the end of an hour I acknowledged defeat. Not only were there no pages from my father's journal discreetly concealed in his colleague's office, there was not even a journal by Wynne-Jones himself. The only link with the mythago wood was the clutter of bizarre, almost Frankensteinian machinery that was Wynne-Jones's 'frontal bridge' equipment. This jumble of invention included headphones, yards of wire, copper coils, heavy car batteries, coloured stroboscopic light discs and bottles of pungent chemicals, labelled in code. All of these were stuffed into a large, wooden chest, covered with a wall drape. The chest was old and intricately patterned. I pressed and prodded at its panels and did indeed discover a concealed compartment, but the narrow space was empty.

As quietly as possible I walked through the rest of the house, peering into each room in turn, trying to intuit whether or not Wynne-Jones might have fashioned himself a hidey-hole away from his study. No such feeling struck me, nothing but the smell of must, damp sheets, decaying paper-back books, and that awful generalized atmosphere of a property that is unused and uncared for.

I went downstairs again. Anne Hayden smiled thinly. 'Any luck?'

'I'm afraid not.'

She nodded her head thoughtfully, then added, 'What exactly were you looking for? A journal?'

'Your father must have kept one. A desk diary, each year. I can't see them.'

'I don't think I've ever seen such a thing,' she said soberly, still thoughtful. 'Which is odd, I grant you.'

'Did he ever talk about his work to you?' I sat on the edge of an armchair. Anne Hayden crossed her legs and placed her magazine down beside her. 'Some nonsense about extinct animals living in deeper woodlands. Boars, wolves, wild bear . . .' She smiled again. 'I think he believed it.'

'So did my father,' I pointed out. 'But my father's journal has been torn. Whole pages missing. I just wondered if they might have been concealed here. What happened to any letters that were sent after your father's disappearance?'

'I'll show you.' She rose, and I followed her to a tall cupboard in the front room, a place of austere furniture, cluttered bric-a-brac, the occasional attractive ornament.

The cupboard was as packed as the cupboard upstairs, with journals still in their envelopes, and faculty newspapers still rolled tight and bound with tape. 'I keep them. God knows why. Perhaps I'll take them to the college later this week. There seems little point. These are the letters . . .'

Beside the journals was a stack nearly a yard high of private correspondence, all the letters neatly opened, and read, no doubt, by the grieving daughter. 'There may be something from your father there. I really can't remember.' She reached in and eased out the pile of mail, thrust it into my arms. I staggered back to the sitting-room and for an hour checked the handwriting of each letter. There was nothing. My back ached with sitting still for so long, and the smell of dust and mould was making me feel sick.

There was nothing I could do. The clock on the mantelpiece ticked loudly in the heavy silence of that room, and I began to feel I was overstaying my welcome. I passed Anne Hayden a sheet of writing, of inconsequential nature, from an earlier diary of my father's. 'The handwriting is reasonably distinctive. If you should discover any loose sheets, or journals . . . I would be very much obliged.'

'I should be glad to oblige, Mister Huxley.' She took me to the front door. It was still raining outside, and she helped me on with my heavy mackintosh. Then she hesitated, staring at me peculiarly. 'Did you ever meet my father when he visited?'

'I was very young. I remember him more from the midthirties, but he never spoke to me, or my brother. He and my father would meet, and immediately go out into the woodland, seeking those mythical beasts . . .'

'In Herefordshire. Where you live now . . . ?' There was pain in the look she gave me. 'I never knew that. None of us knew. Something, perhaps as long ago as those same midthirties, something changed him. I always remained close to him. He trusted me, trusted the affection I felt for him. But he never talked, never confided. We were just . . . close. I envy the times you saw him. I wish I could share your memories of him doing what he loved . . . mythical beasts or no. The life he adored he denied to his family . . .'

'It was the same for me,' I said gently. 'My mother died of heartbreak; my brother and I were cut off from his world. My own father's world, I mean.'

'So perhaps we have both been losers.'

I smiled. 'You more than I, I think. If you would like to visit Oak Lodge, and see the journal, the place—'

She shook her head quickly. 'I'm not sure I dare, Mr Huxley. Thank you all the same. It's just that . . . I wonder, from what you say . . .'

She could hardly speak. In the gloom of the hallway, with the rain a monotonous beat against the stippled window, high above the door, she seemed to burn with anxiety, her eyes wide, now, behind the glasses.

'It's just what?' I prompted, and almost without thinking, without pause, she said, 'Is he in the wood?'

Taken aback for a moment, I realized what she meant. 'It's possible,' I said. What could I tell her? What should I say about my belief that within the woodland edge, in the heart-woods themselves, was a place whose immensity was beyond simple credence? 'Anything is possible.'

Six

I left Oxford, frustrated, filthy, and very tired. The journey home could not have been worse, with one train cancelled, and a traffic jam outside Witney that held my bus up for over half an hour. Mercifully, the rain passed away, though the sky was lowering, threatening, and distinctly wintry, something I did not wish to see in early summer.

It was six in the evening before I got back to Oak Lodge, and I knew at once that I had a visitor: the back door was wide open, and a light was on in the study. I hastened my step, but paused by the door, looking nervously around in case the trigger-happy cavalier, or a mythago of like violence, might be lurking nearby. But it had to be Guiwenneth. The door had been forced open, the paint around the handle scarred and pitted where the shaft of her spear had repeatedly struck. Inside there was a hint of the smell I associated with her, sharp, pungent. She would obviously need to bath a lot more often.

I called her name, walking carefully from room to room. She was not in the study, but I left the light on. Movement upstairs startled me, and I walked to the hallway. 'Guiwenneth?'

'You catch me snooping, I'm afraid,' came Harry Keeton's voice, and he appeared at the top of the stairs, looking embarrassed, smiling to cover his guilt. 'I'm so sorry. But the door *was* open.'

'I thought it was someone else,' I said. 'There's nothing much worth seeing.'

He came down the stairs and I led him back to the sitting-room. 'Was there anybody here when you came in?'

'Someone, I'm not sure who. As I say, I came up the front

way; no answer. Went round the back and found the door open, a funny smell inside, and this . . .' He waved his hand around the room, at the furniture all disarrayed, shelves swept clean, the books and objects cluttered on the floor. 'Not the sort of thing I do by habit,' he said with a smile. 'Someone ran out of the house as I went into the study, but I didn't see who. I thought I'd hang on for you.'

We straightened the room, then sat down at the dining table. It was chilly, but I decided against laying a fire. Keeton relaxed; the burn mark on his lower face had flushed considerably with his embarrassment, but it became paler and less noticeable, although he nervously covered his jaw with his left hand as he spoke. He seemed tired, I thought, not as bright, or as perky as when we had met at Mucklestone Field. He was wearing civilian clothes, which were very creased. When he sat down at the table I could see that he wore a hip holster and pistol on his belt.

'I developed the photographs I took on that flight, a few days back.' He drew out a rolled package from his pocket, straightened it and opened the top, taking out several magazine-sized prints. I had almost forgotten that part of the process, the monitoring and photographing of the land below. 'After that storm we seemed to encounter I didn't expect anything to show up, but I was wrong.'

There was a haunted look to him, now, as he pushed the prints across to me. 'I use a high precision, good spying camera. High grain Kodak film; I've been able to enlarge quite a bit . . .'

He watched me as I stared at the foggy, occasionally blurred, and occasionally ultra-sharp scenes of the mythago wood.

Tree tops and clearings seemed to be the main view, but I could see why he was disturbed, perhaps excited. On the fourth print, taken as the plane had banked to the west, the camera had panned across the woodland, and slightly down, and it showed a clearing and a tall, decaying stone structure, parts of it rising to the foliage level itself.

'A building,' I said unnecessarily, and Harry Keeton added, 'There's an enlargement . . .'

Increasingly blurred, the next sheet showed a close-up of the building: an edifice and tower, rising from a break in the tree-structure of the forest, where a number of figures clustered. No detail was observable, beyond the fact of their humanness: white and grey shapes, suggestive of both male and female, caught in the act of walking about the tower; two shapes crouched, as if climbing the crumbling structure itself.

'Probably built in the middle ages,' Keeton said thoughtfully. 'The wood grew across the access roadway, and the place got cut off . . .'

Less romantic, but far more likely, was that the structure was a Victorian folly, something built more for whim than good reason. But follies had usually been constructed on high hills: tall structures, from whose upper reaches the eccentric, rich, or just plain bored owner could observe distances further than county borders.

If this place, the place we observed on the photograph, *was* a folly, then it was peculiarly inept.

I turned to the next print. This showed the image of a river winding through the densely packed trees; its course meandered, the tree line broken in an aerial reflection of the pathway. At two points, out of focus, the water gleamed, and the river looked wide. This was the *sticklebrook*? I could hardly believe what I was seeing. 'I've enlarged the river parts as well,' Keeton said softly, and when I turned to those prints I realized that I could see more mythagos.

They were blurred again, but there were five of them, close together, wading across the fragment of river that had caught the attention of the camera. They were holding objects above their heads, perhaps weapons, perhaps just staffs. They were as dim and indistinct as a photograph of a lake monster I had once seen, just the suggestion of shape and movement.

Wading across the sticklebrook!

The final photograph was in its way the most dramatic of

them all. It showed only woodland. Only? It showed some-thing more, and I was unwilling, at the time, even to guess at the nature of the forces and structures I could see. What had happened, Keeton explained, was that the negative was underexposed. That simple mistake, caused for no reason he could understand, had captured the winding tendrils of energy arising from across the great span of the woodland. They were eerie, suggestive, tentative . . . I counted twenty of them, like tornadoes, but thinner, knotted and twisted as they probed up from the hidden land below. The nearer vortices were clearly reaching toward the plane, to encompass the unwelcome vehicle . . . to reject it.

'I know what sort of wood it is now,' he said, and I glanced at him, surprised at his words. He was watching me. The expression in his eyes was akin to triumph, but tinged, perhaps, with terror. The burn on his face was flushed, and his lip, in the corner that had been burned, seemed pinched, giving his face a lopsided look. He leaned forward, hands spread palm-flat on the table.

'I've been searching for such a place since the war ended,' he went on. 'In a few days I'd have realized the nature of Ryhope Wood. I'd already heard stories of a haunted wood in the area . . . that's why I've been looking in the county.'

'A haunted wood?'

'A ghost wood,' he said quickly. 'There was one in France. It was where I was shot down. It didn't have the same gloomy aspect, but it was the same.'

I prompted him to speak further. He seemed almost afraid to do so, sitting back in his chair, his gaze drifting away from me as he remembered.

'I'd blanked it out of my mind. I've blanked a lot out . . .'

'But you remember now.'

'Yes. We were close to the Belgian border. I flew on a lot of missions there, mostly dropping supplies to the resistance. I was flying one dusk when the plane was thrown about in the air. Like a tremendous thermal.' He glanced at me. 'You know the sort of thing.'

I nodded my agreement. He went on, 'I couldn't fly over that wood, try as I might. It was quite small. I banked and tried again. The same effect of light on the wings, like the other day. Light streaming from the wings, over the cockpit. And again, tossed about like a leaf. There were faces down below. They looked as if they were floating in the foliage. Like ghosts, like clouds. Tenuous. You know what ghosts are supposed to be like. They looked like clouds, caught in the tree tops, blowing, and shifting . . . but those faces!'

'So you weren't shot down at all,' I said, but he nodded. 'Oh yes. Certainly, the plane was hit. I always say a sniper because . . . well, it's the only explanation I have.' He looked down at his hands. 'One shot, one strike, and the plane went down into that woodland like a stone. I got out, so did John Shackleford. Out of the wreckage. We were damned lucky . . . for a while . . .'

'And then?'

He glanced up sharply, suspiciously. 'And then . . . blank. I got out of the wood. I was wandering around farmland when a German patrol got me. I spent the rest of the war behind barbed wire.'

'Did you see anything in the wood? While you were wandering.'

He hesitated before answering, and there was an edge of irritation to his voice. 'As I said, old boy. Blank.'

I accepted that, for whatever reason, he didn't want to talk about events after the crash. It must have been humiliating for him, a prisoner of war, hideously burned, shot down in bizarre circumstances. I said, 'But this wood, Ryhope Wood, is the same . . .'

'There were faces too, but much closer—'

'I didn't see them,' I said, surprised.

'They were there. If you'd looked. It's a ghost wood. It's the same. You've been haunted by it yourself. Tell me I'm right!'

'Do you need me to tell you what you already know?'

His gaze was intense; his wild, fair hair flopped over his

brow and he looked very boyish; he seemed excited, yet also frightened, or perhaps apprehensive. 'I would like to see inside that woodland,' he said, his voice almost a whisper.

'You won't get very far,' I said. 'I know. I've tried.'

'I don't understand.'

'The wood turns you around. It defends itself . . . well, Good God, man, you know that from the other day. You walk for hours and come in a circle. My father found a way in. And so has Christian.'

'Your brother.'

'The very same. He's been in there, now, for over nine months. He must have found the way through the vortices . . .'

Before Keeton could query my terminology, a movement from the kitchen startled us both, and made us both react with elaborate gestures of silence. It had been a stealthy movement, given away by the shifting of the back door.

I pointed to Keeton's belt. 'May I suggest that you draw your pistol, and if the face that appears around the door doesn't have a frame of red hair . . . then fire a warning shot into the top of the wall.'

As quickly as possible, without making undue noise, Keeton armed himself. It was a regular forces-issue Smith and Wesson .38 calibre, and he eased back the hammer, raising the cocked weapon in one hand, sighting along its barrel. I watched the entrance from the kitchen, and a moment later Guiwenneth stepped carefully, slowly into the room. She glanced at Keeton, then at me, and her face registered the question: Who's he?

'Good God,' Keeton breathed, brightening up, losing his haunted look. He lowered his arm, slotted the pistol back into the holster without taking his gaze from the girl. Guiwenneth came over to me and placed a hand on my shoulder (almost protectively!), standing by me as she scrutinized the burned airman. She giggled and touched her face. She was studying the awful mark of Keeton's accident. She said something in her alien tongue too fast for me to catch.

'You're quite astonishingly beautiful,' Keeton said to her. 'My name's Harry Keeton. You've taken my breath away and I've quite forgotten my manners.' He stood, and stepped towards Guiwenneth, who moved away from him, the grip on my shoulder increasing. Keeton stared at me. 'Foreign? No English at all?'

'English, no. The language of this country? Sort of. She doesn't understand what you say.'

Guiwenneth reached down and kissed the top of my head. Again, I felt it was a possessive, protective gesture, and I couldn't comprehend the reason for it. But I liked it. I believe I flushed as brightly as Keeton had a tendency to do. I reached up and placed my fingers gently on the girl's, and for a brief moment our hands interlocked, a communication that was quite unmistakable. 'Good night, Steven,' she said, her accent strong and strange, the words an astonishing utterance. I looked up at her. Her brown eyes shone, partly with pride, partly with amusement. 'Good *evening*, Guiwenneth,' I corrected, and she made a moue, turned to Keeton and said, 'Good evening . . .' She giggled as she trailed off; she'd forgotten the name. Keeton reminded her and she said it aloud, raising her right hand, palm towards him, then placing the palm across her bosom. Keeton repeated the gesture and bowed, and they both laughed.

Guiwenneth turned her attention back to me, then. She crouched beside me, the spear rising from between her legs as she held it, incongruous, almost obscene. Her tunic was too short, her body too conspicuously young and lithe for an inexperienced man like me to remain cool. She touched my nose with the top of one slender finger, smiling as she recognized the thoughts behind my crimson features. 'Cuningabach,' she said, warningly. Then: 'Food. Cook. Guiwenneth. Food.'

'Food,' I repeated. 'You want food?' I tapped my chest as I spoke, and Guiwenneth shook her head quickly, tapped her own pert bosom and said, 'Food!'

'Ah! *Food!*' I repeated, stabbing a finger towards her. *She* wanted to cook. I understood now.

'Food!' she agreed with a smile. Keeton licked his lips.

'Food,' I said uncertainly, wondering what Guiwenneth's idea of a meal might be. But . . . what did it matter? I was nothing if not experimental. I shrugged and agreed. 'Why not.'

'May I stay . . . just for that part?' Keeton prompted and I said, 'Of course.'

Guiwenneth stood up and touched a finger to the side of her nose. (*You have a treat in store*, she seemed to be saying.) She went into the kitchen and knocked and banged about among the pots and utensils. I heard, quite quickly, the ominous sound of chopping, and the unwelcome, distasteful sound of bones being snapped.

'Awfully impertinent of me,' Keeton said, as he sat in an armchair, still wearing his overcoat. 'Inviting myself like that. But farms always have such lovely supplies. I'll pay, if you like . . .'

I laughed as I watched him. 'I may be paying you . . . not to talk about it. I hate to tell you this, but our cook for the evening doesn't believe, or even know, about traditional liver and bacon. It's as likely that she's going to spit-roast a wild boar.'

Keeton frowned, of course. 'Boar? Extinct, surely.'

'Not in Ryhope Wood. Nor bear. How would you like haunch of bear stuffed with wolves' sweetbreads?'

'Not a lot,' the airman said. 'Is this a joke?'

'The other day I cooked her an ordinary vegetable stew. She thought it was disgusting. I dread to think what she would find passable . . .'

But when I crept to the kitchen door and peered round, she was clearly preparing something a little less ambitious than brown bear. The kitchen table was awash with blood, as were her fingers, which she sucked as easily as I might have sucked honey or gravy. The carcass was long and thin. A rabbit, or a hare. She was boiling water. She had chopped vegetables roughly and was examining the can of Saxa salt as she licked the body fluids from her hands. In the event, the meal was quite tasty, if somewhat revolting in appearance. She served the carcass whole, head and all, but had split the skull so that the brains would cook. These she nicked out with her knife and sliced carefully into three parts. Keeton's refusal of this morsel was an hysterically funny exhibition of courtesy and panic, warring for expression.

Guiwenneth ate with her fingers, using her short knife to stab and cut from the surprisingly meaty rabbit. She dismissed forks as 'R'vannith,' but tried one and clearly recognized its potential.

'How are you getting back to the airfield?' I asked Keeton, later. Guiwenneth had laid a small birchwood fire, the evening being cool. The dining-room seemed cosy, enclosed. She sat cross-legged before the open grate, watching the flames. Keeton remained at the table, dividing his attention between the photographs and the back of the strange girl. I sat on the floor, my back against an armchair, my legs stretched out behind Guiwenneth.

After a while she leaned back on her elbows, across my knees, and reached out with her right hand gently to touch my ankle. The fire made her hair and skin glow. She was deep in thought, and seemed melancholy.

My question to Keeton abruptly broke the contemplative, silent mood. Guiwenneth sat up and looked at me, her face solemn, her eyes almost sad. Keeton stood up and tugged his coat from the back of his chair. 'Yes, it is getting late . . .'

I felt embarrassed. 'That wasn't a hint to go. You're welcome to stay. There's plenty of room.'

He smiled peculiarly, glancing at the girl. 'Next time I might take you up on that offer. But I have an early start tomorrow.'

'How *will* you get back?'

'Same way I came. Motorcycle. I parked it in your woodshed, out of the rain.'

I saw him to the door. His parting words, addressed to me as he stared at the edgewoods, were, 'I'll be back. I hope you won't mind . . . but I'll have to come back.'

'Any time,' I said. A few minutes later the roar of his motorcycle made Guiwenneth jump and question me with her look, alarmed, puzzled. I smiled and told her that it was merely Keeton's chariot. After a few seconds the drone of the cycle had gone, and Guiwenneth relaxed.

Seven

There had been a closeness between us, that early evening, which had affected me strongly. My heart beat loudly, my face flushed, my thoughts were unrestrained, adolescent. The presence of the girl, seated quietly on the floor beside me, her beauty, her strength, her apparent sadness, all combined to play havoc with my emotions. In order to prevent myself reaching for her, grasping her by the shoulders and clumsily attempting to kiss her, I had to grip the arms of my chair, fight to keep my feet motionless on the carpet.

I think she was aware of my confusion. She smiled thinly, glanced at me uncertainly, returned her gaze to the fire. Later she leaned down and rested her head against my legs. I touched her hair tentatively, then more surely. She didn't resist. I stroked her face, brushed my fingers lightly over the tumbling locks of red hair, and began to think my heart would burst.

In truth, I thought that that night she would sleep with me, but she slipped away towards midnight, without a word, without a glance. The room was cold, the fire dead. Perhaps she had slept against me, I don't know. My legs were numb from being held in the same position for hours. I had not wanted to disturb her by any brief motion of my body, other than the gentle caress. And abruptly she stood, gathered up her belt and weapons, and walked from the house. I remained seated, and at some time in the early morning dragged the heavy table-cloth across my body as a blanket.

The next day she returned during the afternoon. She acted with diffidence and distance, not meeting my gaze, not responding to my questions. I decided to busy myself in my usual way: house maintenance (that is, cleaning) and repairing the broken back door. These were not tasks with which I would normally have bothered, but I was reluctant to follow after Guiwenneth as she prowled through the house, lost in her own thoughts.

'Are you hungry?' I asked her later. She smiled, turning to me from her position by my bedroom window, staring out. 'I am hungry,' she said, the accent funny, the words perfect.

'You are learning my language well,' I said with exaggerated emphasis, but she couldn't grasp that.

This time, without my bidding, she ran herself a bath, and squatted in the cool water for some minutes, squeezing the small bar of Lifebuoy soap between her fingers, conducting a murmured conversation with herself, occasionally chuckling. She even ate the cold ham salad spread I prepared.

But there was something wrong, something that was beyond my naïve experience to grasp. She was aware of me, I knew that, and I sensed too, that she needed me. Something was holding her back.

Later in the evening she prowled and poked through the cupboards in the unused bedrooms, and dug out some of Christian's old clothes. She stripped off her tunic and tugged on a collarless white shirt, standing there giggling, arms spread. The shirt was far too big for her, covering her to mid-thigh and hanging loose over her hands. I rolled up the sleeves for her and she flapped her arms like a bird, laughing delightedly. It was back to the cupboard, then, and out with a pair of grey flannel trousers. These we pinned up so that they only reached to her ankle, and the whole lot was tied at the waist with a dressing-gown cord.

In this unlikely garb she seemed to be comfortable. She looked like a child lost in the ballooning clothes of a clown, but how could she judge such things? And being without concern for her appearance, she was happy, I imagined that in her mind she associated the wearing of what she thought to be *my* clothes with being closer to me.

It was a warm night, a more usual summer atmosphere,

and we walked outside the house in the fading light of dusk. She was intrigued by the spread of the sapling growth that now bounded the house and swarmed across the lawns beyond the study. Among these immature oaks she walked in a weaving fashion, letting her hands trail among the flexible stems, bending them, springing them, touching the tiny new season's buds. I followed her, watching the evening breeze catch the voluminous shirt, the incredible cascade of her hair.

She undertook two circuits of the house, walking at near marching pace. I couldn't fathom the reason for the activity, but as she came round to the back yard again her glance at the woodland was almost wistful. She said something in a tone that smacked strongly of frustration.

I grasped it immediately. 'You're waiting for someone. There's someone coming from the wood for you. Is that it? You're waiting!'

And at the same time the sickening thought was occurring to me: Christian!

For the first time I found myself fervently hoping that Christian would not come back. The wish which had obsessed me for months – his return – was reversed as easily, and as cruelly, as one might destroy a litter of kittens. The thought of my brother no longer agonized because of my need for him, and my grief at his disappearance. It agonized because he was searching for Guiwenneth, and because this beautiful girl, this melancholy child warrior, might well have been pining for him in her own turn. She had come to the house outside the woods to wait for him, knowing that it would be to his strange haven that he might one day return.

She was not mine at all. It was not *me* she wanted. It was my elder kinsman, the man whose mind had fashioned her.

Breaking through that moment's angry reflection came the image of Guiwenneth spitting on the floor, and speaking Christian's name with utter contempt. Was it the contempt of one whose affection has been spurned? A contempt now mellowed by time?

Somehow, I thought not. My panic passed away. She had been afraid of Chris, and it was not love that had motivated her earlier violent reference to him.

Back in the house, we sat at the table and Guiwenneth talked to me, staring at me intently, touching her breast, moving her hands in a way that was designed to illustrate the thoughts behind her alien words. She scattered English through her dialogue with amazing frequency, but I still failed to understand the story she was telling. Soon, tiredness, a touch of frustration, shadowed her face, and though she smiled a little grimly, she had grasped that words were useless. With sign language she indicated that *I* should speak to her.

For an hour I told her about my childhood, the family that had once occupied Oak Lodge, the war, my first love. All of these things I illustrated with signs, making exaggerated hugging motions, firing imaginary pistols, walking my fingers along the table, chasing my left hand, finally catching it and illustrating a tentative first kiss. It was pure Chaplin, and Guiwenneth giggled and laughed loudly, made comments and sounds of approval, amazement, disbelief, and in this way we communicated on a level beyond words. I do believe she had understood everything I had told her, and now had gained a strong picture of my early life. She seemed intrigued when I talked of Christian as a child, but fell solemn when I told her how he had disappeared into the woodland.

Finally I said to her, 'Can you understand my words?'

She smiled and shrugged. 'Understand speaking. A little. You speaking. I speaking. A little.' Again she shrugged. 'In woodland. Speaking . . .' She flexed her fingers, struggling to explain the concept. Many? Many languages? 'Yes,' she said. 'Many languages. Some understanding. Some . . .' shaking her head and crossing her opened hands, a clear gesture of negation.

My father's diary had referred to the way a mythago would develop the language of its creator faster than the reverse process. It was uncanny to watch and listen as

Guiwenneth acquired English, acquired concepts, acquired understanding almost with every sentence that I spoke to her.

The rosewood clock chimed eleven. We watched the mantelpiece in silence and when the delicate sound had faded I counted aloud from one to eleven. Guiwenneth answered in her own language. We stared at each other. It had been a long evening and I was tired; my throat was dry with talking, my eyes stinging with dust or ash from the fire. I needed sleep but was reluctant to move from the contact with the girl. I dreaded her walking back into the woodland and not reappearing. As it was, I spent the morning restlessly pacing, waiting for her to return. My need was growing.

I tapped the table. 'Table,' I said, and she said a word which sounded like 'board'.

'Tired,' I said, and let my head drop to one side, making exaggerated snoring motions. She smiled and nodded, rubbing her hands over her brown eyes and blinking rapidly. 'Chusug,' she said, and added, in English, 'Guiwenneth tired.'

'I'm going to sleep. Will you stay?'

I stood up and held my hand to her. She hesitated then reached out to touch my fingers, squeezing the tips with hers. But she remained seated, her gaze on mine, and slowly shook her head. Then she blew me a kiss, pulled the cloth from the table as I had done the other night, and moved over to the floor by the dead fire, where she curled up like an animal, and seemed to drift into sleep immediately.

I went upstairs to my cold bed, and lay awake for more than an hour, disappointed in one way, yet triumphant: for the first time ever she had stayed the night in my house.

Progress was being made!

That night, nature advanced upon Oak Lodge in a frightening and dramatic way.

I had slept fitfully, my mind filled with images of the girl asleep by the fire downstairs, and of her walking through the unnatural growth of saplings that surrounded the house, her shirt billowing, her hands touching the flexible stems of the man-high trees. It seemed to me that the whole house creaked and shifted as the soil below was pierced and penetrated by the spreading roots. And in this way, perhaps, I was anticipating the event that occurred at two in the morning, the dead part of the night.

I awoke to a strange sound, the splintering noise of wood splitting, the groaning of great beams bending and warping. For a second, as I came to my senses, I thought it was a nightmare. Then I realized that the whole house was shaking, that the beech outside my window was being whipped about as if in a hurricane. I could hear Guiwenneth's cry from below, and I grabbed my dressing-gown and raced down the stairs.

A strange, cold wind blew from the direction of the study. Guiwenneth was standing in the dark doorway to that room, a frail shape in her creased clothing. The noise began to abate. A powerful and pungent smell of mud and earth assailed my nostrils as I approached cautiously through the junk-filled lounge, turning on the light.

The oakwood had come to the study, bursting up through the floors, and winding and twisting across the walls and ceiling. The desk was shattered, cabinets broken and pierced by the gnarled fingers of the new growth. Whether it was one tree or more I couldn't tell; perhaps it was no normal tree at all, but, an extension of the forest designed to engulf those flimsy structures that had been made by man.

The room was rank with the smell of dirt and wood. The branches that framed the ceiling trembled; earth fell in small lumps from the dark, scarred trunks that had pierced the flooring at eight points.

Guiwenneth walked into this shadowy cage of wood, reaching out to touch one of the quivering limbs. The whole room seemed to shudder at her touch, but a sensation of calm had enveloped the house, now. It was as if . . . as if once the woodland had grasped the Lodge, had made it a part of its aura, the tension, the need to possess, had gone.

The light in the study no longer worked. Still astonished by what had happened, I followed Guiwenneth into the shadowy, eerie chamber, to rescue my father's journal and diaries from the crumbling desk. A twig of oak twisted, I swear, to stroke my fingers as I tugged the books from the drawer. I was watched as I worked, assessed. The room was cold. Earth fell upon my hair, broke in small lumps on the floor, and where my bare feet touched it, it seemed to burn.

The whole room *rustled*; it whispered. Outside the French windows, which were still intact, the oak saplings crowded closer, taller than me, now, growing towards the house in greater abundance.

The following morning I staggered down from a last few hours of fitful, jumpy sleep, to realize that it was close on ten o'clock, a blustery day outside, with a sky that threatened rain. The tablecloth was crumpled on the floor by the fire, but noise from the kitchen informed me that my guest had not yet departed.

Guiwenneth greeted me with a cheery smile, and words in her Brythonic language that she briefly translated as, 'Good. Eating.' She had discovered a box of Quaker Oats, and had made a thick porridge with water and honey. This she was scooping into her mouth with two fingers, and smacking her lips with loud appreciation. She picked up the box and stared at the dark-robed Quaker who featured on the front, and laughed. 'Meivoroth!' she said, pointing to the thick broth, and nodded vigorously. 'Good.'

She had found something that reminded her of home. When I picked up the box I discovered it was almost empty.

Then something outside caught her attention, and she moved quickly to the back door, opening it and stepping out into the windy day. I followed her, aware of the sound of a horse cantering across the nearer meadow.

It was no mythago who rode up to the fence and leaned down to unlatch the gate, kicking her small mare through into the gardens. Guiwenneth watched the younger girl with interest and half amusement.

She was the eldest daughter of the Ryhopes, an unpleasant girl who conformed to all the worst caricatures of the English upper classes: weak-jawed, dull-eyed, over-opinionated and under-informed; she was horse-obsessed, and hunt-mad, something that I found personally offensive.

She gave Guiwenneth a long, arrogant look, more jealous than curious. Fiona Ryhope was blonde, freckled, and exceedingly plain. Wearing jodhpurs and a black riding jacket, she was – to my eyes – quite indistinguishable from any of the saddle-crazy debutantes who regularly jumped old barrels and fences in the local gymkhana.

'Letter for you. Sent to the house.'

And that was all she said, passing me the buff envelope, then swinging her horse around and cantering back across the garden. She didn't close the gate. From the lack of acknowledgement to the fact that she had not dismounted, every second of her presence on my territory had been insulting, and discourteous. I didn't bother to say thank you. Guiwenneth watched her go, but I walked back into the house, opening the slim package.

It was from Anne Hayden. The letter was simple and short:

Dear Mr Huxley,

I believe the enclosed are the sheets you were looking for when you came to Oxford. They are certainly in your father's handwriting. They were tucked inside an issue of the *Journal of Archaeology*. I believe he had hidden them there, and readdressed his own copy of the journal to my father. In one way you discovered them yourself, since I would not have bothered to send the pile of journals to the university if you hadn't visited. A kind librarian found the sheets and sent them back. I have also enclosed some correspondence that may be of interest to you.

Yours sincerely,
Anne Hayden

Attached to the letter were six folded pages from the journal, six pages that my father had not wanted Christian to discover, six pages that concerned themselves with Guiwenneth, and with the way to penetrate the outer defences of the primal woodland . . .

Eight

May 1942
Encounters with the river tribe, the *shamiga*, with a primitive
form of Arthur, and a Knight, straight out of Malory. This
latter quite risky. Observed a tournament in the older
sense, a crazed battle in a woodland clearing, ten Knights,
all fighting in total silence, except for crash of weapons.
The Knight who triumphed rode around the glade, as the
others departed on horseback. A magnificent looking man in
bright armour and a purple cloak. His horse wore a mantle
and trappings of silk. I could not identify him in terms of
legend, but he talked to me briefly, in a language I could just
recognize: Middle French.

These I list, but it was the fortified village of Cumbarath
that was most significant. Here, staying in a roundhouse for
forty days or more (and yet I was away only two weeks!)
I learned of the legend of Guiwenneth. The village is the
legendary palisaded village, hidden in a valley, or across
a remote mountain, where the pure folk live, the old
inhabitants of the land who have never been found by the
conqueror. A strong and persisting myth through many
centuries, and startling to me since I lived *within* a
mythago . . . the village itself, and all its inhabitants, are
created from the racial unconscious. This, so far, is the
most powerful myth *landscape* in the wood, that I have
discovered.

Learned the language easily, since it was close to the
Brythonic of the girl, and learned fragments of her legend,
although the story is clearly incomplete. Her tale ends in
tragedy, I am sure. Deeply excited by the story. So much that
G talks about when she comes, so many of her strange

obsessions, become clearer to me. She has been generated at age 16 or 17, the time at which her memory becomes important, but the story of her birth is powerfully remembered in the village.

This, then, is part of the dark story of the girl Guiwenneth as told to me:

They were the first days when the legions from the east were in the land.

Two sisters lived in the fort at Dun Emrys, the daughters of the warlord, Morthid, who was old, weak, and had given in to peace. Each daughter was as fair as the other. Each had been born on the same day, the day before the feast of the sun god, Lug. To tell them apart was almost impossible, save that Dierdrath wore a bloom of heather on her right breast, and Rhiathan the flower of a wild rose on her left. Rhiathan fell in love with a Roman commander at the nearby fort Caerwent. She went to the fort to live, and there was a time of harmony between the invader and the tribe at Dun Emrys. But Rhiathan was barren and her jealousy and hate grew, until her face was like iron.

Dierdrath loved the son of a fierce warrior who had been slain in battle against the Romans. The son's name was Peredur, and he had been outcast from the tribe because he had opposed Dierdrath's father. Now he lived, with nine warriors, in the wildwoods, in a stony gorge where not even a hare would dare to run. At night he came to the wildwood edge and called to Dierdrath like a dove. Dierdrath went to him, and in time she carried his child.

When the time came for the birth, the druid, Cathabach, pronounced that she carried a girl, and the name was given: Guiwenneth, which means earth child. But Rhiathan sent soldiers to the Dun, and Dierdrath was taken from her father, and carried against her will to the tents inside the wooden palisade of the Roman fort. Four warriors from the Dun were taken too, and Morthid himself, and he was agreeable that the child, when born, should be fostered by

Rhiathan. Dierdrath was too weak to cry out, and Rhiathan swore silently that when the child was born, her sister would die.

Peredur watched from the forest edge, despairing. His nine were with him and none could console him. Twice, during the night, he attacked the fort, but was repulsed by force of arms. Each time he could hear the voice of Dierdrath, crying to him, 'Be quick. Save my child.'

Beyond the stone gorge, where the woods were darkest, was a place where the oldest tree was older than the land, as round and high as an earth fort. There, Peredur knew, lived the Jagad, an entity as eternal as the rock across which he scrambled, searching. The Jagad was his only hope, for she alone controlled the ways of things, not just in the woods, but in the seas and in the air. She was from the oldest time, and no invader could come near her. She had known the ways of men from the time of the Watching, when men had no tongues to speak.

This is how Peredur found the Jagad.

He found a glen where wild thistle grew, and no sapling was higher than his ankle. Around him, the forest was tall and silent. No tree had fallen and died to form this glade. Only the Jagad could have made it. The nine warriors with him formed a circle, with their backs to Peredur, who stood between them. They held twigs of hazel, blackthorn and oak. Peredur slew a wolf and spread its blood upon the ground, around the nine. The wolf's head he placed facing north. He pushed his sword into the earth at the west of the circle. He laid his dagger at the east. He himself stood to the south, inside his ring, and called for the entity.

This is the way that things were worked in the days before the priests, and the most important thing of all was the circle which bound the caller to his own years and land.

Seven times Peredur called the Jagad.

On the first call he saw only the birds fly from the trees (but what birds they were, crows, sparrows and hawks, each as large as a horse).

On the second call, the hares and foxes of the woodland ran around the circle, and fled to the west.

On the third call, wild boar rushed from the thickets. Each was taller than a man, but the circle held them back (though Oswry speared the smallest for food, and would be called to answer for the act in another season).

On the fourth call, the stags came from the spinneys, followed by the does, and each time their hooves touched the ground the woodland trembled and the circle shook. The eyes of the stags glowed in the night. Guillauc tossed a torque on to the antler of one of them, to mark it as his, and at another time he would be called to answer for the deed.

On the fifth call the glade fell silent, though figures moved beyond vision. Then men on horseback emerged from the treeline, and swarmed about the glade. The horses were black as night, each with a dozen great, grey hounds at its feet, and a rider on its back. Cloaks flowed in silent winds, and torches burned, and this wild hunt circled the nine twenty times, their cries growing loud, their eyes bright. These were no men of the lands of Peredur, but hunters from times past and times yet to come, gathered here, and guarding the Jagad.

On the sixth and seventh call the Jagad came, following behind the horsemen and the hounds. The ground opened and the gates to the world below the land parted, and the Jagad stepped through, a tall figure and faceless, her body swathed in dark robes, with silver and iron on her wrists and ankles. The fallen daughter of the earth, the hateful, vengeful child of the Moon, the Jagad stood before Peredur and in the emptiness that was her face a silent smile appeared, and scornful laughter assailed his ears.

But the Jagad could not break the circle of Year and Land, could not drag Peredur far beyond this place and season, and lose him in a wild place, where he would be at her mercy. Three times she walked around the circle, stopping only to look at Oswry and Guillauc, who knew at once that by killing the boar and marking the stag they had doomed themselves. But their time would be for other years, and another tale.

Then Peredur told the Jagad what he needed. He told her of his love for Dierdrath, and the jealousy of the sister, and the threat to his child. He asked for help.

'I will have the child, then,' said the Jagad, and Peredur answered that she would not.

'I will have the mother, then,' said the Jagad, and Peredur answered that she would not.

'Then I shall have one of the ten,' said the Jagad, and brought to Peredur and his warriors a basket containing hazel nuts. Each warrior, and Peredur himself, took a nut and ate it, none knowing which would have been bound to the Jagad.

The Jagad said, 'You are the hunters of the long night. One of you now is mine, because the magic that I give you must be paid for, and a life is all that can be used. Now break the circle, for the bargaining is done.'

'No,' said Peredur, and the Jagad laughed.

Then the Jagad raised her arms to the dark skies. In the emptiness that was her face Peredur thought he could see the shape of the hag who inhabited the body of the entity. She was older than time itself, and only the wildwoods saved men from her evil glance.

'I will give you your Guiwenneth,' cried the Jagad. 'But each man here will answer for her life. I am the huntress of the first woods, and the ice woods, and the stone woods, and the high tracks, and the bleak moors; I am the daughter of Moon and Saturn; sour herbs cure me, bitter juices sustain me, bright silver and cold iron gird me. I have always been in the earth, and the earth shall ever nourish me, for I am the eternal huntress, and when I have need of you, Peredur, and your nine hunters, I shall call upon you, and whoever I call shall go. There is no time so remote that you shall not wander through it, no land too wide or too cold, or too hot, or too lonely for a quest to take you. Be it known, and be it agreed, then, that when the girl has first known love, each and *all* of you shall be mine . . . to answer my call, or not, depending on the nature of things.'

And Peredur looked grim. But when his friends all gave their consent, he agreed, and so it was done. And thereafter they were known as the *Jaguth*, which is the *night hunt*.

On the day of the child's birth, ten eagles were seen, circling the Roman fort. None knew what to make of the omen, for the bird was a good portent to all concerned, but the number of them was puzzling.

Guiwenneth was born, in a tent, watched only by her aunt and the druid. But as the druid gave thanks with smoke and a small sacrifice, so Rhiathan pressed a cushion to her sister's face, and killed her. None saw her do this deed, and she wept as loudly as the rest for the death.

Then Rhiathan took the girl child and went out into the fort, and raised the child above her head, proclaiming herself foster mother, and her Roman lover the father.

Above the fort, the ten eagles gathered. The sound of their wings was like a distant storm; they were so large that when they grouped they cut off the sun, and threw a great shade across the fort. From this shadow came one of them, swooping fast from the sky. It beat about the head of Rhiathan, and snatched the child in its great talons, flying up again.

Rhiathan screamed her anger. The eagles dispersed quickly towards the country around, but Roman archers loosed a thousand arrows and made their flying difficult.

The eagle with the child in its talons was slowest of all. There was one among the legion who was renowned for his skill with a bow, and his single shot struck through the heart of the eagle, which let the child fall. The other birds, seeing this, came swiftly back, and one flew below the girl so that her fall was broken upon its back. Two others clasped the dead bird in their talons. With the infant and the dead bird, they flew to the wildwoods, to the stone gorge, and there regained their human shape.

It was Peredur who had dived for the child, Peredur himself, her father. He lay, beautiful and pale in death, the arrow still through his heart. About the gorge, the Jagad's laughter was like wind. She had promised Peredur that she would give him his Guiwenneth, and for a few moments he had had her.

The Jaguth took Peredur to the bottom of the stony valley, where the wind was strongest, and buried him there, beneath a stone of white marble. Magidion was now the leader of the group.

They raised Guiwenneth as best they could, these wood-land hunters, outcast warriors. Guiwenneth was happy with them. They suckled her with wild-flower dew and doe's milk. They clothed her in fox hide and cotton. She could walk by the time she was half a year old. She could run by the time she was a full four seasons of age. She knew the names of things in the wildwood soon after she could talk. Her only grief was that the ghost of Peredur called to her, and many mornings she would be found, standing by the marble stone in the wind-swept gorge, crying.

One day, Magidion and the Jaguth hunted south from the valley, the girl with them. They made camp in a secret place, and one of them, Guillauc, remained with the girl, while the others hunted.

This is how Guiwenneth was lost to them.

The Romans had ceaselessly searched the hills and valleys, and the forests around the fort. They smelled the smoke of the camp's fire, now, and twenty men closed in about the clearing. Their approach was betrayed by a crow, and Guiwenneth and the hunter, Guillauc, knew they were lost.

Quickly, Guillauc tied the girl to his back with leather thongs, hurting her, so tight was the binding. Then he sum-moned the magic of the Jagad, and changed to a great stag, and in this form he ran from the Romans.

But the Romans had dogs with them, and the dogs pursued the stag throughout the day. When the stag was exhausted it turned at bay, and the dogs tore it to pieces, but Guiwenneth was saved and taken to the fort. The spirit of Guillauc remained where the stag had fallen, and in the year when Guiwenneth first knew love, the Jagad came for him.

For two years Guiwenneth lived in a tent within the high walls of the Roman stronghold. She was always to be found, struggling to see over the walls of the fort, crying and sobbing, as if she knew that the Jaguth were there, waiting to come for her. No more melancholy child was ever seen during those years, and no bond of love formed between her and her foster mother. But Rhiathan would not part with her.

This is how the Jaguth took her back.

Before dawn, early in the summer, eight doves called to Guiwenneth, and the child woke and listened to them. The next morning, before first light, eight owls called to her. On the third morning she was awake before the call, and walked through the dark camp, to the walls, to the place where she could see the hills around the fort. Eight stags stood there, watching her. After a while they ran swiftly down the hill, and thundered about the fort, calling loudly, before returning to the wild glens.

On the fourth morning, as Rhiathan slept, Guiwenneth rose and stepped out of the tent. The dawn was breaking. The ground was misty and still. She could hear the murmur of voices, the sentries in the watchtowers. The day was chilly.

Out of the mist came eight great hunting dogs. Each towered over the girl. Each had eyes like pools, and jaws like red wounds, and the tongues lolled. But Guiwenneth was unafraid. She lay down and let the largest of the great hounds take her in its jaws and lift her. The dogs padded silently to the north gate. A soldier was there and before he could make a sound his throat had been ripped out. Before the mist lifted, the gate was opened and a foot patrol of men left the fort. Before the gates closed the eight hounds and Guiwenneth slipped away.

She rode with the Jaguth for many years. First they rode north, to the cold moors, through the snows, sheltering with the painted tribes. Guiwenneth was a tiny girl on a huge horse, but when they came north they found smaller steeds, which were still as fast. They rode south again, on the far side of the land, across marshes, fens, woodland and downland. They crossed a great river. Guiwenneth grew, was trained, became skilled. At night she slept in the arms of the leader of the Jaguth.

In this way, many years passed. The girl was beautiful in every way, and her hair was long and red, and her skin pale and smooth. Wherever they rested the young warriors wanted her, but for years she remained unaware of love. It happened, though, that in the east of the land she felt love for the first time, for the son of a Chief, who was determined to have her.

The Jaguth realized that their time with Guiwenneth was ending. They took her west again, and found the valley and the stone of her father, and here they left her, for the one who loved her was close behind, and the Jagad's laughter sounded from beyond the stones. The entity was about to claim them for her own.

The valley was a sad place. The stone above the body of Peredur was always bright, and as Guiwenneth waited there, alone, so the spirit of her father stepped out of the ground, and she saw him for the first time, and he saw her.

'You are the acorn which will grow to oak,' he said, but Guiwenneth did not understand.

Peredur said, 'Your sadness will grow to fury. Outcast like me, you will take my place. You will not rest until the invader is gone from the land. You will haunt him, you will burn him, you will drive him out from his forts and his villas.'

'How will I do this?' Guiwenneth asked.

And around Peredur came the ghostly forms of the great gods and goddesses. For Peredur's spirit was free from the grasping fingers of the Jagad. His bargain fulfilled, she had no claim upon him, and in the spirit world Peredur was renowned, and led the Knights who ran with *Cernunnos*, the antlered Lord of Animals. The antlered God picked Guiwenneth up from the ground and breathed the fire of revenge into her lungs, and the seed of changing, to any form of animal in the wildwood. *Epona* touched her lips and eyes with moon dew, the way to blind the passions of men. *Taranis* gave her strength and thunder, so that now she was strong in every way.

She was a vixen then, slipping into the fort at Caerwent, where her foster mother slept with the Roman. When the man woke he saw the girl standing by his pallet, and was overwhelmed with love for her. He followed her from the fort, through the night, to the river, where they stripped off their clothes and bathed in the cold waters. But Guiwenneth changed to a hawk, and flew about his head, pecking at his eyes until he was blind. The river took him, and when Rhiathan saw the body of her husband, her heart broke, and she flew from the high cliffs, to the sea rocks.

In this way, the girl Guiwenneth came back to the place of her birth.

Nine

I read the short legend to Guiwenneth, emphasizing each word, each expression. She listened intently, her dark eyes searching, enticing. She was less interested in what I was trying to say to her, I felt, than in me. She liked the way I spoke, my smile: features about me, perhaps, that were as exciting to her as her own beauty and that childish, terrifying sexuality were to me.

After a while she reached out and pinched my fingers with hers, silencing me.

I watched her.

No birth, no genesis by whatever strange forest beast, could possibly compare with the generation of a girl by my own mind, and its interaction with the silent forests of Ryhope. She was a creature of a world as divorced from reality as the Moon itself. But what, I wondered, was I to her?

It was the first time the question had arisen. What was I in *her* eyes? Something equally strange, equally alien? Perhaps fascination with me played as large a part in the interest as was the reverse case.

And yet the power that existed between us, that unspoken rapport, that meeting of minds . . . ! I could not believe that I was not in love with Guiwenneth. The passion, the tightness in my chest, the distraction and desire for her, all of these surely added up to love! And I could see that she felt the same for me. I was sure this had to be more than the 'function' of the girl of legend, more than the simple obsession of all males for this forest princess.

Christian had experienced that obsession, and in his frustration – for how could she have responded in kind? She was not *his* mythago – he had driven her back to the woodland, where she had been brutally shot, probably by one of the Jack-in-the-Greens. But the signals between *this* Guiwenneth and myself were far more real, far more true.

How convincing my arguments were to myself! How easily caution could be lost.

That afternoon I forayed again into the woodland, as far as the glade, where the remains of the tent had been totally absorbed into the earth. With my father's map held tightly and protectively in my grasp, I worked out the route inwards, and led the way. Guiwenneth followed quietly behind, eyes alert, body tensed, ready for fight or flight.

The pathway was that along which I had run with Christian, the winter before. To call it a path was overly to dignify the barely perceptible routeway between the towering oak trunks, winding up and down the ragged contours of the land. Dog's mercury and fern stroked my legs; ageing bramble snagged my trousers; birds gave frantic flight above, in the darkening summer canopy. It was here that I had walked before, only to find myself approaching the glade again within a few hundred paces. By following the peculiarly convoluted path that my father had remarked upon, however, I seemed to arrive deeper in the edgewoods, and felt mildly triumphant.

Guiwenneth knew well enough where she was. She called to me and crossed her hands in that negative way that was peculiar to her. 'You don't want me to go on?' I said, and returned through the slick undergrowth towards her. She was slightly cold, I could see, and her luxurious hair was peppered with bits of bramble and splinters of dead bark.

'Pergayal!' she said, and added, 'Not good.' She made stabbing motions at her heart, and I supposed that her message was: *Dangerous*. Immediately she had spoken she reached for my hand, a cold little grasp, but strong. She tugged me back through the trees towards the glade, and I followed unwillingly. After a few paces her hand in mine grew warm, and she grew aware of the contact, letting me go almost with reluctance, but casting a shy glance backwards.

She was waiting still. I couldn't understand for what. As evening gathered, and showers threatened, she stood again at the fence, staring towards the mythago wood, her body tense, looking so very fragile. I went to bed at ten. I was weary after so brief an interlude of sleep the night before. Guiwenneth followed me to my room, watched me undress, then ran giggling away as I approached her. She said something in a warning tone and added a few more words sounding very regretful.

It was to be another interrupted night.

At just after midnight she was by my bed, shaking me awake, excited, glowing. I turned on the bedside lamp. She was almost hysterical in her efforts to get me to follow her, her eyes wide and wild, her lips glistening.

'*Magidion!*' she shouted. 'Steven, *Magidion*! Come! Follow!'

I dressed quickly, and she kept urging me to hurry as I tugged on shoes and socks. Every few seconds she glanced to the woodland, then back at me. And when she looked at me she smiled.

At last I was ready, and she led the way downstairs and to the edgewoods, running like a hare, almost lost to me before I had reached the back door.

She was waiting for me, half-hidden in the scrub before the wood proper. She put a finger to my mouth as I reached her and started to speak. I heard it then, distantly, a sound as eerie as any I have ever heard. It was a horn, or an animal, some creature of the night whose cry was a deep, echoing and mournful monosyllable, rising into the overcast night skies.

Guiwenneth betrayed the hardness of the warrior in her by almost shrieking with delight; excitedly she grabbed my hand and practically tugged me in the direction of the glade. After a few paces she stopped, turned to me, and reached out to grasp me by the shoulders. She was several inches shorter than me, and she stretched slightly and kissed me gently on the lips. It was a moment whose magic, whose wonder, caused the world around me to fade into a summer's day. It took long seconds before the cool, woody night was back, and Guiwenneth was just a flickering grey shape ahead of me, urgently calling me to follow.

Again the cry, sustained and loud; a horn, I was sure now. The calling woodland horn, the cry of the hunter. It was nearer. The sound of Guiwenneth's noisy progress stopped just briefly; the wood seemed to hold its breath as the cry continued, and only when the mournful note had faded away did the whispering night life move again.

I ran into the crouching girl just outside the glade. She tugged me down, gestured to me to be quiet, and together, on our haunches, we surveyed the dark space ahead of us.

There was a distant movement. Light flickered briefly to the left, and again straight ahead. I could hear Guiwenneth's breathing, a strained, excited sound. My own heart was pounding. I had no idea whether it was friend or foe who approached. The horn sounded for the third and last time, so close now that its blast was almost frightening. Around me the wood reacted with terror, small creatures fleeing from one place to another, every square yard of undergrowth moving and murmuring as the woodland fauna fled for safety.

Lights everywhere ahead! They flickered and burned, and soon I could hear the dull crackle of the torches. Torches in woodland! Flames licked high, crackling loud. The restless lights moved side to side, approaching.

Guiwenneth rose to her feet, motioned me to stay where I was, and stepped out into the clearing. Against the brighter torches she was a small silhouette, walking confidently to the middle of the glade, her spear held across her body, ready to be used if necessary.

It seemed, then, that the trunks of the trees moved forward into the clearing, dark shapes detaching themselves from the obscurity of night. My heart missed a beat and I cried out a warning, stifling the final sound as I realized I was behaving foolishly. Guiwenneth stood her ground. The huge black forms closed in upon her, moving slowly, cautiously.

Four of them held the torches and took up positions around the glade. The other three loomed over the doll-like form of the girl. Immense curved antlers grew from their heads; their faces were the hideous skulls of deer, through whose blind sockets very human eyes gleamed in the torchlight. A rank smell, the smell of hides, of skins, of parasite-eaten animals, drifted on the night air, mingling with the sharp smell of pitch, or whatever burned in the lights. Their clothing was ragged, their bodies swathed, with the furs tied by creeper about their lower legs. Metal and stone glinted brightly around necks, arms, waists.

The shambling forms stopped. There was a sound like laughter, a deep growling. The tallest of the three took one step more towards Guiwenneth, then reached up and removed the skull helmet from his head. A face as black as night, as broad as an oak, grinned at her. He made the sound of words, then dropped to one knee and Guiwenneth reached out and laid both hands and her spear across the crown of his head. The others made cries of delight, removed their masks as well, and crowded in closer about the girl. All their faces were painted black, and beards were ragged or plaited, indistinguishable in the half-light from the dark furs and woollens with which they had encased their bodies.

The tallest figure embraced Guiwenneth then, hugging her so hard that her feet lifted from the ground. She laughed, then wriggled out of the stifling embrace, and went to each man in turn touching hands. The noise of chatter grew in the glade, happiness, greeting, delight at renewing an acquaintance.

The talk was incomprehensible. It seemed even less like the Brythonic that Guiwenneth spoke, more of a combination of vaguely recognizable words, and woodland, animal sounds, much clicking, whistling, yapping, a cacophony to which Guiwenneth responded totally in kind. After a few minutes, one of them began to play a bone pipe. The tune was simple, haunting. It reminded me of a folk tune I had heard at a fair once, where Morris dancers had performed their strange routines . . . where had it been? Where had it *been*?

An image of night, of a town in Staffordshire . . . an image of holding tight to my mother's hand, pushed on all sides by crowds. The memory came back . . . a visit to Abbots Bromley, eating roast ox and drinking gallons of lemonade. The streets had milled with people and folk dancers, and Chris and I had followed glumly about, hungry, thirsty, bored.

But in the evening we had packed into the grounds of a huge house, and watched and listened to a dance, performed by men wearing the antlers of stags, the tune played on a violin. That mysterious sound had sent thrills down my spine even at that early age, something in the haunting melody speaking to a part of me that still linked with the past. Here was something I had known all of my life. Only I hadn't known it. Christian had felt it too. The hush that settled upon the crowd suggested that the music being played, as the antlered dancers pranced their circular route, was something so primal that everyone present was reminded, subconsciously, of times gone by.

Here, now, was that same tune. It made the flesh on my arms and neck tingle. Guiwenneth and the horned leader danced joyously to the melody, holding hands, twirling and circling about each other, while the other men edged closer, bringing the light nearer.

Abruptly, with a moment's shared laughter, the awkward dance ceased. Guiwenneth turned to me and beckoned, and I stepped from the cover of the trees, into the clearing. Guiwenneth said something to the leader of the night hunt, and he grinned broadly. He walked slowly over to me, and around me, inspecting me as if I was a piece of sculpture. His smell was overwhelming, his breath stale and fetid. He towered over me by a good twelve inches, and when he reached out to pinch the flesh of my right shoulder the fingers were huge, and that simple gesture, I thought, would break my bones. But he smiled through the heavy layers of black paint, and said, 'Masgoiryth k'k' thas'k hurath. Aur'th. Uh?'

'I agree entirely,' I murmured, and smiled, and gave him a friendly punch on the arm. The muscles below his furs were like steel. He roared with laughter, shook his head, then returned to Guiwenneth. They spoke quickly for a few seconds, then he took her hands in his, raised them to his breast and pressed them there. Guiwenneth seemed delighted, and when this brief ritual was done he knelt before her again, and she leaned down and kissed the top of his head. She came over to me then, and walked more slowly, less excitedly, although in the light of the torches her face was aglow with anticipation, and with affection, I thought. Perhaps love. She took my hands and kissed me on the cheek. Her brutish friend followed her. 'Magidion!' she said, by way of introducing him, and said to him, 'Steven.'

He watched me; his face seemed to indicate pleasure, but there was a sharpness in his gaze, a narrowing of his eyes, that was almost like a warning. This man was Guiwenneth's forest guardian, the leader of the Jaguth. The words of my father's journal were clearly in my mind as I stared at him, and felt Guiwenneth drawing closer to me.

The others came forward then, torches held high, faces dark, yet without threat. Guiwenneth pointed at each in turn and said their names: 'Am'rioch, Cyredich, Dunan, Orien, Cunus, Oswry . . .'

She frowned and glanced at me, her bright face suddenly clouded with sad awareness. Looking at Magidion, she said something, and repeated a word that was clearly a name. 'Rhydderch?'

Magidion drew a breath, shrugged his broad shoulders. He spoke briefly and softly, and Guiwenneth's grip on mine tightened.

When she looked at me there were tears in her eyes. 'Guillauc. Rhydderch. Gone.'

'Gone where?' I asked quietly, and Guiwenneth said, 'Called.'

I understood. First Guillauc, then Rhydderch, had been called by the entity, the Jagad. The Jaguth belonged to her, the price of Guiwenneth's freedom. They quested, now, in other places, other times, in pursuit of whatever the Jagad required of them. Their tales were for another age; their journeys would become the legends of another race.

Magidion drew a short, dull-bladed sword from within the confines of his furs, and detached the scabbard after. These two items he presented to me, speaking softly, his voice an animal growl. Guiwenneth watched delightedly, and I took the gift, sheathed the blade and bowed. His huge hand came down on my shoulder again, squeezing painfully as he leaned closer, still whispering to me. Then he smiled broadly, nudged me closer to the girl, made a whooping night sound, which was echoed by his acquaintances, and drew back from us.

With our arms around each other, Guiwenneth and I watched as the night hunt withdrew deeper into the edge-woods, the torches extinguished by night and distance. A final sounding of the horn drifted towards us, and then the wood was silent.

She slipped into my bed, a nude, cool shape, and reached for me in the darkness. We lay, hugging each other, shivering slightly, even though these dead hours of the morning were by no means cold. All sleep fled from me, my senses heightened, my body tingled. Guiwenneth whispered my name, and I whispered hers, and each time we kissed the embrace grew more passionate, more intimate. In the darkness her breathing was the sweetest sound in the world. With the first stray light of dawn I saw her face again, so pale, so perfect. We lay close, quiet now, staring at each other, occasionally laughing. She took my hand, pressed it to her small breast. She gripped my hair, then my shoulders, then my hips. She wriggled then lay calm, cried then smiled, kissed me, touched me, showed me how to touch her, finally moved easily beneath me. After that first minute of love we could hardly stop staring at each other, and smiling, giggling, rubbing noses, as if we couldn't quite believe that what was happening was *really* happening.

From that moment on, Guiwenneth made Oak Lodge her home, placing her spear against the gate, her way of indicating that she was finished with the wildwoods.

Ten

I loved her more intensely than I would have believed possible. Just to say her name, Guiwenneth, made my head spin. When she whispered my name, and teased me with passionate words in her own tongue, I felt an ache in my chest, and happiness that was almost overwhelming.

We worked on the house, keeping it tidy, rearranging the kitchen to make it more acceptable to Guiwenneth, who enjoyed preparing food as much as I did. She hung hawthorn and birch twigs over every door and window: to keep out ghosts. We moved my father's furniture out of the study, and Guiwenneth created a sort of private nest for herself in that oak-infested room. The forest, having grasped the house so firmly through this one chamber, now seemed to rest. I had half expected that each night more massive roots and trunks would surge through the plaster and the brickwork, until nothing but the occasional window and roof tile could be seen of Oak Lodge among the branches of a tangle of trees. The saplings in the garden and fields grew taller. We worked vigorously clearing them from the garden itself, but they crowded round the fencing and beyond the gate, creating a sort of orchard around us. Now, to get to the main woodland, we had to pick our way through that orchard, stamping out footpaths. This enclosing limb of forest was two hundred yards wide, and on either side was open land. The house rose from the middle of the trees, its roof overgrown with tendrils of the oak that had emerged through the study. The whole area was strangely quiet, uncannily still. Silent, that is, save for the laughter and activity of the two people who inhabited the garden glade.

I loved watching Guiwenneth work. She fashioned clothes

out of every item of Christian's wardrobe she could find. She would have worn shirts and trousers until they rotted on her, but every day we washed ourselves, and every third day our dirty garments, and slowly Guiwenneth's forest smell vanished. She seemed slightly uncomfortable with this, and in this way was unlike the Celtic people of her time, who were fastidiously clean, using soap, which the Romans did not, and regarding the invading legions as quite filthy! I liked her when she smelled faintly of Lifebuoy soap and perspiration; she took every opportunity to squeeze the sap of leaves and plants on to her skin, however.

Within two weeks her command of English was so good that only occasionally did she give herself away with some awkward conjunction, or startling misuse of a word. She insisted that I attempt to acquire some Brythonic, but I proved to be no linguist, finding even the simplest of words impossible to wrap my tongue, palate and lips around. It made her laugh, but it also irritated her. I soon understood why. English, for all its sophistication, its content of other languages, its expressiveness, was not a *natural* language to Guiwenneth. There were things that she could not express in English. Mostly feelings, they were nevertheless of intense importance to her. To tell me she loved me in English was fine, and I shivered each time she used those magic words. But to her, true meaning came in saying 'M'n care pinuth', using her own words to express her love. I never felt as overwhelmed with feeling when she spoke that foreign phrase, though, and here was the simple problem: she needed to see and sense me responding to *her* words of love, but I could only respond to words that meant very little to her.

And there was so much more than love to express. I could see it, of course. Each evening, as we sat on the lawn, or walked quietly through the oak orchard, her eyes glittered, her face was soft with affection. We stopped to kiss, to hug, even to make love in the still woodland, and every single thought and mood was understood by the other. But she needed to *say* things to me, and she could not find the English words to express how she felt, how close to some aspect of nature she felt, how like a bird, or a tree she felt. Something, some way of thinking that I can only crudely translate, could not be put into English, and sometimes she cried because of it, and I felt very sad for her.

Just once, in those two months of the summer – when I could not have conceived of greater happiness, nor have imagined the tragedy that was gaining on us by the hour – just once I tried to get her to move away from the house, to come with me to the bigger towns. With great reluctance, she wrapped one of my jackets around her, belting it at the waist as she belted everything. Looking like the most magnificently pretty of scarecrows, her feet bare but for some home-made leather sandals, she started to walk with me along the track to the main road.

We held hands. The air was hot and still. Guiwenneth's breathing grew more laboured, her look more wild. Suddenly she clenched my hand as if in pain, and drew a sharp breath. I looked at her and she was staring at me, almost pleading with me. Her expression was confused, a mixture of need – the need to please me – and fear.

And equally suddenly she had slapped both hands to her head and screamed, beginning to back away from me.

'It's all right, Guin!' I yelled, and made after her, but she had begun to cry, turning and running back towards the tall wall of young oaks that marked the orchard.

Only when she was standing within their shade did she calm down. Tearfully, she reached for me, and just hugged me, very hard, and very long. She whispered something in her own language, and then said, 'I'm sorry, Steven. It hurts.'

'That's okay. It's okay,' I soothed; and hugged her. She was shaking badly, and later I learned that it had been a physical pain, a shooting pain through her whole body, as if she were being punished for straying so far from the mother wood.

In the evening, after sundown, but at a time when the

world outside was still quite bright, I found Guiwenneth in the cage of oak, the deserted study where the wildwoods grew. She was curled up in the embrace of the thickest trunk, which forked as it sprouted from below the floor, and formed a cradle for her. She stirred as I stepped into the cold, gloomy room. My breath frosted. The branches, with their broad leaves, quivered and trembled, even when I was still. They were aware of me, unhappy with my presence in the room.

'Guin?'

'Steven . . .' she murmured, and sat up, reaching her hand for me. She was dishevelled and had been crying. Her long, luxurious hair was tangled and twisted about the sharp bark of the tree, and she laughed as she tugged the wild strands loose. Then we kissed and I squeezed into the tight fork of the trunk, and we sat there, shivering slightly.

'It's always so cold in here.'

She wrapped her arms around me, rubbed her hands vigorously up and down my back. 'Is that better?'

'It's good just to be with you. I'm sorry you're upset.'

She continued to try and warm me. Her breath was sweet, her eyes large and moist. She snatched a kiss, then rested her lips against the angle of my jaw, and I knew she was thinking hard about something that disturbed her deeply. Around us, the silent forest watched, enclosing us with its supernatural iciness.

'I can't leave here,' she said.

'I know. We won't try again.'

She pulled back, her lips trembling, her face frowning as she verged on tears again. She said something in her own language, and I reached and wiped the two tears that welled up in the corner of her eyes. 'I don't mind,' I said.

'I do,' she said softly. 'I'll lose you.'

'You won't. I love you too much.'

'I love you very much too. And I'll lose you. It's coming, Steven. I can feel it. Terrible loss.'

'Nonsense.'

'I can't leave here. I can't go beyond this place, this wood. I belong here. It won't let me go.'

'We'll stay together. I'll write a book about us. We'll hunt wild pig.'

'My world is small,' she said. 'I can run across my world in days. I stand on a hill and I see a place that is beyond my grasp. My world is tiny compared to yours. You will want to go away, northwards, to the cold place. Southwards to the sun. You will want to go west, to the wild lands. You won't stay here forever, but I have to. They won't let me go.'

'Why are you so worried? If I go away it'll only be for a day or two. To Gloucester, London. You'll be safe. I shan't leave you. I *couldn't* leave you, Guin. My God, if only you could feel what I feel. I've never been so happy in my life. What I feel for you terrifies me, sometimes, it's so strong.'

'Everything about you is strong,' she said. 'You may not realize it now. But when . . .' She trailed off, frowning again, biting back the words until I prompted her to continue. She was a girl, a child. She hugged me, and let her tears come softly and uninhibited. This was not the warrior princess, the fast-running, quick-witted hunter of the day before. Here was that wonderful part of her which, as in all people, had deep and helpless need of another. If ever my Guiwenneth had needed humanizing, now was the time I saw it. Woodland-born though she was, she was flesh and blood, and feeling, and she was more wonderful to me than anything I had ever known in my life.

It grew dark outside, but she spoke of the fear she felt as we sat, frozen stiff, embracing, embraced by our friend, the oak.

'We will not always be together,' she said.

'Impossible.'

She bit her lip, then brushed her nose against mine, coming as close as possible. 'I'm from that other land, Steven. If you don't go from me, then one day I must go from you. But you are strong enough to bear the loss.'

'What are you saying, Guin? Life is just beginning.'

'You are not thinking. You don't want to think!' She was angry. 'I am wood and rock, Steven, not flesh and bone. I am not like you. The wood protects me, rules me. I can't express it properly. I don't have the words. For a time, now, we can be together. But not forever.'

'I'm not going to lose you, Guin. Nothing will stand in the way of us, nothing, not the wood, not my wretched brother, not that beast thing, that *Urscumug.*'

She hugged me again, and in the faintest of voices, almost as if she knew she was asking something that was impossible, she said, 'Look after me.'

Look after me!

It made me smile, at the time. *Me* look after her? It was all I could do to keep her in sight when we hunted the edge-woods. In pursuit of a hare, or wild piglet, a major factor contributing to the logistics of success was my tendency to perspire and gasp myself close to death when running. Guiwenneth was swift, fit and deadly. She never showed any sign of irritation at my failure to reflect her own stamina in mine. She accepted a failed hunt with a shrug and a smile. She never boasted a successful hunt, although, in contrast, I always felt delighted and smug when we were able to supplement our diet with the product of our forest strategy and hunter's skill.

Look after me. Such a simple statement, and it had made me smile. Yes, I could see that in matters of love, she was as vulnerable as me. But I could think of her only as a powerful presence in my life. I looked to Guiwenneth for the lead in almost everything, and it neither shames me, nor embarrasses me to state that. She could run half a mile through undergrowth and slit the throat of a forty-pound wild pig with hardly any effort; I was more orderly and organized than her and brought to her life a degree of comfort that she had not known before.

To each their own. Skills used unselfishly make for co-operation. In six weeks of living with, and deeply loving Guiwenneth, I had learned how easy it was to look to her for the lead, for she was an expert in survival, a hunter, an individual in every way, who had chosen to combine her life essence with mine, and in that I basked.

Look after me!

If only I had. If only I could have learned her language, and learned, thus, the terrible fear that haunted this most beautiful and innocent of girls.

'What is your earliest memory, Guin?'

We were walking in the later afternoon, skirting the wood to the south, between the trees and Ryhope. It was cloudy, but warm. The depression of the day before had passed, and as is the way with young lovers, somehow the anxiety and pain of what we had talked about so briefly had brought us closer, and made us more cheerful. Hand in hand we kicked through long grass, picked carefully between the sprawling, fly-infested pats of cow dung, and walked always with the Norman tower of St Michael's church in the distance.

Guiwenneth remained silent, although she hummed softly to herself, a broken tune, weird, rather like the music of the Jaguth. Some children were running across the Lower Grubbings, throwing a stick for a dog, and shrieking with boyish laughter. They saw us and obviously realized that they were trespassing, and cut off away from us, vanishing over a rise of ground. The dog's hysterical barking drifted on the still air. I saw one of the Ryhope girls riding at a canter along the bridle-way towards St Michael's.

'Guin? Is that too tough a question?'

'What question, Steven?' She glanced at me, dark eyes gleaming, mouth touched with a smile. In her way she was teasing me, and before I could restate my query, she broke from me and raced – all flapping white shirt and baggy flannels – to the woodland edge and peered inside.

Raising a finger to her lips as I approached, she murmured, 'Quiet . . . quiet . . . oh, by the God Cernunnos . . . !'

My heart began to beat faster. I peered into the darkness

of the wood, seeking among the tangled growth for whatever she had seen.

By the God Cernunnos?

The words were like pinches and punches to my mind, teasing strokes, and slowly I became aware that Guiwenneth was in a very playful mood.

'By the God Cernunnos!' I repeated, and she laughed and began to run along the track. I chased her. She had listened to the way I blasphemed and adapted such blasphemy to the beliefs of her own age. Normally she would never have expressed surprise with such a religious oath. It would have been a reference to animal dung, or death.

I caught her – and therefore she had intended me to catch her – and we wrestled on the warm grass, struggling and twisting until one of us gave in. Soft hair tickled my face as she leaned to kiss me.

'So answer my question,' I said.

She looked irritated, but couldn't escape my sudden bear hug. She looked resigned, then sighed. 'Why do you ask me questions?'

'Because I want answers. You fascinate me. You frighten me. I need to know.'

'Why can't you accept?'

'Accept what?'

'That I love you. That we're together.'

'Last night you said we wouldn't be together always . . .'

'I was sad!'

'But you believe it's true. I don't,' I added sternly, 'but in case . . . just in case . . . anything *did* happen to you. Well. I want to know about you, all about you. You. Not the image figure that you represent . . .'

She frowned.

'Not the history of the mythago . . .'

She frowned even more deeply. The word meant something to her, but the concept nothing.

I tried again. 'There have been Guiwenneths before; perhaps there will be Guiwenneths again. New versions of you.

But it's *this* one that I want to know about.' I emphasized the word with a wiggle and a squeeze. She smiled.

'What about you? I want to know about you too.'

'Later,' I said. 'You first. What were your first memories? Tell me about your childhood.'

As I suspected would happen, a shadow passed across her face, that brief frown that says the questions has touched an area of blankness. And that blankness had been known, before, but never acknowledged.

She sat up and straightened her shirt, shook her hair back, then leaned forward and began to pluck the dry grass from the ground, knotting each fibrous stem around her finger. 'The first memory . . .' she said, then looked into the distance. 'The stag!'

I remembered the discovered pages of my father's diary, but tried to blot his own record of the story from my mind, concentrating totally upon Guiwenneth's uncertain recollection.

'He was so big. Such a broad back, so powerful. I was tied to him, leather knots on my wrists, holding me firm against the stag's back. I called him Gwil. He called me Acorn. I lay between his great antlers. I can remember them so well. They were like the branches of trees, rising up above me, snapping and cracking at the real trees, scraping the bark and the leaves. He was running. I can still smell him, still feel the sweat on his broad back. His skin was so tough, and sharp. My legs were sore with rubbing. I was so young. I think I cried, and yelled at Gwil, "Not so fast!" But he ran though the forest, and I clung on, and the leather ropes cut at my wrists. I can remember the baying of hounds. They were pursuing him through the wood. There was a horn, too, a huntsman's horn. "Slower," I cried to the stag, but he just shook his great head and told me to cling on tighter. "We have a long chase, little Acorn," he said to me, and the smell of him choked me, and the sweat, and the hurt of his wild chase on my body. I remember the sunlight, among the trees. It was blinding. I kept trying to see the sky, but each time the sun came through it blinded me. The hounds came closer. There were so many of them. I could see men running through the forest. The horn was loud and harsh. I was crying. Birds seemed to hover over us, and when I looked up their wings were black against the sun. Suddenly he stopped. His breath was like a loud wind. His whole body was shaking. I remember crawling forward, tugging at the leather ropes, and seeing the high rock that blocked the way. He turned. His antlers were like black knives, and he lowered his head and cut and jabbed at the dogs that came for him. One of them was like a black demon. Its jaws gaped, all wet. Its teeth were huge. It lunged at my face, but Gwil caught him on the prong of one antler and shook him until his guts spilled. But then there was just the sudden wind-sound of an arrow. My poor Gwil. He fell and the dogs tore at his throat, but still he kept them from me. The arrow was longer than my body. It stuck out of his heaving flesh, and I can remember reaching to touch it, and the blood on it, and I couldn't move the shaft, it was so hard, like a rock, like something growing from the stag. Men cut me loose and dragged me away and I clung to Gwil as he died, and the dogs worried at his entrails. He was still alive, and he looked at me and whispered something, like a forest breeze and then snorted once and was gone . . .' She turned to me. Touched me. Tears stained her cheeks, glistened in the bright day. 'As you will go, everything will go, everything that I love . . .' I touched her hand, kissed her fingers.

'I'll lose you. I'll lose you,' she said sadly, and I couldn't find the words to respond. My mind was too filled with images of that wild chase. 'Everything I love is stolen from me.'

We sat for a long time in silence. The children, with their wretchedly vociferous dog, chased back along the edge of the wood, and again saw us, and scampered, abashed and afraid, out of sight. Guiwenneth's fingers were a nest of entwined grasses, and she laced small golden flowers into them, then wiggled her hand, like some strange harvest puppet. I touched her shoulder.

'How old were you when this happened?' I asked.

She shrugged. 'Very young. I can't remember, it was several summers ago.'

Several summers ago. I smiled as she said the words, thinking that only two summers ago she had not yet existed. How *did* the generic process work, I wondered, watching this beautiful, solid, soft and warm human creature. Did she form out of the leaf litter? Did wild animals carry sticks together and shape them into bones, and then, over the autumn, dying leaves fall and coat the bones in wildwood flesh? Was there a moment, in the wood, when something approximating to a human creature rose from the under-brush, and was shaped to perfection by the intensity of the human will, operating outside the woodland?

Or was she just suddenly . . . there. One moment a wraith, the next a reality, the uncertain, dreamlike vision that suddenly clears and can be seen to be real.

I remembered phrases from the journal: *The Twigling is fading, more tenuous than the last time I encountered him . . . found traces of the dead Jack-in-the-Green, worried by animals, but showing an unusual pattern of decom-position . . . ghostly, running shape in the hogback, not a pre-mythago, the next phase perhaps?*

I reached for Guiwenneth, but she was stiff, rigid in my arms, disturbed by memories, disturbed by my insistence that she talk about something that was clearly painful to her.

I am wood and rock, not flesh and bone.

The words she had used several days before sent a thrill of shock through me as I remembered them. *I am wood and rock.* So she knew. She knew that she was not human. And yet she behaved as if she *were.* Perhaps she had spoken metaphorically; perhaps it was her life in the woods to which she had referred, as I might have said *I am dust and ashes.*

Did she know? I longed to ask her, burned to see inside her head, to the silent glade where she loved and remembered.

'What are little girls made of?' I asked her and she looked

round sharply, frowning, then smiling, puzzled by the question, half-amused as she realized, from my own smile, that there was a riddle-like answer.

'Sweet acorns, crushed honeybees and the nectar of bluebells,' she said.

I grimaced with disgust. 'How horrible.'

'What then?'

'Sugar and spices and all things . . . er . . .' How did it go? '. . . nicest.'

She frowned. 'You don't like sweet acorns or honeybees? They're nice.'

'I don't believe you. Not even grubby Celts would eat honeybees.'

'What are little *boys* made of?' she asked quickly, and answered with a giggle, 'Cow dung and questions.'

'Slugs and snails, actually.' She seemed duly satisfied. I added, 'The occasional hindquarters of an immature hound.'

'We have things like that. I remember Magidion telling me. He taught me a lot.' She held up her hand for silence, while she thought. Then she said, 'Eight calls for a battle. Nine calls for a fortune. Ten calls for a dead son. Eleven calls for sadness. Twelve calls at dusk for a new king. What am I?'

'A cuckoo,' I said, and Guiwenneth stared at me.

'You knew!'

Surprised, I said, 'I guessed.'

'You knew! Anyway, it's the *first* cuckoo.' She thought hard for a moment, and then said, 'One white is luck for me. Two white is luck for you. Three white for a death. Four white, and a shoe, will bring love.'

She stared at me, smiling.

'Horse's hooves,' I said, and Guiwenneth slapped me hard on the leg. 'You *knew*!'

I laughed. 'I'm just guessing.'

'It's the first strange horse you see at the end of winter,' she said. 'If it has four white hooves, then forge a shoe and you'll see your loved one riding the same horse in the clouds.'

'Tell me about the valley. And the white stone.'

She stared at me, then frowned. She was suddenly very sad. 'That is the place where my father lies.'

'Where is it?' I asked.

'A long way from here. One day—' She looked away. What memories did she entertain now, I wondered? What sad recollections?

'One day, what?'

Quietly, she said, 'One day I would like to go there. One day I would like to see the place where Magidion buried him.'

'I would like to go with you,' I said, and for a moment her moist gaze met mine, and then she smiled.

And then she brightened. 'A hole in a stone. An eye on a bone. A ring made of thorn. The sound of a forge. All of these things . . .' She hesitated, watching me.

'Keep away ghosts?' I suggested, and she tumbled on top of me with a cry of, '*How* do you *know?*'

We walked slowly back to the house in the very late afternoon. Guiwenneth was slightly chilly. It was August 27th, if I remember, and sometimes the day would seem like autumn, and sometimes like summer. There had been a crispness in the air that morning, the first shivery portent of the new season; summer had flourished during the day, and now autumn again showed its shadow. The leaves at the very tips of the trees had begun to show signs of turning. For some reason I felt depressed, walking with my arm round the girl, feeling her windblown hair tickle my face, the touch of her right hand on my breast. My suddenly gloomy mood was not helped by the distant sound of a motorcycle.

'Keeton!' said Guiwenneth brightly, and led me at a trot the rest of the way, to the stand of thin trees that was the orchard. We wove through the copse, to the overgrown gate. We forced our way through the tangled undergrowth that swamped the fence around the cleared garden, much of which was in shadow, and darkly overhung by the branches of the oak that wound about the house.

Keeton was standing at the back door, waving and holding up a flagon of the Mucklestone Field homebrew. 'I've got something else,' he called as Guiwenneth ran to him and kissed his cheek. 'Hello, Steven. Why so glum?'

'Change of season,' I said. He looked bright and happy, his fair hair awry from the ride here, his face dirt-stained except around his eyes, where his goggles had been. He smelled of oil, and slightly of pigs.

His extra surprise was half a side of spitting pig. It looked a pale and feeble cadaver compared to the grey and scrawny creatures that Guiwenneth speared in the deep runs of the wood. But the thought of a pork more succulent and less strong than the wild pigs I had become used to was immensely cheering.

'A barbecue!' Keeton announced. 'Two Americans at the field showed me how. Outside. This evening. After I've washed. A barbecue for three, with ale, song, and party games.' He looked suddenly a little concerned. 'Not interrupting something, am I, old boy?'

'Not at all. Old boy,' I said. His Englishisms often sounded affected, and irritated me.

'He's fed up,' advised Guiwenneth, and gave me an amused look.

By the Good God Cernunnos, how glad I am, now, that Keeton gatecrashed that moment, those hours between us. Resentful though I was of his presence, when I was trying to get a little closer to Guin, I have never given greater thanks to that Celestial Watching-Being than I did later that night. Even though, in one way, I would be wishing that I were dead.

The fire burned. Guiwenneth had built it up while Keeton had constructed the rough-and-ready spit. The pig was his payment for two days' work on the farm attached to the airfield; his plane was out of service at the moment, and the farm work was welcome, as was his help. Well paid rebuilding work at Coventry and Birmingham had called away many of the farmhands from the counties of the Midlands.

It takes a lot longer to spit-roast a pig than Keeton had realized. Darkness enveloped woodland and orchard, and we turned the lights on in the house so that the garden area, where we squatted and chatted around the sizzling meat and the brightly flaring wood fire, was bathed in a cosy glow. I attended to records, playing through the collection of dance-hall music that my parents had built up over the years. The battered old Master's Voice gramophone kept running down, and under the influence of the beer that Keeton had purloined, the continual droning down of the voices became hysterically funny.

At ten o'clock we poked the jacket potatoes out of the fire and ate them with butter and pickle and a thin slice of the blackened outer flesh of the piglet. Hunger appeased, Guiwenneth sang us a song in her own tongue, which Keeton was able to accompany, after a while, on his small harmonica. When I asked her to translate she just smiled, tapped my nose, and said, 'Imagine!'

'It was about you and me,' I ventured. 'Love, passion, need, long life and children.'

She shook her head, and licked a finger that she'd just smeared along the remains of our precious butter ration.

I said, 'What, then? Happiness? Friendship?'

'You incorrigible romantic,' murmured Keeton, and was proved right, for Guiwenneth's song had not really been about love at all, not as I had imagined it. She translated as best she could.

'I am the daughter of the early hour of the morning. I am the huntress who by dawnlight . . . who by dawnlight . . .' She made frantic throwing motions.

'Casts?' suggested Keeton. 'Throws the net?'

'Who by dawnlight throws the net into the glade of the woodcocks. I am the falcon who watches as the woodcocks rise and are caught in the net. I am the fish that . . . the fish that . . .' She made exaggerated side to side motions of her hips and shoulders.

'Wiggles,' I said.

'Struggles,' Keeton corrected.

She went on, 'I am the fish that struggles in the water, swimming towards the great grey rock that marks the deep pool. I am the daughter of the fisher who spears the fish. I am the shadow of the tall white stone where my father lies, the shadow that moves with the day towards the river where the fish swims, towards the forests where the glade of the wood-cocks is blue with flowers. I am the rain that makes the hare run, sends the doe to the thicket, stops the fire in the middle of the round house. My enemies are thunder and the beasts of the earth who crawl by night, but I am not afraid. I am the heart of my father, and his father. Bright as iron, swift as arrow, strong as oak. I am the land.'

These last words – 'Bright as iron, swift as arrow, strong as oak. I am the land' – she sang in her reedy voice, match-ing the words to the tune and the rhythm of the original. When she had finished she smiled and bowed, and Keeton applauded loudly, 'Bravo.'

I stared at her for a moment, puzzled. 'Not about me at all, then,' I said, and Guiwenneth laughed. 'About nothing else but you,' she said. 'That's why I sang it.'

I had meant it as a joke, but now she had confused me. I didn't understand. Somehow, in some fashion, the wretched Keeton did. He winked at me. 'Why don't you check the grounds, the two of you. I'll be all right here. Go on!' He smiled.

'What the hell's going on?' I said, although I said it softly. But as I rose to my feet, Guiwenneth rose too, tugging down the vivid red cardigan and licking the remains of the butter and pork fat from her fingers before holding her sticky hand out to me.

We walked to the garden's edge, and kissed quickly in the darkness where the young oaks grew. There was stealthy movement in the woodland; foxes, perhaps, or wild dogs, drawn to the smell of the cooking meat. Keeton was an oddly crouched shape, silhouetted against the flame and flaring sparks of the fire.

'He understands you more than I do,' I said.

'He sees both of us. You only see me. I like him. He's a very gentle man. But he's not my *flintspear*.'

The wood seemed alive with movement. Even Guiwenneth was puzzled. 'We should be careful of wolves and wild dogs,' she said. 'The meat . . .'

'There can't be wolves in the forest,' I said, 'surely. Boar I've seen, and you've told me of a wild bear . . .'

'Not every creature comes to the edge so quickly. Wolves are pack animals. The pack may have been in the deep forest, in the wildwoods. They have taken a long time to get here. Perhaps.'

I glanced into the darkness, and the night seemed to whisper ominously; shivering. I turned back to the garden, and reached for Guiwenneth. 'Let's go back and keep him company.'

Even as I spoke, the dark shape of Keeton was rising to its feet. His voice was subdued, but urgent. 'We've got company.'

Through the trees that crowded about the garden fence, I could see the flicker of torchlight. The sound of men approaching was a sudden, loud intrusion in the wild night. I walked with Guiwenneth back to the fire, into the spill of light from the kitchen. Behind us, where we had stood, there too torches showed. They closed in upon the garden in a wide arc, and we waited, listening for some sign of their nature.

From ahead of us there came the eerie tune of the Jaguth, played on the reedy pipes I had heard before. Guiwenneth and I exchanged a quick, delighted glance, and then she said, 'The Jaguth. They've come again!'

'Just in time to finish off our pig,' I said ruefully. Keeton was frozen to the spot with fear, not liking the stealthy approach through the darkness of these strange men-creatures.

Guiwenneth walked towards the gate, to greet them, shouting out something in her strange language. I began to step after her, picking up a firebrand from the fire, to hold as they held their torches. The sweet piping continued.

Keeton said, 'Who are they?' And I said, 'Old friends, new friends. The Jaguth. There's nothing to fear . . .'

And at that moment I realized that the piping had stopped, and Guiwenneth too had stopped, a few paces away from me. She stared around her, at the flickering lights in the darkness. A moment later she looked back at me, her face pale, her eyes wide, her mouth open; from being delighted, she suddenly was terrified. She took a step towards me, my name on her lips, and I was caught in her sudden panic, and reached for her . . .

There was a strange sound, like wind, like a hoarse, tuneless whistle, and then the sound of a thump and Keeton's gasping cry. I glanced at him and he was stepping rapidly backwards, arched back, clutching at the top of his chest, his eyes screwed shut with pain. A moment later he fell to the ground, arms outstretched. Three feet of wood shaft jutted from his body. 'Guin!' I screamed, tearing my gaze from Keeton. And then all around us the woodland burst into brilliant fire, the trunks catching, the branches, the leaves, so that the garden was surrounded by a great, roaring wall of flame. Two dark human shapes came bursting through that fire, light glinting on metal armour and the short-bladed weapons held in their hands. For a moment they hesitated, staring at us; one had the golden mask of a hawk, its eyes mere slits, the ears rising like short horns from the crown. The other wore a dull leather helmet, the cheek straps broad. The hawk laughed loudly.

'Oh God no . . . !' I cried, but Guiwenneth screamed at me, 'Arm yourself!' as she raced past me to where her own weapons were lodged against the back wall of the house.

I followed her, grabbing up my flintspear and the sword

that Magidion had presented to me. And we turned, backs to the wall, and watched the gruesome band of armoured men who emerged, dark silhouettes, through the burning forest, and spread out around the garden.

The two warriors suddenly ran at us, one at Guiwenneth, one at me. It was the hawk who chose me.

He came at me so fast that I hardly had time to raise and thrust my spear at him; the events happened in a blur of burnished metal, dark hair, and sweaty flesh, as he deflected my blow with his small round shield, then clubbed me heavily on the side of the head with the blunt pommel of his sword. I staggered to my knees, then struggled to rise, but the shield was struck against my head and the ground hit my face, hard and dry. The next I knew he had tied my arms behind my back, worked my spear under my armpits, and trussed me like a turkeycock.

For a moment or two I watched Guiwenneth fight, and she fought with a fury that astonished me. I saw her bring her dagger down into her own attacker's shoulder; then a second hawk ran from the garden's edge, and she swung to face him, and firelight glinted on metal and the man's hand seemed to fly towards the woodshed. A third came, and a fourth. Guiwenneth's war-cry was a screech of indignation. She moved so fast that I became confused watching her.

And of course, there were too many of them for her. Suddenly she had been bowled over, disarmed, then flung high into the air. She was caught between the hawks, and though she struggled, they tied and trussed her in the same fashion as me.

Five tall, dark warriors remained at the garden's edge, crouching, watching the end of the affray.

My own hawk reached for my hair and dragged me to my feet, hauling me, bent double, across the garden towards the fire. He dropped me to the ground a few feet from Guiwenneth. She looked at me through bloody eyes and the fall of dishevelled hair across her face. Her lips were wet, and I could see tears glistening, bright specks in the fire. 'Steven,' she murmured, and I realized that her lips were swollen and painful. 'Steven . . .'

'This can't be happening,' I whispered, and felt my own tears rise. My head was spinning; everything seemed so unreal. My body was numb, with shock, with anger. The sound of the burning forest was loud, almost deafening.

Men continued to step through the fire, some leading large, dark-maned horses, which whickered and reared in discomfort. The sharp cries of command were loud against the crackle of burning wood. Brands from our own small fire were taken and used to start a small smithy, close to the house. Others of this band of men began to break wood from the coops and shed. During these brief minutes of confusion, the five dark figures had remained, crouching, just inside the ring of fire. Now they rose to their feet and approached. The oldest, who was the leader, stepped past the fire, where already several of the hawks were crouching, waiting to divide up the spitted pig. This man reached down and with a broad-bladed knife, carved himself a generous portion from the rump, stuffed it into his mouth and wiped his fingers on his heavy cloak. He came towards Guiwenneth, and shrugged the cloak off, revealing a naked upper torso, his belly full and sagging, his arms thick, his chest deep. This was a strong man going to seed in late middle age. The flesh of his body, I noticed, was a latticework of scars and weals. Around his neck he carried a bone pipe, and he trilled on it, mocking us.

He dropped to a crouch by the girl and reached a hand to lift up her chin. He brushed the hair from her face, and twisted her jaw roughly to look at her, grinning through his greying beard. Guiwenneth spat at him and he laughed; and that laugh . . .

I frowned, completely unnerved. I sat in the firelight, in pain, unable to move, and stared at this coarse, ageing warlord.

'I've found you at last,' he said, and the voice sent a long thrill of anguish through me.

'She's mine!' I cried through sudden tears.

And Christian looked at me and slowly rose to his feet.

He towered over me, an old man, war-worn and ragged. His breeches stank of urine. The sword he wore on his wide, leather belt, hung ominously close to my face. He jerked my head up by the hair, and with his other hand stroked his matted, greying beard.

'It's been a long time, brother,' he said, in a hoarse, animal whisper. 'What *am* I going to do with you?'

Behind him, the side of pig had been reduced to nothing, and the hawks chewed vigorously, and spat into the fire while they talked in murmuring voices. From the house came the sounds of hammer on metal. A furious activity of repair was occurring, on weapons and on the harnessing of the great horses, which were tethered close by to me.

'She's mine,' I said quietly, staring at him through my tears. 'Leave us alone, Chris.'

He kept looking at me for several seconds, a frightening silence. Abruptly he reached down and jerked me to my feet, and ran me backwards until I fetched up hard against the wooden wall of the shed. As he moved he roared with anger, and his stale, fetid breath made me gag. His face, inches from my own as he glared at me, was the face of an animal, not a man, and yet I could now begin to discern the eyes, the nose, the lips of my brother, the handsome youth who had left the house just a year before.

He shouted something gruffly, and one of his older warriors flung him a length of rope with a noose on the end. The rope was coarse and sharp, and he tugged the noose over my head and tightened it on my neck, tossing the free rope over the shed. A moment later the slack was taken up and the noose tugged me to my toes. I could breathe, but I couldn't relax. I began to gasp, and Christian smiled, reaching up a stinking hand to block my nostrils and my mouth.

He ran his finger over my face. It was an almost sensuous touch. When I struggled for breath he released my mouth and I sucked air into my lungs gratefully. All the time he had watched me curiously as if desperately searching for some memory of friendship between us. His fingers were like a woman's caressing my brow, my cheeks, my chin, the junction of the rope and the torn skin of my neck. In this way he found the oak leaf amulet that I wore, and he frowned as he saw it. He rested the silver leaf in his hand and stared at it. Without looking at me he said, 'Where did you get this?' He sounded quite astonished.

'I found it.'

He said nothing for a second, then snapped the thong from my neck, and held the oak leaf to his lips. 'I would have been dead but for this. When I lost it I thought my fate was sealed. I have it back, now. I have everything back . . .'

He turned to look at me, then, searching my eyes, my face. 'It's been many years . . .' he whispered.

'What's happened to you?' I managed to breathe. The rope tugged at me, irritated me. He watched my discomfort, the movement of my lips, through gleaming dark eyes that showed no compassion.

'Too much,' he said. 'I've searched too long. But I've found her at last. I've run too long . . .' He looked wistful, glancing away from me. 'Perhaps the running will never end. He still pursues me.'

'Who?'

He glanced at me again. 'The beast. The Urscumug. The old man. Damn his eyes. Damn his soul, he follows me like a hound on the scent. He is always there, always in the woodland, always just outside the fort. Always, always the beast. I'm tired, brother. I truly am. At last—' he glanced at the slumped form of the girl, 'At last I have the one thing I have sought. Guiwenneth, my Guiwenneth. If I die, we die together. I no longer care if she loves me. I shall have her, I shall use her. She will make the dying good. She will inspire me to make a last effort to kill the beast.'

'I can't let you take her,' I said hopelessly, and Christian frowned, then smiled. But he said nothing, moving away from me, back towards the fire. He walked slowly, thoughtfully. He stopped and stared at the house. One of his men, a long-haired, raggedly dressed warrior, moved to the body of Harry Keeton, turned it over and split through the man's shirt with a knife, raising the blade above Keeton's breast. He stopped and said something in an alien tongue. Christian looked at me, then spoke back to the man, and the warrior rose angrily to his feet and stalked back to the fire.

Christian said, 'The Fenlander is angry. They want to eat his liver. They're hungry. The pig was small.' He smiled. 'I said no. To spare your feelings.'

He walked to the house then, and vanished inside. It seemed he was gone for a long time. Guiwenneth looked up only once, and her face was wet with tears. She stared at me, and her lips moved, but I could make out no sound, nor what she was trying to say. 'I love you, Guin,' I called back to her. 'I'll get us out of this. Don't worry.'

But my words had no effect on her, and her battered face fell down again as she knelt by the fire, trussed and guarded.

Around me, the garden was a scene of confusing activity. One of the horses had panicked, and was rearing and kicking against its tether. Men walked to and fro, others were digging a pit, still others crouched by the fires and talked and laughed in loud voices. In the night, the burning woodland was a terrifying sight.

When Christian emerged from the house again, he had shaved off the ragged grey-black beard, and combed his long, greasy hair back into a pigtail. His face was broad, strong, even if his jowls were slightly loose. He looked uncannily as I remembered our father, in the years before I went to France. But bulkier, harder. He carried his sword and belt in one hand. In the other he held a bottle of wine, the top neatly broken off. Wine?

He came over to me and drank from the bottle, smacking his lips appreciatively. 'I didn't think you'd find the store,' he said. 'Forty bottles of the best Bordeaux. A taste more sweet I can't imagine. Will you have some?' He waved the broken

173

bottle at me. 'A drink before dying. A toast to brother-hood, to the past. To a battle won and lost. Drink with me, Steve.'

I shook my head. Christian seemed momentarily disap-pointed, then flung back his head and poured the red wine into his mouth, stopping only when he choked, laughing as he choked. He passed the bottle to the most sinister of his compatriots, the Fenlander, the man who had wanted to slit open the corpse of Harry Keeton, and the man drank the remnants down, tossing the bottle into the woodland. The rest of the secret store of wine that I had failed to discover was carried out in improvised sacks, and distributed among the hawks for carriage.

The woodland fire burned down and began to die out. Whatever had caused it, whatever magic, the spell was waning, and the smell of wood ash was strong on the air. But two very strange figures suddenly appeared at the gar-den's edge, and began to run about the perimeter. They were almost naked, their bodies covered with white chalk, except for their faces, which were black. Their hair was long, but held back by a leathery band around the crown. They carried long, bone batons, and waved these at the trees, and where they passed, so the flames sprang up again, the fire rekindled as furious as before.

At last Christian came back to me, and I realized that the delay, the strange sense of pause, was because he did not know what to do with me. He drew his knife and stuck it hard into the shed beside me, and he leaned on the hilt, taking his weight, resting his chin on his hands, and focusing not upon me, but upon the grain of the pitch-painted wood slats. He was a tired man, a weary man. Everything about him, from his breathing to the shadows around his eyes, told me that.

'You've aged,' I said, pointing out the obvious.

'Have I?' He smiled wearily, then spoke slowly. 'Yes. I suppose I have. Many years have passed, for me. I went a long way inwards, trying to escape the beast. But the beast belonged in the heartwoods, and I couldn't outrun it. It's a strange world, Steven. A strange and terrible world beyond the hogback glade. The old man knew so much, and he knew so little. He knew of the heartwoods; he had seen, or heard, or imagined the heartwoods, but his only way to get there . . .' He broke off and looked at me curiously. Then he smiled again and straightened up. Touching me on the cheek, he shook his head. 'What in the name of the woodnymph Handryama am I going to do with you?'

'What is to stop you leaving me, and leaving Guiwenneth, to live happily for as long as we can? And do whatever you must do, go back, or leave the wood and go abroad. Come back to us, Christian.'

He leaned back on the knife, so close to me that I could easily have touched his face with my lips, but not looking at me. 'I could no longer do that,' he said. 'For a while, when I journeyed inwards, yes, I might have come back. But I wanted her. I knew she would be somewhere there, somewhere deep. I followed stories of her, ventured to mountains, and valleys, where stories told of her. Always I seemed to be a few days late. The beast stalked me. Twice I battled with it, but the battle was not resolved. I have stood, my brother, upon the hill, the tallest hill, where the stone folly was built, and seen into the heartwoods of the forest, the place where I shall be safe. And now that I have found my Guiwenneth, that is where I shall go. Once there, I have a life to finish, a love to find; but I shall be safe. Safe from the beast. The old man.'

'Go there alone, Chris,' I said. 'Guiwenneth loves me, and nothing will change that.'

'Nothing?' he repeated, and smiled wearily. 'Time can change anything. With no-one else to love, she will come to love me . . .'

'Look at her, Chris,' I said angrily. 'A captive. Dejected. You care no more for her than you do for your hawks.'

'I care about the having of her,' he said quietly, menacingly. 'I have hunted too far, too long to worry about the finer aspects of love. I shall make her love me before dying; I shall enjoy her until then . . .'

'She is not yours, Chris. She is *my* mythago—'

He reacted with sudden violence, smashing his fist into the side of my face so hard that two of my teeth were buckled inward. Through the pain, blood flooding my mouth, I heard him say, 'Your mythago is dead! This one is mine. Yours I killed years ago. She is *mine*! If not for that I wouldn't take her.'

I spat the blood from my mouth. 'Perhaps she belongs to neither of us. She has her own life, Chris.'

He shook his head. 'I claim her. There is nothing more to be said.' As I began to speak, he raised a hand and roughly pinched my lips together, silencing me. The spear shaft beneath my arms was so painful that I felt sure my bones would soon break. The noose ate deeper into my skin.

'Shall I let you live?' he said, almost musingly. I made sounds in my throat, and he pinched my lips tighter. He wrenched the knife from the shed and held it before me, touching my nose with its cold point, then lowering the blade and tapping it gently against my lower belly. 'I might allow the life to remain in your body . . . but the cost—' he tapped me again – 'the cost would be very high. I couldn't let you live . . . as a man . . . not having known the woman I claim . . .'

The idea froze me with the horror of it. I could hardly see him for the sudden pulsing of blood through my head, the sudden shock.

He let go of my lips, but held his hand over my mouth. Through fear, through pure terror, I had started to cry, and my body shuddered with the sobs that came from deep within me. Christian came close, his eyes narrow, but frowning, unhappy about many things.

'Oh Steve . . .' he said, and repeated the tired, sad statement. 'It could have been . . . what could it have been? Good? I don't suppose it could have been good. But I would have liked to have known you during the last fifteen years. There were times when I yearned for your company, to talk to you, to be . . .' He smiled and used his forefinger to wipe the tears from my cheeks. 'Just to be a normal man among normal company.'

'It could be that way again,' I whispered, but he shook his head, still sad.

'Alas no.' And added, after a thoughtful pause, regarding me, 'And I regret that.'

Before either of us could speak further, a terrifying sound came from beyond the burning trees. Christian turned from me, and looked towards the woodland. He seemed shocked; almost furious with shock. 'Not so close . . . he can't be so close . . .'

The sound had been the roar of a wild beast. Tempered by distance, and the noise of the warrior band about me, I had not recognized the cry of the boar creature, the Urscumug. Now the sound became familiar, for it came a second time, and with it the distant groan and crack of trees and branches being snapped and pushed aside. In the garden, the hawks, the warriors, the strange men from cultures unrecognizable, began to move swiftly into action, gathering equipment, slinging the harnesses on to the five horses, calling orders, preparing to leave.

Christian made a motion to two of his hawks, who tugged Guiwenneth to her feet, removed the spear-shaft from beneath her arms, and slung her over the broad back of a horse, tying her securely below its belly.

'Steven!' she screamed, struggling to see me.

'Guiwenneth! Oh my God, no!'

'Quickly!' shouted Christian, repeating the order in another language. The sound of the Urscumug grew closer. I struggled against the restraining rope, but it was too tight, too secure.

The company of mercenaries were moving swiftly towards the woodland to the south side of the garden, where two of them hacked the fencing down, before beginning the process of leaping through the flames of the burning orchard, to escape the garden glade.

Soon, most of them had gone, only Christian, the Fenlander and one of the strange, white-painted Neoliths remaining behind. This ancient warrior held the horse over which Guiwenneth was tied. The Fenlander went behind the shed and I felt his tug on the rope around my neck.

Christian walked close to me, and shook his head again. The fire around us burned brightly, but the sound of the approaching beast was loud. My eyes filled with tears, and Christian became a dark blur against the bright flame.

Without a word he reached his hands to my face, and leaned close to me, pressing his lips to mine, holding the kiss for two or three seconds.

'I have missed you,' he said quietly. 'I shall continue to do so.'

Then he stepped away from me, glanced at the Fenlander and said, without pause, without concern, 'Hang him.'

And turned his back, calling a command to the man by the horse, who led the beast towards the burning orchard.

'*Chris!*' I screamed, but he ignored me.

A moment later I felt myself wrenched from the ground, and the noose bit deeply, strangling me swiftly. And yet awareness remained, and though my feet dangled above the ground, I managed to keep breathing. Water blurred my vision. And the last I saw of Guiwenneth was her long, beautiful hair, flowing down the side of the beast which carried her. It snagged on the broken fencing, and I thought a strand or two of the auburn hair had remained there, caught in the wood.

Then darkness began to close about me. There was the sound of a sea, pounding against rocks, and the deafening screech of a bird of prey, or some similar carrion creature. The bright fire became a bright blur. My lips moved but I could utter no sound . . .

Something dark came between my dangling body and the flame trees. I blinked, and desperately tried to scream. In that brief action, my vision cleared, and I realized that I was looking at the legs and lower torso of the Urscumug. The stench of animal sweat and dung was overwhelming. The creature bent towards me, and through watering eyes I saw the stark, hideous features of the man-boar, painted white, bristling with hawthorn and leaves. The mouth opened and closed in a curious semblance of speech. All I heard was a hissing sound. All I was aware of were those slanted, penetrating eyes, the eyes of my father, the facial features around it grimacing and grinning, as if triumphant at having caught up with one of his errant sons at last.

A clawed fist closed about my waist, squeezing hard, lifting me towards the glistening jaws. I heard laughter, human laughter, or so it seemed, and then I was shaken so violently – as a dog worries at a bird – that at last unconsciousness claimed me, and that terrifying moment passed into the realm of dreams.

There was a sound like a swarm of wasps, which gradually faded. I could hear bird-song. My eyes were open. Patterns and shadows swirled and shifted, slowly resolving into a night vision of stars, clouds, and a human face.

My body was numb, everywhere except my neck, which began to feel as if needles were being pressed into the bone. The hanging-rope was still tied in place, but its cut end lay beside me, on the cold ground.

Slowly I sat up. The cooking fire still burned brightly. The air smelled powerfully of ash, blood, and animal. I turned and saw Harry Keeton.

I tried to speak, but nothing moved, no sound came. My eyes watered and Keeton reached out and patted my arm. He was sprawled on his side, propped up by one elbow. The broken arrow shaft stuck obscenely from his shoulder, rising and falling with each of his laboured breaths.

'They took her,' he said, shaking his head, sharing my grief. I nodded as best I could. Keeton said, 'I couldn't do anything . . .'

I reached for the cut rope, made a hoarse sound, querying what had happened.

'That beast,' he said. 'The boar thing. It picked you up. It shook you. My God, what a creature. I think it thought you were dead. It sniffed you hard, then let you dangle again. I cut the rope with your own sword. I thought I was too late.'

I tried to say thank you, but still no sound came.

'They left this, though,' Keeton said, and held up the silver oak leaf. Christian must have dropped it. I reached for it and closed my fingers around the cold metal.

We lay there in the darkening garden, watching the bright streams of sparks rise skywards from the smouldering trees. Keeton's face was ghastly pale in the glow of the fire. Somehow we had both survived, and towards dawn we helped each other into the house, and collapsed again, two woebegone, wounded creatures, shivering and shaken.

I cried for an hour at least, for Guiwenneth, with anger, for the loss of all I had loved. Keeton remained silent, his jaw set firm, his right hand pressed against the arrow wound, as if staunching the flow of blood.

We were a desperate pair of warriors.

But we survived the day, and when I had the strength, I walked to the manor house, and summoned help for the wounded airman.

PART THREE

The Heartwoods

Inwards

From my father's diary, December 1941:

Wrote to Wynne-Jones, urging him to return to the Lodge. I have been more than five weeks in the deep woodland, but only a fortnight or so has passed at home. For me, there has been no *sense* of the time shift, the winter being as mild and as persistent in the woods as at home. There was a little snow, no more than a flurry. No doubt the effect – which I am led to believe is an effect of 'relativity' – is more pronounced the closer to the heartwoods one journeys.

I have discovered a fourth pathway into the woods, a way of travelling *beyond* the outer defensive zones, although the feeling of disorientation is strong. This route is almost too obvious: the stream that passes through the wood, which C & S call 'stickle-brook'. Since this tiny rivulet expands to full flood within two days' journey inwards, I cannot imagine how the water balance is worked! Does it become a full torrent at some point? A river like the Thames?

The track reaches beyond the Horse Shrine, beyond the Stone Falls, even beyond the place of ruins. I encountered the *shamiga*. They are from the early Bronze Age in Europe, perhaps two thousand years BC. Their storytelling ability is prolific. The so-called 'life-speaker' is a young girl – painted green – with clear 'psychic' talents. They are a legendary people themselves, the eternal guardians of river fords. From them I have learned of the nature of the inner realm, of the way to the heartwoods that will take one beyond the zone of ruins, and the 'great rift'. I have heard of a great fire that holds back the primal woodland at the very heart of the realm itself.

My difficulty is still exhaustion. I need to return to Oak Lodge because the journey is too daunting, too demanding. A younger man, perhaps . . . who knows? I must organize an expedition. The wood continues to obstruct me, defending itself with the same vigour that originally made travelling through even its periphery a frightening experience. The *shamiga*, however, hold many keys. They are the traveller's friend, and I shall attempt to rediscover them before the coming summer is out.

The shamiga are the traveller's friend. They hold many keys . . .

I have no sense of the time shift . . .

The girl affects me totally. J has sent his, but what can I do? It is the nature of the mythago itself . . .

How comforting the incomplete and obsessive journal became in the days after that painful and heartbreaking night. The *shamiga* held the keys to many things. The sticklebrook was the way in to the deeper woods. And since Christian was from the outside I found it comforting to think that he, too, was bound to the 'routeways', and I would be able to follow him.

I read the diary as if my life depended upon it; perhaps there *was* value in the obsession. I intended to follow my brother as soon as my strength was back, and Keeton felt up to journeying. There was no way of telling what simple observations or comments of my father's might have been of crucial value at some later stage.

Harry Keeton received medical attention at the airforce base from which he operated. The wound was not dangerous, but was certainly severe. He came back to Oak Lodge three days after the attack, his arm in a sling, his body weak, but his spirit strong and vital. He was *willing* himself better. He knew what was on my mind, and he wanted to come with me; and the thought of his companionship was agreeable.

For my part, there were two wounds to heal. I couldn't speak for three days, and could only manage to swallow liquids. I felt weak and distraught. The strength returned to my limbs, but distress came in the persistent image of

Guiwenneth, slung crudely across the back of a horse and dragged from my sight. I couldn't sleep for thinking of her. I wept more tears than I would have believed possible. For a while, three days or so after the abduction, my anger peaked, and became irrationally expressed in a series of hysterical fits, one of which was witnessed by the airman, who braved my abusive assault upon him and helped to calm me down.

I *had* to get her back. Legendary role or no, Guiwenneth from the greenwood was the woman I loved, and my life could not continue until she was safe again. I wanted to smash and crush my brother's skull in the same way that I smashed vases and chairs in that sequence of physically powerful tantrums.

But I had to wait a week. I just couldn't see myself heading through tangled woodland without becoming completely exhausted. My voice came back, my strength returned, and I made my preparations and plans.

The day of departure would be the 7th of September.

An hour before dawn Harry Keeton arrived at the Lodge. I listened to the sound of his motorcycle for some minutes before the bright beam of his headlight swept through the darkened hallways, and the noisy engine was cut. I was in the oak cage, curled up in the tree hollow where I had spent so much time with Guiwenneth. I was thinking of her, of course, and impatient with Keeton for being late. I was also irritated with the man for arriving and breaking through my melancholy.

'I'm ready,' he said as he stepped in through the front door. He was wet with condensation and smelled of leather and petrol. We went into the dining-room.

'We'll leave at first light,' I said. 'That is, if you can move.'

Keeton had prepared himself well, and taken the prospective journey very seriously. He was wearing his motorcycle leathers, with heavy boots and a leather pilot's cap. His rucksack was bulging. He carried two knives at his waist, one a wide-bladed object, which he presumably intended to use as a machete as we forced through the underwood. Pots and pans rattled as he moved.

As he eased the immense pack from his shoulder he said, 'Thought it would be wise to be prepared.'

'Prepared for what?' I asked with a smile. 'Sunday roast? A forest waltz? You've brought your life-style with you. You're not going to need it. And you're certainly not going to be able to carry it.'

He stripped off the tight pilot's helmet and scratched his tawny hair. The burn-mark on the lower part of his face was flushed brightly; his eyes twinkled, partly with excitement, partly with embarrassment.

'You think I've overdone it?'

'How's the shoulder?'

He stretched his arm, made a tentative swinging motion. 'Healing well. Intact. Two or three days and it'll be good as new.'

'Then you've obviously overdone it. You'll never carry that pack on one shoulder.'

He looked slightly worried. 'How about this?'

As he spoke he shrugged off the Lee-Enfield rifle which had been slung behind his back. It was a heavy rifle, as I knew from experience, and smelled of oil where he had cleaned and waterproofed it. From his leather coat pocket he produced boxes of ammunition. From his breast pocket he produced his pistol, with ammunition for *that* from the zip pocket of his leggings. By the time this process of unloading had been completed his volume had withered by half. He suddenly seemed far more the slender airman of days before.

'Thought they might come in useful,' he said.

In a way he was right, but I shook my head. One of us would have to carry them, and a trek through dense wild-wood did not lend itself to carrying unreasonably heavy loads. Keeton's shoulder had healed quickly, but he would clearly begin to suffer if the wound was subjected to too much abrasion and pressure. My own wounds had healed as well, and I felt strong, but not so strong that I could add twenty pounds of rifle to my neck.

And yet, there would be rifles in the woodland. I had already encountered a matchlock. I had no idea whether or not heroic figures from more recent years were present in the forest, and what weaponry they might possess.

'Perhaps the pistol,' I said. 'But Harry . . . the man we're going in to find is primitive. He has opted for sword and spear and I intend to challenge him in the same fashion.'

'I can understand that,' said Keeton softly. He reached out for the pistol and returned it to its shoulder holster.

We unpacked his rucksack, removing a plethora of items that we agreed would be more of an encumbrance than a comfort. We carried food enough for a week, in the form of bread, cheese, fruit and salt beef. A ground sheet and light-weight tent seemed a good idea. Water flasks in case we found only poisoned water. Brandy, medicinal alcohol, plasters, antiseptic cream, antifungal ointment, bandages: all of these seemed of the highest importance. A plate each to eat off, enamel mugs, matches and a small supply of very dry straw. The rest of our packs consisted of clothing, one complete change each. The heaviest item was the oilskin which I had obtained from the manor. Keeton's leather outfit, likewise, would be a burden to carry, but for warmth and waterproofing seemed a good idea.

All this for a journey through a stand of trees around which I could run in little more than an hour! How quickly we had both come to accept the occult nature of Ryhope Wood.

Christian had taken the original map. I spread out the copy I had made from memory and showed Keeton the route I proposed to take, along the rivulet, to the place marked 'Stone Falls'. This meant crossing two zones, one of which I could remember as having been labelled 'oscillating traverse zone'.

Christian was a week or so ahead of us, but I felt confident that we could still find traces of his passage inwards.

At first light I picked up my stone-bladed spear, and buckled on the Celtic sword that Magidion had given me. Then, ceremonially, I closed and locked the back door of Oak Lodge. Keeton made some feeble joke about notes for milkmen, but went quiet as I turned towards the oak orchard and began to walk. Images of Guiwenneth were everywhere. My heart raced when I remembered the Hawks leaping through the burning trees, which had rapidly regenerated and were in full summer leaf. The day was going to be hot and still. The oak orchard seemed unnaturally silent. We walked through its thin underbrush and emerged on to the dew-glistening open land beyond, trekking down the slope to the sticklebrook, and the mossy fence that seemed to guard the ghost wood from the mortal land outside.

I have discovered a fourth pathway into the deeper zones of the wood. The brook itself. So obvious, now, a water track! I believe it could be used to enter the heartwoods themselves. But time, always time!

Keeton helped me wrench the old gate from where it had been nailed to a tree. It was half-buried in the bank of the stream. It came away from its attachments, trailing weed, rot, moss and briar rose. Beyond the gate the stream widened and deepened to form a dangerous pool, bordered by tangled hawthorns. Barefoot, and with trousers rolled up, I stepped into that pool and waded around its edge, carefully holding on to the roots and branches of that first, quite natural defensive zone. The pool's bottom was at first slippery, then soft. The water swirled about my legs, cold and scummy. The moment we entered the dank woodland in this way, a chill came over us, the sensation of being cut off from the brightening day outside.

Keeton slipped and slid his way after, and I helped him from the pool on to the muddy bank. We had to stoop and force our way through the tangle of snagging thorn and briar, easing our way along the stream's edge. There were bits and pieces of fencing here, decades old, so rotten that they crumbled at the touch. The dawn chorus was subdued, I thought, although there was much bird motion above us in the high, dark foliage.

The gloom lifted suddenly and we came to a more open patch of bank, and here sat down to dry our feet and put boots back on.

'That wasn't so hard,' Keeton said, wiping blood from a thorn scratch on his cheek.

'We've barely started,' I said, and he laughed.

'Just trying to keep the spirits high.' He looked about him. 'One thing's for sure. Your brother and his troop didn't come this way.'

'They'll be heading for the river, though. We'll pick up the trail soon enough.'

I am going to keep this diary as a record of what happens to me. There are several reasons. I have left a letter explaining them. I hope the diary will be read. My name is Harry Keeton, of 27 Middleton Gardens, Buxford. I am 34 years of age. Today is the 7th September 1948. The date, though, no longer matters. It is DAY ONE.

We are spending our first night in the ghostwood. We have walked for twelve hours. No sign of Christian, or horses, or G. We are in the place that Steven's father discovered and named Little Stone Glade. We reached the glade before last light, and it is a perfect site to recoup from the exertions of the walk, and to eat. The so-called 'little stone' is a massive sandstone block, fourteen feet high (we estimate) and twenty paces round. Much chipped, eroded, weathered etc. Steven has found faint markings upon it, including his father's initials GH. If this is the *little* stone, what I wonder . . . ?

Totally exhausted. Shoulder very troublesome, but have opted for 'hero's' way out, and shall not mention it unless S notices. I can carry my pack quite adequately, but there is far more scrambling and physical effort than I had anticipated. Tent is pitched. A warm evening. The woodland seems very normal. The sound of the stream is clear, although it is less a stream, more a small river. We have been forced away from its bank by the density of the under-brush. Already there is a quality about the woodland that defies experience, the size of certain trees, gigantic, natural, no sign of having been trimmed or coppiced. They seem to enfold whole areas of underwood, and feel very protective. When the leaf cover is so complete, the underwood is thin, and walking is easy. But of course, it is very dark. We rest below these giant trees quite naturally, though. The whole wood breathes and sighs. Many horse-chestnuts, so the wood is not 'primal', but a great abundance of oak and hazel, with whole stands of ash and beech. A hundred forests in one.

Keeton began to keep his diary from that first night, but maintained the journal for only a few days. It was intended to be a secret, I believe, his last testament to the world should anything happen to him. The skirmish in the garden, the arrow wound that nearly killed him, my account of how close he had come to being cooked liver, all this inspired him with a sense of foreboding, whose deeper nature I failed to grasp until much later.

Sneaking a look at the diary each night as he slept, I dis-covered I was glad of this little focus of normality. I knew, for example, that his shoulder was causing him trouble, and made sure he put no undue exertion upon it. He was also quite flattering to me: *Steven a fine walker, determined. His purpose, whether consciously or unconsciously guides him inwards with accuracy. He is a great comfort, despite the anger and grief that seethe just below the surface.*

Thank you, Harry. In those first few days of the journey you were a great comfort too.

If the first day had been a long, but straightforward jour-ney, the second was not. Although we were following the 'water track', the woodland defences were still a great nuisance.

First, there was disorientation. We found ourselves walk-ing *back* the way we had come. At times it was almost possible to experience the switch in perception. We felt dizzy; the underwood became preternaturally dark; the sound of the river changed from our left to our right. It frightened Keeton. It disturbed me. The closer we hugged the riverside, the less pronounced the effect. But the river itself was defended from us by a screen of thorns which was quite impenetrable.

Somehow we passed that first defensive zone. The wood began to haunt us. Trees seemed to move. Branches fell upon us . . . in our mind's eyes only, but not before we had reacted with exhausting shock. The ground seemed to writhe at times, and split open. We smelled fumes, fire, a stench like decay. If we persisted, the illusions passed.

And Keeton wrote in his diary. *The same haunting that I experienced before. And just as frightening. But does it mean I'm close? I must not begin to expect too much.*

A wind blew at us, then, and this storm was certainly no illusion. It howled through the forest; leaves were stripped from the trees; twigs, brambles, earth, stones, all came surging towards us, so that we had to shelter, clinging on to trees for dear life, threatened with being blown back the way we had come. To escape that incredible gale we had to hack through the thorn on the riverside. It took us a full day to move no more than half a mile or so, and we were bruised, cut and exhausted when we finally camped for the night . . .

And during the night the sounds of beasts haunted us. The earth vibrated, the tent was shaken violently, and lights glowed in the darkness, throwing eerie, wispy shadows across the canvas. We didn't sleep for a minute. But the following day we seemed to have overcome the defences. We made good progress, and eventually found we could encroach upon the river with greater facility.

Keeton began to experience the formation of pre-mythagos. He became jumpy during the fourth day, starting with shock, hissing for silence, crouching and searching the woodland. I explained to him how to distinguish between real movement and the hallucinatory forms of the pre-mythagos, but after the terrors of the first few days he was not at ease, and didn't become so until much later. As for real mythago forms, we heard one on that easy first day, but saw none.

Or is that true?

We had come to a place marked on my father's map as 'Stone Falls', a place he had often referred to. The river – our tiny sticklebrook – had widened to about ten feet, and was a crystal torrent of water, swirling through the thin woodland that crowded banks more sandy than muddy. The place felt open, a delightful site for a camp, and indeed we found the signs of such an encampment, traces of rope, the marks where fastenings had been driven into trees. But there were no tracks, no signs of fire, and though my spirits leapt at the thought of being on Christian's trail, I had to acknowledge that the site had been constructed by a mythago, at some time long in the past.

Away from the river the land sloped steeply upwards, a rising woodland of thin trees, mostly beech. They sprouted from an earth that was strewn with great boulders and jagged promontories of dark rock. The map had shown a track over this rise of ground, cutting off a meander in the river, where the bank was marked as 'dangerous passage'.

We rested, then moved away from the river and through the beechwood, pulling ourselves up the steep slopes by hanging on to the slender trunks of the trees. Each outcrop of stone was like a cave, and there were traces of animal life outside many of them.

It was hard going. The river dropped away below us, in sight and sound. The silence of the wood enveloped us totally. Keeton was labouring with his sore shoulder, his face so red that the ferocious burn didn't show at all.

We crossed the mossy rocks on the ridge and began to descend to the river on the other side. A great stone was leaning at a sharp angle from the slope. It looked – and Keeton remarked upon the fact as well – like a standing stone that had slipped. We skidded and ran towards it, fetching up sharp and hard against its smooth side. Keeton was breathless.

'How *about* this!' he exclaimed, running his finger around the design that had been deeply chipped into the rock. It was the face of a wolf against a diamond background; weather had blurred the finer detail. 'Is someone buried here, I wonder?'

He stepped round the rock, still leaning against it. I glanced about me and realized that there were at least ten such stones, although smaller, rising from the underbrush of the beechwood.

'It's a cemetery,' I murmured.

Keeton was standing below the imposing monument, staring up at it. From somewhere on the slope came the sound of wood cracking, and the noisy tumbling of a stone down towards the river.

Then the ground shook slightly. I glanced about apprehensively, wondering if something was approaching. Keeton's cry of, 'Oh Christ!' jerked my attention back to him, and I saw him madly scrambling towards me. It took me a second to realize what was happening.

The great stone was beginning to move, slowly toppling forwards.

Keeton got clear. The monolith slipped majestically over, crashed through two slender young trees and slid heavily down the slope for about forty yards, leaving a great gaping hole behind it.

We edged forward to the pit and cautiously peered in. At the bottom of the hole, just visible through the packed earth, were the bones of a man, still clad in armour. The skull, which stared up at us, had been cracked open by a blow. A slender, pointed helmet, of green but bright metal, had been placed above the head. The warrior's arms were crossed on the flattened breastplate. The metal looked polished, even though it had tarnished. Keeton thought it was bronze.

As we stood staring reverently down at the corpse, earth

fell from the breastplate, and the skeleton began to move. Keeton cried out in shock, and I felt every organ in my body twist with fright. But it was just a snake, a brightly coloured adder. It came sliding from the ribcage, below the breastplate, and tried to ascend the earthy slope of the grave.

That brief moment had totally unnerved the two of us.

'God Almighty,' was all Keeton said, save to add, 'Let's get out of here.'

'It's only a skeleton,' I said. 'It can't harm us.'

'*Somebody* buried him,' Keeton pointed out correctly.

We grabbed our packs and slipped and slid our way down the slope, to the more protective trees of the riverside. I laughed when we got back to what felt like safety, but Keeton stared back through the crowded trees, up towards the stone ridge where the megalith lay.

Following his solemn gaze I saw the unmistakable flash of light on green metal. After a second it vanished.

Day five. Fifth night. colder. I am very tired, shoulder in great pain. Steven tired too, but very determined. The incident with the standing stone was more terrifying than I can admit. The warrior is pursuing us. *Convinced* it is. I see flashes of light on its armour. Noisy progress through underbrush. Steven says I should put it from my mind. We are well equipped to deal with pursuers. He has confidence. The thought of battling with *that* thing, though. Horrible!

I am haunted by these edge of vision images. S explained them to me, but I had no idea of how distracting they could be. Figures, groups, even animals. I see them, sometimes, very clearly. Frightening visions. He says I am beginning to shape them, and they do not exist, to try and concentrate only on the forward vision until I am used to them.

Tonight, wolves have sniffed at us from across the river. Five in all, great beasts, rancid to smell, so confident. They made no sound. They were quite real. Padded off silently back towards the edgewoods.

We have walked, now, for five days. A total of sixty hours by my reckoning. My watch is broken for no reason that I can fathom. Steven came without. But sixty hours is about right, and that means eighty or ninety miles *at least*. We have not yet reached the place where my photographs showed figures/buildings. We looked at the photographs by torch-light. We could have walked through the wood twenty times over, and we are still at the edge.

I am frightened. But this is certainly a ghost wood. And if S is right in everything he tells me, then the avatar and the city will be here too, and the damage can be undone. God watch me, guide me!

The avatar and the city will be here . . .
The damage can be undone . . .

I read the words through again, while Keeton slept silently close by. The fire was low, no more than a flickering flame, and I pushed two more pieces of wood upon it. Sparks flew into the night. In the darkness around us there was stealthy sound, clear and unnerving against the perpetual rush of the sticklebrook.

The avatar and the city will be here . . .

I watched Keeton's slumbering form, then gently replaced the small notebook in the sealed pocket of his haversack.

So Keeton's relationship with Ryhope Wood – the ghost-wood, as he called it – was more than a companion-out-of-curiosity to me. He had been in such a wood before, and more had happened to him there than he had told me.

Had he encountered a mythago form in *that* woodland? An avatar, the earthly form of a God? And what damage did he mean? His burnmark?

How dearly I would have liked to have talked to him about it. But I couldn't reveal that I had read his diary, and he had mentioned the ghost wood in France only briefly. I hoped that in time he would entrust me with whatever secret he carried, whether dread, or guilt, or revenge.

We broke camp an hour after first light, having been disturbed by wild animals, probably wolves. Looking at the map we carried, it was uncanny to recognize how far we had *not* come, how close to the edge of the woodland we remained. We had walked for so many days, and yet had hardly begun our journey. Keeton was having great difficulty in accepting the changing relationship of space and time. For my part, I wondered what the wildwoods themselves would do to us.

For these, as yet, were not the wildwoods. The cemetery, Keeton told me, had been an area of ancient coppice. Ryhope Wood, growing wild, had returned to a natural form at its edges, but the signs of man were everywhere abundant. Keeton showed me what he meant: that the large, standard oak we passed below had self-seeded and grown to its majestic size without being affected by man, but close by was a beech that had been neatly lopped ten feet from the ground, albeit hundreds of years before, and the resulting cluster of new shoots that had grown from this pollard had thickened to give the several immense trunk-like limbs that reached skywards, and cast such gloom across the underwood.

But had the coppicing been performed by man or mythago?

We were passing through the zones of habitation of such strange forest beings as the Twigling, the Jack-in-the-Greens, Arthur; and of communities too, according to my father's journal: the *shamiga*, outlaw bands, gypsy villages, all of the mythic peoples associated, either in fear or magic, with thick woodland.

And perhaps, too, we were passing through the genesis zone of Guiwenneth himself. How many Guiwenneth mech Penn Evs were there? Guiwenneth, daughter of the Chief. How many wandered this expansive forest? It was a world of mind and earth, a realm outside of real laws of space and time, a giant world, with room enough for a thousand such girls, each the product of a human mind, drawn from the towns and villages around the estate where Ryhope Wood grew.

How I missed her. How right Keeton was to refer to the fury bubbling just below. There were times when an uncontrollable rage overcame me, and I could hardly bear to be with the other man, stalking ahead into the brush, striking at anything and everything, shaking with rage at what my brother had done to us.

It had been days since the attack, and he would be miles ahead of us. I should not have delayed! I had so little chance of finding her, now. The woodland was a gigantic landscape, a primal place, endlessly wide.

The depressions passed. And halfway through that sixth day's trek I found evidence of Christian in a form I had not expected, evidence which made it clear that he was not so far ahead of us after all.

We had been following a deer track for nearly an hour along the river's edge. The carpet of dog's mercury and bracken was thin, here, and the spoor of a small stag was so obvious in the soft mud patches that a child could have followed it. The trees crowded closer to the water. Their outer branches almost closed over the river, forming an eerie, silent tunnel. Light shafted through the broken foliage and formed a gloriously-lit underworld, into which we pursued our prey.

The animal was smaller than I had expected, and was standing, proud and alert, near to a spinney, where the river bank was wide and dry. Keeton had trouble seeing the beast, it was so perfectly camouflaged against the dark wood behind. I approached cautiously under cover, holding Keeton's pistol. I was too hungry for fresh meat to care about the ignominity of this kill. I placed a single shot, just above the animal's anus, and splinters of backbone perforated the hide for two feet along the spine. The stag was maimed, and I fell upon it, swiftly ending its agony. After butchering it as Guiwenneth had showed me, I tossed a raw haunch to Keeton, with a smile, and told him to get a fire going. Keeton was pale and disgusted. He jumped back from the blood-raw meat, then looked at me startled. 'You've done this before.'

'Indeed I have. We'll feed well, for the moment. Keep several pounds of cooked meat for tomorrow, and carry two joints, as much as we can manage.'

'And the rest?'

'Leave it. It'll keep the wolves off our back for a while.'

'Will it, though?' he murmured, and gingerly picked up the deer haunch and began to brush the leaf litter and dirt from it.

It was as he was gathering wood for the fire that Keeton gasped with horror and called to me. He was standing beyond the spinney, staring at the ground. I walked up to him, conscious, again, of an odour I confess I had noticed as soon as I had gone stalking the deer: the decay of an animal of large size.

The offending objects were human animals, two in number. Keeton gagged slightly, then closed his eyes. 'Look at the man,' he said, and I stooped, peering through the gloom, and saw what he meant. The man's breastbone had been split, the same motion that the Fenlander had been about to make upon Keeton himself, to extract the liver from the corpse.

'It's Christian,' I said. 'He killed them.'

'Two, three days ahead,' said Keeton. 'I've seen corpses in France. They're flexible, do you see?' He leaned down, still shaking, and moved the girl's ankle. 'But beginning to swell. Damn. She was young . . . look at her . . .'

I cleared the brush from around the bodies. They were certainly young. Lovers, I imagined, both quite naked, although the girl still had a necklace of bone around her neck, and the boy had strands of leather around his calves, as if the sandals that he had been wearing had been too crudely looted from his corpse. The girl's fists were clenched. I reached out and the fingers unfurled quite easily. In each hand she held a broken partridge feather, and I thought of Christian's cloak, which had been fringed by such things.

'We should bury them,' Keeton said. I noticed that he had tears in his eyes. His nose was wet. He reached down and moved the boy's hand into his lover's, then turned, presumably to see where a good site for burial might be.

'Trouble,' he whispered, and I turned too, and felt a sudden shock as I saw the ring of angry-looking men around us. All but one – an older man in authority – had a bow drawn, the arrow pointed either at myself or Keeton. One of them was shaking, the bow trembling, the arrow wavering between my face and chest. Tears marked this man's face in a great streak through the grey paint with which he was decorated.

'He's going to shoot,' Keeton hissed, and before I could say, 'I know,' this manifestly distressed man had loosed the arrow. In the same instant the older man next to him had raised his staff, clipping the edge of the bow. The arrow was nothing but a sudden, shocking sound, passing between Keeton and myself and impacting with a tree, deeper in the woods.

The ring remained, the arrows pointed. The distressed man stood, crestfallen, angry, his bow held limply by his side. His chief came forward, searching our eyes with his, aware of the stone-bladed spear I held. He smelled sweet, a strange phenomenon, sweet like apple, as if he had daubed his body with apple juice. His hair was braided five times, and painted with blue and red whorls.

He looked between us at the bodies of the youngsters, then spoke to the men around him. Bows were lowered, arrows unnocked. He could see that they had been dead for days, but to check his point he ran a finger over the blade of my spear, sniggered, then checked my sword, which impressed him, and Keeton's knives, which puzzled him.

The two bodies were dragged out into the clear space by the river and bound with twine. Two litters were made, crude affairs, and the corpses reverently placed upon them. The band's leader crouched above the girl, staring at her face. I heard him say, 'Uth guerig . . . uth guerig . . .'

The man who had been the girl's father (or the boy's, it was hard to tell) wept silently again.

'Uth guerig,' I murmured aloud, and the older man glanced up at me. He tugged the partridge feather from the girl's right hand and crushed it in his own. 'Uth guerig!' he said angrily.

So they knew of Christian. He was *uth guerig*, whatever that meant.

Killer. Rapist. Man without compassion.

Uth guerig! I dared not tell them that I was the brother of that murderous creature.

The deer gave cause for some concern. After all, it belonged to us. The haunches and cadaver were brought close by, and the ring of men stood back, some of them smiling and indicating that we should take the meat. It took very little in the way of gesturing to indicate that the meat would be a gift from us to them. I had hardly smiled and shaken my head before six of them swooped upon the pile and slung the great joints over their shoulders, walking briskly along the river's edge, towards their community.

Life-Speaker

Sixth night. We are with a people who guard river crossings, called the *shamiga* according to Steven, who remembered their name from his father's account. A strangely touching burial for the two youngsters we found. Also unnervingly sexual. They were buried across the river, in the woods, among other graves, the earth piled high above the ground. Each was painted with white spirals, circles and crosses, the pattern on the girl different from that on the boy. They were laid in the same grave, straight out, arms crossed on chest. A piece of thin twine was tied to the tip of the boy's member, and tugged around his neck to simulate erection. The girl's passage was opened with a painted stone. Steven believes this is to make sure they are sexually active in the other world. A large mound of earth was raised over the grave.

The *shamiga* are mythagos, a legendary *group*, a tribe out of fable. Odd to think of it. Odder than being with Guiwenneth. They are a legendary people who guard – and haunt, after death – the river crossings. They transform into stepping stones when the river floods, or so the legend goes. There are several fables associated with the *shamiga*, all lost in our own time, but Steven learned a fragment of one such tale, concerning a girl who stepped into the water, ducked down to assist the crossing of a Chieftain and was taken to help build the wall of a stone fort.

The *shamiga* do not appear to specialize in happy endings. This became clear later when the 'life-speaker' came to us. A girl in her early teens, quite naked, painted green. Quite alarming. Something happened to Steven and he seemed to understand her perfectly.

At dusk, after the burial, the *shamiga* feasted on our fresh kill of venison. A great fire was kindled, and a ring of torches placed around us, about twenty feet away. Around the fire gathered the *shamiga*, more menfolk than women, I noticed, with only four children, but all wearing brightly coloured tunics, or skirts, and waist-length cloaks. Their huts – away from the river, where the ground had been cleared – were crude affairs, square plan, with shallow thatch roofs, each building supported by a simple frame of hardwood. From the waste-tips and the remains of old buildings – indeed, from the graveyard itself – we could see that this community had been here for many generations.

The venison, spit-roasted and basted with a herb and wild-cherry sauce, was delicious. Politeness required the use of twigs, sharpened and split into forks, with which to consume meat. Fingers were used to tear the meat from the carcass, however.

It was still quite light when the feast finished. I discovered that the grieving man had been the father of the girl. The boy was *inshan*: from another place. A crude communication by sign language continued for some while. We were not suspected of being evil; reference to *uth guerig* were rudely shrugged away – it was not our business; questions about our own origins produced answers that puzzled the gathered adults, and after a while made them suspicious.

And then a change came over our hosts, a buzz of anticipation, a great deal of understated excitement. Those among the gathered clan who did not watch Keeton and myself with a sort of amiable curiosity, glanced around, searching beyond the torches, watching the dusk, the woodland, the gentle river. Somewhere a bird shrilled unnaturally and there was a moment's cry of excitement. The tribe's elder, who was called Durium, leaned towards me and whispered, 'Kushar!'

She was among us before I realized it, passing among the *shamiga*, a dark, slim shape, silhouetted against the burning ring of torches. She touched each adult on the ears, eyes and mouth, and to some she gave a small, twisted twig of wood. These were held reverently by most, though two or three of the *shamiga* made little graves in the ground and buried the offerings at their feet.

Kushar dropped to a crouch before Keeton and myself and examined us closely. She was daubed with green paint, though her eyes were ringed with thin circles of white and black ochre. Even her teeth were green. Her hair was long and dark, combed out very straight. Her breasts were mere buds, and her limbs thin. She had no body hair. The feeling I had was that she was only ten or twelve years old, but how hard it was to gauge!

She spoke to us and we spoke back in our language. Her dark eyes, gleaming by torchlight, focused more upon me than upon Keeton, and it was to me that she gave the small twig. I kissed it, and she laughed briefly, then closed her small hand around mine, squeezing gently.

Two torches were brought and placed on each side of her and she settled into a more comfortable kneeling position, facing me, then started to speak. The *shamiga* all turned to face us. The girl – was she *called* Kushar? Or was *kushar* a word for what she was? – closed her eyes and spoke in a slightly higher pitch than I thought was normal for her.

The words flowed from her tongue, eloquent, sibilant, incomprehensible. Keeton glanced uncomfortably at me, and I shrugged. A minute or so passed and I whispered, 'My father managed to understand somehow—'

I said no more than that because Durium glanced at me sharply, leaning towards me, his hand outstretched in an angry gesture that clearly indicated, 'Be silent!'

Kushar kept talking, her eyes still closed, unaware of the gesturing going on around her. I grew very conscious of the sounds of the river, the torches, the rustle of the woodland. So I almost jumped when the girl said, and repeated, 'Uth guerig! Uth guerig!'

Aloud I said, 'Uth guerig! Tell me about him!'

The girl's eyes opened. She stopped speaking. Her face looked shocked. Around me the rest of the *shamiga* were shocked as well. Then they became restless, upset, Durium loudly expressing his own irritation.

'I'm sorry,' I said quietly, looking at him, then back at the girl.

. . . tells all stories with her eyes closed, so that the smiles or frowns of those who listen cannot effect a shape-change upon the characters within the story.

The words, from my father's letter to Wynne-Jones, were haunting fragments of guilt in my mind. I wondered if I had changed something at a crucial point, and the story would never be the same again.

Kushar continued to stare at me, her lower lip trembling slightly. I thought tears welled up in her eyes for a second, but her suddenly moist gaze became clear again. Keeton remained dutifully silent, his hand resting against his pocket where he carried the pistol.

'Now I know you,' Kushar said, and for a moment I was too surprised to react.

'I'm sorry,' I said to her again.

'So am I,' she said. 'But no harm has been done. The story has not changed. I did not recognize you.'

'I'm not so sure I understand—' I said. Keeton had been watching the two of us peculiarly. He said, 'What don't you understand?'

'What she means . . .'

He frowned. 'You can understand her words?'

I looked at him briefly. 'You don't?'

'I don't know the language.'

The *shamiga* began to make a hissing sound, a certain sign that they wished silence, that they wanted the history to continue.

To Keeton, the girl was still speaking the language of two thousand years before Christ. But I understood her, now. Somehow I had entered the awareness of this young life-speaker. Is that what my father had meant when he referred to a girl with 'clear psychic talents'? And yet, the astonishing fact of our establishing communication stopped me thinking about what had really happened. I could not have known, then, what a devastating change had occurred in me, as I sat by the river and listened to the whispered voice of the past.

'I am the speaker of the life of this people,' she said, and closed her eyes again. 'Listen without speaking. The life must not be changed.'

'Tell me of *uth guerig*,' I said.

'The life of the Outsider has gone for the moment. I can tell only the life that I see. *Listen!*'

And with that urgent statement I fell silent –

Outsider! Christian was the *Outsider!*

– and attended to the sequence of tales that the life-speaker recounted.

The first tale I remember easily; others have faded from mind because they meant little, and were obscure. The final tale affected me strongly, for it concerned both Christian and Guiwenneth.

This was Kushar's first tale:

On that far day, during the life of this people, the Chieftain, Parthorlas took the head of his brother, Diermadas, and ran back to his stone fort. The pursuit was fierce. Forty men with spears, forty men with swords, forty dogs the height of deer, but Parthorlas outran them, holding the head of his brother in the palm of his left hand.

On that day the river had flooded and the *shamiga* were hunting, all save the girl Swithoran, whose lover was the son of Diermadas, known as Kimuth Hawkspeaker. The girl Swithoran stepped into the water and ducked her head, to aid the crossing of Parthorlas. She was a stone as smooth as any stepping stone, with her back so white and pure as it rose above the water. Parthorlas stepped upon her and jumped to the far bank, then reached back and plucked the stone from the river.

It nestled in his right hand. His fort was stone built and there was a gap in the southern wall. And on that day Swithoran became a part of the fort, stuck in the hole to stop the winter winds.

Kimuth Hawkspeaker summoned the clans of his *tuad*, which is to say of the lands he controlled, and made them swear allegiance to him, now that Diermadas was dead. This they did, after a month of bargaining. Then Kimuth Hawkspeaker led them and charged them to lay siege to the stone fort.

This they did, for seven years.

For the first year, Parthorlas alone shot arrows at the assembled host of the plain, below the fort. For the second year Parthorlas flung metal spears at the host. For the third year he fashioned knives from the wood of carts, and so kept the furious host at bay. In the fourth year he flung the cattle and wild pigs that he kept in the fort, keeping just enough to sustain him and his family. In the fifth year, with no weapons and little food and water, he flung his wife and daughters at the army on the plain, and this scattered them for more than six seasons. Then he flung his sons, but Hawkspeaker flung them back, and this frightened Porthorlas even more, for his sons were like broken-backed hens, and pecked for favours. In the seventh year Parthorlas began to fling the stones from the walls of his fort. Each stone was ten times the weight of a man, but Parthorlas flung them to the far horizon. In time he came to the last bits of the wall, where the winter draughts were blocked. He failed to recognize the smooth white stone from the river and flung it at the War Chief Kimuth Hawkspeaker himself, killing him.

Swithoran was released from the stone-shape and wept for the dead chieftain. 'A thousand men have died because of a hole in a wall,' she said. 'Now there is a hole in my breast. Shall we slaughter a thousand more because of that?' The clan chiefs discussed the matter, then returned to the river, because it was the season when the big fish swam up from the sea. The place in the valley became known as *Issaga ukirik*, which means *where the river girl stopped the war*.

As she spoke the history, the *shamiga* murmured and laughed, involved with every phrase, very image. I could see very little amusing in the story at all. Why did they laugh more loudly at the description of pursuit (eighty men and forty dogs) and of the stone fort than at the image of

Parthorlas flinging his wife, daughters and sons? (And why, for that matter, did they allow themselves to laugh at all? Surely Kushar could hear that response!)

Other histories followed. Keeton, listening only to the fluent sound of an alien language, looked glum, yet resigned to patience. The stories were inconsequential, and most of them I have now forgotten.

Then, after an hour of speaking, and without pausing for breath, Kushar told a story about the Outsider, and I scribbled it down with pen and paper, searching for clues as I wrote, unaware that the story itself contained the seeds of the final conflict that was still so far away in time, and woodland.

On that far day, during the life of this people, the Outsider came to the bare hill behind the stones that stood in a ring around the magic place called Veruambas. The Outsider thrust his spear into the earth, and squatted down beside it, watching the place of stones for many hours. The people gathered outside the great circle, and then came inside the ditch. The circle was four hundred paces across. The ditch around it had been sunk to five man heights. The stones were all animals, which had once been men, and earth had a stone-talker, who whispered the prayers of the priests to them.

The youngest of the three sons of the Chieftain Aubriagas was sent up the hill to study the Outsider. He came back, breathless and bleeding from a wound to his neck. The Outsider, he said, was like a beast, clad in leggings and jerkin of bear hide, with a great bear's skull for a helmet, and boots made of ashwood and leather.

The second youngest son of Aubriagas was sent up the hill. He returned, bruised about the face and shoulders. The Outsider, he said, carried forty spears and seven shields. About this belt hung the shrivelled heads of five great warriors, all of them chieftains, none of them with the eyes left in the skulls. Behind the hill, camped out of sight, he had an entourage of twenty warriors, each a champion, all of them frightened of their leader.

Then the eldest of the brothers was sent to study the Outsider.

He came back with his head held in his hands. The head spoke briefly before the Outsider on the hill rattled his heaviest shield.

This is what the head said:

'He is not of us, nor of our kin, nor of our race, nor of our land, nor of this season, nor of any season during which our tribe has lived. His words are not our words; his metal comes from deeper in the earth than the place of ghouls; his animals are beasts from the dark places; his words have the sound of a man dying, without meaning; his compassion cannot be seen; to him, love is something meaningless; to him, sorrow is laughter; to him, the great clans of our people are cattle, to be harvested and serviced. He is here to destroy us, for he destroys all that is strange to him. He is the violent wind of time, and we must stand or fall against him, because we can never be one tribe with him. He is the Outsider. The one who can kill him is still a long way away. He has eaten three hills, drunk four rivers, and slept for a year in a valley close to the brightest star. Now he needs a hundred women, and four hundred heads, and then he will leave these lands for his own strange realm.'

The Outsider rattled his heaviest war-shield and the head of the eldest brother cried, casting forlorn glances at the one he loved. Then a wild dog was brought, and the head was tied to its back. It was sent to the Outsider, who pricked out the eyes and tied the skull to his belt.

For ten days and nights the Outsider walked around the stone shrine, always out of reach of arrows. The ten best warriors were sent to speak to him and came back with their heads in their hands, weeping, to say goodbye to their wives and children. In this way, all the wild dogs were sent from the shrine, carrying the combat trophies of the alien.

The wolf stones in the great circle were daubed with wolf blood and the speakers whispered the names of *Gulgaroth* and *Olgarog*, the great Wolf Gods from the time of the wildwoods.

The deer stones were painted with the patterns of the stags and the speakers called for *Munnos* and *Clumug*, the stags who walk with the hearts of men.

And on the great boar stone the carcass of a boar that had killed ten men was placed, and its heart blood smeared on the ground. The speaker for this stone, who was the oldest and wisest of the speakers, called for *Urshacam* to appear, and destroy the Outsider.

On the dawn of the eleventh night, the bones of the strangers who guarded the gates rose and ran, screeching, into the boggy woods. There were eight of them, ghastly white, and still wearing the garments from the time of their sacrifice. The ghosts of these strangers fled in the form of black crows, and so the shrine was unguarded.

Now, from the wolf stone came the great spirits of the wolves, huge shapes, grey and fierce, leaping through the fires and across the great ditch. They were followed by the horned beasts of old, the stags which ran on their hind legs. They too went through the smoke of the fires, and their cries were frightening to hear. They were dim shapes in the mist on that cold morning. They could not kill the Outsider, and they fled back to the ghost caves in the earth.

Finally, the boar spirit squeezed from the pores of the stone and grunted, sniffing the morning air, lapping at the dew that had formed on the wild grass around the stone. The boar was twice the height of a man. Its tusks were as sharp as a chieftain's dagger, and the spread of a full-grown man's arms. It watched as the Outsider ran swiftly around the circle, spears and shields held so easily in his hands. Then it ran towards the north gate of the circle.

In that dawn, in the mist, the Outsider cried out for the first time, and though he stood his ground, the spirit of the Urshacam terrified him. Using amethysts for eyes, he sent the head of the eldest son of Aubriagas back to the shrine, where the tribes were huddled in their hide tents, to tell them that all he required was their strongest spear, their sweetest ox, freshly slaughtered, their oldest clay flagon of wine, and their fairest daughter. Then he would go.

All of these things were sent, but the daughter – fairer, it was thought, than the fabled Swithoran – returned, having been rejected by the Outsider as ugly. (She was not at all unhappy about this.) Others were sent, but though they were beautiful in all the various ways of women, all were rejected by the Outsider.

At last the young Warrior-shaman Ebbrega gathered twigs and

branches of oak, elder and hawthorn and fashioned the bones of a girl. He fleshed them with the rotten leaves and litter from the sties, the hard droppings of hare and sheep. All this he covered with scented flowers from the woodland glades, blue, pink and white, the colours of true beauty. He brought her to life with love, and when she sat before him, naked and cold, he dressed her in a fine white tunic, and braided her hair. When Aubriagas and the other elders saw her they could not speak. She was beautiful in a way they had never seen, and it stilled their tongues. When she cried, Ebbrega saw what he had done and tried to take her for his own, but the chieftain restrained him and the girl was taken. She was called *Muarthan*, which means *loving one made from fear*. She went to the Outsider and gave him an oak leaf, shaped from thin bronze. The Outsider lost his reason and loved her. What happened to them after does not concern the life of this people, except to say that Ebbrega never ceased to search for the child he had made, and searches still.

Kushar finished the tale and opened her eyes. She smiled at me briefly, then shifted her body into a more comfortable position. Keeton looked glum, his chin resting on his knees, his gaze vacant and bored. As the girl stopped speaking he looked up, glanced at me and said, 'All over?'

'I've got to write it down,' I said. I had managed to take notes only on the first third of the tale, becoming too absorbed in the unfolding images, too fascinated by what Kushar had been saying. Keeton noticed the excitement in my voice, and the girl cocked her head and looked at me, puzzled. She too had seen that her story had affected me strongly. Around us, the *shamiga* were drifting away from the torches. The evening was finished, for them. Understanding was just beginning for me, however, and I tried to keep Kushar with us.

Christian was the Outsider, then. The stranger who is too strong to subdue, too alien, too powerful. The Outsider must have been an image of terror to very many communities. There was a difference between *strangers* and the Outsiders.

Strangers, travellers from other communities, needed the assistance of the tribes. They could be helped, or sacrificed, according to whim. Indeed, the story that Kushar had just told had referred to the bones of the strangers who guarded the gates into the great circle, which was surely Avebury, in Wiltshire.

But the Outsider was different. He was terrifying because he was unrecognizable, incomprehensible. He used unfamiliar weapons; he spoke a totally foreign tongue; his behaviour did not conform; his attitude to love and honour were very different from what was familiar. And it was that alien quality that made him destructive and without compassion in the eyes of the community. And Christian had indeed now become destructive and compassionless.

He had taken Guiwenneth because that is what he had dedicated his life to achieving. He no longer loved her, was no longer strongly under the effect of her, but he had taken her. What had he said? 'I care about the having of her. I have hunted too far, too long, to worry about the finer aspects of love.'

The story that Kushar had told was fascinating, for there were so many ingredients I could recognize: the girl made from the wild, nature sent to subdue the unnatural; the symbol of the oak leaf, the talisman which I still wore; the creator of the girl reluctant to part with her; the Outsider himself terrified of one thing only, the spirit of the boar, Urshacam: the Urscumug! And his willingness to accept the tribute of cattle, wine and girl and return to his 'own strange realm', as Christian was now making for the very heart of Ryhope Wood.

What had happened in the tale afterwards, I wondered, and perhaps, I would never know. The girl, the life-speaker, seemed attuned only to the folk memories of her people; events, stories, passed down by word of mouth, changing, perhaps, with each telling, which is why they insisted on the strange rule of silence during the recounting, frightened of the truth slipping away because of the responses of the listeners.

Clearly, much truth had already gone from the story. Heads that talked, girls made from wild flowers and dung . . . perhaps all that had happened was that a band of warriors from another culture had threatened the community at Avebury and had been appeased with cattle, wine and marriage to one of the daughters of a minor chief. But the myth of the Outsider was still terrifying, and the sheer anxiety of encompassing the unknown was a persistent and deep-rooted concern.

'I'm hunting *uth guerig*,' I said, and Kushar shrugged.

'Of course. It will be a long and difficult pursuit.'

'How long ago did he kill the girl?'

'Two days. But perhaps it was not the Outsider himself. His warriors guard his retreat through the wildwoods, to *Lavondyss*. *Uth guerig* himself may be a week or more ahead of you.'

'What is *Lavondyss*?'

'The realm beyond the fire. The place where the spirits of men are not tied to the seasons.'

'Do the *shamiga* know of the boar-like beast? The Urscumug?'

Kushar shivered, wrapping her thin arms around her body. 'The beast is close. Two days ago it was heard in the stag glen, near to the broch.'

Two days ago the Urscumug had been in the area! That almost certainly meant that Christian had been close by as well. Whatever he was doing, wherever he was going, he was *not* as far ahead of me as I'd thought.

'The Urshacam,' she went on, 'was the first Outsider. It walked the great valleys of ice; it watched the tall trees sprout from the barren ground; it guarded the woodlands against our people, and the people before us, and the people who came to the land after us. It is an ever-living beast. It draws nourishment from the earth and sun. It was once a man, and with others was sent to live in exile in the ice valleys of this land. Magic had changed them all to the appearance of beasts. Magic made them ever-living. Many of my people have died because the Urshacam and his kin were angry.'

I stared at Kushar for a moment, amazed by what she was saying. The end of the Ice Age had been seven or eight thousand years before the time of her own people (which I took to be an early Bronze Age culture that had settled in Wessex). And yet she knew of the ice, and of the retreat of the ice . . . Was it possible that the stories could survive that long? Tales of the glaciers, and the new forests, and the advance of human societies northwards across the marshes and the frozen hills?

The Urscumug. The first Outsider. What had my father written in his journal? *I am anxious to find the primary image . . . I suspect that the legend of the Urscumug was powerful enough to carry through all the Neolithic and on into the second millennium* BC, *perhaps even later. Wynne-Jones thinks the Urscumug may pre-date even the Neolithic.*

The trouble with the *shamiga* was that their life-speaker could not spin tales to order. During my father's contact with them, references to *Urshacam* had not occurred. But clearly the primary mythago, the first of the legendary characters that had so fascinated my father, came from the Ice Age itself. It had been created in the minds of the flint-workers and hunter-gatherers of that cold time, as they struggled to keep the forests back, following the retreating cold northwards, settling the fertile vales and dales that were so gradually exposed over the generations-long spring.

Then, without another word, Kushar slipped away from me, and the two torches were extinguished. It was late, and the *shamiga* had all gone to their low huts, although a few of them had dragged hides to the fireside and were sleeping there. Keeton and I erected our tiny tent and crawled in.

During the night an owl cried loudly, an irritating, haunting call. The river was an endless sound, breaking and splashing over the stepping stones which the *shamiga* guarded.

In the morning they were gone. Their huts were deserted.

A dog, or a jackal, had worried at the grave of the two youngsters. The fire still smouldered.

'Where the hell are they?' Keeton murmured, as we stood by the river and stretched, after splashing our faces. They had left us several strips of meat, carefully wrapped in thin linen. It was an odd and unexpected departure. This place seemed to be the community home, and I should have thought that some of them would have remained. The river was high; the stepping stones were below the surface. Keeton stared at them and said, 'I think there are more stones than yesterday.'

I followed his gaze. Was he right? With the river swollen by rains somewhere behind us, were there suddenly three times the number of stones than the day before?

'Pure imagination,' I said, shivering slightly. I shrugged on my pack.

'I'm not so sure,' Keeton said as he followed me along the river shore, deeper into the woodland.

Abandoned Places

Two days after leaving the *shamiga* we found the ruined stone tower, the 'broch', the same structure that Keeton had photographed from his plane. It stood back from the river and was much overgrown. We hovered in the underbrush and stared across the clearing at the imposing grey walls, the window slits, the vine and creeper that were slowly smothering the building.

Keeton said, 'What do you think it is? A watchtower? A folly?'

The tower had no top. Its doorway was square and lined with heavy blocks of stone. The lintel was intricately carved.

'I have no idea.'

We stepped towards the place and noticed at once how the ground was churned and trodden, the clear tracks of horses. There were signs of two fires. And most obvious of all, the deeper, broader marks of some large creature, obliterating the earlier tracks.

'They were here!' I said, my heart racing. At last I had a *tangible* sign of how close to Christian we were. He had been held up. He was two days or less ahead of me.

Inside the broch the smell of ash was still strong, and here the marauding band had again set about the task of repair and reforging of weapons. Light shafted into the gloomy interior from the window slits; the hole where the roof had been was covered with foliage. I could see well enough, however, to notice, the corner place where Guiwenneth had been held with a cloak, perhaps, cast over the rotting straw that was still piled there. Two long, glistening strands of her hair were caught on the rough stone of this barbarian place; I unsnagged them and carefully wound them around my finger. I stared at them in the half-light for a long time, fighting back the sudden despair that threatened to overwhelm me.

'Look at this!' Keeton called suddenly, and I walked back to the low doorway. I stepped out through the tangle of briar and vine and saw that he had hacked away the plant life from the lintel, to expose the carving more clearly.

It was a panoramic scene, of forest and fire. At each side of the lintel, trees were shown, all growing from a single, snake-like root that stretched across the stone. From the root dangled eight blind, human heads. The woodland was shown crowding towards a central fire. Standing in the middle of the fire was a naked human man, his form pecked out in detail, save for the face. The erect phallus was disproportionately large; the figure's arms were held above the head, grasping a sword and a shield.

'Hercules,' ventured Keeton. 'Like the chalk giant at Cerne Abbas. You know, that hillside figure.'

It was as good a guess as any.

My first thought about the ruined stone broch was that it had been constructed thousands of years ago and had been consumed by the woodland in much the same way as Oak Lodge was being engulfed. But we had come so *far* into this strange landscape, already many miles further from the edge than was physically possible, so how could the broch have been erected by human hand? There remained the possibility that as the forest expanded so the distortion of time within it expanded . . .

Keeton said the words that I knew to be true: 'The whole building is a mythago. And yet it means nothing to me . . .'

The lost broch. The ruined place of stone, fascinating to the minds of men who lived below steep thatch, inside structures of wicker and mud. There could be no other explanation.

And indeed, the broch marked the outskirts of an eerie and haunting landscape of such legendary, lost buildings.

The forest felt no different, but as we followed animal

paths and natural ridges through the bright undergrowth, so we could see the walls and gardens of these ruined, abandoned structures. We saw an ornately gabled house, its windows empty, its roof half-collapsed. There was a Tudor building of exquisite design, its walls grey-green with mossy growth, its timbers corroded and crumbling. In its garden, statues rose like white marble wraiths, faces peering at us from the tangle of ivy and rose, arms outstretched, fingers pointing.

In one place the wood itself changed subtly, becoming darker, more pungent. The heavy predominance of deciduous trees altered dramatically. Now a sparsely foliaged pine-forest covered the descending slope of the land.

The air felt rarefied, sharp with the odour of the trees. And we came at once upon a tall wooden house, its windows, shuttered, its tiled roof bright. A great wolf lay curled in the glade that surrounded it: a bare garden, not grassy but heavy with pine needles, and dry as a bone. The wolf smelled us and rose to its feet, raising its muzzle and emitting a haunting, terrifying cry.

We retreated into the thin pinewoods and retraced our steps, away from this old Germanic location within the forest.

Sometimes the deciduous woodland thinned and the undergrowth grew too dense for us to move through it, so that we had to skirt the impenetrable tangle, striving to keep our sense of direction. In such expansive thickets we saw corrupted thatch, wicker and daub walls, sometimes the heavy posts or stone pillars of cultures unrecognizable from these remains. We peered into one well-hidden glade and saw canvas-and-hide canopies, the remains of a fire, the piled bones of deer and sheep, and encampment in the dark forest – and from the sharp smell of ash on the air, a place still used.

It was towards the end of that day, however, that we emerged from the wood and confronted the most astonishing and memorable of these mythagos. We had glimpsed it through the thinning trees: high towers, crenellated walls; a dark, brooding stone presence in the near distance.

It was a castle out of the wildest dreams of faerie, a gloomy, overgrown fortress from the time of Knights, when chivalry had been more romantic than cruel. Twelfth century, I thought, or perhaps a century earlier. It made no difference. This was the image of the stronghold from times after the sacking and abandonment of the great Keeps, when many of the castles had fallen into ruin, and some had become lost in the more remote forests of Europe. The land around it was grassy, well-grazed by a small flock of scrawny grey sheep. As we walked from the cover towards the stagnant waters of the moat, so these animals scattered, bleating angrily.

The sun was low and we stepped into the shadow of the great walls, and began a slow tour of the castle. We kept away from the treacherous slope that bordered the moat. High, slitted windows had once given archers a wide view of sieging forces, and when we remembered this we moved back towards the scrub wood. But we neither saw nor heard the signs of any human presence inside the fort.

We stopped and stared at the tallest of the watch towers. From such a prison maidens of myth like Rapunzel had let down their golden hair, a rope for chivalrous knights to climb.

'A painful experience, no doubt,' Keeton reflected, and we laughed and walked on.

Back into the sun, and we came to the gate. The drawbridge was up, but looked rotten and decayed. Keeton wanted to look inside, but I felt a vague apprehension. It was then that I noticed the ropes, hanging from two of the crenellations on the wall. Keeton, simultaneously, saw the signs of a fire on the sheep-grazed bank. We looked around us and sure enough, the grassland was quite churned with hoofprints.

It could only have been Christian. We were still following him. He had preceded us to this castle, and had scaled the walls to plunder the inside.

Or had he?

Floating face down in the moat was a human shape. I became aware of it by stages. It was naked. The dark hair and pale buttocks were greened with slime. A thin patch of pink about the middle of the back, like a pale red algal growth, informed me of the wound that had sent this Hawk to his doom.

I had hardly recovered from the frisson of apprehension that the sight of this dead warrior elicited in me when I heard movement beyond the drawbridge.

'A horse,' Keeton said, and I heard the whickering of such a beast and nodded.

'I suggest we make a strategic withdrawal,' I said.

But Keeton hesitated, staring at the wooden gate.

'Come on, Harry . . .'

'No. Wait . . . I'd like to see inside . . .'

And even as he stepped forward, scanning the arrow slits above the gate, there came the sound of wood creaking, and ropes singing with strain. The huge drawbridge came crashing down. It struck the near bank just inches from Keeton's startled figure, and the jarring shock in the earth made me bite my tongue.

'Christ!' was all Keeton said, and backed towards me, fumbling for the pistol in his waist pocket. A figure on horseback was revealed in the high gateway. It kicked its mount forward, and lowered its short, blue-pennanted lance.

We turned and ran for the woodland. The steed galloped after us, hooves loud on the hard ground. The Knight cried out at us, his voice angry, his words familiar yet meaningless, with a suggestion of French. I had had time to take in only very little about him. He was fair-haired and thinly-bearded, and wore a dark band around his head, although a heavy steel helmet was slung on the back of his saddle. He was clad in a mail shirt and dark leather breeches. The horse was black with three white hooves –

Three white for a death! Guiwenneth's rhyme came back to me with numbing force.

– and was decorated in the simplest of red trappings: on the reins, across its neck, with a patterned saddlecloth hanging below its belly.

The horse snorted behind us, thumping heavily across the turf, nearer with every stride. The Knight kicked and urged it faster. His mail shirt rattled, and the bright helmet struck noisily against some metal part of his saddle. Glancing back as we ran for cover, I could see how he leaned slightly to the left, the lance held low, ready to be jerked up as it struck at our bodies.

But we plunged into the cool undergrowth seconds before the lance was struck angrily against a towering blackthorn. He kicked his steed into the woodland, leaning low across the beast's withers, and holding the lance carefully against the flank. Keeton and I circled him, hugging bush and trunk, trying to avoid his eyes.

After a moment or two he turned and went out into the dusk light again, galloped up and down the length of the scrub for a few minutes, and then dismounted.

Now I realized how truly huge this man was, at least six and a half feet tall. He swung his double-edged sword and hacked his way through the thorn, shouting all the time in his quasi-French.

'Why is he so damned angry?' Keeton whispered from a few feet away, and the words were overheard. The Knight glanced towards us, saw us, and began to run in our direction; sunlight caught in glinting flashes on his mail shirt.

Then there was a shot. Not from Keeton. It was a strange, muffled sound, and the moist, mossy air was suddenly acrid with the smell of sulphur. The Knight was flung back, but didn't fall. He stared in astonishment to our right, holding the shoulder where the ball had made its glancing strike. I looked too. The shadowy form of the cavalier who had shot at me by the mill-pond could just be glimpsed. He was frantically re-priming his heavy match-lock rifle.

'It can't be the same man,' I said aloud, but the mythago

turned towards me and smiled, and even if it was a different genesis, it was the same form which I had previously encountered.

The Knight walked out of the bosk and called his horse. He began to strip the trappings from the animal. With a slap of his broad blade on its hindquarters, he gave the horse its freedom.

The cavalier had vanished into the gloom. Once before he had tried to kill me. Now he had saved me from a potentially murderous attack. Was he following me?

As the uncanny thought occurred to me, Keeton drew my attention to the part of the encroaching woodland from which we had first seen the castle. A figure stood there, gleaming greenly in the fading light. Its face was ghastly and drawn, but it was armoured, and was watching us. It had probably been following us since our encounter at the Stone Falls.

Unnerved by this third apparition, Keeton led the way through the greenwood, following the course we had set ourselves before. We were soon out of sight of the great fortress, and from behind there came no obvious sound of pursuit.

We found the road on the fourth day after leaving the *shamiga*. Keeton and I had separated, forcing our way through the tangled forest, seeking a boar run, or stag track, anything to make the going easier. The river was away to our left, dropping into a shallow gorge, where the bank was unmanageable.

Keeton's cry did not startle me because it was not anguished. I cut through the thorn and bramble towards him, realizing at once that he was in a sort of clearing.

I emerged from the underbrush on to an overgrown and decaying brick roadway, about fifteen feet wide and with gutters on either side. The trees formed a sort of arch across it, a tunnel of foliage, through which sunlight filtered.

'Good God,' I said, and Keeton, standing in the middle of

this unlikely track, agreed with me. He had shrugged off his pack, and was resting, hands on hips.

'Roman, I think,' he said. Another guess, and in this case a good one.

We followed the road for a few minutes, glad of the freedom of movement after so many hours picking our way through the forest. Around us, birds sang shrilly, feeding, no doubt, on the flying insects that swarmed in the clear air.

Keeton was inclined to think of the road as a real structure, overtaken by woodland, but we were surely too deep for that to have been the case.

'Then what's the purpose of it? I don't have fantasies about lost roads, lost tracks.'

But that wasn't the way it worked. At one time, a mysterious road, leading beyond the known land, might have been a strong myth image; over the centuries it degenerated, but I could remember my grandparents talking about 'fairy tracks' that could only be seen on certain nights.

After a few hundred yards, Keeton stopped and indicated the bizarre totems that had been placed on each side of the crumbling road. They had been half-hidden in the underbrush, and I cleared the leaves from one, disturbed by the sight which greeted me: a decaying human head, its jaw stretched open and an animal's long-bone rammed through the mouth. It had been impaled upon three sharpened stakes of wood. Across the road Keeton was holding his nose against the stink of decay. 'This one's a woman,' he said. 'I get the feeling we're being warned.'

Warned or not, we continued to walk. It may have been imagination, but a hush enveloped the enclosing trees. There was movement in the branches, but no song.

We noticed other totems. They were tied to the low branches, sometimes strung on bushes. They were in the form of rag creatures, little bags of coloured cloth, with the crude representations of limbs drawn upon them. Some had been impaled with bones and nails, and the whole unnerving presence of the offerings was suggestive of witchcraft.

We passed below a brick archway which spanned the road, and scrambled over the dead tree that had fallen beyond it. We found we had come into a cleared space, a ruined garden, pillars and statues rising from a tangle of weeds, wild flowers and a bramble thorn gone wild. Ahead of us was a villa of clear Roman design.

The red tiled roof had partly fallen in. The walls, once white, were dulled by time and the elements. The entrance door was open and we stepped into the cold, eerie place. Some of the mosaic and marble flooring was intact. The mosaics were exquisite, showing animals, hunters, scenes of country life, and gods. We stepped carefully across them. Much of the floor space had already collapsed into the hypocaust.

We toured the villa, exploring the bath-house, with its three, deep pools, still lined with marble. In two of the rooms the walls were painted, and the features of an elderly Roman couple gazed at us, serene and perfectly groomed . . . the only blemishes were the savage sword cuts that had been made across the throats of each, hacking into the wall itself.

In the main room, on the marble floor, there were the signs of several fires, and the charred, chewed bones of animals had been flung into a waste pit in the corner. But the fires were cold, long dead.

We decided to stay here for the night, a change from pitching the small tent in the cramped and lumpy spaces between insect-infested trees. We were both on edge in the ruined villa, aware that we were spending the night in the product of fear, or hope, of some other age.

In its way, the villa was the equivalent of the broch, and of the great castle whose walls we had skirted a couple of days before. It was a place of mystery, lost and no doubt romanced about. But to which race did it belong? Was it the end of the Roman dream, the villa where the last Romans lived? The legions had pulled out of Britain in the early fifth century, leaving thousands of their people vulnerable to attack by the invading Anglo-Saxons. Was this villa linked with a Romano-British myth of survival? Or was it a Saxon dream, the villa where gold might be buried, or where the ghosts of the legions remained? A place of quest, or of fear? In Keeton and myself it inspired only fear.

We built a small fire, from wood that we found in the remains of the heating system. As darkness came down, so the smell of our fire, or perhaps the smell of food, attracted visitors.

I heard it first, a stealthy movement in the bath-house, followed by the whispered sound of a warning. Then there was silence. Keeton rose to his feet and drew his revolver. I walked to the cold passage that led from our room to the bath area, and used my small torch to expose the intruders.

They were startled, but not frightened, and stared at me beyond the circle of light, shielding their eyes slightly. The man was tall and heavily built. The woman, tall as well, carried a small bundle of cloth in her arms. The boy who was with them stood motionless and blank faced.

The man spoke to me. It sounded like German. I noticed how he kept his left hand resting on the pommel of a long, sheathed sword. Then the woman smiled and spoke too, and the tension evaporated for the moment.

I led them back to the enclosed room. Keeton made up the fire and began to spit-cook some more of the meat we carried. Our guests crouched across the fire from us, looking at the food, at the room, at Keeton and myself.

They were obviously Saxons. The man's clothing was heavy and woollen, and he used leather straps to tie his leggings and baggy shirt. He wore a great fur topcoat. His hair, long and blond, had been tied into two braids at the front. The woman was also fair-haired, and wore a loose, check-patterned tunic, tied at the waist. The boy was a miniature version of the man, but sat in silence, staring at the fire.

When they had eaten they expressed gratitude, and then introduced themselves: the man was Ealdwulf, the woman Egwearda, the boy Hurthig. They were afraid of the villa, that much was clear. But they were puzzled by us. With gestures I tried to explain that we were exploring the woodlands, but for some minutes the message failed to penetrate. Egwearda stared at me, frowning, her face quite pale, quite lovely, despite the lines of tension and hardship that were etched around her eyes.

All at once she said something – the word sounded like *Cunnasman* – and Ealdwulf gasped, comprehension brightening his rugged face.

He asked me a question, repeating the word. I shrugged, not understanding.

He said another word, or words. *Elchempa*. He pointed at me. He repeated *Cunnasman*. He used his hand to indicate *following*. He was asking me if I was following someone, and I nodded vigorously.

'Yes,' I said, and added, 'Ja!'

'Cunnasman,' Egwearda breathed, and shifted position so she could reach across the fire and touch my hand.

'There's something odd about you,' Keeton said. 'To these people, at least. And to the *shamiga*.'

The woman had reached for her bundle. Little Hurthig whimpered and squirmed away, looking anxiously as the cloths were unfolded. She had placed the bundle by the fire, and I was discomfited by what the flickering light revealed to me.

What Egwearda had been carrying, as if it were a child, was the mummified hand and arm of a man, severed just below the elbow. The fingers were long and powerful; on the middle finger was a bright red stone. In the same parcel was the broken blade of a steel dagger, its jewelled haft just a fragment of the decorative weapon it had once been.

'Aelfric,' she said softly, and laid her own hand gently on the dead limb. The man, Ealdwulf, did the same. And then Egwearda covered the gruesome relic. The boy made a sound, and at that moment I realized that he was mute. He was quite deaf. His eyes shone, though, with an awareness that was quite uncanny.

Who were they?

I sat there and stared at them. Who were they? From what historical period, I wondered. They were almost certainly from the fifth century after Christ, the early decades of the Germanic infiltrations into Britain. How else could they be associated with a Roman villa? By the sixth century, woodland and earth-slip had covered most of the Roman remains of this sort.

What they represented I couldn't imagine, but at some time a tale had been told of the strange family, the mute son, the husband and wife, carrying the precious relic of a King, or a warrior, seeking for something, seeking for a resolution to their tale.

I could think of no story of Aelfric. The legend had been lost from the written accounts; in time, it had been lost from the oral traditions. Thereafter it had remained only as an unconscious memory.

The Saxons may have meant nothing to me, but as Keeton had pointed out, I certainly meant something to them. It was as if . . . as if they *knew* me, or at least knew of me.

Ealdwulf was talking to me, scratching patterns on the marble. After a while I began to grasp that he was drawing a map, and I gave him paper and a pencil from the small supply I carried. Now I could see what he was representing. He marked the villa and the road, and the distant curving river – the sticklebrook – now a gigantic flow, cutting through the forestlands. It seemed that ahead of us was a gorge, steep-sided and wooded, with the river curling through its narrow valley bottom.

Ealdwulf said the word, '*Freya!*' and indicated that I should go up the river. He repeated the word, looking for signs of understanding. He said, 'Drichtan! Freya!'

I shrugged to indicate complete bafflement, and Ealdwulf gasped with exasperation and looked at Egwearda.

'Freya!' said the woman. She made funny motions with her hands. 'Drichtan.'

'I'm sorry. It's all Saxon to me.'

'Wiccan,' she said, and searched for more ways to express the concept, but then shrugged and gave up.

I asked what was across the gorge. When Ealdwulf understood the question he drew flames, pointed to our own small fire, and indicated a fire of gigantic proportions. He also seemed to be very much against my going there.

'Elchempa,' he said, stabbing the fire. He watched me. He stabbed at the flames again. 'Feor buend! Elchempa!' He shook his head. Then he tapped me on the chest. 'Cunnasman. Freya. Her. *Her!*' He was touching the map where it showed the river, some way from the nearest point of crossing of the gorge.

'I think,' said Keeton softly, 'I think he's saying . . . *kinsman.*'

'Kinsman?'

'Cunnasman. Kinsman.' Keeton looked at me. 'It's a possibility.'

'And *Elchempa?* Outsider, I suppose.'

'El. Alien. Yes. I think that could be right. Your brother is heading towards the fire, but Ealdwulf wants *you* to go up the river and find the *Freya.*'

'Whatever that is . . .'

'Egwearda referred to *wiccan,*' Keeton said. 'That could be witch. Or wise one. It probably doesn't mean quite what they intend . . .'

With some difficulty I asked Ealdwulf about *Elchempa,* and his dramatic gestures of killing, burning and dismembering left me in no doubt that we were talking of Christian. He had pillaged his way through the forest, and was known and feared throughout.

But now Ealdwulf seemed to have a new hope. And I was that hope. Little Kushar's words came back to me:

Now I know you. But no harm has been done. The story has not been changed. I did not recognize you.

Keeton said, 'They've been waiting for you. They know you.'

'How is that possible?'

'Word spread from the *shamiga*, perhaps. Perhaps Christian himself has talked about you.'

'The important thing is, they know I'm here. But why the relief? Do they think I can control Christian?' I touched my neck where the scars of the rope were rough and still sensitive. 'They're wrong if they do.'

'Then why are you following him?' Keeton asked quietly.

And I said, without thinking, 'To kill him and release Guiwenneth.'

Keeton laughed. 'I think that might do the trick.'

I was tired, but the towering presence of the early Saxon unnerved me. Nevertheless, Ealdwulf was adamant that Keeton and I should sleep. He gestured and repeated the word *slaip!* which was clear enough.

'Slaip! Ich willa where d'yon!'

'I'll guard you,' Keeton said with a grin. 'It's easy once you get the rhythm.'

Egwearda came around to us and spread out her cloak, curling up safely beside us. Ealdwulf walked to the open doorway and stepped out into the night. He drew his long-sword and drove it into the ground, dropping to a crouch behind it, his knees to either side of the bright blade.

In this position he guarded us through the night that remained. In the morning his beard and clothes were dew-drenched. When he heard me stir he rose from his crouch and grinned, coming back into the room and brushing the wetness from his body. He reached for my sword and drew it from the leather scabbard. He frowned as he held the Celtic toy before his eyes, and compared it with his own hardened steel blade. My sword was curved and tapered, and only half the length of Ealdwulf's weapon. He shook his head in doubt, but then struck each blade against the other and seemed to change his mind. He weighed and hefted Magidion's gift to me, struck through the air with it twice, and then nodded approval.

Repeating his guttural advice to me that I should follow the river and forget all notion of pursuing the Outsider, he and Egwearda departed. Their mute, miserable son walked ahead of them, brushing his hand through the damp ferns that grew in abundance in the deserted garden.

Keeton and I breakfasted, which is to say we forced down a handful of oats, moistened with water. Somehow this simple ritual, the putting aside of time for a moment's eating and contemplation, made a cheering start to the day.

We retraced our steps along the Roman road, then went back into the woodland where there seemed to be a natural causeway through the tight brush. Quite where we would come out I had no idea, although if the sticklebrook continued to curve as Ealdwulf's map had indicated, then we would intersect it again.

We had seen no trace of Christian for a day or more, and had totally lost his tracks. My only hope, now, was to find the place at which he had crossed the river. To that end, Keeton and I would have to part company for a while, exploring the sticklebrook in both directions.

Keeton said, 'You'll not be taking the Saxon's advice, then?'

'It's Guiwenneth I want, not the blessing of some superstitious pagan. I'm sure he meant well, but I can't afford to let Christian get that far ahead . . .'

In my mind was my father's diary . . .

. . . *away for ninety days, though only a fortnight has passed at Oak Lodge . . .*

And Christian, always Christian, the shock of the sight of him as an ageing man.

I would have liked to have known you during the last fifteen years.

And he had only been gone twelve months or so!

Each day that Christian gained on me might have been a week, or a month. Perhaps, at the centre of the wildwoods, beyond the fire – the heart of the realm, which Kushar had called *Lavondyss* – was a place where time had no meaning at all. When my brother crossed that line he would go too far from me, into a realm as alien to me as London would have been to Kushar herself. And all hope of finding him would be gone.

The thought thrilled me. It also terrified me. It had surfaced unbidden, as if planted and waiting its time to be known. And now I remembered Kushar's description of *Lavondyss*:

The place where the spirits of men are not tied to the seasons.

As the image of Christian drifting into time's endless realm sent a cold chill of anguish through me. I knew that I was right.

There was not an hour to be lost, not a moment to be wasted . . .

Necromancer

Shortly after our departure from the villa we crossed the border between two zones of woodland. The land cleared and we entered a wide, bright glade. The long grass was sticky with dew and matted with spider's webs, which glistened and quivered in the breeze.

In the middle of the glade stood an imposing tree, a horse-chestnut, its swell of foliage broad and dense, reaching close to the ground.

On the far side, however, the tree had lost is magnificence in a shocking way. It was blighted, and grotesquely parasitized. Its foliage was brown and rotting, and great ropes of creeper and sucking plant parasites, like a net of tendrils, had reached across the glade from the wood and were entangled with the branches.

At times the tree quivered and great ripples of writhing activity coursed down the sucker net, back to the tree line. The very ground itself was a mess of roots and bindweed, and strange sticky protrusions that reached inches into the air and waved, as if searching for prey.

Horse-chestnut was a recent addition to the British landscape, only a few hundred years a native. Keeton felt that we had moved beyond the mediaeval wood, now, and were stepping into a more primitive forest. Indeed, he soon pointed out the greater preponderance of hazel and elm, with oak and ash, and the towering beech standards, beginning to be less in evidence.

There was a new quality to this forest, a darker, heavier feel. The smell was more rank and cloying, like rotting leaves and dung. The sound of bird life was more muted. The foliage quivered in breezes that we could not feel. The underwood about us was far gloomier, and the sunlight that pierced the dense leaf cover did so in startlingly brilliant shafts of yellow, a hazy light that picked out dripping leaves, and shining bark, giving me the impression that all around us there were silent figures, watching.

Everywhere we looked we could see the rotting hulks of trees. Some were still standing, held by their neighbours, but most had crashed at angles through the wood, and were now overgrown with vine and moss, and crawling with insect life.

We remained trapped in this endless twilight for hours.

At one point it began to rain. The broken light about us faded altogether so that we trudged through the saturated underbrush in an appalling gloom. When the rain stopped the trees continued to drip uncomfortably, though the patchy light returned.

We had heard the sound of the river for some time without really being aware of it. Suddenly Keeton, who was taking the lead, stopped and turned back to me, frowning. 'Hear that?'

Now I noticed the distant sound of the sticklebrook. The rushing of the water had an odd quality to it, as if it echoed and came from very far away.

'The river,' I said, and Keeton shook his head irritably.

'No. Not the river . . . the voices.'

I approached him and we stood for a few further seconds in silence.

And there it was! The sound of a man's voice, coming to us with that same echoing quality, followed by the whickering complaint of a horse and the distant rumble and clatter of rocks falling from a slope.

'Christian!' I cried, and pushed past Keeton at a run. He stumbled after me, and we surged through the brush, veering between the crowded trees, and using our staffs to strike violently at the tangles of thorn that blocked our way.

I saw light ahead of me and the woodland began to thin. It was a hazy, green light, difficult to distinguish. I raced on, my pack making movement awkward. I burst out of the light wood and only a frantic leap to my right, clutching desperately at the gnarled root of a tree, stopped me from plummeting head-first over the ravine that was suddenly revealed there.

Keeton came running after me. I hauled myself up and reached for him, dragging him to a stop just before he too realized that the ground had gone, dropping away in an almost sheer cliff to the sparkling band of the river, half a mile below.

We struggled back to safety, and then edged closer to the precipice. There was certainly no path down here. The opposite cliff was less dramatically sheer, and was quite heavily wooded. The trees, sparse forms of whitebeam and oak, clung desperately to every crevice and ledge. A denser woodland resumed at the cliff's top.

Again I heard the distant, hollow sound of a voice. This time as I searched the far side of the gorge I began to detect movement. Rocks slipped and fell through the clinging scrub, plunging down to the river below.

And a man emerged, leading a straining and rearing horse, tugging the beast up what seemed to be an almost impossibly narrow pathway.

Behind the horse came other figures, armour and leathers shining. They were pushing and pulling at several reluctant pack-animals. A cart was being drawn slowly up the same ledge, and it slipped and got stuck for a few seconds as the wheel went off the path. There was a flurry of activity, and much shouting and ordering.

As I watched, I grew aware that this straggling column of warriors stretched a long way up the cliff. Suddenly the bulky, cloaked form of Christian was there, leading a horse with black trappings! The shape that was slumped over the animal's withers seemed to be female. Sunlight glanced off red hair, or was that just the desperate deception of my imagination?

Before I could reflect upon the wisdom of the act, I had bellowed Christian's name across the gulf, and the whole

233

column stopped and stared at me as the sound echoed and reverberated away to nothing. Keeton sucked in his breath, in a gesture of frustration.

'*Now* you've done it,' he whispered.

'I want him to know I'm following,' I retorted, but felt embarrassed at having lost the element of surprise. 'There's *got* to be a path down,' I said, and began to move through the undergrowth parallel with the cliff top.

Keeton restrained me for a moment, then pointed across the ravine. Four or five shapes were slipping back along the steep ledge, dropping swiftly through the trees.

'Hawks,' Keeton said. 'I made six. Six, I think. Yes, there! Look.'

The small band were heading down the slope, weapons held loosely as they grabbed for support and steadied themselves for the treacherous slide back to the river.

This time Keeton followed me, and we raced through the wood at the cliff edge, wary for loose rock or hidden roots that might have tripped us.

Where was the path?

My frustration grew as the minutes passed and the Hawks dropped lower, and out of sight. They would be at the river within the hour, and could be there waiting for us. We *had* to be there first.

I was so absorbed with searching for signs of the path which my brother had used that for a few seconds I failed to notice the quivering black shape ahead of me.

It rose abruptly and dramatically to its feet, exhaling breath in a powerful and vibrant gust, a deep hissing sound that deafened as well as assailed with its stink. Keeton ran into me, then cried out and staggered back.

The Urscumug swayed from side to side, its mouth working, the distorted white features of the man I had so feared writhing and grinning upon its tusked features. The great spear it held seemed to have been made from the entire trunk of a tree.

Keeton vanished into the underbrush and I stepped quietly

after him. For a moment it seemed that the great boar-beast hadn't really seen us, but now it grew aware of us by sound, and began to chase. It wove between the trees, moving in that same startling fashion as before, fast and determined. Keeton raced in one direction and I fled in another. The Urscumug stopped, cocked its head and listened. Its chest rose and fell, the sharp hair on its body bristling, the crown-of-thorn branches that it wore rustling as it turned this way and that. In the subdued light its tusks were high, bright points. It reached out and snapped the branch from a tree, which it used to smash at the undergrowth, still listening.

Then it turned and walked in its stooped, swaying manner, back to the ravine. There it stood, staring across the gorge at Christian's train of horse and warrior. It flung the branch into the chasm, then again looked back towards me, and cocked its head.

I swear it seemed to follow my movements as I stealthily crept back to the place it had been guarding. Perhaps it was ill, or wounded. I almost cried out with shock when Keeton's hand touched my shoulder. Indicating total silence he pointed to the top of the narrow pathway that began to lead down the cliff.

Ever watchful, we began to walk down that track. The last I saw of my father's mythago was its towering black form, swaying slightly as it stared into the distance, its nostrils quivering, its breathing a quiet, calm, contemplative sound.

No journey was ever more difficult, or more terrifying, than that climb down to the river valley. I lost count of the number of times that I lost my grip, slipped and went skidding down the sharp-stoned, tangle-rooted ledge, avoiding oblivion only by reflex grasping and the occasional helping hand from Keeton. I returned the favour to him just as often. We took to descending with our hands almost touching, ready for a frantic grab.

Horse manure, wheel-tracks, and the sign of rope supports on the trunks of the wind-twisted trees told of Christian's equally perilous passage, hours or perhaps a day or so before.

We could no longer see the Hawks who were coming to confront us. When we stopped and listened to the heavy silence we could hear only the chatter of birds, though once or twice we heard voices from very far away, Christian and the main band, now nearly on to the plateau of the inner realm.

For over an hour we descended. At last the ledge widened, becoming more of a natural path, leading down towards the great green swathe of woodland, a carpet of foliage through which we could see the occasional gleam of the great river, and above which the grey walls of the gorge were sinister and concealing.

On level ground at last there was a sinister hush, a sense of watching and being watched. The undergrowth was sparse. The river surged past, a hundred yards or so away, invisible through the heavy shade of the silent wood.

'They're here already,' Keeton whispered. He was holding his Smith and Wesson. He crouched behind a heavy stand of gorse and peered towards the river.

I ran to the nearest tree and Keeton followed, overtaking me and approaching the river. A bird fluttered noisily above us. To our right an animal, perhaps a small deer, shifted restlessly in a thicket. I could see the long line of its back and hear the slight snorting of its breathing.

By dint of stealth, and a darting motion from tree to tree, we came to the dry, slightly sandy shore of the river, where the snaking roots of hazel and elm formed a series of pits and wells, into which we slipped for cover. The river here was about forty yards wide, deep and swirling. Its centre was bright, but the canopy of the trees along its bank threw much of it into shade. And now that it was late afternoon, the light was going and the far bank was darkening. It looked a threatening place.

Perhaps the Hawks had not arrived yet after all. Or were they watching us from the gloom of the far side?

We had to get across the river. Keeton was nervous about attempting that crossing now. We should wait until dawn, he said. For the long night ahead, one of us would watch and one would sleep. The Hawks *had* to be here somewhere, and were simply waiting for the best moment to attack.

I agreed with him. For the first time I was glad that he had brought the pistol. The gun should at least give us a tactical advantage, a chance to send them scattering while we completed our crossing.

I had entertained these idle thoughts for no more than ten minutes when they came at us. I was crouched by the river, half in the lee of an elmwood trunk, searching the shadows across the water for a sign of movement. Keeton rose to his feet and cautiously stepped to the water's edge. I heard his gasping cry and then the *whoosh* of an arrow, which splashed distantly in the river. Keeton began to run.

They were *already* on our side of the sticklebrook, and they came at us suddenly and swiftly, running and leaping in a zig-zagging, wild fashion. Two carried bows, and a second arrow clattered off the tree next to me, its shaft broken. Following Keeton, I ran as fast as I could. I was thrown forward by a heavy thump in my back, and knew without looking that my haversack had saved my life.

Then there was a single shot and a terrible scream. I glanced back and one of the Hawks was motionless, hands to face, blood gouting from between his fingers. His compatriots scattered sideways, and this unfortunate warrior collapsed to knee and belly, quite dead.

Keeton had found a deeper depression in the ground, with a screen of tight gorse, and a fence of tree root between us and the Hawks. Arrows skimmed above our heads, one snagging my ankle as it rebounded from a branch. It was a shallow but incredibly painful cut.

Then Harry Keeton did something very foolish. He stood up and aimed very deliberately at the most active of the attackers. Simultaneous with the discharge of the pistol, a sling-stone knocked the weapon from his hand, sending it skidding yards away across the dry ground. Keeton ducked back into cover, holding his hand, nursing the bruised and cut finger.

Christian's guardians came at us then, like five hounds from hell, whooping and howling: lithe, near-nude shapes, protected by the most basic of leather armour. Only the gleaming hawk masks were of metal – and the short, glinting blades they held.

Keeton and I ran from these warriors like deer from a fire. We were fleet, despite our packs and heavy protective clothing. The imagined pain of a knife drawn across our throats gave us great incentive to find the energy for retreat.

What appalled me most, as I veered from cover to cover, was how unprepared we had been. For all our talk, for all my feeling of strength, when it came down to it we were totally vulnerable, not even a .38 calibre pistol serving us well against the simple skills of trained soldiers. We were children in the woods, naïve kids playing at survival.

If I *had* been called upon to confront Christian, he would have made mincemeat of me. To go against him with a stone-bladed spear, a Celtic blade, and a lot of anger would have been scarcely more effective than shouting at him.

The ground dropped away beneath me, and Keeton dragged me down into yet another 'shell-hole'. I turned and raised my spear, and watched as one of the Hawks came jumping towards us.

What happened next was quite odd.

The warrior stopped, and in every sinuous, tense movement of his body I could see that he was suddenly frightened, even though the yellow bird-mask gave nothing away. He backed away from us, and I became aware of the sudden, chill wind that blew around us.

The air became dark, all light draining from the riverside as if a sudden thunderous black cloud had come across the sun. The trees about me began to whip and strain, branches creaked, leafy twigs trembled and rustled in a shiver of disturbance. Something misty and wraithlike curled around the leading Hawk. He screamed and ran back towards his companions.

Dust rose from the ground in great columns. The waters of the river spouted as if great marine beasts fought there. The trees around us became almost frantically shaken, shedding branches noisily. The air was freezing cold, and the ghastly, grinning shapes of elementals darted and flowed through an eerie mist which hovered, refusing to be dispersed by the wind.

Keeton was terrified. Crystals of ice formed on his eyebrows and the tip of his nose. He shivered violently, huddling deeper into his motorcycle leathers. I shivered too, my breath frosting, and eyes smarting with ice. The trees became white, laced with a fine fall of snow. Strange laughter, and the banshee shrieking of violent mind-forms, cut this part of the woodland off from all that was natural.

Through chattering teeth Harry Keeton stammered, 'What the devil is it?'

'A friend,' I said, and reached out reassuringly.

The *Freya* had come to me after all.

Keeton glanced at me through frosted lids, wiping a hand across his face. Around us the whole landscape was white with ice and snow. Tall, flowing shapes ran silently through the air, some coming towards us, peering at us with sharp faces and narrow eyes full of mischief. Others were simply swirls of size and sombre shape that caused the air to *thud* and *bang* as they passed, like some weird implosion.

The Hawks ran screaming. I saw one lifted from his feet and crushed double, then twisted and crushed further until a sticky exudate dripped from his suspended corpse . . . a corpse that hovered in the air, held by invisible hands. The ragged, splintered remains were tossed into the river and vanished below the crystal surface. Another Hawk was sent squirming and struggling to his doom on the far side of the water, impaled on a jagged stump of branch. What happened to the others I couldn't tell, but the screaming went on for some minutes, and the poltergeist activity remained as intense as ever.

Eventually there was silence. The air warmed, the sheen of white vanished, and Keeton and I rubbed our frozen hands vigorously. Several tall, wraithlike forms approached us, tenuous mist-shapes, vaguely human. They hovered above us, peering down, hair flowing in eerie slow motion. Their hands trembled, long tapered fingers pointing, grasping. The glow of their eyes was focused upon us, gleaming wells of awareness above wide, grinning mouths. Keeton watched these ghosts, aghast and terrified. One of them reached down and pinched his nose, and he whimpered with fear, causing the elementals to laugh in a cackling way. It sounded wrong, a sound of malice, a woodland echo that did not issue from their lips, but seemed to bray from all around us.

The light came then, the golden, diffuse light which marked the solemn arrival of the boat. The elementals surrounding us shivered and quavered, still making sounds of laughter. Those that were naked seemed to dissolve into smoke, others drifted away from us, hugging the shadowy places, the nooks and crevices of branch and root, bright eyes still fixed upon us.

Keeton gasped as he saw the boat. I watched, feeling greatly relieved. For the first time since the beginning of this journey I thought of the silver oak leaf amulet, and reached into my saturated shirt to draw the medallion out, and hold it towards the man who watched us from the vessel.

The boat seemed far more at home on this wide stretch of water than on the impossibly narrow sticklebrook near to the Lodge. Its sail was slack. It drifted out of the gloom and the tall, cloaked man leapt ashore, tying a mooring rope to a stump of root. The light came from a glowing torch on the boat's prow. It had been an illusion that he himself shone. He no longer wore the elaborately crested helmet, and as Keeton and I watched he flung off his cloak, reached for the bright firebrand and drove the shaft into the river bank, stepping past it so that its aura radiated around his massive frame.

He came over to us and leaned down to lift us to our feet.

'Sorthalan!' he said loudly, and repeated the word, this time striking his chest with his fist. 'Sorthalan!'

He reached to the amulet around my neck, touched it and smiled through his thick beard. What he said then, in a flowing tongue reminiscent of Kushar's language, meant nothing to me. And yet I felt again that what was being said was: *I have been waiting for you.*

An hour after dusk the Urscumug came down from the high cliff, to cross the water in pursuit of Christian. Stealthy movement in the woodland was the first sign of its approach, and Sorthalan extinguished the torch. There was a half-full moon, high above the river, and the clear night allowed the first stars to show through. It must have been about nine o'clock, the dusk made darker by the canopy.

The Urscumug appeared through the trees, walking slowly, making a strange snuffling sound in the still evening. We watched from cover as the great boar-shape stopped at the water's edge and stooped to pick up the limp, crushed body of one of the Hawks. It used its tusks to rend open the body and crouched, in a startlingly human way, as it sucked the soft innards of the dead mythago. The cadaver was flung into the river, and the Urscumug, growling deeply, looked along the shore. For a long moment its gleaming gaze rested upon us, but it surely could have seen nothing in the gloom.

Yet the white mask of the human face seemed to glow in the moonlight, and I swear the lips were parting in an unheard communication, as if the spirit of my father were speaking silently, and smiling as he spoke.

Then the beast rose from its haunches and waded into the water, raising its huge arms to shoulder level, holding the gnarled spear slightly above its head. The thorn antlers it wore snagged in the trees on the far side, but apart from a grumble or two there was no further sound from the Urscumug, save that an hour or so later rocks clattered down through the woodland, and splashed gently into the river.

On the river the boat bobbed noisily, caught by the current and straining at its tethering rope. I peered into its hull. It was of simple, yet elegant design; it had a narrow draught, but with space enough for perhaps twenty people to huddle beneath the skin coverings which could be slung to weather-proof the craft. A single sail, simply rigged, could let it take the wind, but there were rowlocks of crude design, and four oars for calmer waters.

It was the figurines that caught my attention again, the gargoyles carved at stern and prow. They sent shivers of recognition and horror through me, touching a part of my racial memory that I had long since suppressed. Wide-faced, narrow-eyed, bulbous-lipped, the features were an art form of their own, unrecognizable yet haunting.

Sorthalan dug a fire pit and struck flame into dry wood from a flint apparatus of his own making. He wood-roasted two pigeons and a woodcock, yet there was scarcely enough meat upon the fowl to satisfy my own hunger, let alone the appetites of the three of us.

For once we did not begin the pointless ritual of communication and misunderstanding. Sorthalan ate in silence, watching me, but more intent upon his own thoughts. It was I who tried to communicate. I pointed in the direction of the primary mythago and said, 'Urscumug.'

Sorthalan shrugged. 'Urshucum.'

Almost the same name that Kushar had used.

I tried something else. Using my fingers to indicate movement I said, 'I'm following *uth guerig*. Do you know of him?'

Sorthalan chewed and watched me, then licked the bird grease from two fingers. He reached over and used the same two sticky digits to press my lips together.

Whatever it was he said, it meant, 'Be quiet and eat,' and I did just that.

I estimated Sorthalan to be a man in his fifties, heavily lined, yet still quite dark of hair. His clothing was simple, a cloth shirt with a ribbed leather corselet that seemed quite effective. His trousers were long and bound with cloth strips. For shoes he had stitched leather. He seemed, it must be said, a colourless man, since all these fabrics were the same monotonous brown hue. All, that is, except the necklet of coloured bones that he wore. He had left the intricately patterned helmet in the boat, but didn't object when Keeton fetched it to the fireside and ran his fingers over the beautifully depicted scenes of hunting and war.

Indeed, it soon occurred to Keeton that the pattern of silver on bronze on the helmet depicted Sorthalan's life itself. It began above the left eyebrow ridge and ran in a subtly continuous scene around the crest to the panel above the elaborate cheek guard. There was room, still, for a scene or two to be etched.

The pattern showed boats on a stormy sea; a forested river estuary; a settlement; tall, sinister figures; wraiths and fire; and, finally, a single boat with the shape of a man at the prow.

Keeton said nothing, but was clearly impressed and moved by the exquisite artistry involved in the etching.

Sorthalan wrapped his cloak around his body and appeared to drift into a light sleep. Keeton poked the fire and put a new piece of wood on to the bright embers. It must have been close to midnight and we both tried to sleep.

But I could only doze fitfully, and at some time in the dead part of the night I became conscious of Sorthalan's voice whispering softly. I opened my eyes and sat up, and saw him seated next to the deeply sleeping Keeton, one hand resting on the airman's head. The words were like a ritual chant. The fire was very low and I again made it up. By its renewed light I saw the sweat that was saturating Sorthalan's face. Keeton shifted, but stayed asleep. Sorthalan raised his free hand to his lips as he glanced at me, and I trusted him.

After a while the softly chanted words ended. Sorthalan rose to his feet, shrugged off his cloak and walked to the water, stooping to wash his hands and splash his face. Then he crouched on his haunches, staring into the night sky, and his voice grew louder, the sibilant, hesitant sounds of his language echoing into the darkness. Keeton woke and sat up, rubbing his eyes. 'What's going on?'

'I don't know.'

We watched for a few minutes, our puzzlement increasing. I told Harry Keeton what Sorthalan had been doing to him, but he showed neither fear nor concern.

'What is he?' Keeton said.

'A shaman. A magic man. A necromancer.'

'The Saxon called him *Freya*. I thought that was a Viking god or something.'

'God grew out of the memories of powerful men,' I suggested. 'Perhaps an early form of Freya was a witch.'

'Too complicated too early,' Keeton said with a yawn, and then we both reacted with startled surprise at a movement in the underwood behind us. Sorthalan remained where he was, still stooped by the water, but silent now.

Keeton and I rose to our feet and stared into the darkness. An increasing amount of rustling heralded the approach of a vaguely human shape. It hesitated, swaying slightly in the gloom, its outline only just picked out by the fire.

'Hello!' came a man's voice, not cultured, very uncertain. The word had sounded more like ''Allo!'

Following the hailing cry, the figure stepped closer, and soon a young man came into view. He hovered in the zone of elementals, surrounded by the wraiths and ghostly forms of Sorthalan's entourage, which seemed to urge him forward, though he was reluctant to come. All I recognized at this time was his uniform. He was ragged, certainly and without equipment, neither pack nor rifle. His khaki jacket was open at the neck. His breeches were loose at the thigh and bound tight to his calves with cloth puttees. On the sleeves of his jacket he wore a single stripe.

He was so obviously a soldier from the British Army of the First World War that at first I refused to trust my senses. Used to a visual diet of primitive, iron-wielding forms, so familiar and comprehensible a sight did not ring true.

Then he spoke again, still hesitant, his voice rich with cockney vowels.

'Can I approach? Come on, mates, it's bleedin' cold out here.'

'Come on in,' Keeton said.

'At last!' said our night guest cheerfully, and took several paces towards us. And I saw his face . . .

And so did Keeton!

I think Harry Keeton gasped. I just looked from one to the other of the men and said, 'Oh God.'

Keeton backed away from his alter-image. The infantry-man didn't appear to notice anything. He came into the camp and rubbed his arms vigorously. When he smiled at me I tried to smile back, but confronted with the spitting image of my travelling companion my uncertainty must have shown.

'I thought I could smell chicken.'

'Pigeon,' I said. 'But all gone.'

The cockney infantryman shrugged. 'Can't be 'elped. Bleedin' starvin' though. I ain't got the equipment to hunt properly.' He looked from one to the other of us. 'Any chance of a fag?'

'Sorry,' was said in unison. He shrugged.

'Can't be 'elped,' he repeated, then brightened. 'Name's Billy Frampton. You get lost from your unit?'

We introduced ourselves. Frampton crouched by the fire, which burned brightly, now. I noticed Sorthalan approach us, and circle round to come behind the new arrival. Framp-ton appeared to be unaware of the shaman. His fresh face, sparkling eyes, and flop of fair hair were a vision of a younger Harry Keeton – and without the burn mark.

'Meself, I'm heading back to the lines,' said Frampton. 'Got this sixth sense, y'see? Always did, even in London as a sprog. Got lost in Soho once, about four years old. Found me way back to Mile End, though. Good sense of direction. So you'll be okay, mates. Stick with me. You'll be right as rain.'

Even as he spoke he was frowning, looking anxiously at

the river. A moment later he glanced at me, and there was a wild sort of expression in his eyes, an almost panicked uncertainty.

'Thanks, Billy,' I said. 'We're heading inwards. Up the far cliff.'

'Call me Spud. All me mates call me Spud.'

Keeton exhaled loudly and shivered. The two men exchanged a long stare, and Keeton whispered, 'Spud Frampton. I was at school with him. But this isn't him. He was fat, and dark . . .'

'Spud Frampton, that's me,' said our guest, and smiled. 'Stick with me, mates. We'll get back to the lines. Getting to know these woods like the inside of the old Cockney Pride.'

He was another mythago, of course. I watched him as he talked. He continually glanced around: he seemed to be in a deep and growing state of distress. Something was wrong, and he knew it. His existence was wrong. Inasmuch as any mythago could be called a natural woodland presence, Spud Frampton was *unnatural*. I intuited why, and murmured my theory to Keeton, while Spud stared at the fire and kept repeating, in an increasingly pointless tone, 'Stick with me, mates.'

'Sorthalan created him out of your mind.'

'While I was sleeping . . .'

Indeed. Sorthalan did not have the same talent as little Kushar, and so he had reached into Harry Keeton's stored race memory and found the most recent mythago-form secured there. By magic, or by a psychic power of his own possession, the necromancer had formed the mythago in an hour or so, and had brought it to the camp. He had given him Keeton's features, and named him from a schoolboy memory. Through Spud Frampton, the Bronze Age magician would speak to us.

Keeton said, 'I *know* him, then. Yes. My father spoke of him. Or of *them*. Shellhole Sam was one. And he told me several stories of a cockney corporal – Hellfire Harry, he called him. They were all about "getting home". Hellfire

Harry was the corporal who'd slip down into your shell hole, in the mist, where you were crouched, utterly buggered, utterly lost, and would somehow get you home. Hellfire Harry used to do things in style, though. He got one group of lost soldiers from the Somme in France right back to their croft in the Scottish Isles. "Well bugger me, mates, I *thought* me feet was sore . . ."' Keeton grinned. 'That sort of thing.'

'Mythago forms as recently as that,' I said quietly. I was astonished. But I could well imagine how the horrors and disorientation of the Flanders trenches could cause the anguished generation of a 'hope' form, a figure that could confidently lead, give new inspiration, reinvest the lost and terrified soldiers with courage.

Yet looking at our acquaintance, this rapidly created heroic figure, I could see only disorientation and confusion. He had been created for a purpose, and the purpose was language, not myth.

Sorthalan approached and eased his bulky form into a crouch, resting a hand lightly on the soldier's shoulder. Frampton jumped slightly, then looked up at me. 'He's glad you found the courage to come.'

'Who is?' I asked, frowning, and then realized what was happening. Sorthalan's lips moved, though no sound came. As he spoke silently, so Frampton addressed me, his cockney tones sounding strange against the legend he spoke. He reiterated in words the picture story on Sorthalan's helmet.

'His name is Sorthalan, which means "the first boat-man". In the land of Sorthalan's people a great storm was coming. That land is far away from this. The storm was of a new magic, and new Gods. The land itself was rejecting Sorthalan's people. At that time, Sorthalan was still a ghost in the loins of the old priest, Mithan. Mithan could see the dark cloud in the future, but there were none to lead the tribes across the land, and the sea, to the forested isles beyond. Mithan was too old for his ghosts to form infants in the bellies of women.

'He found a large boulder with a water-worn furrow in its

surface. He placed his ghost in the stone, and the stone on a high pinnacle. The stone grew for two seasons, then Mithan pushed it from the pinnacle. It broke open and an infant was curled up inside. That was how Sorthalan was born.

'Mithan nourished the child on secret herbs from the grasslands and the woodlands. When he had reached manhood Sorthalan returned from the wild lands to the tribes, and gathered families from each. Every family built a boat, and carried the boats by cart to the grey sea.

'The first boatman led them across the sea and along the coast of the isle, searching the cliffs and the dark woods, and the river estuaries, for a safe place of landing. He found reed-choked marshlands, where wild geese and moorhens swam. They slipped into the land through a hundred channels, and soon found a deeper riverway, leading inwards, cutting between wooded hills and steep gorges.

'One by one the boats moored on the bank, and the families trekked away from the river to form their tribes. Some survived, some did not. It was a journey into the dark ghost places of the world, a journey more terrifying than any that had ever been contemplated. The land was inhabited, and these hidden folk came against the intruders with their stones and spears. They summoned the earth forces, and the river forces, and the spirits that united all of nature, and sent them against the intruders. But Sorthalan had been well taught by the old priest. He absorbed the malevolent spirits into his body, and controlled them.

'Soon only the first boatman remained upon the river, and he sailed north, the land's ghosts with him. He sails the rivers always, waiting for the call from his tribes, and he is always there to help, with his entourage of these ancient forces.'

Sorthalan, through his human medium, had told us of his own legend. That marked, more than anything, the power of the man. And yet his powers were limited; he could not achieve what Kushar had achieved. And he, too, seemed to be waiting for me, as the *shamiga*, as the Knight, and as the Saxon family had been waiting.

'Why is he glad that I've come?' I asked. Now it was Frampton's turn to mouth the silent words, and a moment later he said aloud,

'The Outlander must be destroyed. It's an alien thing. It is destroying the woodland.'

'You seem powerful enough to destroy any man,' I said. Sorthalan smiled and shook his head, answering in his cockney way.

'The legend is clear. It's the Kin who kills the Outlander – or is killed. Only the Kin.'

The legend was clear? At last, then, the words had been spoken to confirm my growing suspicion. I had become a part of legend myself. Christian and his brother, the Outlander and his Kin, working through roles laid down by myth, perhaps from the beginnings of time.

'You've been waiting for me,' I said.

'The realm has been waiting,' Sorthalan said. 'I wasn't sure that you were the Kin, but I saw what effect the oak leaf had upon you. I began to will it to be.'

'I've been expected.'

'Yes.'

'To fulfil my part of a legend.'

'To do what must be done. To remove the alien from the realm. To take his life. To stop the destruction.'

'Can one simple man be so powerful?'

Sorthalan laughed, though his mouthpiece remained solemn, saying, 'The Outlander is not simple, and is not a simple man. He doesn't belong—'

'Nor do I—'

'But you are the *Kin*. You're the bright side of the alien. It's the dark that destroys. He has come so far since the guardian was lured to the edge.'

'Which guardian?'

'The Urshucum. The Urshuca were the oldest of the Outlanders, but they grew close to the earth. The Urshucum you have seen had always guarded the pass to the valley of the flame-talkers, but it was called to the edge. There is a great magic beyond these forests. A voice called. The guardian went, and the heart of the realm was exposed. The Outlander is eating at that heart. Only the Kin can stop him.'

'Or be killed by him.'

Sorthalan made no comment at that. His piercing grey eyes regarded me narrowly, as if still searching for signs that I was the man to fulfil the myth role.

I said, 'But how can the Urshucum have always guarded these—' what had he referred to? – 'flame-talkers. My father *created* the Urshucum. From here,' I tapped my head. 'From his mind. As you have just created *this* man.'

Spud Frampton made no response that would have indicated his understanding of my cruel words. He watched me sadly, then spoke as the necromancer directed him. 'Your father merely summoned the guardian. All that is in the realm has always been here. The Urshucum was summoned to the edge of the realm and changed as Sion had changed it before.'

This meant nothing to me.

'Who was Sion?'

'A great Lord. A shaman. Lord of Power. He controlled the seasons so that Spring followed Summer, then Summer followed Spring. He could give men the power to fly like kestrels. His voice was so loud that it reached the heavens.'

'And he *changed* the Urshuca?'

'There were ten minor Lords,' Sorthalan said. 'They were afraid of Sion's spreading power so they came against him. But they were defeated. Sion used magic to transform them into beasts of the wood. He sent them into exile, to a land where the longest winter was just ending. That land was this place, which once had been buried by ice. The ice melted, and the forests returned, and the Urshuca became the guardians of that forest. Sion had given them the power of near immortality. Like trees, the Urshuca grew but did not wither. Each went to a river, or a land valley, and built his castle to guard the way into the newly growing greenwood. They became close to the earth, and were friends of those who came to settle and hunt and live from the land.'

I asked the obvious question. 'If the Urshuca were friends of man, why is this one so violent? It's hunting my brother; it would kill me without thinking if it could catch me.'

Sorthalan nodded, and Frampton's lips hardly moved as the words of his creator emerged.

'A people came who had flame-talkers with them. The flame-talkers could control fire. They could make fire jump from the sky. They could point their fingers to the east and the flame would spread to the east. They could spit upon the fire and it would become a glowing ember. The flame-talkers came and began to burn the forests. The Urshuca opposed them violently.'

The communication stopped for a minute or so as Sortha-lan rose to his feet, turned from us, and urinated impressively into the night.

'There were men controlling the fire that night when Christian came,' Keeton whispered. I had not forgotten them. I had called them Neoliths. They seemed the most primitive of Christian's entourage, but apparently they had a mind control over fire and flame itself.

I could well imagine the simple historical basis from which legends of the Urscumug and the flame-talkers had sprung. The vision I had was of a time when the last Ice Age was rapidly declining. The ice had advanced as far as the English Midlands. Over the centuries, as it withdrew, the climate had been cold, the land in the valleys marshy and treacherous, the slopes bare and frozen. The pines had arrived, a sparse fir forest, foreshadowing the great Bavarian forests of our own time. Then the first of the deciduous trees had begun to take root, the elms, the thorns, the hazels, followed by the limes, oaks and ashes, pushing the evergreen forest northwards, creating the dense greenwood cover that partially survived to this day.

In the dark, empty spaces below the canopy, boars, bears and wolves had run, deer had grazed the glades and glens, emerging occasionally on to the high ridges, where the forest thinned and the bramble and thorn formed bright spinneys.

But human animals had come back to the greenwood, advancing north into the cold. And they had begun to clear the forest. They had used fire. What a skill it must have been to set a fire, control it, and clear the site for a settlement. And what a greater skill it must have been to have resisted the re-encroachment of the forest.

There would have been a bitter struggle for survival. The wood was desperate and determined to keep its mastery of the land. Man and his fire had been determined that it should not. The beasts of that primal woodland had become dark forces, dark Gods; the wood itself would have been seen to be sentient, creating ghosts and banshees to send against the puny human invader. Stories of the Urscumug, the forest guardian, had become associated with the fear of strangers, new invaders, speaking other languages, bringing other skills.

The Outsiders.

And later, the men who had used fire had become almost deified as 'flame-talkers'.

'What is the end of the legend of the Outsider?' I asked Sorthalan as he sat down again. He shrugged, a very modern gesture, and drew his heavy cloak around his shoulders, tying the rough cords at the front. He seemed tired.

'Each Outlander is different,' he said. 'The Kinsman will come against him. The outcome cannot be known. It's not the certainty of success that makes us welcome your presence in the realm. It's the *hope* of success. Without you, the realm will wither like a cut flower.'

'Tell me about the girl, then,' I said. Sorthalan was clearly very tired. Keeton too was restless and yawning. Only the infantryman seemed alert and awake, but his gaze was fixed at some point in the distance, and there was nothing behind his eyes except the controlling presence of the shaman.

'Which girl?'

'Guiwenneth.'

Sorthalan shrugged again and shook his head. 'The name is meaningless.'

What had Kushar called her? I checked my notes.

Again, Sorthalan shook his head.

'The girl created from love out of hate,' I suggested, and this time the necromancer understood.

He leaned towards me and rested his hand on my knee, saying something aloud in his language, and staring at me quizzically. As if remembering himself, he inclined his head slightly towards the vacant infantryman, whose gaze sharpened.

'The girl is with the Outlander.'

'I know,' I said, and added, 'That's my reason for pursuing him. I want her back.'

'The girl is happy with him.'

'She is not.'

'The girl belongs to him.'

'I don't accept that. He stole her from me—'

Sorthalan reacted with startled surprise. I went on. 'He stole her from me and I'm going to take her back.'

'She has no life outside the realm,' Sorthalan said.

'I believe she does. A life with me. She chose that life, and Christian acted against her choice. I don't intend to own her, or possess her. I just love her. And she loves me, of that I'm sure.' I leaned closer. 'Do you know her story?'

Sorthalan turned away, thinking deeply, evidently disturbed by my revelations.

I persisted: 'She was raised by the friends of her father. She was trained in the way of the woods and magic, and trained with weapons too. Am I right? She was kept until she was a woman, guarded by the Night Hunt. She fell in love for the first time and the Night Hunt brought her back to the land of her father, to the valley where he was buried. This much I know. The ghost of her father linked her with the Horned God. This much I know. But what happened then? What happened to the one who loved her?'

It happened, then, that she fell in love with the son of a chief who was determined to have her. The words of the diary were strong and clear in my mind. But was this version too recent for Sorthalan to recognize the details?

Suddenly Sorthalan turned sharply on me, and his eyes blazed; through his beard he seemed to be smiling. He was excited, and very positively so. 'Nothing has happened until it happens,' he said through Frampton. 'I had not understood the presence of the girl. Now I do. The task is easier, Kinsman!'

'How?'

'Because of what she is,' said Sorthalan. 'She has been subdued by the Outlander, but now she is beyond the river. She will not stay with him. She will find the powers to escape—'

'And return to the edge of the wood!'

'No,' said Sorthalan, shaking his head as Frampton articulated the sound. 'She will go to the valley. She will go to the white stone, to the place where her father is buried. She will know that it is her only hope for release.'

'But she won't know how to get there!' My father's journal had referred to Guiwenneth's 'sadness' that she could not find the valley which breathed.

'She will run to the fire,' Sorthalan said. 'The valley leads to the place where the fire burns. Trust me, Kinsman. Once beyond the river she is closer to her father than she has ever been. She will find the way. You must be there to meet her – and to confront her pursuer!'

'But what *happened* after that confrontation? The stories must say . . . !'

Sorthalan laughed and grasped me by the shoulders, shaking me. 'In years to come they will say *everything*. At the moment the story is unfinished.'

I stood there stupidly. Harry Keeton was shaking his head in a sort of disbelief. Then Sorthalan thought of something else. His gaze went past me and he released me from his powerful grip. Frampton said on his behalf, 'The three who are following will have to be abandoned.'

'The three who are following?'

'The Outlander gathered a band of men as he devastated the realm. The Kinsman too. But if the girl goes to the valley, there is a better way for you to meet her, and the three must be abandoned for a while.'

He stepped past me and called into the darkness. Keeton rose to his feet, apprehensive and puzzled. Sorthalan spoke words in his own language and the elementals gathered about us, forming a shimmering bright veil.

Three figures stepped from the obscurity of night into the glow of the elementals. They walked uncertainly. First came the cavalier, then the Knight. Behind them, his sword and shield held loosely at his side, came the cadaverous form of the man from the stone grave. He kept apart from the other two, a ghastly myth creature, born more from horror than hope.

'You will meet them again, at another time,' Sorthalan said to me. I kept thinking that I hadn't even heard them coming down the cliff! But the sensation of being followed was borne out as a genuine awareness and not an irrational fear.

Whatever passed between the shaman and the warriors, the three men who might have accompanied me in another tale stepped back into the stygian wood and vanished from my sight.

The consciousness of Billy Frampton returned briefly to the mythago form that sat with us. The infantryman's eyes lit up a little and he smiled. 'We should get some kip, mates. It's going to be a long hike tomorrow, back to the lines. Bit of shut-eye, do us the power of good.'

'Will you be able to guide us inwards?' Keeton asked his alter-image. 'Can you lead us to the valley of the white stone?'

Frampton looked utterly blank. 'Blimey, mate. What's all that about? I'll be bleedin' glad just to get back to a trench and a nice plate of bully . . .'

As he spoke the words he frowned, shivered, and glanced around. That cascade of uncertainty returned to his features, and he began to tremble violently. 'This ain't right . . .' he whispered, looking from one to the other of us.

'What isn't right?' I asked.

'This whole place. I think I'm dreaming. I can't hear gunfire. I don't feel right.' He rubbed his fingers on his cheeks and chin, like a frozen man rubbing circulation back into his flesh. 'This just ain't right,' he repeated, and looked up into the night sky, at the breeze-blown foliage. I thought tears glistened in his eyes. He smiled. 'Maybe I'll pinch meself. Maybe I'm dreaming. I'll wake up in a little while. That's it. I'll wake up and everything will be right again.'

And with that he tugged at Sorthalan's cloak and curled up by the shaman, like a child, sleeping.

For my part, I managed to sleep a little too. So did Keeton, I think. We were woken abruptly, some time before dawn. The riverside was beginning to become visible with the approaching day.

What had woken us was a sudden, distant shot.

Sorthalan, hugged in his cloak, was watching us through narrowed, dew-touched eyes. He remained expressionless. There was no sign of Billy Frampton.

'A shot,' Keeton said.

'Yes. I heard it.'

'My pistol . . .'

We looked back towards the place where the Hawks had attached us, then shrugged off our simple coverings. Chilled and aching from the hard ground, we ran together along the river shore.

Keeton saw it, and shouted to me. We stood by the tree and stared at his pistol, which was hooked on to a thin branch. Touching it gently, Keeton sniffed the barrel and confirmed that it had just been fired.

'He must have fixed it like that so that it wouldn't follow him into the river,' Keeton said. We turned and stared at the flowing waters, but there was no sign of blood or of the infantryman himself.

'He knew,' Keeton said. 'He knew what he was. He knew that he had no real life. He ended it in the only honourable way.'

Maybe I'm dreaming. That's it. I'll wake up and everything will be right again.

I don't really know why, but for a while I felt inordinately sad, and rather irrationally angry with Sorthalan, who seemed to me to have created a human being simply to be used and expended. The truth of the matter, of course, was that Billy Frampton had been no more real than the ghosts which hovered in the foliage around our camp.

The Valley

There was little time available for brooding over Frampton's death, however. When we got back to the camp, Sorthalan had already rolled up the hides from the camp, and was aboard the small boat, making preparations to sail.

I picked up my haversack and spear and waved to the boatman, finding it hard to smile.

But a hand pushed me forward from behind, and I stumbled towards the river. Keeton had likewise been propelled towards the boat, and Sorthalan shouted a word at us, indicating that we should jump aboard.

Around us, the elementals were like a perpetual breeze, and the touch of fingers on my face and neck was both disturbing and comforting. Sorthalan extended a hand to help us board, and we hunkered down in the midships, on the rough seats. Symbols and faces had been painted and carved, or simply scratched, all around the inner hull – the marks, perhaps, of the families who had originally sailed with the first boatman. At the prow, peering towards us, was the grimacing face of a bear, its eyes peculiarly slanted, two stubby horns suggesting more of an amalgamation of deity-figures than the simple bear itself.

Suddenly the sail flapped noisily and unfurled. Sorthalan walked about the boat, tethering the rigging. The vessel rocked once, then spun out into the river, turned about, and went with the flow. The sail billowed and stretched, the ropes creaked and snapped, and the boat listed sharply. Sorthalan stood at the long rudder, his cloak wrapped about him, his gaze fixed now on the deepening gorge ahead of us. A fine spray cut from the water's surface and cooled our skins. The sun was low and the shadow of the high cliffs was still cast darkly across the surging river. The elementals flowed through the trees, and across the waters ahead of us, making the water ripple with an eerie light.

At Sorthalan's instruction, Keeton and I took positions at various rigging stations. We soon learned how to tug and loosen the sail to take full advantage of the dawn winds. The river curved and meandered through the chasm. We skipped over the waters, surging ahead faster than a man could run.

It grew colder, and I was glad of my oilskin. The landscape around us began to show signs of seasonal change, a darkening of the foliage, then a thinning. It became a cold, late autumnal forest, in a bleak, seemingly endless gorge. The cliff tops were so far above us that few details could be seen, though squinting against the bright sky on several occasions I saw movement up there. Occasionally, great boulders fell heavily and noisily into the river behind us, causing the boat to rock violently. Sorthalan just grinned and shrugged.

It seemed that the boat was dragged by a current, faster and faster. It shot over rapids, with Sorthalan working the rudder expertly, and Keeton and myself hanging on to the rowlocks for dear life. Once we came perilously close to the chasm's sides, and only frantic tacking of the sail avoided disaster.

Sorthalan seemed unbothered. His elementals were now a dark and brooding swarm of shape behind and above us, although occasionally a streak of sinuous light would dart ahead, winding up through the autumnal forest which lined the gorge.

Where were we going? Attempts to get an answer to that question were met with a single finger prodded upwards, towards the plateau on the inward side of the river.

We came into the sun, the river a blinding, brilliant gold. The elementals crowded ahead of us, forming a gloomy veil through which the sun was dimly filtered. In shadow again, we gasped as we saw an immense stone fortress, rising from the water's edge and built up the whole of the cliff to our right. It was an astonishing sight, a series of towers, turrets, and crenellated walls, seemingly crawling up the rock itself. Sorthalan urged the boat to the far side of the river and beckoned us to lower our heads. I soon saw why. A hail of bolts struck the boat and the water around us.

When we were beyond firing range I was instructed to wrench the short wooden shafts from the outer hull, a job more difficult than it sounds.

We saw other things on the walls of the ravine, most notably a huge, rusting metal shape, in the form of a man.

'Talos!' Keeton breathed as we sailed rapidly past, the wind tugging noisily at the sail. The giant metal machine, a hundred feet high or more, was crushed against the rocks, partly consumed by trees. One arm was out-stretched across the river and we sailed through the shadow of the huge hand, half expecting it to suddenly fall and grasp us. But this Talos was dead, and we passed on from its sad, blind face.

A strong surge of anxiety made me demand repeatedly in English, 'Where the hell *are* we going, Sorthalan?'

Christian, by now, was miles away, days away.

The river could be seen to be curving as if around the plateau. We had covered many many miles ourselves, and the day was nearly done. Indeed, abruptly Sorthalan pulled the boat to the shore, moored it and made camp. It was a cold evening, very wintry. We huddled by the fire, and spent several hours in silence before curling up to sleep.

There followed another day of the same, a terrifying journey across rocky shallows, down endless rapids, around great swirling pools, where silver-backed fish of incredible size darted at us.

Another day's sailing, another day of watching ruins, shapes and the signs of primitive activity on the enclosing cliffs. At one point we passed below a cave community. The scrubby trees had been cleared, exposing the cliff face, and there were nearly twenty caverns carved, or fashioned, in that vertiginous wall. Faces peered down at us as we sailed past, but I could see no more detail than that.

It was on the third day that Sorthalan cried out cheerfully, and pointed ahead. I peered over the side, squinting against the bright sun, and saw that the river was spanned by a high, crumbling bridge, which extended from cliff top to cliff top.

Sorthalan guided the boat to the inward shore, furled the sail, and let the little vessel coast on the current until it was below the huge stone edifice. A great shadow passed over us. The immensity of that bridge was breathtaking. Bizarre faces and animal forms had been carved on the span. The supporting pillars were shaped from the cliff itself. The whole bridge was falling into decay, and even as we were clambering ashore a huge stone, twice my height, detached itself noisily from the arch above us and curled silently and terrifyingly down to the water, where its splash nearly swamped the three of us.

We began to climb almost at once. What was a daunting prospect proved to be far easier than I had expected, since there were ample hand- and footholds in the crudely-carved supporting pillars. The tenuous shapes of Sorthalan's entourage were clearly visible around us, and I realized they were actually *helping* us, for my pack and spear seemed lighter than I'd expected.

Abruptly the full weight of my pack returned. Keeton gasped too. He was poised precariously on the sheer pillar, three hundred yards or more above the river, and suddenly unaided for the first time. Sorthalan scrambled on, calling to us in his ancient tongue.

I risked only one glance down. The boat was so tiny, and the river so distant, that my stomach gave way and I groaned aloud.

'Hang on,' called Keeton, and I looked up, and took reassurance from his grin.

'They were helping us,' I said as I hauled myself after him.

'Tied to the boat,' he said. 'Limited distance they can move, no doubt. Never mind. Nearly there. Only about half a mile to go . . .'

For the last hundred yards we climbed up the vertical face of the bridge itself. The wind tugged and teased at me, as if hands were pulling at my pack, trying to dislodge me from the great structure. We climbed over one of the grinning gargoyle faces, using its nostrils, eyes and lips as handholds. Eventually I felt Sorthalan's strong hands clutching at my arms, dragging me to safety.

We walked briskly to the plateau, over the crumbling bridge gate and through the trees beyond. The land sloped up, and then down, and we emerged on to a rocky knoll from where we could see across the wide, winter landscape of the inner realm.

This, clearly, was as far as Sorthalan would accompany us. His legend, his purpose, bound him to the river. In our time of need he had come to our aid, and now he had shown me the way to Guiwenneth, the shortest way.

He found a bare patch of rock, and used a sharp stone to scratch out the map that I would memorize. Distantly, mere vague outlines on the far horizon, I could see twin peaks, snow-capped mountains. He indicated them on the rock, and drew the valley between them, and the standing stone. He showed how the valley led to forest that bordered a part of the great wall of flame. I could see no smoke from here; the distance was too great. He marked, then, the way we had sailed. We were closer to the valley than at the place where Christian had crossed the river. If Guiwenneth *did* escape from my brother, and made her way, by whim or instinct to the valley of her father's grave, then Christian would have several more days' journey.

We were closer to the stone than he was.

Sorthalan's last gesture was an interesting one. He drew my flint-bladed spear from where I had secured it in my pack and made the mark of an eye upon the shaft, about two feet from the stone blade. Through the eye he scratched a rune like an inverted 'V', with a squiggle on one tail. Then he stood between the two of us, a hand on each of our shoulders, and propelled us gently towards the winter land.

The last I saw of him, he was crouched on the bare rock, staring into the far distance. As I waved so he waved back, then rose and vanished into the trees behind him, making his way back to the bridge.

I have lost track of time, so this is DAY X. The cold is growing more severe. Both of us concerned that we may not be equipped for an intensely cold environment. Twice during the last four days, snow has fallen. On each occasion only flurries, which drifted through the bare branches of the winter wood and hardly settled. But an ominous portent of what is to come. From higher ground, where the forest thins, the mountains look uninviting and sinister. We are getting closer to them, certainly, but the days go past and we seem to make no real ground.

Steven is becoming more on edge. Sometimes he is sullenly silent, at others he shouts angrily, blaming Sorthalan for what he sees as an interminable delay. He is growing so strange. He looks more like his brother. I had a fleeting glimpse of C in the garden, and while S is younger, his hair is wild, his beard thick, now. He walks in the same swaggering manner. He is increasingly adept with sword and spear, while my own facility with a spear or knives is non-existent. I have seven rounds left for the pistol.

For my part I find it continually fascinating to think that Steven has become a myth character himself! He is the mythago realm's mythago. When he kills C the decay of the landscape will reverse. And since I am with him, I suppose I am part of the myth myself. Will there be stories told one day of the Kinsman and his companion, the stigmatized Kee, or Kitten, or however the names get changed? Kitten, who had once been able to fly above the land, now accompanying the Kinsman through strange landscapes, ascending a giant bridge, adventuring against strange beasts. If we *do* become legends to the various historical peoples scattered throughout this realm . . . what would that *mean*? Will we somehow have become a *real* part of history? Will the *real* world have distorted tales of Steven and myself, and our quest to avenge the Outsider's abduction? I cannot remember my folklore well enough, but it intrigues me to think that tales – of Arthur and his Knights, perhaps (Sir Kay?) – are elaborate versions of *what we are undertaking now*!

Names change with time and culture. Peregu, Peredur, Percival? And the Urscumug – also called Urshucum. I have been thinking a lot about the fragmentary legend associated with the Urscumug. Sent into exile in a very far-off land, but that land was England, and an England at the very end of the Ice Age. So who sent them? And from where? I keep thinking of the Lord of Power, who could change the weather, whose voice echoed around the stars. Sion. Lord Sion. I think of names, words, half remembered. Ursh. Sion. Earth, perhaps. Science, perhaps. Earth watchers exiled by Science?

Do the earliest of folk-heroes, or legendary characters, come not from the *past* but from . . .

Whimsy! Simple whimsy. And there is the rational man in me again. I am hundreds of miles into a realm outside the normal laws of space and time, but I have come to accept the strangeness as normal. That said, I *still* cannot accept what I *believe* to be abnormal.

What happened, I wonder, to the Kinsman's friend? What has legend told of faithful Kitten? What will happen to me if I do not find the Avatar?

We began to starve. The woodland was a desolate and seemingly uninhabited place. I saw certain fowl birds, but had no means of catching them. We crossed brooks and skirted small lakes, but if there were fish in them then they chose to hide well from our sight. The one time we saw a small hind I called for Keeton's pistol, but he refused to give it, and in my momentary confusion I let the beast escape, even though I charged between the sparse thickets in pursuit and flung my spear with all my might.

Keeton was becoming superstitious. At some point in the last few days he had managed to lose all but seven bullets. These he guarded with his life. I found him examining them. He had marked one with his initials. 'This is mine,' he said. 'But one of the others . . .'

'One of the others what?'

He looked at me, hollow-eyed and haunted. 'We can't *take* from the realm without sacrifice,' he said. He looked down at the other six bullets in his hand. 'One of these belongs to the Huntsman. One is his, and he'll destroy something precious if I should use it by mistake.'

Perhaps he was thinking of the legend of the Jagad. I don't know. But he would no longer use the pistol. We had taken too much from the realm. There had to be a time of repaying favour.

'So you'll force us to starve,' I said angrily, 'through a silly whim!'

His breath frosted, moisture forming on the sparse hair of his moustache. The burned skin of his chin and jaw was quite pale. 'We won't starve,' he said quietly. 'There are villages along the way. Sorthalan showed us that.'

We stood, tense and angry in the frozen forest, watching as a fall of light snow drifted from the grey heavens.

'I smelled wood smoke a few minutes ago,' he said suddenly. 'We can't be far.'

'Let's see, shall we?' I replied, and pushed past him, walking briskly on the hard forest floor.

My face was suffering badly from the cold, despite my growth of beard. Keeton's enclosing leathers kept him warm. But my oilskin cape, though a good waterproof, was not good thermal wear. I needed an animal skin, and a thick fur hat.

Within minutes of that brief and hostile confrontation, I too smelled a wood-burning fire. It was a charcoal maker, in fact, in a cleared woodland glade, an earth mound over a deep fire pit, untended. We followed the beaten track to the stockade of the village, just visible ahead, then hailed the occupants in as friendly a tone as possible.

They were an early Scandinavian community – I can't say 'Viking', although their original legend must surely have included *some* elements of warriorhood. Three long houses, warmed by large open fires, peered out into a yard overrun with animals and children. But the signs of past destruction were evident, for a fourth house was burned to a ruin, and outside the village was an earth mound of a different sort from the charcoal maker – a tumulus in which, we were told, eighty kinsfolk lay, slaughtered some years before by . . .

Well, of course.

The Outsider.

They fed us well, although eating food from human crania was unnerving. They sat around us, tall, fair-haired men in great furs; tall, angular women in patterned cloaks; tall, bright-eyed children, their hair, boy and girl alike, braided over the crown. They supplied us with dried meat and vegetables, and a flagon of sour ale that we would jettison as soon as we were beyond the stockade. They offered us weapons, which was astonishing, since a sword to *any* early culture represented not just *wealth*, but possession of an implement that was normally very difficult to obtain. We refused. We did accept, though, their gifts of heavy reindeer-hide cloaks, which I substituted for my own cape. The cloak was hooded. Warm at last!

Swathed in these new clothes, we took our leave on a mist-shrouded, icy dawn. We followed tracks back through the woodland, but during the day the fog became denser, slowing us down. It was a frustrating experience, which did not help my humour. Always at the back of my mind was a picture of Christian, getting closer to the fire, approaching the realm of Lavondyss where the spirits of men were not tied to the seasons. I could also clearly see Guiwenneth, trussed and despondent behind him. Even the thought of her riding like the wind towards her father's valley was becoming hopelessly anguished. This trek was taking so long. Surely they would be there before us!

The fog lifted later in the day, though the temperature dropped still further. The wood was a bleak, grey place, stretching endlessly around us; the sky was overcast and sombre. I frequently shinned up the taller trees to look for the twin peaks ahead of us, for reassurance.

The wood, too, was increasingly primitive, thick stands of hazel and elm, and an increasing preponderance of birch on the higher ground, but the comforting oak seemed almost gone, except that occasionally there would be a brooding stand of the trees, around a clear, cold glade. Rather than being afraid of these clearings, Keeton and I found them to be sanctuaries, heart-easing and welcoming. Towards each dusk, the moment of finding such a dell was the moment of camping.

For a week we trekked across the icy land. Lakes were frozen. Icicles hung from the exposed branches of trees at the edge of clearings, or open land. When it rained we huddled, miserable and depressed. The rain froze, and the landscape glittered.

Soon the mountains were a lot closer. There was a smell of snow on the air. The woodland thinned, and we peered along ridges where old tracks would once have passed. And from this high land we saw the smoke of fires in the distance, a village haven. Keeton became very quiet, but also very agitated. When I asked him what was wrong he couldn't say, except that he felt very lonely, that the time of parting was coming.

The thought of not having Keeton's company was not pleasant to contemplate. But he had changed over the days, becoming increasingly superstitious, more and more aware of his own mythological role. His diary, essentially a mundane account of journey and pain (his shoulder was still hurting him) repeatedly asked the question: what is the future for *me*? What has legend told of Brave K?

For my part I had ceased to worry about how the legend of the Outsider ended. Sorthalan had said that the story was unfinished. I took that to mean that there was no pre-ordination of events, that time and situation were mutable. My concern was only for Guiwenneth, whose face both haunted and inspired me. She seemed always to be with me. Sometimes, when the wind was mournful, I thought I could hear her cry. I longed for pre-mythago activity: I might have glimpsed a doppelgänger, then, and taken comfort from that illusory closeness. But since passing the zone of abandoned places all that activity had gone – for Keeton too, although in his case, the loss of the shifting peripheral shapes was a mercy.

We came within sight of the village and realized that we had come back, now, to something almost alien in its primitiveness. There was a wooden palisade on a raised earth bank. Outside the bank were a few yards of chipped and razor sharp rocks, rammed into the ground like crude spikes, a simple defence, simply overcome. Beyond the wall the huts were of stone, built around sunken floors. Crossed wooden beams formed the support for roofs of turf and occasionally a primitive sort of thatch. The whole community had the feel of being more subterranean than earthbound, and as we entered the gateway through the earth wall we were conscious only of the dull stone, and the heavy smell of turf, both fresh and burning.

An old man, supported by two younger bloods, came towards us; they all wielded long, curved staffs. Their clothing was the ragged and stitched hides of animals, formed into tunics with trousers below, tied at the calves with leather. They wore bright headbands, from which dangled feathers and bones. The younger men were clean-shaven; the old man had a ragged white growth of beard that grew to his chest.

He reached towards us as we approached, and held out a clay pot. In the pot was a dark red cream. I accepted the gift, but more was obviously required. Behind them a few huddled figures had appeared, men and women, wrapped against the cold, watching us. I noticed bones lying on raised platforms beyond the squat huts.

And on the air came the smell of grilled onions!

I passed the clay pot to the old man, and leaned forward, imagining that I was expected to daub my features in some way. He seemed pleased and touched his finger to the ochre, then quickly drew a line on each of my cheeks, repeating the decoration on Keeton. I took the pot back, and we went deeper into the village. Keeton was still agitated, and after a moment said, 'He's here.'

'Who's here?'

But there was no answer to my question. Keeton was totally absorbed in his own thoughts.

This was a Neolithic people. Their language was a sinister series of gutturals and extended diphthongs, a weird and incomprehensible communication that defies even phonetic reproduction. I looked around the bleak and uninviting community for some sign of the connection with myth, but there was nothing to demand interest save for an enormous, white-façaded tumulus being constructed on a knoll of high land towards the mountains, and an elaborate display of intricately patterned boulders surrounding the central house. Work was still continuing on the carving of these stones, supervised by a boy of no more than twelve years of age. He was introduced as *Ennik-tig-encruik*, but I noticed he was referred to as 'tig'. He watched us searchingly as we, in turn, watched the work of pecking out patterns using antler and stone.

I was reminded of the megalithic tombs of the west, of Ireland in particular, a country I had visited with my parents when I had been about seven years old. Those great tombs had been silent repositories of myth and folklore for thousands of years. They were fairy castles, and the golden-armoured little folk could often be seen by night, riding from the hidden passages in the mounds.

Were these people associated with the earliest memories of the tombs?

It was a question never to be answered. We had come too far inwards; we had journeyed too far back into the hidden memories of man. Only the Outsider myth could be related to these primitive times, and the earliest Outsiders of them all: the Urshuca.

A grey and shivery dusk enveloped the land. Freezing mist shrouded the mountains and the valleys around. The woodland was a stand of sinister black bones, arms raised through the icy fog. The fires in the earth huts belched smoke from the holes in the turf roofs, and the air became sweet with the smell of burning hazelwood.

Keeton abruptly stripped off his furs and pack, letting them fall to the ground. Despite my query, he ignored me, and ignored the old man, walking past him towards the far side of the enclosure. The white-haired elder watched him, frowning. I called Keeton's name, but was aware of the futility of the act. Whatever had suddenly come to obsess the airman, it was his business alone.

I was taken to the main hut and fed fully on a vegetable broth in which rather unpleasant chunks of fowl were floating. The tastiest food presented to me was a biscuit, made from a grain, nutty in flavour, with a slight aftertaste of straw – not at all bad.

In the early evening, replete but feeling very isolated, I stepped out into the yard beyond the huts, where torches burned brightly, throwing the palisade into shadowy relief. A brisk, freezing wind blew, and the torches guttered noisily. Two or three of the Neoliths watched me from their furs, talking together quietly. From below a canopy, where light burned, came the sharp strike of bone on stone, where an artist worked late into the night, anxious to express the earth symbols that the boy 'tig' was summoning.

In the distance, as I peered into the nightland, other fires burned between the mountains. These pinpricks of light were clearly communities. But in the far distance, eerily illuminating the mist, was a stronger, widely diffuse glow. We were already coming into range of the barrier of fire, the wall of flame maintained by flame-talkers, the boundary between the encroaching forest and the clear land beyond. There, the world of mythago wood entered a timeless zone that would be unexplorable.

Keeton called my name. I turned and saw him standing in the darkness, a thin figure without his protective clothing.

'What's going on, Harry?' I asked as I stepped up to him.

'Time to go, Steve,' he said, and I saw that there were tears in his eyes. 'I did warn you . . .'

He turned and led me to the hut where he had been sheltering.

'I don't understand, Harry. Go where?'

'God knows,' he said quietly, as he ducked through the low doorway into the warm, smelly interior. 'But I knew it would come to this. I didn't come with you just for fun.'

'You're making no sense, Harry,' I said as I straightened up.

The hut was small, but could have slept about ten adults. The fire burned healthily in the centre of the earth floor. A matting of sorts had been laid around the edge of the floor space. Clay vessels cluttered one corner; implements of bone and wood were stacked in another. Strands of grass and reed thatch dangled from the low roof.

There was only one other occupant of the hut. He sat across from the fire, frowning as I entered, recognizing me even as I recognized him. His sword was resting against the supporting pillar for the roof. I doubt if he could have stood in that tiny place even if he'd wanted to.

'Stiv'in!' he exclaimed, his accent so like Guiwenneth's.

And I crossed the floor to him, dropped to my knees, and with a sense of incredible confusion, and yet a great pleasure, greeted Magidion, the Chieftain of the Jaguth.

My first thought, strangely, was that Magidion would be angry with me for having failed to protect Guiwenneth. This sudden surge of anxiety must have made me seem as a child at his knees. The feeling passed. It was Magidion himself, and his Jaguth, who had failed her. And besides: there was something not right with the man. For a start, he was alone. Secondly, he seemed distracted and sad, and his grip on my arm – a welcoming gesture – was uncertain and short-lived.

'I've lost her,' I said to him. 'Guiwenneth. She was taken from me.'

'Guiwenneth,' he repeated, his voice soft. He reached out and pushed a branch deeper into the fire, causing a shower of sparks and a sudden wave of heat from the declining embers. I saw then that there were tears glistening in the big man's eyes. I glanced at Keeton. Harry Keeton was watching the other man with an intensity, and a concern, that I could not fathom.

'He's been called,' Keeton said.

'Called?'

'You told me the story of the Jaguth yourself—'

I understood at once! Magidion, in his own time, had been summoned by the Jagad. First Guillauc, then Rhydderch, and now Magidion. He was apart from the others now, a solitary, questing figure, following the whim of a woodland deity as strange as she was ancient.

'When was he summoned?'

'A few days ago.'

'Have you spoken to him about it?'

Keeton merely shrugged. 'As much as is possible. As usual. But it was enough . . .'

'Enough? I still don't understand.'

Keeton looked at me, and he seemed slightly anguished. Then he smiled thinly. 'Enough to give me a slight hope, Steve.'

'The "avatar"?'

If I felt embarrassed as I said the word, Keeton just laughed. 'In a way I wanted you to read what I was writing.' He reached into the pocket of his motorcycle trousers and drew out the damp, slightly dog-eared notebook. After cradling it in his hand for a moment he passed it to me. I thought there was a certain hope in his eyes, a change from the brooding man who had developed over the last few days. 'Keep it, Steve. I always intended that you should.'

I accepted the notebook. 'My life is full of diaries.'

'This one's very scruffy. But there are one or two people in England . . .' He laughed as he said that, then shook his head. 'One or two people back home . . . well, their names are written at the back. Important people to me. Just tell them, will you?'

'Tell them what?'

'Where I am. Where I've gone. That I'm happy. Especially that, Steve. That I'm happy. You may not want to give the wood's secret away . . .'

I felt a tremendous sadness. Keeton's face in the firelight

was calm, almost radiant, and he stared at Magidion, who watched us both, puzzled by us, I thought.

'You're going with Magidion . . .' I said.

'He's reluctant to take me. But he will. The Jagad has called him, but his quest involves a place I saw in that wood in France. I only glimpsed it briefly. But it was enough. Such a place, Steve, a magic place. I know I can get rid of this . . .' He touched the burn mark on his face. His hand was shaking, his lips trembling. It was the first time, I realized, that he had ever referred to his wound. 'I have never felt whole. Can you understand that? Men lost arms and legs in the war and went on normally. But I have never felt whole with *this*. I was lost in that ghost wood. It was a wood like Ryhope, I'm sure of it. I was attacked by . . . something . . .' A hollow-eyed, frightened look. 'I'm glad we didn't come across it, Steve. I'm glad, now. It burned me with its touch. It was defending the place I saw. Such a beautiful place. What can burn can unburn. It's not just weapons that are hidden in this realm, and legends of warriors and defenders of the right, and that sort of thing. There is beauty too, wish-fulfilment of a more . . . I don't know how to describe it. Utopia? Peace? A sort of future vision of every people. A place like heaven. Maybe heaven itself.'

'You've come all this way to find heaven,' I said softly.

'To find peace,' he said. 'That's the word, I think.'

'And Magidion knows of this . . . peaceful place?'

'He saw it once. He knows of the beast god that guards it, the "avatar" as I call it. He saw the city. He saw its lights, and the glimmer of its streets and windows. He walked around it by watching its spires, and listening to the night-calls of its priests. An incredible place, Steve. Images of that city have always haunted me. And that's true, you know . . .' He frowned, realizing something even as he spoke. 'I think I dreamed of that place even in childhood, long before I crashed in the ghost wood. I dreamed of it. Did I create it?' He laughed with a sort of weary confusion. 'Maybe I did. My first mythago. Maybe I did.'

I was bone-weary, but I felt I had to know as much from Keeton as possible. I was about to lose him. The thought of his departure filled me with a powerful dread. To be alone in this realm, to be utterly alone . . .

He could tell me very little more. The full facts of his story were that he had crashed in ghost woodland, with his navigator, and the two of them had stumbled, terrified and starving, through a forest as dense and as uncanny as Ryhope Wood. They had struggled to survive for two months. How they had come across the city was pure chance. They had been attracted by what they thought were the lights of a town, at the edge of the wood. The city had glowed in the night. It was alien to them, unlike any city of history, a glowing, gorgeous place, which beckoned them emotionally and had them stumbling blindly towards it. But the city was guarded by creatures with terrifying powers, and one of these 'avatars' had projected fire at Keeton, and burned him from mouth to belly. His companion, however, had slipped past the guardian and the last Keeton had seen blinded by tears, hardly able to restrain the screams of pain, was the navigator walking the bright streets, a distant silhouette, swallowed by colour.

The avatar itself had carried him away from the city and set him loose in the woodland fringes. It had been a warning to him. He was captured by a German patrol and spent the rest of the war in a prison camp hospital. And after the war he had been unable to find that ghost wood, no matter how hard he tried.

Concerning Magidion, there was little more to tell. The call had come a few days before. Magidion had left the Jaguth and moved towards the heart of the realm, to the same valley which was my own destination. For Magidion, and his sword-kin, the valley was also a potent symbol, a place of spiritual strength. Their leader lay buried there, brave Peredur. Each, on being summoned, made the trek to the stone, before passing either inwards, through the flame and thence into no-time, or back out again, as seemed to be Magidion's destiny.

He knew nothing of Guiwenneth. She had loved with her heart, and the tie with the Jaguth was broken. Her anguish had summoned them to Oak Lodge, all those weeks ago, to comfort her, to reassure her that she might, with their blessing, take this strange, thin young man as her lover. But Guiwenneth had passed beyond them in her tale. They had trained her and nurtured her; now she needed to go to the valley which breathed, to raise the spirit of her father. In the story which my own father had told, the Jaguth had ridden with her. But time and circumstances changed the details of a story and in the version that I was living out, Guiwenneth had been a lost soul, destined to return to her valley as the captive of an evil and compassionless brother.

She would triumph, of course. How could it be otherwise? Her legend would have been meaningless unless she overcame her oppressor, to triumph, to become the girl of power.

The valley was close. Magidion had already been there, and was now retracing his steps across the inner realm of forest.

When the fire finally died down, I slept like a log. Keeton slept too, though during the night I woke to the sound of a man crying. We rose together before first light. It was bitterly cold, and even in the hut our breath frosted. A woman came in and began to make up the fire. Magidion freshened himself, and Keeton did likewise, breaking the ice that had formed on a heavy stone pot of water.

We stepped outside into the enclosure. No-one else was about, although from all the huts came the first thin streamers of smoke. Shivering violently, I realized that snow was on its way. The whole Neolithic compound was bright with frost. The trees that loomed around its walls looked like crystal.

Keeton reached into his leathers and drew out the pistol, holding it towards me.

'Perhaps you should have this,' he said, but I shook my head.

'Thanks. But I don't think so. It wouldn't seem right to go against Christian with artillery.'

He stared at me for a second, then smiled in a forlorn, almost fatalistic way. He pocketed the weapon again and said, 'It's probably for the best.'

Then, with the briefest of goodbyes, Magidion began to walk towards the gate. Keeton followed him, his pack large upon his back. His body was bulky in the fur cloak. Even so, he seemed tiny next to the antlered man who led the way into the dawn. At the gate Keeton hesitated and turned, raising a hand to wave.

'I hope you find her,' he called.

'I will, Harry. I'll find her and take her back.'

He hovered in the gateway, a long, uncertain pause before he called, 'Goodbye, Steve. You've been the best of friends.'

I was almost too choked to speak. 'Goodbye, Harry. Take care.'

And then there was a barked order from Magidion. The airman turned and walked swiftly into the gloom of the trees.

May you find your peace of mind, brave K. May your story be a happy one.

A terrible depression swamped me for hours. I huddled in the small hut, watching the fire, occasionally reading and re-reading the entries in Harry Keeton's notebook. I felt overwhelmed by panic and loneliness, and for a while was quite unable to continue my journey.

The old man with the white beard came and sat with me, and I was glad of his studious presence.

The depression passed, of course.

Harry was gone. Good luck to Harry. He had indicated to me that it was just two or three days' journey to the valley. Magidion had been there already and there was a huntsman's shelter close by the stone. I could wait there for Guiwenneth to arrive.

And Christian too. The time of confrontation was scant days away.

I took my leave of the enclosure in the early afternoon and paced away through the thin flurries of snow that swirled from the grey skies. The old man had marked my face with different ochres, and presented me with a small ivory figurine in the shape of a bear. What purpose was served by paint and icon I have no idea, but I was glad of both contributions and tucked the bear-talisman deeply into my trouser-pocket.

I nearly froze to death that night, huddled under my canvas tent in a glade that had seemed sheltered but through which an evil wind blew continually from midnight to dawn. I survived the cold, and the following day I emerged on to clear ground, at the top of a slope, and was able to look over the woodland at the distant mountains.

It had been my impression that the valley of Peredur's stone lay between those imposing, snow-capped slopes. Now I saw how wrong that belief was, how misleading Sorthalan's map had been.

From this vantage point, I could glimpse for the first time the great wall of fire. The land rose and fell in a series of steep, wooded hills. Somewhere among them was the valley, but the barrier of fire, rising above the dark forest in a band of brilliant yellow which merged with a pall of grey smoke, was clearly on *this* side of the mountains.

The mountains were in the realm beyond, the no-place where time ceased to have meaning.

Another night, this time spent huddled in a sheltered overhang of rock, which could be made warm by a small fire. I was reluctant to light that fire, since my shelter was on higher ground and the flame might have been noticed. But warmth was a precious thing in that bleak and frozen landscape.

I sat in my cave, starving, yet without any interest in the meagre supplies I carried. I watched the darkness of the land, and the distant glow of the flame-talker's fire. It seemed, at times, that I could hear the sounds of the burning wood.

During the night I heard a horse whinny. It was somewhere out among the moonlit trees, below the overhang where I huddled. I moved in front of my dimming fire to try to block the light. The sound had been muffled and distant.

Had there been voices as well? Would anyone be travelling on so dark and cold a night?

There was no further sound. Shaking with apprehension I crept back into my cave, and waited for dawn.

In the morning the land was shrouded in snow. It wasn't deep, but it made walking hazardous. Among the trees it was easier to see the ground and avoid the twisting roots and trap-holes. The woodland rustled and whispered in the white stillness. Animals scampered within earshot, but were never visible. Black birds screeched and circled above the bare branches.

The fall of snow grew heaver. I began to feel haunted by it as I pushed on through the forest. Each time a branch shifted and spilled snow on to the ground I jumped out of my skin.

At some time during the morning a strange compulsion affected me. It was partly fear, I suppose, and partly the memory of that horse, whinnying and complaining in the frozen night. I became convinced I was being followed and started to run.

I ran easily for a while, cautiously picking my way through the snow-bound forest, careful of roots and covered pot-holes. Each time I stopped and stared back into the silent wood I thought I could hear a furtive movement. The place was a shadowy, confusing mix of white and grey. Nothing moved in those shadows, save the sprinkle of snowflakes that drifted through the branches, a gentle accompaniment to my increasingly panicky flight.

A few minutes later I heard it. The unmistakable sound of a horse, and the sound of men running. I peered hard through the snow, and into the grey places between the trees. A voice called quietly and was answered from my right. The horse whinnied again. I could hear the whisper of feet on the soft ground.

Now I turned towards the valley and began to run for my life. Behind me there was soon no attempt to disguise the pursuit. The whickering of the horse was loud and regular. The cries of the men hinted at triumph. When I glanced back

I saw shapes weaving through the forest. The rider and his horse loomed large through the white veil.

I tripped as I ran, and stumbled hard against a tree, turning like an animal at bay and bringing down my flint-bladed spear. To my astonishment, wolves were leaping through the snow on either side of me, some casting nervous glances at me, but running on. Looking round, I saw the tall stag weaving between the trees, pursued by this voracious pack. For a second I was confused. Had the whole sensation of being chased been nothing but the sound of nature?

But the horseman was there. The beast shook its head as its rider kicked it forward, each step sending the snow flying. The Fenlander sat astride it, cloaked and dark, holding his own lethally-tipped javelin with arrogant ease. He watched me through narrowed eyes, then abruptly urged the horse into a run, bringing up the javelin to strike.

I darted to one side, tangled in tree roots, my haversack swinging awkwardly. As I moved I blindly swung the spear at my attacker. There was an animal sound of pain, and the spear was jerked roughly in my hands. I had caught the horse in the flank, ripping its flesh. It shook, then reared, and the Fenlander was thrown from its back. He laughed as he sat in the snow, still watching me. Then he began to climb to his feet, reaching for his javelin.

I reacted without thinking, stabbing at him. The spear broke where Sorthalan had carved his watching eye. The Fenlander stared stupidly at the stump of wood in his breast, then looked up at my shaking figure, the broken shaft of the spear still held towards him. His eyes rolled up and he toppled backwards, mouth open.

Snow began to coat his features.

I left him where he lay. What else should I do? I threw the broken shaft aside and walked unsteadily on through the woodland, wondering where the rest of the pack were. And where Christian was hiding.

And in this way, trembling with the shock of the kill and lost in my nervous thoughts, I emerged from the forest at the top of the valley, where a mournful wind blew.

Peredur's stone rose from the snow before me, a huge, wind-scoured pinnacle, towering above the land to a height of at least sixty feet. I walked towards the grey megalith, awestruck and deeply moved by the silent authority of the monument. Undecorated, the stone had been formed from a single hew, and had been roughly dressed with the most primitive of tools. It tapered slightly towards its top, and was leaning slightly towards the wall of fire at the end of the valley. Snow had drifted against one side of the stone and half obscured the crudely etched shape of a bird, whose species was not clear. This was the earliest symbol representing Peredur, the simple association with the myth of rescue. Here, then, was Peredur's stone for all the ages of legend: a stone for Peredur by whatever name he had been known, a place of quest for the girl who had been rescued on the wing, in whatever form she had been known through the centuries.

Guiwenneth. Her face was before me, more beautiful than before, her eyes twinkling with amusement. Wherever I looked I could see her – in the hills, in the white branches, against the distant dark wall of smoke. '*Inos c'da, Stivv'n,*' she said, and laughed, her hand across her mouth.

'I've missed you,' I said.

'*My flintspear,*' she murmured, touching a finger to my nose. '*You have the strength. My own precious flintspear . . .*'

The wind was bitterly cold. It blew from the hills behind, feeding and fanning the flame-talker's barrier to the innermost realm. Her voice faded, her pale features became lost against the snow. I walked around the stone, wary of surprise by Christian's Hawks, almost crying out for Guiwenneth to be huddled there, waiting for me.

The first thing I noticed was the trail of shallow prints, leading towards the trees and the far flame. The snow had almost filled them in, but it was plain enough that *someone* had been to the stone, and had walked on down the valley.

I began to follow them, hardly daring to think of the identity of their maker. The trees were densely clustered in the deep valley bottom. The snow was thick for a while, but soon vanished from the ground as the warmth of the fire wall grew intense.

The crackle and roar of the flames mounted in volume. Soon I could see the fire through the wood. And soon the whole wood ahead of me was a blazing wall, and I stepped through a zone of charred and skeletal trunks, their blackened branches like the stiffened limbs of fire victims. Small, charred remnants of oak and hazel, and all the rest of the primitive wood, were silhouetted against the brilliance of the flame; they looked like twisted human figures.

One of the figures moved, stepping parallel to the fire and disappearing behind the tall shadow of a tree. I moved quickly into cover and watched, then darted to a closer vantage point, trying to hug the sparse cover and squinting to see against the brilliance of the firelight before me. Again there was furtive movement. A tall shape – too tall for Guiwenneth – it carried something that glinted.

I dropped to a crouch, then ran to a small boulder and ducked behind it. I saw no more movement and stepped cautiously into the lee of a stooping, carbonized oak.

He rose from the ground like a wraith, no more than five paces from me, a shadow emerging from the shade. I recognized him at once. He was holding a long-bladed sword. He was dripping with sweat and had stripped down to a saturated dark-grey woollen shirt, opened to the waist, and loose cloth trousers, tied at the calves to stop them flapping. There were two recent cuts on his face, one of which had gashed across his eye. He looked vile and violent, grinning through the dark beard. He held his sword as easily as if it was made of wood, and came slowly towards me as he spoke.

'So you've come to kill me, brother. You've come to do the deed.'

'Did you think I wouldn't?'

He stopped, smiled and shrugged. Ramming his sword into the ground he seemed to lean on it. 'I'm disappointed, though,' he said evenly. 'No stone-age spear.'

'I left the sharp end in your right-hand man. The Fenlander. Back in the woods.'

Christian looked surprised at that, frowning slightly and glancing beyond Peredur's stone. 'The Fenlander? I thought I'd sent him to the Underworld myself.'

'Apparently not,' I said calmly, but my thoughts were racing. What was Christian saying? Was he implying that there had been a civil war within his band? Was he alone, now, alone and abandoned by his troop?

There was something weary, almost fatalistic, about my brother. He kept glancing at the fire, but when I moved slightly in his direction he reacted promptly, and the red, gleaming blade stabbed towards me. He slowly circled me, the fire becoming bright in his eyes, and on the dried blood of his face.

'I must say, Steven, I'm impressed by your doggedness. I thought I'd hanged you at Oak Lodge. Then I sent six men back to settle with you by the river. What happened to them, I wonder?'

'They're all face down in the river, well eaten by fish by now.'

'Shot, I suppose,' he said bitterly.

'Only one,' I murmured. 'The rest just weren't good enough swordsmen.'

Christian laughed disbelievingly, shaking his head. 'I like your tone, Steve. Arrogant. That's a strength. You really *are* determined to be the avenging Kinsman.'

'I want Guiwenneth. That's all. Killing you is less important. I'll do it if I have to. I'd prefer not.'

Christian's slow circling motion stopped. I held my Celtic blade menacingly and he cocked his head, examining the weapon. 'Nice little toy,' he said with cynicism, scratching his belly through the dark grey material of his shirt. 'Useful for vegetables, I don't doubt.'

'And Hawks,' I lied.

Christian was surprised. 'You killed one of my men with that?'

'Two heads, two hearts . . .'

For a second my brother was silent, but then he just laughed again. 'What a liar you are, Steve. What a noble liar. I would do the same myself.'

'Where's Guiwenneth?'

'Well, now. There's a question. Where's Guiwenneth? Where indeed?'

'She escaped from you, then.'

Relief, like a bird, had begun to flutter in my chest.

Christian's smile was sour, however. I felt blood burning in my face, and the heat from the fire wall was almost overwhelming. It roared and hissed as it blazed, a torrent of sound close by. 'Not exactly,' Christian said slowly. 'Not escaped so much as . . . let go . . .'

'Answer me, Chris! Or I swear I'll cut you down!' Anger made me sound ridiculous.

'I've had a little trouble, Steve. I let her go. I let them all go.'

'Your band turned against you, then.'

'They're turning in their graves, now.' He chuckled coldly. 'They were foolish to think they could overpower me. They hadn't been reading their folklore. Why, only the *Kinsman* can kill the Outsider. I'm honoured, brother. Honoured that you've come this far to put an end to me.'

His words were hammer blows. By 'let go' he meant killed. Oh God, had he killed Guiwenneth too? The thought overpowered my reason. Already hot enough to drop, I felt only anger, and the red heat of hate. I ran at Christian, swinging my sword wide and hard. He backed away raising his own blade and laughing as iron rang on steel. I struck again, low down. The sound was like the dull tolling of a bell. And again, at his head – and again, a thrusting blow to his belly. My arm ached as each stroke was parried with a jarring, ferocious blow from Christian's own sword. Exhausted, I stopped, and stared at the flickering shadows cast by the fire across his savage, grinning features. 'What's happened to her?' I said, breathless and aching.

'She'll be here,' he said. 'In her own time. A handy little girl, that . . . with a knife . . .'

And as he spoke he pulled open his dark shirt and showed me the spreading bloodstain over his belly that I had taken for dark sweat. 'A good strike. Not fatal, but close to fatal. I'm draining away, but of course . . . I shan't *die* . . .' He growled as he spoke, then. 'Because only the *Kinsman* can kill me!'

As he said the words so an animal look of rage came into his stare and he came at me in a blur of speed, his sword invisible against the fire. I felt it slice the air on each side of my head and a second later my own blade was struck from my hand. It spun across the clearing. I staggered back slightly and tried to duck below the fourth of Christian's strokes, which cut horizontally towards my neck and stopped dead against the skin.

I was shaking like a leaf, my lips slack, my mouth dry with shock.

'So this is the great Kinsman,' he roared, irony and anger tainting the words. 'This is the warrior who came to kill his brother. Knees knocking, teeth chattering, a pathetic excuse for a soldier!'

There was nothing useful to be said. The hot blade was gently cutting more deeply into my neck. Christian's eyes seemed almost literally to blaze.

'I think they'll have to rewrite the legend,' he murmured with a smile. 'You've come a long way to be humiliated, Steve. A long way to end up a grinning, fly-blown head on his own sword.'

In desperation I flung myself away from his blade, ducking down and more than half hoping for a miracle. I faced him again and was shocked at the death mask that was his face, his lips drawn back exposing white teeth that now glowed yellow. He swept his sword from side to side, a blur of speed and wind, as regular as a heartbeat. Each time the point passed by, the tip touched my eyelids, my nose, my lips. I backed steadily away. Christian stepped steadily after me, taunting me with his skill.

All at once he tripped me with the sword, dealt me a stinging blow to the buttocks, then lifted me to my feet, the sharp edge below my chin. As before, in the garden, he pushed me back against a tree. As before, he had the better of me. As before, the scene was ringed by fire.

And Christian was an old and weary man.

'I don't care about legends,' he said quietly, and again looked at the roaring flames. The bright fire shone on the blood and sweat that caked his features. He turned back to me, speaking slowly, his face close to mine, his breath surprisingly sweet. 'I'm not going to kill you . . . *Kinsman*. I'm beyond killing, now. I'm beyond everything.'

'I don't understand.'

Christian hesitated for a moment and then, to my surprise, released me and backed away. He walked a few paces towards the fire. I remained where I was, clutching the tree for support, but aware that my own sword was close by.

With his back to me, stooping slightly as if in pain, he said, 'Do you remember the boat, Steve? The *Voyager*?'

'Of course I do.'

I was astonished. What a time to get nostalgic. But this was no mere soft memory. Christian turned back towards me and now he glowed with a new emotion: excitement. 'Remember when we found it? The day with the old Aunt? That little ship came out of Ryhope Wood as good as new. Remember that, Steve?'

'As good as new,' I agreed. 'And six weeks later.'

'Six weeks,' Christian said dreamily. 'The old man knew. Or thought he did.'

I pushed away from the tree and gingerly stepped towards my brother. 'He referred to the distortion of time. In his diary. It was one of his first real insights.'

Christian nodded. He had let his sword relax. The perspiration poured from him. He looked vacant, then in pain. He seemed almost to sway. Then his focus sharpened.

'I've been thinking a lot about our little *Voyager*,' he said, and looked up and around. 'There's more to this realm than

Robin Hood and the Twigling.' His gaze fixed on me. 'There's more to legend than heroes. Do you know what's beyond the fire? Do you know what's through there?' With great difficulty he used his sword to point behind him.

'They call it *Lavondyss*,' I said.

He took a difficult step forward, one hand on his side, the other using his sword as a stick.

'They can call it what they like,' he said. 'But it's the Ice Age. The Ice Age that covered Britain more than ten thousand years ago!'

'And beyond the Ice Age, the interglacial, I suppose. And then the Ice Age before that, and so on, back to the Dinosaurs . . .'

Christian shook his head, contemplating me with deadly seriousness. 'Just the Ice Age, Steve. Or so I'm told. After all—' another grin – 'Ryhope Wood is a very *small* wood.'

'What's your point, Chris?'

'Beyond the fire is the Ice,' he said. 'And within the Ice . . . a secret place . . . something to do with the Urscumug. And then, beyond the Ice there's the fire again. Beyond the fire, the wildwood. And then England. Normal time. I've been thinking about the *Voyager*. Was it scarred and damaged as it sailed through the realm? It must have been. It must have been here a lot longer than six weeks! But what happened to that damage? Maybe . . . maybe it fell away. Maybe as it came through the wood the realm took *back* the time it had imposed upon it. Do you see what I'm saying? You've been here, how long? Three weeks? Four? But outside, only a few days have passed, perhaps. The realm has *imposed* time upon you. But perhaps it takes back that time if you go through it in the right way.'

'Eternal youth . . .' I said.

'Not in the least!' he exclaimed, as if frustrated by my failure to understand. 'Regeneration. Compensation. I'm fourteen, fifteen years older than I would have been if I'd stayed at Oak Lodge. I think the realm will let me shed those years, and the scars, and the pain, and the anger . . .' He suddenly sounded as if he was imploring me. 'I've got to try, Steve. There's nothing left for me now.'

'You've destroyed the realm,' I said. 'I've seen the decay. We have to fight, Chris. You have to be killed.'

For a moment he said nothing to that, then made a sound halfway between scorn and uncertainty.

'Could you really kill me, Steve?' he asked, with a quiet tone of menace in his voice.

I made no answer. He was right, of course. I probably couldn't. I could have done it in the heat of the moment, but watching this wounded, failing man, I knew I could probably not strike the blow.

And yet . . .

And yet so much depended on me, on my courage, on my resolve.

I began to feel dizzy. The heat from the fire was exhausting, draining.

My brother said, 'In a way you *have* killed me. All I wanted was Guiwenneth. But I couldn't have her. She loved you too much. It destroyed me. I'd looked for her for too many years. The pain of finding her was too great. I want to leave the realm, Steve. Let me go—'

Surprised by his words, I said, 'I can't stop you going.'

'You'll hunt me. I need peace. I need to find my own peace. I *must* know that you won't be behind me.'

'Kill me then,' I said bluntly.

But he just shook his head and laughed ironically. 'You've risen from the dead twice, Steven. I'm beginning to be afraid of you. I don't think I'll try it a third time.'

'Well, thank you for that at least.'

I hesitated, then asked quietly, 'Is she alive?'

Christian nodded slowly. 'She's yours, Steve. That's how the story will be told. The Kinsman showed compassion. The Outsider was reformed and left the realm. The girl from the greenwood was reunited with her lover. They kissed by the tall white stone . . .'

I watched him. I believed him. His words were like a song that brings tears to the eyes.

'I shall wait for her, then. And thank you for sparing her.'

'She's a handy little girl,' Christian repeated, touching his stomach wound again. 'I had very little choice.'

Something in his words . . .

He turned from me and walked towards the fire. The thought that I was about to bid a glad adieu to my brother stopped me thinking about Guiwenneth for a moment.

'How will you get through?'

'Earth,' he said, and reached for his cloak. He had piled soil into the hood. He held the garment like a sling; with his free hand he gouged a handful of dirt from the ground and flung it into the fire. There was a splutter and a sudden darkening of the flame, as if the earth had swamped the conflagration.

'It's a question of the right words and sufficient dirt to scatter through the flames,' he said. 'I learned the words, but the quantity of Mother Earth is a problem.' He glanced round. 'I'm a pretty poor shaman.'

'Why not go along the river?' I said as he began to swing the cloak. 'That's your easiest option, surely. The *Voyager* made it through that way.'

'River's blocked to people like me,' he said. The cloak was swinging in a great circle around his head. 'And besides, that's *Lavondyss* beyond the fire. *Tir-na-nOc*, dear Steven. Avalon. Heaven. Call it what you like. It's the unknown land, the beginning of the labyrinth. The place of mystery. The realm guarded not against *Man* but against Man's curiosity. The inaccessible place. The unknowable, forgotten past.' He looked round at me, as he swung the heavily laden cloak. 'When so much is lost in the dark of time there must be a myth to glorify that lost knowledge.' Back to the fire, stepping forward as he spoke. 'But in *Lavondyss* the place of that knowledge still exists. And that's where I'm going first, brother. *Wish me luck!*'

'*Luck!*' I cried, as he flung the dirt from the cloak. The

flames roared, then died, and for an instant I saw the icy lands beyond, through the charred corpses of trees.

Christian ran towards that temporary pathway through the surging fire, an old man, heavily built, limping slightly as his wound jarred painfully. He was about to achieve something that I had committed myself to preventing – save that he was alone, now, and not with Guiwenneth. And yet I could scarcely bear to think of what would happen to him in timeless *Lavondyss*. From hatred I had come full circle and now felt an uncontrollable sadness that I would probably never see him again. I wanted to give him something. I wanted something of his, some memento, some piece of the life I had lost. And as I felt this, so I thought of the oak-leaf amulet, still around my neck and warm against my chest. I began to chase after him, tearing at the necklet, ripping the heavy silver leaf from its leather binding.

'Chris!' I shouted. 'Wait! The oak leaf! For luck!'

And I threw it after him.

He stopped and turned. The silver talisman curved towards him and I realized immediately what would happen. I watched in numb horror as the heavy object struck him on the face, knocking him back.

'*Chris!*'

The fire closed in about him. There was a long, piercing scream, then only the roar of the flames; maintained by earth magic, they cut me off from my brother's terrible fate.

I could hardly believe what had happened. I dropped to my knees, staring at the fire, deeply shocked and shaking as if with a fever.

But I couldn't cry. No matter how hard I tried, I couldn't cry.

Heartwood

It was done, then, Christian was dead. The Outsider was dead. The Kinsman had triumphed. The legend had resolved in favour of the realm. The destruction and decay would cease henceforth.

I turned from the fire and walked back through the crowded wood, to the snow line and on up the valley. Around me, the land was blanketed with white. The bright stone that towered above me was almost invisible in the heavy fall. I walked past it, no longer afraid of confronting Christian's mercenaries.

I struck the stone with my sword. If I had expected the note to ring out across the valley I was wrong. The clang died almost immediately, though no more quickly than my bellowed cry for Guiwenneth. Three times I called her name. Three times I was answered by nothing but the whisper of snow.

She had either been and gone, or had not yet arrived. Christian had implied that the stone *was* her destination. Why had he laughed? What did he know that he had kept so secret?

I suppose I knew even then, but after such an agonizing journey in pursuit of her the thought was too painful to contemplate, I was unprepared to acknowledge the obvious. And yet that same thought tied me to the place, stopped me leaving. I had to wait for her, no matter what.

There was nothing else in the world which mattered so much.

For a night and a full day I waited in the hunter's shelter, close to Peredur's monument, warming myself by a fire of elm. When it stopped snowing I walked the land around the stone, calling for her, but to no avail. I ventured down the valley as far as I dared and stood in the forest, staring at the huge wall of fire, feeling its heat melt the snow around, bringing an uncanny sense of summer to this most primitive of all woodlands.

She came to the valley during the second night, walking so softly across the snow carpet that I almost missed her. The moon was half full, the night bright and clear, and I saw her. She was a hunched and miserable shape walking slowly through the trees, towards the imposing rise of the monolith.

For some reason I didn't shout her name. I tugged on my cloak and stepped from my tiny enclosure, wading through the drifts in pursuit of the girl. She seemed to be staggering as she walked. She remained hunched up, folded in on herself. The Moon, behind the monolith, made the stone a sort of beacon, beckoning to her.

She reached the place of her father's burial and stood, for a moment, staring up at the rock marker. She called for him then, and her voice was hoarse, breaking with cold and pain, and pure exhaustion.

'Guiwenneth!' I said aloud, as I stepped through the trees. She visibly jumped, and turned in the night. 'It's me. Steven.'

She looked pale. Her arms were folded across her body and she seemed tiny. Her long hair was lank, soaked with snow.

I realized that she was trembling. She watched me in terror as I approached. I remembered, then, how like Christian I must have seemed to her, darkly bearded, bulky with furs.

'Christian is dead,' I said. 'I killed him. I've found you again, Guin. We can go back to the Lodge. We can be together without fear.'

Go back to the Lodge. The thought filled me with warm hope. A lifetime without distress, without worry. Oh God, at that moment I wanted it so much!

'Steve . . .' she said, her voice a mere whisper.

And collapsed against the stone, clutching herself as if in

pain. She was exhausted. The walk had taken so much out of her.

I walked quickly to her and lifted her into my arms, and she gasped, as if I'd hurt her.

'It's all right, Guin. There's a village close by. We can rest for as long as you like.'

I put my hands into the warmth of her cloak, and with a sense of terrible shock, felt the cold stickiness on her belly.

'Oh Guin! Oh God, no . . .'

Christian had had the last word after all.

Her hand, lifted with the last of her strength, touched my face. Her eyes misted, the sad gaze lingering on me. I could hardly hear her breathing.

I looked up at the stone. '*Peredur!*' I called desperately. '*Peredur? Show yourself!*'

The stone stood silently above us. Guiwenneth folded herself more deeply into my embrace and sighed, a small sound in the cold night. I hugged her so hard I was afraid she would snap like a twig, but I had to keep the warmth in her body somehow.

Then the ground shook a little, and again. Snow fell from the top of the stone and was dislodged from the branches of trees. Another vibration, and another . . .

'He's coming,' I said to the silent girl. 'Your father. He's coming. He'll help.'

But it was not Guiwenneth's father that appeared around the stone, holding the limp carcass of the Fenlander in its left hand. It was not the ghost of brave Peredur which stood above us, swaying slightly, its breathing a steady, ominous sound in the darkness. I stared up at the moonlit features of the man who had begun all this, and had no strength to do anything but bitterly shout my disappointment as I tucked Guiwenneth deeper into my cloak, bending my head above her, trying to make her invisible.

It must have stood there for a minute or more, and in all that time I waited for the feel of its fingers pinching about my shoulders, lifting me to my doom. When nothing happened I looked up. The Urscumug was still there, watching me, eyes blinking, mouth opening and closing, showing the glistening teeth within. It still held the Fenlander's body, but with a single, sudden motion that made me jump with fright, it flung the corpse away, and reached for me.

Its touch was more gentle than I would have thought possible. It tugged at my arm, making me release my protective grip upon Guiwenneth. It picked her up and cradled her body in its right arm as easily as a child cradles a toy.

He was going to take her from me. The thought was too much to bear and I started to cry, watching the shape of my father through a blur of tears.

Then the Urscumug stretched out its left hand to me. I stared at it for a moment, and then I realized what it wanted. I stood up and reached out to the hand, which enclosed mine totally.

In this way we walked round the stone, through the snow to the trees, and through the trees to the fire wall ahead.

So much passed through my mind as I walked with my father. The look on his face was not a scowl of hate, but a soft and sad expression of sympathy. In the garden of Oak Lodge, when the Urscumug had shaken me so hard, perhaps he had been trying to shake life *back* into my body. At the wooded gorge, when my father had hesitated, listening for us, perhaps he had known where we were all the time, and was waiting for us to pass him by. He had helped me in my pursuit of the Outsider, not hindered. When he – as all things in the realm – had come to need me, he had rediscovered compassion.

My father placed Guiwenneth on the hot ground. The fire roared into the sky. Trees blistered and charred, branches falling in flames as they reached towards the barrier. It was an odd place. The sweat poured from me, the heat of that supernatural inferno soaking me. The struggle was eternal, I realized. The wall of fire probably never moved – trees grew into it and were consumed. All the time it was maintained by the flame-talkers, the first real heroes of modern humankind.

I had imagined that the three of us were to pass through the flames, but I was wrong. My father reached towards me and pushed me away.

'Don't take her from me!' I implored him. How beautiful she looked, face framed in red hair, skin glowing with the brightness of the fire. '*Please!* I *must* be with her!'

The Urscumug watched me. The great beast's head slowly shook.

No. I could not be with her.

But then he did something wonderful, something that was to give me courage and hope for the long years to come – a gesture that would live with me as a friend through the eternal winter, while I waited with the Neolithic peoples of the nearby village, guarding Peredur's stone.

He touched a finger to the girl's body, then pointed to the fire wall. And then he indicated that she would return. To me. She would come back to me, alive again, my Guiwenneth.

'How long?' I begged the Urscumug. 'How long will I wait? How long will it take?'

The Urscumug bent to the girl and picked her up. He held her towards me and I pressed my lips to Guiwenneth's cold lips, and held the kiss, my eyes closed, my whole body shaking.

My father curled her up into his safe grasp and turned to the flames. He flung a great handful of earth at the wall and the flames died down. I had the briefest of glimpses of the mountains beyond, and then the shape of the boar passed through the charred trees into the timeless realm. As it walked, so it brushed past a blackened tree stump that looked uncannily like a human figure, arms raised to its head. The shape disintegrated. A second later the flames grew bright again and I was alone, left with the memory of a kiss, and the joy of seeing tears in my father's eyes.

Coda

At that time, in the life of this people, Mogoch the giant was set a task by the fates, and walked north for a hundred days without resting. This brought him to the furthest limits of the known world, facing the gate of fire that guarded *Lavondyss*.

At the top of the valley was a stone, ten times the height of a man. Mogoch rested his left foot on the stone, and wondered for what reason the fates had brought him this far from his tribal territory.

A voice hailed him, 'Take your foot from the stone.'

Mogoch looked about him and saw a hunter, standing on a cairn of rocks, staring up.

'I shall not,' said Mogoch.

'Take your foot from the stone,' shouted the hunter. 'A brave man is buried there.'

'I know,' said Mogoch, not moving his foot. 'I buried him myself. I placed the stone on his body with my own hands. I found the stone in my mouth. Look!' And Mogoch grinned, showing the hunter the great gap in his teeth where he had found the brave man's marker.

'Well, then,' said the hunter. 'I suppose that's all right.'

'Thank you,' said Mogoch, glad that he would not have to fight the man. 'And what great deed brings *you* to the borders of *Lavondyss*?'

'I'm waiting for someone,' the hunter said.

'Well,' said Mogoch. 'I hope they'll be by shortly.'

'I'm sure she will,' the hunter said, and turned from the giant.

Mogoch used an oak tree to scratch his back, then ate a deer for his supper, wondering why he had been summoned to this place. Eventually he left, but named the valley *ritha muireog*, which means 'where the hunter waits'.

Later, however, the valley was called *imarn uklyss*, which means 'where the girl came back through the fire'.

But that is a story for another time, and another people.

But the story doesn't end with

MYTHAGO WOOD

Other books in the Ryhope Wood sequence are:

**LAVONDYSS
THE BONE FOREST
THE HOLLOWING
MERLIN'S WOOD
GATE OF IVORY, GATE OF HORN**

And turn the page for an extract from **AVILION**,
Robert Holdstock's final Ryhope Wood novel,
published in the summer of 2009

JACK AT THE EDGE

Wood Haunter

The man materialised from the edge of the wood so suddenly that the two boys, fishing from the opposite bank of the brook, almost slipped into the water with shock. He stood midstream in the shadows for a while, the water bubbling around his crude soft leather boots. He was wearing buckskin trousers, had a jacket or cloak slung casually over his right shoulder, and a pack over his left. His filthy shirt was open to the waist, revealing a heavily tattooed torso.

The boys scrambled back onto the bank and stared at the stranger, who met their look with a cool, pale, searching gaze of his own. His face was lean and lightly bearded, scars on the skin visible in places through the black hair. On his left arm a strip of white fabric, bulging with moss that dangled from its edges, was stained with red, suggesting a recent wound. He seemed unbothered by it.

After watching the boys for a while he looked towards the spire of the church in Shadoxhurst, squinting against the sun.

'Shadokhurze?' he asked, still staring at the distant village. Though his pronunciation was strange, they recognised his meaning.

'That's right, mister,' said the older of the boys, a gangling, ginger-haired youth who spoke nervously.

'How far in paces?'

The boys exchanged a confused, wide-eyed look. The younger, much smaller boy, said, 'A thousand, maybe.'

'Maybe a million,' the other added.

The man looked quizzically at each of them before his face broke into a broad grin. 'Depends on the size of the paces, I suppose.'

The boys smiled as well, one less willingly than the other.

Now the stranger came towards them, tossing his pack onto the bank, bundling up his odd-looking jacket and crouching down between them. He ran his free hand through the water as it flowed beneath him, towards the edge. He inspected the moss patch on his arm briefly, then glanced up quickly. 'What do you call this stream?'

'We don't call it anything.'

'It's the *sticklebrook*. Do you know where it flows to?'

The boys shook their heads. 'Nobody does,' said the older one. 'Can't follow it in. You try and follow it in and you end up coming back. It twists you about in there. I've tried it. It's scary. When did you go in?'

The man glanced up. 'I didn't go *in*,' he said softly. 'I came *out*.'

'Came out of where?'

'Came out of what's in there. There's a lot to see in Ryhope Wood. That *is* its name, isn't it?'

They nodded agreement. Then the older boy made a sound of surprise, his mouth gaping. 'You're one of the wood haunters! You're speaking English, so I didn't realise it. But that's what you are. A wood haunter.' He hesitated, nervous. 'Aren't you?'

The stranger considered the question, then splashed water onto his face and slowly stood up.

'Perhaps. Perhaps not. I don't know what you mean by that. But you'd be amazed,' he went on, 'at what this little stream becomes a few thousand paces in. It's very big, very deep, very rough. There are tributaries that run into it and I used a boat to get here along most of it. From inwards. Hauled it onto a sandbank in a beech forest, maybe four thousand paces from here. Hid it among rocks. The *Muurngoth* hunt in those places, not far from the edge. The rivers run in all directions; and they know how to trim a sail too. I don't want to lose my boat.'

He smiled then, and stepped onto the bank. 'This is where the stream goes in. My father's directions were right. I'm on the right side of the wood.'

He looked around, inspecting the landscape. 'Do you know the house here? Oak Lodge?'

The boys watched him blankly, then shook their heads. Again, it was the older one who spoke. 'There's no house near this wood. Just fields and pastures and sheep. And old fencing. And some earthworks. The Manor House is over the hill.'

'Oak Lodge? You've never heard of it?'

'There's no house anywhere near here, mister. That's the truth.'

'Oh, but there is.'

'What makes you think so?' the other boy asked, with a frown.

'What makes me think so? Because my father lived there for a lot of his life. And so did my grandfather, who was a scientist and an explorer. His name was George Huxley. My father's name was Steven. And I'm John Huxley. Jack, if you like. And I've come a long way to find my home. What are you two called?'

'Eddie,' said the fair-haired older boy.

'Won't tell,' said the younger, with a glare.

'I understand. More than you might know.' He smiled. ' "Won't Tell." '

He gave the boys a friendly look and turned away to pick up his heavy pack, then thought of something and came back. He reached into the pack and pulled out two odd circular objects, bits of twig and small thorny briars, interwoven intricately, with two longer twigs curling out and down like inverted tusks. He tossed one of the objects to each of the boys, who caught them and studied them curiously. They looked up and the older one, Eddie, asked, 'What is it?'

'It's what we call a *daurbrak*.'

'What's it for?'

'It's a shield. It keeps a Green Man away if he comes at you. You put it in your mouth with the twigs pointing down. It confuses him. They're called *daurog*. He doesn't have very good eyesight, you see?'

With a wave and a twinkle in his eye, Jack Huxley turned away and began walking briskly round the edge of Ryhope Wood. Looking back after a few seconds he called out, 'There *is* a house here, you know. It's just that you boys can't see it.'

Robert Paul Holdstock was born in 1948 in a remote corner of Kent, sharing his childhood years between the bleak Romney Marsh and the dense woodlands of the Kentish heartlands. He received an MSc in medical zoology and spent several years in the early 1970s in medical research before becoming a full-time writer in 1976. His first published story appeared in the *New Worlds* magazine in 1968 and for the early part of his career he wrote science fiction. However, it is with fantasy that he is most closely associated.

1984 saw the publication of *Mythago Wood*, winner of the BSFA and World Fantasy Awards for Best Novel, and widely regarded as one of the key texts of modern fantasy. It and the subsequent 'mythago' novels (including *Lavondyss*, which won the BSFA Award for Best Novel in 1988) cemented his reputation as the definitive portrayer of the wild wood. His interest in Celtic and Nordic mythology was a consistent theme throughout his fantasy and is most prominently reflected in the acclaimed Merlin Codex trilogy, consisting of *Celtika*, *The Iron Grail* and *The Broken Kings*, published between 2001 and 2007.

Among many other works, Holdstock co-wrote *Tour of the Universe* with Malcolm Edwards, for which rights were sold for a space shuttle simulation ride at the CN Tower in Toronto, and *The Emerald Forest*, based on John Boorman's film of the same name. His story, 'The Ragthorn', written with friend and fellow author Garry Kilworth, won the World Fantasy Award for Best Novella and the BSFA Award for Short Fiction.

Robert Holdstock died in November 2009, just four months after the publication of *Avilion*, the long-awaited, and sadly final, return to Ryhope Wood.

www.robertholdstock.com

A full list of Fantasy Masterworks can be found at
www.gollancz.co.uk